I wiggled out the narrow opening of the car door, which was wedged against the dirt bank. I felt my foot slip against the soft earth and lost my balance.

"Ouch!" I said, as my hand hit some sharp, slaty stones buried in the dirt. It was an undignified sound but it saved our lives. As Gideon started forward past the front of the car to help me, a shot rang out. There was a whizzing past my ear as the bullet missed him by inches.

"Run!" Gideon yelled as more shots sounded.

I felt my hand yanked forward, and I was dragged up over the dirt bank.

"My God!" I said. All of a sudden my knees were shaking. "Somebody tried to kill us!"

# The deMaury Papers

## Isabelle Holland

FAWCETT CREST • NEW YORK

*THE deMAURY PAPERS*

THIS BOOK CONTAINS THE COMPLETE TEXT OF
THE ORIGINAL HARDCOVER EDITION.

Published by Fawcett Crest Books, a unit of CBS Publications, the Consumer Publishing Division of CBS Inc., by arrangement with Rawson Associates Publishers, Inc.

Copyright © 1977 by Isabelle Holland

ISBN: 0-449-23606-4

The lines from *Murder in the Cathedral* by T. S. Eliot are reprinted with the permission of Harcourt Brace Jovanovich Inc.

Printed in the United States of America

10   9   8   7   6   5   4   3   2   1

*For Philip and Margaret Holland*

The last temptation is the greatest treason:
To do the right deed for the wrong reason.

T. S. ELIOT, *Murder in the Cathedral*

# one

WHEN GIDEON LIGHTWOOD's letter arrived, I was fairly sure, as I started to open it, that it would be less than cordial. After all, despite, or perhaps because of, our relationship—he had been, until her death, my cousin Rosemary's husband—we had met only twice: once at his wedding when he was understandably preoccupied with Rosemary; once after her death, when his attitude towards me was one of guarded hostility, originating, perhaps, in the fact that he associated me with the tragic accident that took her life.

Even so, I was somewhat started by his brusque rebuff.

*Dear Janet:*

*I received your letter of June 28. Unfortunately, the first three weeks of September that you suggested for your visit are not convenient. Benedict and I will both be in London and the house closed. If Bridewell wants you to do this book about your father, perhaps he should come and look over the deMaury papers himself before we leave.*

I stared at the letter, which had been sent to my office at Bridewell and Denby, Publishers, sighed and then groped in my personal correspondence file for the carbon of my original letter to Gideon. By comparison, my letter had been a model of decorous indifference.

> *Dear Gideon:*
>
> *I have some holiday coming up and would like to visit Tenton for the purpose of collecting what's left of my father's papers. The Society has been talking about a biography for some time. Bridewell has now suggested I write it and—mirabile dictu—offered a contract. Please let me know if the first three weeks of September will be convenient.*

Gideon's uncivil note had been the response. Well, I thought, given everything that had happened, and Gideon's understanding of it, what could I expect?

I was stapling Gideon's letter to the carbon of mine to him when Jason Bradshaw strolled in. Jason looked about twenty-six, a good five years junior to my thirty-one and it was always faintly irritating to have people who had just met Jason refer to him as that "nice" or (more frequently) "that extraordinarily bright" young man in tones that clearly conveyed their assumption that Jason was far junior to me. As Ann Merriman, the publisher's assistant, who had been with the firm for twenty years, said, "Jason has looked twenty-six for the past fifteen years, which is pretty good for a man getting on forty. One day, all of a sudden-like, he'll look sixty."

Jason inserted his slight, graceful body between my filing cabinet and the door.

"Bad news, Janet dear?" he said, his sherry-colored eyes riveted to the letters.

I slipped them into the file. "Not really." It wasn't a lie, but it felt like one and, inevitably, I could feel my cheeks start to burn.

"Then why are you looking so guilty?"

"And why are you being so nosy?" I counterattacked, always a good ploy with Jason.

"My dear, if Tony Bridewell offers you, a member of the staff, a contract, then *anyone* would be nosy. It's against the sacred rule: never publish with your own house—as *everyone* knows."

I'd had a hope, faint but persistent, that the news of the contract for my father's biography that Tony had—most surpisingly—offered would remain a secret, at least until I'd written the book. After all, Tony, as owner and publisher of Bridewell and Denby, could offer, draw up and sign his own contract without having to announce it at the monthly editorial meeting where all contracts were introduced and discussed.

But it hadn't happened that way.

The current secretary of the Society—Towards a World Union—which my father had founded in 1930, and which had gone steadily downhill since his death in 1970, knew Tony Bridewell socially and approached him at some literary cocktail party they both attended. The secretary, Myron Weatherby, had suggested the book and Tony had not only welcomed the idea with enthusiasm, but—to my vast astonishment—insisted that I write it. A few days later I found myself signing a contract and accepting a surprisingly large advance. And the whole project was announced as a *fait accompli* at the following editorial meeting.

"Steam rollered through," Jason reported to me afterwards. The day of the meeting had been suddenly changed, by Tony Bridewell's order, from its usual Wednesday to Thursday. This meant that because of having to work with an author who was in New York for the one day only, I would not be able to attend.

"Tony probably wanted people to feel free to object," I said, beginning to see a method in Tony's arbitrary change of date for the meeting. After all, since the author I was to work with all that Thursday was his own, he knew I would be tied up. So much for my desire to keep my share in my father's biography a secret.

Although I had known for some time the Society's occasionally expressed wish to memorialize the founder —my father—in a biography, the actual proposal to

Tony Bridewell, and his appropriation of my services as author, had happened so fast I still wasn't sure myself what I thought of it. I had done a lot of journeyman writing, one way or another—advertising and jacket copy and book releases—during my years in the publicity and promotion department before going over to the editorial side. After that there were a couple of extensive rewrite projects I had done on books whose original authors had good ideas but no craft in setting them down. Despite this, I had never really considered myself a writer. But when I raised this point to Tony Bridewell, he brushed it aside with that almost hypnotic combination of high-handedness and charm that—ten years before, when he was thirty-three—had marked his brilliant if short-lived career as a member of the House of Representatives. Before and after that interlude he had served in the family firm of Bridewell and Denby, the firm founded by his grandfather. During the past few years he had served there as publisher and editor-in-chief, a position he had earned by the same charismatic blend of characteristics that he had displayed in Congress, and an overwhelming confidence in his own judgment—a judgment almost monotonously justified by rising sales among the books he had brought in and the resulting rising status for the house as a whole.

"Nonsense," he'd said then. "Of course you can do it."

And because he had said it, I believed him, and stilled the small voice inside me that murmured that if he had stated with the same conviction that I could sing an aria standing on my head on a high wire, I'd believe that, too. I spent a great deal of time stilling that small voice, because at the root of what it had a habit of saying to me was that I was in love with Tony Bridewell. Fortunately for my peace of mind that voice broke through the firm control of my conscious mind only in occasional, unguarded moments, such as a wakeful three o'clock in the morning, or that first second when I saw Tony's tall, burnished head appear in a doorway. And since most of the time I had myself convinced that those moments were the tail end leftover of a bit of adolescent nonsense, I was reasonably sure that no one would suspect the efficient, ambitious editor, Janet deMaury, of such uncharacteristic idiocy. But that reasonable sureness sometimes faltered before Jason's unnerving radar when it came to human emotions. He would walk into a crowded cocktail party, thick with smoke and idle, brittle chatter, and be able to gossip all over the office the next morning about who was feeling what about whom. It was an intuition approaching genius. Fortunately for Bridewell and Denby, he was almost as good in his job of advertising and publicity director as he was at nosing out gossip.

"It may be against traditional publishing wisdom to publish with your own house," I said now, firmly putting my personal correspondence file into my bottom drawer, and remembering to refrain from locking it in Jason's presence—nothing would ignite his curiosity as much as that. "But it's not a novel, or anything remotely creative, and if Tony is right—and he usually is about such matters—then I'm the obvious person to do it, Bridewell is the obvious house, given the closeness of the families, and since I happen to work for the house, it's silly to make the usual fuss."

"Yes," Jason said thoughtfully. "That skilled rationalization does indeed sound like our Tony when he's got the bit between his teeth."

"What do you mean by that?" I asked sharply, before I could remember to hang on to my cool.

"If you ask me," Jason said, "which you haven't, I think Tony dreamed up the whole thing himself, including having you as the writer."

What he said was so absurd that it restored my balance. "Now why on earth would he do that?"

"You're fishing," Jason said. "However," he went on hurriedly, as I opened my mouth, "I'll feed your vanity. Because, as you know very well indeed, our beloved leader has a large crush on you, and has had, furthermore, since long before his divorce."

I did not have to act my astonishment. I was stunned.

And then I broke out laughing. "Jason, you're a wiley one," I said. "Too clever by half, and *much* too clever for your own good."

"What do you mean?" he protested, for once caught off balance.

I grinned, but didn't say anything. As a matter of fact, I was rather pleased with myself for having tumbled so fast to Jason's little method. It was so very like him: titillate my interest by suggesting that Tony Bridewell might nurse a *tendresse* for me, and thus flush out an admission that the shoe was on the other foot.

"Clever, Jason," I said. "But it won't work, love. You're wrong."

"Wrong about what?"

"Wrong about all your little romantic plots and ploys. The Society may be gripped with sentiment over my father, but Tony's interest is firmly grounded in the business of selling books. There are still about fifteen thousand members, worldwide, and while that may be puny compared to the million and a half back in the fifties, they're all pretty well heeled, and they'd every last one of them troop out to buy any book about my father. As a matter of fact, the Society will probably buy fifteen thousand copies and distribute them."

Jason pouted, looking rather like a cross child, which he often did when his bluff was called. "Then if it isn't because he has a yen for you, why should Tony not only gleefully appoint you the writer, but rush the whole thing through the editorial board?"

Since the same question had been occurring to me, ever since Tony broached the matter, Jason rather had me in a corner. There were several members of the Society, all professional writers, who would have been a far more obvious choice than I. But I gave him the overwhelmingly obvious answer I had given myself.

"Item one," I said, checking off a finger, "I am Robert deMaury's daughter. Item two"—I moved to another finger—"I'm here, like Mount Everest. Yes, I know you consider that argument against, rather than for, but in this case I think you're wrong. Item three," I finished firmly, forestalling Jason, who had opened his mouth and then closed it again, "I can probably be had a lot cheaper than any of the Society's writers. And our Tony, like most men born to money, can be extremely tight with the dollar."

"Speaking of being born to money," Jason said, and I saw with relief that he was—at least for the time being —momentarily deflected from his investigative insinuations, "have you heard that the White House is going to offer Tony that ambassadorship—one of the big ones, London or Paris? Anyway, the one that fell vacant recently when the man there resigned."

"Another of your fantasies, Jason?"

He raised his hand. "Scout's honor."

"Where did you hear that?"

"I don't reveal my sources," he said piously. "But I got it from a friend on one of the newspapers, who got it from a friend in the administration in Washington."

I stared at him thoughtfully. The idea was not as fantastic as all that. The Bridewells had always been active in politics, and both Tony's father and grandfather had been appointed ambassadors, one to France and one to Russia, although which was which I could never remember. And, most of all, Tony himself had served in Congress, making a name for himself as one of the House's outstanding young liberal lions.

"Didn't all this come up about five years ago? I mean that Tony was about to go to the embassy in Rome or Paris or somewhere?"

"Yes, but it didn't come to anything or it fell through or something."

"No, it wasn't that," I said slowly, groping around in my memory. "He turned it down. It even got to the point where he had to make a statement to the press because somebody at the White House or State Department had leaked something and the media was badgering him."

"So he said something like, 'Not now but later. Give me a raincheck,'" Jason chimed in. "Yes, I remember now. But about the book you're going to write—"

I was never more glad to hear the phone ring.

"Sorry, Jason," I said with a grin, reaching for the receiver, "not now but later. Give me a raincheck." Jason flicked a salute with his hand and left.

It was Cynthia, Tony Bridewell's secretary. "Janet? Mr. Bridewell would like to see you and wonders if you could come by the office?"

"Of course." I gave the obvious answer. But I sat staring at the receiver for a moment after I put it down. Cynthia Harris was a funny kid, recently promoted to being Tony's secretary after Ann Merriman had been made assistant. Her phone manner left a lot to be desired, and she was famous for replying to a voice on the telephone that announced itself as a noted celebrity, "Yeah? And I'm Barbra Streisand," only to be told rather grimly by Tony that the celebrity, an old friend, was exactly who he said he was.

But she kept Tony's office running with crack efficiency and her intuitions, where Tony was concerned, were infallible, if partly unconscious. More often than not, she'd pick up the phone and say, "Janet, Tony wants to see you." Occasionally, as in this case, it was "Mr. Bridewell." And yet her shift from the formal to the informal, was, I was convinced, neither deliberate nor conscious. Which made it all the more significant. If "Mr. Bridewell" wanted to see me, it conveyed a certain atmosphere around his office that meant he was very probably about to present me with something I wouldn't like, and was going to be official about it.

The auguries, I felt, were not altogether good, at least not from my point of view. But I still had to go. Pulling out a mirror, I ran a comb through my short hair, about which the most that could be said was that it was thick and curly—its brown had been variously described by hopeful hairdressers as chestnut, ash and/or reddish, but mouse was a fairer description—dashed some powder on my nose and freshened my lipstick. My hazel eyes stared back at me. "It doesn't look good," I said aloud. Then I went down the hall to Tony's office.

"You wanted to see me?" I said, stepping into Tony's

big, square, corner office that was high enough to have a view of both the East and the Hudson rivers.

"Yes, Janet. Sit down."

I knew then why Cynthia had been formal. Tony was sitting back in his chair, his handsomely tailored English jacket open, looking relaxed and at ease. But it was deceptive. He was coiled tight as a spring. I had known Tony since I was a child of ten and he was a young man of twenty-two who occasionally showed up at the Bridewell and deMaury family parties looking, to my adoring eyes, unbearably glamorous. He was also, as an admirer of my father's work, around our house a fair amount. But there were times when his tension seemed tightened to an extraordinarily high pitch and when underneath the casual manner ran something that both attracted and frightened me. Once, when I struggled with my child's vocabulary to express this to my father, he said simply, "Yes. Tony burns."

I had known Tony now for twenty-one years and worked for him for seven, yet, seated in front of his desk, trying to look as at ease as possible, I still felt that quiver of . . . something . . . that was not fear, but akin to it.

"Made any plans for going to England, yet?" he asked.

"I wrote to Gideon Lightwood, telling him I wanted to come and look for the papers . . ."

"He was the one who put your father's papers in order, wasn't he?"

"Yes. It was one of those queer things where Father had left all his personal papers with the Society's headquarters in London, meaning to go back and put them in order before bringing them over here. But then he died, and a year or so ago the Society had to move its quarters and without anyone's by your leave they shipped the papers to Tenton."

"And there they've been, resting in peace, ever since, I take it."

It sounded like a question. So I said, "Yes, of course. As far as I know, anyway."

Tony's brilliant blue eyes rested on me. For a minute

I had the odd feeling that he wasn't seeing me at all. I had caught that look on Tony's face at sales conferences, when he was pushing a book that he was trying to convince the salesmen would be a winner. "It's the look he gets," Jason once irreverently said, "when he's envisioning sales in the tens of thousands and wants everyone else to have the same clear view."

Then Tony did one of his characteristic volte-faces. His eyes focused on me. He smiled, and became a totally different person. I thought about Jason's romantic insinuation that Tony had a *tendresse* for me. Would that that were true!

Tony said now, "Am I right in assuming that it was Lightwood who actually sorted the papers out and knows which are where?"

"Exactly right," I said. "Which is what makes things a trifle difficult."

"Yes. You and Lightwood have never been too fond of one another, have you?"

I smiled. "You could put it that way. His wife, Rosemary, was my first cousin, as you know. I think you also know that Rosemary and I were practically brought up together and were tremendously close, especially as she was orphaned when she was a child and spent so much time with us. A lot of people thought I was a bad influence on her because I was the family rebel. I always assumed that was the reason for Gideon's hostility. And then, of course, on top of that, I was with her on that fatal trip in Italy when she died."

"How old was her son when this happened?"

"Benedict? Well, he's eleven now. He must have been six."

"And Lightfoot has brought him up alone?"

"Because of his handicap there's some kind of governess."

Tony grinned. "There'll always be an England, especially as long as there are governesses or nannies. When did you say you were going to be there?"

"Well, I wanted to go the first three weeks of September. But when I wrote suggesting that, I got one of Gideon's chilly put-downs. He said he and Benedict would be in London then and the house closed. And added that if you wanted the book done, perhaps you should come and look at the papers yourself now."

It was at that point that Tony dropped his bombshell.

"Impossible! You'll have to go immediately."

"But I can't! My desk's piled high."

"Other people can do the stuff that's on your desk now, Janet. But only you—with Gideon—can make sense out of your father's papers. So I want you to go over there right away."

"But—" My head was spinning. The books I was working on, the authors I had appointments with, the production schedules I was hovering over and pushing along went through my head like a speeded-up film. "I can't, Tony," I repeated. "There's the Cartwell manuscript . . . if that's not ready in three weeks, at the most, it'll never make the winter list, and if it doesn't make that list, after all the postponements, he's threatening some kind of suit. Then there's that political biography. If that isn't in the bookstores by fall—"

Tony held up a hand. "Let's take them one at a time. I'm quite sure it can all be worked out."

Rebel and general family firecracker I might be, bucking against the family's almost missionary-like idealism, but I had inherited my father's tenacity and firmly held conviction that if you started a job you finished it, and I fought against Tony's various suggestions as to how others would complete work on the books I had brought into the house.

"But what's the hurry?" I protested.

"Two things. The first and lesser reason is that I want you here in September. That series of wildlife books that we've been dickering with the museum over for the past two years has suddenly come through. The writer of the first volume will be ready to hand in a manuscript by Labor Day, and since all the future volumes have to tie in with the first, I want you to be here to receive it and work with the author while he's in New York and before he goes back to Alaska or wherever he hides out. The second reason is more important. Have you given much thought to how short a time you need to write the biography?"

I stared at Tony. "Well, the contract calls for delivery in two years."

"And two years is 1979. Do you know when your father founded World Union?"

"1930."

"That's what everyone thinks. But it's not so. Read this." And he handed a letter over the desk.

I stared at the familiar letterhead, unchanged since my father, indulging a minor hobby in graphics, designed it himself. At the bottom of the letter was Myron's spiky signature. My eye ran down the letter.

> *It's astonishing, after all these years, to find that the Society was actually founded towards the end of 1929. I suppose the mistake was made because the announcement about the Royal patron, and the opening of the new quarters in London, did not take place until the following year. But there's no question: our copies of the very early letters confirm the fact that the first meeting summoned by Robert deMaury in his own flat occurred several months earlier.*

Even in my mental turmoil, I saw the import of what Myron was saying. "So the fiftieth anniversary of the founding will be in 1979."

"Precisely. And, of course, that's the obvious time for publishing the book. I'd like to make the publication day the exact anniversary of that first meeting held in your father's flat. Think of the publicity that we'd get! Since your father's death the Society has dwindled to nothing. Without his personality it couldn't withstand the changing times. But there are still a few prominent people around who remember how powerful it was—especially in the thirties and mid-fifties. Jason's department could have a field day with that. . . . But it means having finished books no later than the summer of seventy-nine. This time we're not going to repeat our previous bloopers when some much touted book actually arrived in the stores weeks after all the publicity about it. The books are going to be ready and waiting in the warehouse before Jason cranks up the promotion machine. But that means that you, my dear, have to deliver your manuscript no later than the fall of seventy-eight. Which is why I want you to drop everything now and get over to England to do your basic research."

"Why don't you give me a sabbatical in which I can write the book in peace and quiet, instead of in odd moments around my job?" I asked brazenly.

"Because then I'd have to hire an editor to do the work you're doing," Tony replied. "And that extra salary would come out of the profit I'm expecting on your father's book."

"I could live on the advance you've given me," I suggested rather tentatively, because I had been looking upon that (to me) large sum as gravy in the bank.

"I'd still have to have somebody take your place. Don't be so overwhelmed with modesty, Janet. You get a lot of work done around here. More than most of the other editors, many of whom seem to have large ideas accompanied by a small capacity for the nuts and bolts of daily work."

I made a gigantic effort not to succumb to the pleasure that flowed through me at his words. And failed. "Flattery," I said, uttering the feeble cliché, "will get you almost anywhere. As you well know."

"I'm not flattering you, Janet. We're too old friends for that. Aren't we?"

Feeling like I was drowning in those blue eyes, I stared at the big, handsome man across the desk. Tony married when I was twelve. That marriage ended with his wife's death in a car accident seven years later. Three years after that, he married again. Eight years later, that marriage ended in divorce. If Tony had played around outside his marriages—which rumor said he had—it certainly wasn't with me. But sometimes I toyed with a fantasy that one day, when I was sitting in front of his desk as I was now, he would get up and come around and pull me to my feet. . . .

I therefore felt as though I was caught in my own dream when I saw him get up and come around the desk and reach out to pull me to my feet.

"Besides," he said, holding on to my hands, "I like to have you around. And I won't be looking too close if you shut your door and work on your book here."

For reasons I didn't fully understand myself, I withdrew my hands. "All right, Tony. You're the boss. I'll turn over my current work and get to England by the end of the week. Which will," I said, after a moment, "be an unpleasant surprise for Gideon."

"Oh, I'm sure you can manage Gideon," Tony said, going back around his desk and beginning to shift the papers on his blotter, always a sure sign that he was ready for his visitor to leave. As I got to the door he looked up and smiled again. "Let me know when exactly you're leaving."

It was, after all, not that difficult to get off. With the way smoothed by Tony's iron hand, the work proved surprisingly easy to delegate. At home, all I had to do was lock my apartment and ask the super to keep an eye on it, which by itself was unusual. My apartment has frequently been occupied by the cats and dogs that I have almost inadvertently acquired because of a tendency—Jason calls it my reigning weakness—to pick up forlorn and abandoned strays. But all recent tenants had found good homes, and my own Tobias, canine roommate for many happy years, had, the previous month, succumbed to old age. Now packing, I reflected it was just as well that I had not taken my planned journey to the Humane Society, Tobias's ancestral home, to find another of my preferred breed—mutts.

Getting out to the airport proved equally painless. Having discovered my flight and departure time, Tony had laid on a limousine.

"That's pretty expensive of you, Tony," I said, when I went in the afternoon before I left to send Gideon a cable and say good-bye to Tony and thank him.

He waved a hand. "Nothing is too good, etcetera.

Have a good flight. Don't worry about anything here. Keep in touch."

Twelve hours later I was in a London hotel, making arrangements to hire a car the following day to drive to Tenton. When I hung up I sat on the side of the bed and stared sleepily at the telephone. Another of Tony's gifts to the departing worker was a first-class ticket, a delicious luxury which I reveled in all the way over. But whether traveling first or tourist, I still didn't sleep on planes, and while it was bright midmorning in London, according to my body-clock it was three A.M. without having been to bed. So I decided to give in to native cowardice and not to call Gideon telling him that I had arrived. My cable had been fairly explicit about hiring a car and driving myself up the following day. Time enough to talk to him when I got there.

I allowed myself only a short nap, since I wanted a good night's sleep before setting out on my journey the next morning. Then I got up, bathed and dressed and indulged myself in one of my favorite English lunches—pork pie and salad. Then, in the interests of establishing the right mental atmosphere, walked to the Bloomsbury section of London where, fifty years before, my father had his first flat, the meeting place, according to Myron Weatherby, of the Society's first gathering, and where, on another side of the square, stood the house that became the Society's first headquarters a year later.

Sold the previous year, the tall Regency building now, according to the directory in the foyer, housed two literary agencies and a magazine. I was standing in the foyer, staring at the short listing, when the glass-paneled front door opened and a tall, stooped man of about forty came out.

"May I help you?" he asked courteously, but with a slight guttural accent.

"No. Thank you just the same."

He continued to look at me with bright brown eyes, and I felt so foolish, loitering there for apparently no reason, that I succumbed to the rather weak-kneed urge to explain my presence.

"This was once the headquarters of the Society Towards a World Union, wasn't it?"

The man was shaking out and then furling a large black umbrella, a sensible preparation for the gray day outside. But the alert eyes never left my face. "I believe so," he said. "Are you looking for their present whereabouts?"

"No, not really, I don't think they have any here in London now. It was really just a sentimental journey."

"Oh? Are you interested in the Society?"

Why, I thought, had I got myself into this? Because I suddenly discovered that I had no wish to make any further revelation to this civil stranger of my connection to the Society or my relationship to its founder.

"Oh, just a general historical interest. I'm behaving like a rather typical tourist."

"But you sound partly English?"

"My mother was English and I spent part of my childhood over here." With his body and his umbrella, which he seemed to have some trouble furling, he was effectively blocking my way out of the small foyer. "Excuse me," I said firmly, and, pushing his umbrella aside, got out onto the porch and the steps.

"Because," the man said, as though he were continuing a sentence already started, "all inquiries about the Society can be made at the magazine office on the top floor."

I was surprised at that. Neither Myron Weatherby nor anyone else in the Society in New York had told me that some magazine was acting as an agent for inquiries.

"Here," the man said, opening up the glass-paneled door. "Let me show you to the lift."

One of the stubborn streaks for which I was famous in the family took hold of me then. For some reason I didn't understand, this stranger, whom I had never seen before, wanted to get me up to the magazine on the top floor to pose questions about the Society which I had no interest in asking.

"Thank you," I said, "but I'm in a rush and must go. Some other time, perhaps." And I all but ran down the steps and walked briskly to the end of the square. It was only then that I felt able to turn and look back. The man was nowhere in sight. All of which meant that either he had sprinted to the other end of the square, which somehow seemed unlikely, or he had gone back into the house. To the magazine? Moving back a little to where I could see them, I stared at the windows of what must have been the house's servants' quarters. But it was a gesture that had little meaning. What did I expect to see? A face peering out? Gazing up, I realized, with a certain irony, that if there'd been half a dozen faces in the window, with the sun reflected off the glass, I wouldn't have seen them. And if I changed my position by moving any farther back, the big trees in the square would block my view.

Odd, I thought, turning and walking much more slowly back towards the hotel.

The next morning, with my bags stowed away in the trunk, I pointed the hired car in a northwesterly direction, heading for the upper reaches of the Welsh border country and the village of Tenton, outside of which stood Tenton Hall, where Sir Gideon Lightwood, former soldier and landowner, lived with his and his late wife Rosemary's son, Benedict.

I had met Gideon at his wedding in New York, when he had come over to marry Rosemary. Owing to a delayed flight, he had arrived barely in time to get to the big church on Madison Avenue, and my first sight of him was as I preceded Rosemary down the aisle. That moment was one that stayed in my mind from then on. As I, Rosemary's maid-of-honor, walked slowly towards the chancel steps, the lights and blaze of flowers that had at first distracted my eyes seemed to recede. I was, naturally, consumed with curiosity about the man who was to marry the cousin who had been brought up with me as though she were my sister. We were both nineteen, and until a year or so before, we had shared practically everything —schools, friends, homes and, perhaps most of all, my father's somewhat erratic affection.

But at eighteen, when I went off to college, our paths

diverged. I had chosen to attend a large state university in the Midwest, ostensibly to follow a boyfriend who was going there. Rosemary instead went to London, where she had been offered a job in the Society's headquarters. It was there in London that she'd met Gideon. Rosemary was not much of a letter writer, so the announcement of her engagement, dutifully placed in the *New York Times* by our Aunt Cecilia, my father's sister, was almost as much of a surprise to me as it was to some of our more casual friends.

Rosemary came back from London for the wedding, I flew east, and the first question I asked her when we finally came together in Aunt Cecilia's New York apartment was, "Rosemary—what's he like?"

Her cool, beautiful, almost remote face broke into a smile. "Devastating," she said, and we both broke into laughter over the reminder that at twelve years old, when we had both just read *Jane Eyre,* we had sworn an oath that neither of us would settle for a husband who was any less devastating than that hero of heroes, Edward Fairfax Rochester.

"Show me a picture," I had said, ever literal-minded. But Rosemary didn't have one, which I thought very odd. "It all happened so fast," she explained.

I thought that was a rather poor excuse, knowing that I would, if necessary, have bought or stolen a camera and backed my beloved to the nearest wall and used up endless reels until I had a likeness that satisfied me. But then, as Rosemary pointed out when I said this to her, I was both bossier and more romantic than she was.

"I may *look* more romantic," she said, trying on Aunt Cecilia's lace veil, handed down in the family for several generations, "but, as we both know, you're much more old-fashioned in that way than I am." She glanced up at me in the big mirror in front of which she was sitting. *"N'est-ce pas?"*

It was true. Rosemary, who looked almost a stereotype of the classic debutante, was much more caught up in the family tradition of good works than I, which was one reason she had turned down college to work in the

Society's London office, an act of devotion to my father's cause that I, at the cost of a great deal of guilt, refused. (Since my name was, after all, deMaury, it was originally offered to me.) There was, for one thing, my current boyfriend, an excuse that Rosemary looked upon with shocked disbelief. There was another reason, lying deep where my conscious mind could not reach it. I couldn't define it, and was ashamed of it, whatever it was. All I knew was that no matter how many lectures I gave myself about carrying on my father's work, about his lifelong, selfless dedication to world union and brotherhood in a world that sorely needed it, I couldn't make myself quit everything and go over to London to prop up what was left of his cherished cause.

Unlike me, Rosemary did not question this. She simply went in my place. And found Gideon. Or was found by him.

Pacing slowly up the aisle to the Bach fugue, measuring my steps so as not to gain on two little page boys in kilts, I finally saw the two men standing to the right of the chancel steps. The redhead standing slightly in front I knew immediately to be the best man, because one of the few details that Rosemary had offered was that Gideon was dark. A second later and I caught sight of a tall head with thick black hair, a pair of black brows that bisected the face and, thrust between them, a powerful nose. A few steps farther on and I saw the silvery lightness of the eyes set deep behind the brows, eyes that looked to me for a moment with cool indifference. Then they slid past me and I knew, as they softened, that they had found Rosemary.

That had been twelve years ago. I had seen Gideon only once since he and Rosemary left the reception following the wedding.

In the seven years before her death, I saw Rosemary twice: once when she came back to the States for my father's funeral in 1970; the second time when she and I took that ill-fated trip to Italy where, in Rome, when coming from a party to meet me in the piazza below, she was struck and killed by a hit-and-run car.

It was then, while I was questioned endlessly by the Italian police, that I saw Gideon again. He had flown from England and sat with me while the interrogation went on:

How far away had I been when it happened?

Across the piazza sitting at an outdoor table having coffee.

Why wasn't I with Rosemary at her party?

Because I had gone to a party of my own nearby and we were to meet at the piazza café and walk back to the hotel.

Did I see or hear anything that could help them find the car?

No, all I saw and heard were a sudden blaze of headlights and the sound of the motor accelerating.

Nothing else? Not the color of the car, the license plate? The make?

No, it was dark . . .

Gideon, sitting there, was remote and guarded and, understandably I supposed, antagonistic, as though angry that I was alive while Rosemary was dead.

The police then almost casually asked if Rosemary and I had quarreled in any way.

No, I said. Why should they think that?

Wasn't it unusual for two young women, closely related, not to attend the same parties?

Not at all, I replied. By that time we had lived on different sides of the Atlantic for some years and had different sets of friends. Besides which, the party I had been to had been given by an Italian author of mine and came under the general heading of business.

So we hadn't quarreled in any way?

Absolutely not.

I tried not to let their questioning upset me, realizing that the police, with nothing to go on, were looking anywhere possible for clues. But later, still jolted somewhat by the police probings, I asked myself that question and came up with the conclusion that as a matter of fact, almost curiously, we had never quarreled. This was undoubtedly more to Rosemary's credit than mine because while I didn't hold grudges, I could flare up with all the ease of an Irish grandmother, and had never been hesitant about expressing myself. But Rosemary didn't have that Irish grandmother. That feisty old lady had been my father's mother. My own mother, sister to Rosemary's, had been English. She had married an American, Robert deMaury, who was living in England at that time, a year before her sister married William Farnborough, an Englishman. A year after that, Rosemary and I were born, but on different sides of the Atlantic, because my own parents had come to New York. Then, when she was eleven, Rosemary's parents were killed in a car accident, and after that she divided her time between our home in New York and that of her English grandparents. Eight years later she married Gideon.

But in those eight years, when we were so much together—all the more, after my mother's death when we were fourteen—we had never quarreled, a fact that I had not looked upon as particularly remarkable until the subject was brought up by the police. Then, in the months that followed her death and my eventual return to the States, I examined every moment of our lives together that I could remember. It was at that point that I made the curious discovery: how complete Rosemary's reserve had been. It was not only that we had not quarreled. Rosemary had seldom, if ever, discussed her deep feelings about anything. But, having made that discovery, I also realized that I had known that fact, at some level, all along, because I had even, when I was about fifteen, commented on it to my father.

"Yes," he'd said, "you're right. She doesn't discuss how she feels. That's her great strength."

Naturally enough, since I discussed my feelings all the time, I bristled. "Why should that be a strength?"

"Because she holds fast to the integrity of those feelings. You—born communicator that you are—talk over how you feel about practically anything with practically anybody all the time. So you end up with a mixture of feelings—yours and theirs—which you then think are entirely your own."

I sorted that out, staring at him. Strangely, and for all his volubility about his pet causes, my father had something of Rosemary's guarded reserve.

"You mean she's more like you," I said slowly, feeling oddly hurt.

"Yes," he said. And then made the kind of personal gesture which so often won him so much devotion. Reaching out with both of his hands he grasped my head and planted a kiss on the top of it. "But you're my daughter, and I love you very much." The trouble was that at that point I didn't really believe him.

Eventually the Roman police gave up and I returned to the States. I wrote then to Gideon and offered to take Benedict, the six-year-old son Rosemary had left behind, at least for a while. Gideon's refusal was curt. When, three years after that, Benedict was severely injured in a fall from his pony, I heard the news from relatives in England, not from Gideon. Again I wrote, prompted as much as anything else by the feeling that Rosemary would want me to. This time Gideon's extremely brusque reply left me in no doubt that he intended his refusal to be taken as final.

So there the matter rested and, what with my own work and life, Rosemary slid to the back of my mind until one day, some time later, when Tony and I were talking about my father and his Society, Rosemary's name came up in the course of conversation. Tony then astonished me by saying, "You are—and were—a much stronger person than Rosemary, Janet. You've always come over with much more impact. People liked you better."

"That's nonsense, Tony." (But even as I spoke I felt a surge of reassurance that Tony was saying this to me.) "Rosemary was far, far more beautiful."

"Granted," he said. "Rosemary had the kind of face that launched ships and over which empires and thrones are lost. And that reserve of hers just added to the mystic attraction. But you were brighter—and nicer—and people liked you more. And for all her staggering beauty, I think Rosemary felt, around you, cast into the shade.

You know, Janet, it's only us ordinary mortals that place such a high premium on beauty. Frequently people who possess it find it less than an unmixed blessing. I've always thought that was why she married Gideon Lightwood—Sir Gideon Lightwood. She not only married before you—and even in the wild sixties in the circles you both moved in that was still a coup—but getting Lightwood was an achievement in itself. It may only be a baronetcy, but the name is one of the oldest in England, and that property has been in the family since the fourteenth century."

I was still reeling from the shock of hearing that Rosemary might have felt outshone by me.

"Tony—are you *sure?* I mean about the way Rosemary felt. I can hardly believe it. And am I dumb not to have picked this up?"

"No. Just not one to suffer the torments of self-doubt. And there was also the fact that Rosemary was not given—ever—to discuss her feelings. After all, Janet, she didn't have to confront them that much. She was always going back and forth between the two countries. So, in a sense, whatever she might have felt was relieved by a change of scene. Probably that had something to do with her reason for taking that job with the Society in London. When you turned it down, it was one up to her to take your place. After all, she was always jealous of your father's affection for you."

"Oh, Tony. What rubbish. My father thought the world of her. More, I sometimes thought, than he did of me. In fact—" and I reported the scene in which he had spoken of Rosemary's integrity. "I think he thought she was even stronger than I."

"Your father had his blind spots, Janet. Rosemary shared some of his views and enthusiasms. Naturally he would see that as strength, and, to some extent, your constant verbal questioning as defection. Not that he didn't adore you," Tony added hastily, and, I felt, untruthfully, "but it did affect his view of Rosemary."

It took me some while to accept what Tony had said. But eventually I did, because it made sense of so much, especially Gideon's dislike. Obviously, loving her, he would see me as dominant and overbearing. Strangely, having come to realize that, I lost some of the rage I had been building up against him. I still disliked Gideon, finding him arrogant, stuffy and narrow. But his prejudice against me seemed somehow a logical outcome of his love for Rosemary.

Thus, when I wrote saying I wished to come and examine the Society's papers now at Tenton, I did so with some trepidation and was therefore not overly surprised at his less than civil answer.

But then came Tony's high-handed maneuverings, and so that day as I pointed the car in a northwesterly direction out of London towards Tenton Hall, I found myself not entirely sure of the kind of reception I would get. Well, I thought, if Gideon didn't like it, he would have to lump it.

I held on to that admirable sentiment while I drove through the village of Tenton, a straggle of houses on either side of a road, and inquired directions at the Tenton Arms, a rather depressed-looking pub at the northern end of the village. It took all my concentration to understand the directions when I got them, because the local accent had more than a touch of Welsh, wording and lilt. But at the second run-through I thought I understood and, sure enough, two winding miles later found myself following along a high stone wall that eventually curved into a tall iron gate whose stone posts on either side each sported a stone leopard, paw on shield.

I have never seen a place look more deserted, and, for the first time, my faith in the wisdom of following Tony's orders as blindly as I had was shaken. A drive led from the gate, with the line of trees on either side and thick branches meeting overhead. It must, at one time, when it, was cared for, have been a beautiful vista. But the grass lining the drive needed attention and seemed to be losing a battle against shrubbery that, tangled and overgrown, had crept up between the trees. At the far end was a yellowish stone house, looking, from what I could see of it, to be a Georgian structure. But anything less hospitable was hard to imagine.

Getting out of the car, I went up to the gate to see if I could open it or if there was a bell. I discovered immediately that the gate would not open from the outside. After groping around the tall, creeper-covered post, I did discover a metal contraption which I pulled. At which point a man came out of what I saw was a small gatehouse tucked beneath the wall, wiped his mouth—it was, I realized, his tea time—and, in the same local accent, asked my name and purpose.

I gave him my name, Janet deMaury, and my purpose, to see Sir Gideon Lightwood. The man went back into the house. I stood there, waiting, and discovered, to my chagrin, that I would not be all that upset if the man came back and said something like, "The master said no. You can't come in." I would have done my best, I thought, walking back and forth, and I would not, therefore, have to meet Gideon. Curious, I thought, stopping in my pacing. I hadn't realized how much I was dreading that encounter. Well— But the man was back, and without further words, was unlocking the gate.

I drove through and up the avenue, and saw, in the rear-view mirror, the gates being shut. At that moment, the temptation to turn the car around, order the man to reopen the gates and drive out again was astonishingly strong. So strong that the car seemed to slow to a stop of its own accord. It was almost, my scattered mind seemed to tell me, as though those gates behind me were prison gates, and I had voluntarily walked into a prison. Or was a trap a better analogy?

It had been cold, wet and rainy ever since I had come into the west country. But that hardly accounted for the shiver that quivered over me.

"Come on, Janet." I said the words aloud to myself. What were the terms used so often to describe me that I found them irritating? Practical, extrovert Janet. I said those aloud too. And then the mental picture of myself, sitting in my hired car, in the middle of this rundown, desolate estate, talking to myself about myself, tickled my sense of humor, and I started to laugh.

Putting the car in gear, I drove up to the front and, again, stopped. The house was taller than I had thought, and its Georgian simplicity was marred by obvious additions that had been built on either side. The soft lemony color that I had seen from the end of the drive was a wash, rather similar to those used on French châteaux, and was surprising, somehow, in this country-side. I knew from what Rosemary had told me, that though the land had been in the Lightwood family since the fourteenth century, this was the third house to be built on it, the two previous having been a small castle, which was torn down and replaced by a Tudor house which, in the eighteenth century, was burned down and replaced by the present building.

Well, I thought, whatever money, revenue or whatnot the family had lived on for all these centuries must be dwindling out. The place could certainly use another coat of wash and a general sprucing up. What a surrounding, I thought, for a child, already an invalid, to be brought up in.

Following the drive around to the side, I took the car into what was obviously once a stable, got out, shut the door, and walked out of the courtyard, meaning to go back around to the front.

The sound of a side door opening was drowned out by sudden, deep barking. I stood frozen. Loping down the steps around the house was a magnificent German shepherd, his intent clear by the savagery of his bark and lips drawn back over his teeth. When it comes to angry guard dogs I am not in the least brave. Some power that was not courage kept my feet rooted, instead of bearing me away, futilely, no doubt, but at top speed. Then something made me raise my head. Standing at the top of the steps, watching me grimly, was Gideon.

# two

"GOOD AFTERNOON," Gideon said.

The dog had slowed and was now growling instead of barking, but the lips were still curved up, the back legs tensed, ready to thrust him forward.

"Please call your dog off, Gideon." I was surprised—and proud—that my voice came out as normal-sounding as it did. If it had reflected the way I felt, it would have been a quiver or a squeak.

Gideon stared at me for a minute, frowning, his silver-gray eyes barely visible under the heavy black bar of his brows. Then he said, "Back Gelert. Heel."

The lips lowered. The growling stopped. The dog turned and obediently ran back to Gideon, pushing his nose against Gideon's hand, looking like any affectionate animal.

Only as it slowed I become aware of how rapidly my heart had been pounding. "That's a rather dangerous pet, isn't it?" Now that my fear had receded, I was also aware of my anger.

"He's a trained guard dog," Gideon said, his hand

touching the handsome head. "He was merely doing his job. This is an isolated house."

"Since your gatekeeper announced me, you can hardly claim to have been taken by surprise. You got my cable, didn't you?"

"Yes. Why the rush?"

"Well, for one thing, you said you wouldn't be here in September when I suggested I'd come, and then, for a variety of technical reasons connected with getting the book out on time, Tony insisted I come over right away."

"Why didn't Bridewell come himself?"

"Why should he, if he could send me? Why do you ask?"

Gideon shrugged. "It just seems to me it's the kind of operation he'd want to carry out himself."

"You don't know Tony. He's a master delegator." At that point the rain, which had been falling off and on since I entered this part of the country, started down again, and this time with more force. I could feel the big drops splash on my head and face.

"You'd better come in," Gideon said, and turned back up the steps, the dog, Gelert, beside him. Reflecting that among welcomes this must rate zero in cordiality, I followed him.

The glass-paneled side door led straight into a large, square room with high ceilings and two walls covered with books. Opposite the door, a fire crackled in the big fireplace. As we came in, another, much smaller dog got up from the rug in front of the fire and took one or two uncertain steps in our direction. Moving towards her, I saw she was balanced on three legs. She was also painfully thin. As long as they are not large and threatening to bite me, I am a patsy when it comes to animals, so as I came up to her I held out my hand. Shakily, because the leg she was favoring was one of her hind ones, she rose on her one good back leg and put her paws on my raincoat.

"Down," Gideon said, walking over to the other side of the fireplace.

But I was stroking her and she was licking my hand. "She doesn't bother me. What's her name?"

"She doesn't have one. She's only here temporarily."

"Why? Doesn't she belong to you?"

"No. If she belonged to me, she wouldn't be here temporarily."

I opened my mouth to reply in kind, but decided, at least for the time, to maintain civility on my side even if it killed me. Some of my reasons for this were muddled and I didn't have time to sort them out. But one was obvious: I needed Gideon's help, and, having stolen a march on him in coming here uninvited and two months early, it behooved me, insofar as I could without allowing myself to be trodden on, to keep the peace.

Evidently Gideon repented of his surliness, because he said, reaching down to poke the fire, "She doesn't belong to anybody. I found her when I was walking in the fields back of the house. Her foot was caught in a trap."

"You have traps on your land?"

"Of course not. But poachers put them out."

"You don't know who she belongs to?"

"Nobody around here owns her. I've asked in the village."

"Well, what will you do with her?"

"I don't know. Why are you so interested?"

I felt a familiar impulse coming over me. There was something about the small, tan, pointed muzzle and skinny body that I found endearing. I looked at her carefully. "She's not very old, is she? She looks barely out of puppyhood."

"The vet said she was about nine months."

Grudgingly I conceded the point that Gideon had at least had her seen by a veterinary surgeon. "What do you plan to do with her, then, if she's only going to be here temporarily?"

"I'm not going to do anything with her. I've put an advertisement in the local paper and the owner may show up. I repeat, why are you so interested?"

"Because I like her."

"Well, if you like her that much and the owner doesn't come to light, you can take her with you. Gelert is not that fond of her."

"I see," I said. "Jealousy."

"Something like that. I—Ah, come in, Sheila."

I turned. Standing in the door was a young woman of about my own age and of striking good looks. Red hair and a pretty face topped an excellent figure and she was a good four inches taller than I.

"Sorry," she said with a smile of great charm. "I didn't know you had guests."

"Janet, this is Sheila Maitland, who represents Benedict's only hope of getting into a good school once his leg is put right. Sheila, this is my sister-in-law, Janet deMaury."

"Oh." Sheila came into the room with her hand out. "I didn't realize you were coming so early. Gideon said something about your wanting to come in September."

I explained again about the book.

"Oh, well, you'll probably hit better weather by coming early," she said, and then glanced outside the window at the steadily falling rain. "Not that it would look that way. Did you have a good journey?"

I was as happy to see her as though she were an old friend, because the atmosphere in the room, which had been tense and crackling, suddenly eased. And I answered her queries about my flight from New York and my hotel in London with more enthusiasm than such commonplaces deserved. Finally she said, "Have you offered Miss deMaury any tea, Gideon?"

"No. Sorry. I'll ring for some."

"Don't worry if it's a bother," I said, somewhat insincerely. A cup of tea would be very welcome. I hadn't realized how chilled I had become.

"It's time for it anyway," Gideon said, touching a bell beside the chimney piece.

An elderly woman who looked as though she might be a housekeeper came in.

"Is tea ready, Mrs. Lowndes?" Gideon said. "By the way, this is Benedict's cousin, Miss deMaury. She's come for a visit."

"How do you do, madam? Yes, I'll bring tea in right

away. Shall I get your bag? It's your car, isn't it, in the court?"

"Yes, thank you. That would be kind of you."

Well, I thought, as she left. That was that hurdle taken. I had been planning to ask Gideon if someone could bring my suitcase in. His statement that I had come for a visit was the first acknowledgment from him that I would be staying. Sitting down in the armchair beside the fire, I prepared to enjoy my tea.

"Sheila's been tutoring Benedict for the last year," Gideon said, after tea, and after Sheila had gone up to see Benedict before leaving for the day.

"How is he?"

"They're going to have to put a steel plate in his hip, but, for medical reasons I don't understand, feel it would be better to wait. Something to do with the last operation he had."

Gideon was frowning, staring at the fire.

"It must be hard for a boy of eleven to be an invalid," I said tentatively. "I take it he's completely bedridden."

Gideon didn't answer for a minute, then he said, "What? Oh—no, he's not always bedridden. Periodically he gets up, and with the aid of a cane or a crutch, gets about quite well. That's the baffling part. The best specialists in London have looked at him, X-rayed him and examined him from head to toe and from A to Z, to say nothing of Dr. Maitland, Sheila's father. Nobody can give any explanation for the fact that there are times when he hops about like a relatively normal boy with a bad leg, and other times when he lies in bed, practically as though he'd been paralyzed, and yet other occasions, especially lately, when he flies into temper tantrums."

The firelight played over Gideon's face, throwing the forehead and nose and square chin into sharp relief, making the already deep lines seem deeper. Gideon must be, I thought, calculating, forty-three or -four. Unlike Tony Bridewell, who looked considerably younger than his forty-three years, Gideon looked older than his age. It couldn't, I found myself thinking, have been easy for him. First his wife died and then three years later his son was injured severely enough to leave him physically damaged. And now, I wondered, had whatever happened to Benedict affected his mind?

"Is it psychological?" I asked Gideon, following this train of thought, and then wondered if he would take offense. Even in this day there were traditionalists who resisted any explanation that seemed to owe anything to disturbed emotions. And I strongly suspected that Gideon might be just such a product of the old school. But he surprised me.

"I wondered that myself. The doctors themselves seemed divided. So a psychiatrist came down here."

"What did he say?" I asked, when Gideon didn't go on.

"Well, as often happens, when the doctor comes the symptoms disappear. The day the psychiatrist came Benedict seemed fully his old self, except for his physical condition. In the psychiatrist's words he appeared to be a lively, intelligent, curious boy, remarkably well adjusted to his injury. Then, of course, after the doctor left, Benedict's . . . emotional . . . condition proceeded to grow worse."

"Back to square one," I said.

"As you say, back to square one."

The door opened, and the housekeeper, Mrs. Lowndes, came in to collect the tea things. "Will Miss Maitland be staying for dinner, Sir Gideon?" she asked.

He looked up. "No. Not tonight. Just Miss deMaury, Mr. Roger and me."

I was wondering who Roger was when I remembered that he must be, of course, Gideon's much younger half brother. Gideon's father, Sir Gareth Lightwood, after a few years of being a widower, had married again late in life and had produced a second son before he finally himself died. I tried to recall whether the second Lady Lightwood, much younger than her husband, was still alive. I glanced at Gideon's withdrawn face and decided not to ask. Instead I said, feeling far more sympathetic to

Gideon than I would have believed possible, "I'm sorry about Benedict."

And promptly got set back on my heels. Gideon turned from the fire and looked at me as though something I'd said had tripped some warning or danger signal. The look of baffled pain that had touched my sympathy was replaced by the expression I knew much better: one of cold dislike.

"Thank you," he replied, in a voice that matched his face. "But there is no reason why Benedict should concern you in any way."

I was angered into a retort. "Oh yes there is. His mother was my cousin. I am his blood relative. Of course I have a legitimate interest in him."

"Let me assure you—"

"Hello, hello," said a cheerful voice from the door. "Fighting already, Gideon? And with such a pretty girl?"

The young man who was strolling into the room was a younger and far handsomer version of the scowling figure in front of the fire. Smiling, he came towards me with his hand out. "Gideon is in such a foul temper he probably won't introduce us. I'm Roger Lightwood, the family prodigal. I gather from advance reports that you're Janet deMaury, Rosemary's cousin."

"The reports are correct," I said, shaking his hand. "I'm delighted to meet you."

"How super that you've come early. In September I'd probably not be here. If Gideon is trying to terrorize you, pay no attention. He's known for miles around for his surly disposition."

"Kind of you," Gideon said. But the look of frozen hostility had gone, to my relief. "Now that you're here," he went on, getting up and going towards the door, "you can help entertain Janet. I'm going up to see Benedict. Dinner is at seven, Janet. I need hardly tell you that in this day and time, with only the three of us, we don't dress."

"That's a pity," I said, as the door closed behind Gideon. "I'd rather hoped that Gideon would be one of the last outposts of the Empire. You know, black tie in the jungle."

Roger grinned. "Yes, I can just see him upholding the ancient disciplines while all around crumbled. Sherry?" He went over to a side table on which were a decanter and glasses.

"Yes, thanks."

He poured out two glasses and brought one over to me. "Cheers," I said, and took a sip.

He raised his glass. *"Salut!"* He swallowed some of the wine. "And where is the divine Sheila?"

"Upstairs with Benedict, I think. She said she wanted to settle him before leaving."

"Ah! Then I take it she's not joining us for dinner."

"I gather not." Over my glass I stared at the face that was so like, and yet so unlike, Gideon's. There was the same high brow, pronounced bones and black hair. Unlike Gideon's, Roger's nose was shorter and straighter and his eyes were more blue than gray. The big difference, though, lay in expression. Even in the few minutes I had known him, a dozen expressions had played over Roger's volatile face: interest, amusement, distaste . . . and the flicker of distaste, I suddenly realized, had been discernible when he mentioned Sheila's name. What did he call her—"the divine Sheila"?

I hesitated. I was in a strange country and, for all the fact that my mother was English, among a strange people. Even at home my tendency to bluntness had got me into occasional trouble. Here—? Yet I could be nothing but myself, I decided.

"Don't you like Miss Maitland?" I asked.

He held his sherry glass up to the light, looking at it through the dark gold liquid. "Now that," he said slowly, "is very perceptive of you."

I burst out laughing. "Not in the least. Anybody could have picked that up."

He grinned. "I would have said so, but do you know, neither Sheila nor my brother have, so wrapped up are they in mutual approval."

"Oh." I absorbed this piece of information. "Like that."

"Just like that," Roger said gently.

"But—" I said.

"But what?"

"I suppose I mean, what's stopping them? She's not married to anyone else."

"Oh—Gideon's not one to rush into anything as . . . final . . . as marriage."

"Well," I said thoughtfully, "it wasn't a world record, but his courtship of Rosemary was fairly speedy."

"You were there when she died, weren't you?"

"Yes."

"I never quite knew what happened. The newspaper accounts seemed vague, and I didn't like to question Gideon." He looked at me inquiringly.

"As you probably know, it was a hit-and-run thing. Rosemary and I were going to meet after our separate parties at a sidewalk café and walk home together. I was there first, sipping my coffee, waiting for her. It wasn't late. Then I saw her come out of the house on the side at right angles to the café and start to come towards me. I remember, she had on a white dress. The next thing I saw were headlights and I heard the sound of a car roaring up. Then she seemed to go up in the air . . ." My voice faltered. It was a while since I had relived it for someone else.

"Sorry," Roger said. "That was a stupid thing to ask. It must bring it all back."

I sat there, rather shaken as I always was by the memory of those lights rushing towards Rosemary. "It's all right," I said, and got to my feet. "I think I'll freshen up before dinner. I wonder where Mrs. Lowndes has taken my bag."

He put down his sherry. "Please let me show you where the guest room is. I'm pretty sure which one she'll have put you in." He smiled then. "It isn't as though Gideon had dozens of rooms all made up and ready to be occupied by a guest. This way."

I followed him out into a wide hall that led, after we had passed a few doors, into the center of the ground floor, from which rose a staircase, branching to either side from a landing halfway up. Portraits hung around the hall, nearly all of men dressed in clothes going as far back in time and fashion as a gentleman in full-bottom wig and Caroline dress. I waved a hand towards it. "A cavalier ancestor?" I inquired.

Roger glanced down from the stairs. "Of course. That was also a Sir Gideon. I'm afraid he lost his head around the time that Charles I did."

When we got to the top of the stairs we turned left and were proceeding down another long hall, twin to the one downstairs, when I heard a high voice. "No, I will *not* do as you say, and you can't make me."

"Benedict," I said the name aloud.

Roger turned a little. "Yes." He hesitated. "He can be difficult. And it's not just because Gideon is often strict with him. Being a cripple, Benedict knows that his father and, of course, Sheila, will let him get away with a lot that they wouldn't otherwise. And I'm afraid he uses that fact."

"I'm looking forward to meeting him."

Roger had stopped at a door and turned, an odd smile on his face. "I wonder if you'll feel the same enthusiasm after you've come to know him. Here's your room."

The room he showed me to must have been on one of the corners of the original building before the wings were added to the sides. Like the room downstairs, it was big and square with a high ceiling. A double bed jutted out from one wall. There was an old-fashioned wardrobe and basin with running water to the right. On the left was a chest of drawers, beyond that a fireplace with a newly lit fire crackling in it, and across the far corner a dressing table with three mirrors. On either side of the bed was a night table, and extending beyond those, bookcases.

"It's such a filthy day, I'll put on some lights."

Roger pressed a switch on the wall beside him that turned on two wall lamps, then walked towards the bed and switched on the lamp standing on the nearest night table. It certainly made a difference. The room, which had, despite the fire, looked cold and gray, seemed now warm. I could see the color and pattern of the wall-

papers—a soft apple green with tiny yellow and blue
flowers on it, a green that was picked up by green curtains
and a green patterned eiderdown folded on the bed. My
bag, I noticed, had been placed on a trunk stand beside
the washbasin.

"It looks very nice, Roger. Thanks for showing me up."

"Dinner will be in"—he checked his watch—"about
half an hour." He smiled. "See you then." He was about
to close the door when he poked his head back in. "Oh—
the bathroom is next door to your left down the hall.
You'll have it to yourself since Gideon and I use the one
in the other wing."

Ten minutes later I had unpacked my bag, hung my
clothes in the wardrobe and placed my underthings in the
chest of drawers beside the fire. Gideon might have said
not to dress, I thought, but he didn't say not to take a
bath, and standing there in front of the fire, I was suddenly overcome with a sense of fatigue, even a slight
depression. Since these were feelings I had seldom had
to cope with in my life, I gave myself an impatient shake
and decided that a hot bath would make me feel better.

Picking up the towel and washcloth that were hanging
beside the basin, I opened my door and then paused.
Where had Roger said the bathroom was? Left or right?

I couldn't remember. Shrugging, I turned right. Far
down in front of me I could see the square central hall
with the two branches of the stairs leading from it. Between there and where I stood were four doors on either
side of the hall. There was no way on earth to tell whether
one was a bathroom or not. I walked forward to the first
door on my right and gave a cautious knock. When there
was no reply, I knocked a little more loudly. If there was
one thing I certainly didn't want to do it was walk into
someone's bedroom. But hadn't Roger said that he and
Gideon had their rooms at the other end of the opposite
wing? I stood in front of the door, irresolute. What is the
matter with me? I thought. Why don't I just open the door
and walk in? The answer made no sense. Beyond all
reason I was quite convinced that someone was on the
other side of the door.

Well, if that's the case, the rational side of me argued, why doesn't whoever it is answer my knock?

Again I paused. Then, irritated with myself, and even amused at the picture I must make, standing in the hall in my red robe, with towel and washrag over my arm, clutching bath powder in one hand, I turned the doorknob with the other and pushed open the door. As I did so, I heard, from within the room, a door close softly. Putting out a hand, I flicked on a switch. I was right. It was not a bathroom. Nor was it a bedroom.

Bookshelves lined three walls to shoulder height on two sides, and all the way to the ceiling on my right. A blackboard stood on an easel across from me. There was an old-fashioned school desk facing it, and a few feet from the blackboard, a desk that looked as though it might be a teacher's. Of course, I thought. What was it Gideon had said? Something about Miss Maitland being Benedict's only hope of getting into a good school once his leg was put right. This must be the schoolroom where that good-looking red-haired young woman taught Benedict the subjects he would have to be prepared in.

Unlike Rosemary, with her steady progress of A's and B's, I had been an erratic student. All A's when I worked with subjects that interested me and an equal flurry of D's or even F's when I was bored. Yet despite my ups and downs I had—mostly—enjoyed school, so the sight of the blackboard, the faint smell of chalk and the slightly musty odor of schoolbooks all had cheerful connotations. Yet, again, I experienced that curious flatness of feeling that I had been aware of in my bedroom.

"There are no such things as ghosts," my passionately humanist father had said one Christmas when some aunt or godmother had sent Rosemary and me a collection of ghost stories. And Rosemary and I, reading the stories and poking a little fun at them as we went along, had agreed with him. I still agreed with him. But, standing there in the door of the schoolroom, I began to wonder if there was, indeed, such a thing as atmosphere held by insentient objects like furniture and walls that could make itself known. My eyes strayed around the book-lined walls, and at that moment I remembered the soft, barely audible sound of the closing door that I had heard when I came in.

But I must, I decided, have been mistaken. Old houses had curious acoustics. By some curious quirk of sound waves, a door closing down the hall must have been responsible for the noise I'd heard. Because there was no door in this room other than the one I had come in by.

Unaccountably, I shivered. Well, no wonder, I thought, it was cold in here. It might be July by the calendar, but from everything I'd read and heard and remembered, that meant nothing to the English climate. Besides which, it was more than time I had my bath. I had just turned when Gideon's voice said,

"May I help you?"

I felt as guilty and foolish as a child caught with her hand in the cookie jar. "Sorry, Gideon. I guess I took the wrong turning. I was looking for the bathroom, and then when I saw this was a schoolroom, I was standing here remembering my own school days." I knew I was rattling on like an idiot, but somehow I couldn't stop myself. Perhaps it had to do with the rather grim look around Gideon's mouth.

"Your bathroom is to the left of your bedroom," he said. And then: "It's almost seven."

"I'll be as quick as I can," I said, sweeping past him. "I'm a bit chilled and I would like to have a hot bath."

"That's why I ordered a fire in your room. After New York, you'll find it both cold and damp. And the schoolroom is not heated unless Benedict is studying in there."

"Hasn't he been studying lately?"

"No. I'll ask Mrs. Lowndes to hold back dinner for twenty minutes. That should give you enough time. Here you are." We had been walking down the hall past my bedroom. Opening the door of the first room beyond it, he turned on the light, revealing a bathtub that looked the size of a battleship and other accoutrements of a bathroom, including a towel rack made of heated pipes for the purpose of drying towels.

Ten minutes later, when I returned to my room, I

found, sitting outside my door, my little canine friend from downstairs, her sore leg tucked up under her.

"Hello," I said.

Once again she got shakily to her feet and put her front paws up against me. I patted the tan head. Down went the ears. Her skinny tail waved frantically.

"All right. You can come in. But I don't know if you're allowed upstairs."

She herself seemed to be in no doubt, though when she was in the room she went around investigating it in a way that made me fairly certain she'd never been in this particular room before.

"You ought to have a name," I said, taking off my robe and getting into fresh clothes as quickly as I could. Opening up the wardrobe, I decided to lift my spirits with a bright red dress. Red, I found myself complacently thinking, was not a color that a redhead would wear with any success. With the dress on and my hair brushed, I examined myself in the three-way mirror. Some people, I thought, recalling the magnificently proportioned Sheila, could definitely be said to have a capital F figure. Those who had admired my style had usually used the term slight or boyish. Even Rosemary, for all her fragility, had a tendency to go in and out in the right places.

"Boadicea," I said to myself gloomily, thinking of the ancient and warlike British queen, usually portrayed massively in bronze or marble, driving a chariot drawn by equally fearsome horses.

There was a short, quick bark. I looked down. There my companion was, sitting on my robe which she had plainly pulled off the bed where I had thrown it.

"Don't tell me you want to be called Boadicea," I said. "The name suits you about as well as it suits me."

Another bark.

"All right, Boadicea it is. But I shall call you Buff for short."

When I entered the sitting room downstairs a few minutes later, Buff was at my heels and the gong was being sounded.

"Exactly on time," Roger said cheerfully.

"Where did you find her?" Gideon asked, looking at Buff. "Mrs. Lowndes was looking for her to give her some dinner."

"Her name," I announced, "is Boadicea, after the British queen. But you may call her Buff for short."

"I see," Gideon said drily, looking down at Buff, who was making up to him in what I thought was rather a flirtatious way. "I take it you have accepted my suggestion of adopting her."

"Yes," I surprised myself by saying. "I have." And wondered how much red tape I would have to submit to to get her back to New York. I glanced down at her. "Does she speak anything but Welsh?"

Roger gave a snort of laughter. "I don't know about her Welsh, but there's one person who'll be happy if you take her away."

Gideon, who was swallowing the last of his sherry, put the frail crystal down on a side table with a snap. "What nonsense are you talking about? Come along, let's go into the dining room. Mrs. Lowndes has been kept waiting long enough."

The room we entered was across the hall, a high, rectangular paneled room with a long polished wood table, at one end of which three places had been laid. A heavy sideboard ran along one side, and a fire crackled in a chimney piece on the other. Gideon sat at the head, with me on the right and Roger opposite. We had barely sat down when Mrs. Lowndes came in with a tray carrying three soup plates.

I decided to pursue the interesting lead Roger had provided just before we arrived in the dining room. "Who is the person who's going to be happy when I take Buff away?"

"Nobody," Gideon snapped. "Roger was talking rubbish—as he often does."

"Thank you for the kind words, brother mine," Roger said, grinning.

"Which of the Society's papers, specifically, are you looking for?" Gideon asked abruptly, with such an obvious turning of the subject that I almost wanted to laugh. Plainly he was anxious that Roger should not answer my question. Which itself, I thought, was a dead giveaway. But I could certainly check it later.

"All of them," I replied. "After all, if this is going to be a complete biography of my father almost anything to do with the Society is relevant."

"Whew! You'll have yourself quite a job, Janet." Roger reached for some salt. "How many months do you plan to stay?"

I found the little tinge of alarm that went through me when he said that as surprising as it was unpleasant. I had been in the house only an hour or two. Yet the thought of spending more than the minimum time I'd allotted was astonishingly unwelcome.

"Months! Three weeks at the most."

"With how many helpers?"

"Well—Gideon."

Gideon said nothing. After a second Roger said carefully, "That is what I call trust and optimism."

"What do you mean?" I could feel my tension tightening. There was an undercurrent to the conversation that I could sense and that was making me uneasy. "What are you talking about?"

Roger moved while Mrs. Lowndes removed his soup plate. Vaguely I found myself wondering if she were the only house servant, and if so, how on earth she took care of a place this size.

After a short silence Gideon said, "Roger is referring to a—er—mishap that befell the papers since they arrived here. They were packed in not very sturdy cardboard boxes which I had ordered to be taken straight up to the attics. Since I had no particular reason to look at them again, I didn't go near them until I received your cable, when I thought I'd make sure they were placed where you could easily open them when you arrived. When I got up there I found that they had all been opened and their contents scattered all over the floor of the attic room—as a matter of fact, the floor was a foot deep in them. I got some more cartons from a supplier in the nearest town and with the aid of a couple of helpers flung the papers in them in no order at all. I would have written to you about the matter, only there wasn't enough time."

I stared at him, my hunger now gone for the evening. "And you have no idea who could have done it?"

"None at all—or I would have told you. Further—I have no idea *when* it was done. The papers have been here for more than a year. The attic floor of the house, which is a rabbit warren of rooms—ex-servants' quarters and old box rooms—are almost never gone into now. Certainly not at that end which is chockfull of rubbish that's been collecting for centuries."

I sat there, my mind in a turmoil. Finally I said, "But *why?* It's hard to think of anything more innocuous—even boring—than the papers of an idealistic society that reached its peak in the late forties and fifties and had, to my father's undying disappointment, little impact on world events."

"I don't know the answer to that, either," Gideon said, placing his knife and fork across his plate. His appetite, I saw, had not been destroyed the way mine had, though I had noticed that he had served himself sparingly from the not-very-interesting-looking dishes Mrs. Lowndes had offered around.

"You don't know who, or when or why," I said. And then, after a pause. "Did you call the police?"

Roger gave a short laugh.

I looked at him. "What's so funny?"

"The local police force," Gideon said, "consists of P.C.—for Police Constable—Thomas, a good man in dealing with a rowdy drunk, a barking dog or a stolen bicycle."

"But not, I take it," I said, "with the vandalization of several boxes of papers."

"Precisely," Gideon said.

I sat there, bothered by something that it took me a moment or two to identify. I saw then that it was a general dissatisfaction—even disbelief—in Gideon's reaction. "You mean to say," I said, "that not knowing who or when or why, you've just accepted it as the work of elves, or an Act of God, for which there's no explanation, and have done nothing to get at the bottom of it?"

"Gideon's reactions are rather like the mills of the gods." Roger said. "They grind very slowly."

"But," I pointed out, "according to the rest of that quotation, they grind exceedingly fine." I glanced questioningly at Gideon.

"I'm not quite sure what you'd expect me to do," Gideon said, allowing Mrs. Lowndes to take his plate. "To my knowledge, nothing was stolen. There was certainly no sign of breaking and entering—for one thing it would be impossible, with as few servants as we have, to keep a place this size properly locked up. There must be a dozen ways someone could enter without the least difficulty. And if I did call the local CID men in all they would say was that the vandalization was almost certainly the result of some personal spite."

I absorbed that while Mrs. Lowndes brought in the sweet and offered it around. Having sent back most of my main course, and feeling somewhat guilty about it, I took no more than a teaspoonful of the custardy-looking concoction. Gideon took little more, I noticed. Only Roger seemed to eat a full plateful with youthful enthusiasm.

"Coffee will be served in the sitting room," Gideon said, rising to his feet as soon as we had finished. "I'll join you there in a minute." And he disappeared through the door that led to what I supposed was the kitchen.

"Still," I burst out, as Roger and I were walking back across the hall into the book-lined sitting room. "I do think it's strange that Gideon did nothing about the vandalizing of the boxes."

Roger held the door for me and followed me in. "It's not really strange when once you understand what was really in Gideon's mind," he said.

I looked back from the fireplace, where I was still searching for warmth. "What was in his mind? What do you mean?"

"I mean," Roger said easily, "that he thinks that Benedict did it."

# three

I STARED AT HIM. "Benedict? I thought he was bedridden, practically immobile—Oh." Suddenly I remembered what Gideon had said about his son.

"Oh, what?" Roger asked, stepping behind me to put another log on the fire.

"I just remembered that Gideon said one of the baffling things about Benedict's illness was that from time to time he could get about quite well with the aid of a cane or a crutch, while the rest of the time he was all but paralyzed. But even if he was that ambulatory, could he tear open carefully packed cardboard cartons and scatter their contents to the degree Gideon described?"

Roger straightened. "Why not? It's not as though the cartons were made of wood and nailed down. There's nothing wrong with Benedict's hands. If anything, his hands and arms are stronger than those of the average boy of eleven—probably because he's had to swing himself about on crutches and in and out of wheelchairs."

"But *why?*"

51

"Why, why, why," Roger said smiling. "You always want to know why."

"Don't you? I've always thought that the answer to why was much more interesting than the answer to what."

"No. I've always been a what person myself. Deed over motive."

I smiled back. "Why?"

"Because I think that all motive is the same—self-interest."

"That's pretty cynical."

Roger merely grinned.

"All right," I said. "I don't agree with you, which probably makes me naïve. But given your premise, what could Benedict get out of tearing open those boxes and throwing the papers all over the place?"

"That's easy—he'd annoy his father. After all, Benedict didn't know that the papers hold practically no interest for Gideon; that the reason they're here, so to speak, is simply because Gideon married into the family. He probably thought they were something his father valued. But there's something I should remind you of. I said Gideon thought Benedict had done it. I didn't say that I thought so."

"You mean you don't think he did."

"What a definite person you are! Is that a typically American quality? I don't know whether Benedict did or didn't. I—"

The door opened and Mrs. Lowndes entered carrying a silver tray bearing a small but exquisite silver coffee pot, a tiny silver cream jug and sugar bowl, and three china demitasse cups and saucers. Following her was Gideon.

"Thank you, Mrs. Lowndes," he said, and then, when the housekeeper had left the room, "Janet, would you like to pour?"

As I handed Roger his cup I saw him shake his head faintly, and understood, without too much trouble that he was telling me not to mention our discussion about Benedict and Gideon's suspicions concerning him. Which was a pity, I thought, adding both cream and sugar to the excellent but very strong coffee Mrs. Lowndes had made.

"Queen Anne?" I asked, with a wave in the direction of the pot.

"Yes," Gideon said.

I turned the pot. The letters G and L formed part of the delicate chasing of the silver. "And I take it this belonged to your family at that time."

"I believe so." Gideon sounded impatient.

Although I hadn't totally acceded to Roger's request, indicated by the shaking of his head, I felt, at least for the moment, bound to honor it. Which was a pity, because I would like very much to have asked Gideon what motive he ascribed to his son for the vandalization. Instead, I said into an awkward silence that had fallen, "Gideon, I would like so much to meet Benedict."

Gideon's feelings about this were, I thought, plain when I saw the heavy black brows draw together in a bar over his imperious nose. "He isn't well, just at the moment, Janet. It might, perhaps, be better to wait. As I think I mentioned to you, he has periods when he seems immobilized. And during those times he often reacts poorly to any outsider being brought in to see him."

I hesitated, expecting, for some reason, Roger to come to my aid. But he simply sat in his chair, his eyes on the fire, a faraway look on his face, giving every appearance of having heard neither my request nor Gideon's refusal.

Instead of discouraging me, this poured a little ginger into my spirit.

"He didn't sound too immobilized this evening before dinner when I heard his voice telling someone that he would not do as they said, and that furthermore whoever it was couldn't make him."

I don't know what I expected from Gideon—a blast, one of his flat categorical statements that, as a guest in his house, I was subject to his wishes, a reminder that I was not here in the same house as Benedict at anyone's invitation. Certainly Gideon's expression was anything but conciliatory. But all he said was, "Yes, I'm afraid Benedict can be difficult at times." A comment that was probably all too true, but which answered nothing.

"Still," Roger said lazily, "Janet is his aunt."

"Cousin," Gideon corrected. "Rosemary and Janet were cousins, not sisters."

"Ah, yes, I keep forgetting. I suppose it was the sister-like quality of their relationship. Their closeness."

Why, as a result of that innocuous and entirely accurate statement, the atmosphere seemed suddenly taut, strung with live wires, I didn't know. But it was palpable. Gently Gideon put down his cup, his strong long-fingered hand seeming to dwarf the delicate porcelain. For some reason I found myself intensely aware of his physical presence. Gideon was a tall man, well over six feet, rangy rather than bulky, with big bones and powerful shoulders. It would take two men of ordinary size and strength, I mused, to put the slightest restraint on any act he'd made up his mind to engage in, and even then I wouldn't bet too much on their chances. So what chance would an eleven-year-old boy have against such a father? None. And no one would be more aware of his powerlessness than the boy himself. My respect for the child, whose voice clearly announced his refusal to knuckle under, increased. So did my determination to see him.

"And now, if you'll excuse me," Gideon said. "There's work I'm afraid I must do. And I'm sure, after your long drive, Janet, that you won't want to be staying up too late. Don't let Roger keep you up. His preference is to sleep all day and gad all night."

"Not fair, brother. Not fair. And I assure you, anyway, that I won't subject Janet to my night-owl tendencies."

Gideon, at the door, turned. "See that you don't." A slight smile touched his mouth. "Good night," he said, and left.

Roger put down his cup. "I don't know what Gideon thought I would talk you into. It's not as though the village were rampant with night life."

"I think he was just expressing his general disapproval of my being here."

"Well, Gideon disapproves of most people. He's something of a misanthropist, and his misanthropic instincts are fed and watered by his staying so much in this isolated barn that he inherited. He's a little better in London, after some of his friends have had time to invite him out and warm him up and humanize him. But of course the trouble with that is that he's there less and less."

"I should think if Benedict needed medical attention he'd be there more and more."

"Yes, but against that is the undoubted fact that to inherit an estate of this size that has been in his family for as long as it has, is a responsibility he can hardly ignore. Even in this day and age."

"And it outweighs Benedict's good?"

Roger didn't answer immediately. Then, "Let's just say that they're two powerful pressures pulling in opposite directions."

"And the inheritance comes first."

Roger laughed. "Spoken like a true republican—with a small R. No more social hierarchy. No more landed ownership—let's pour some more tea into Boston harbor."

I grinned. "Oh, I'm not that much of a small R republican, or even a small D democrat. I just think that Gideon has his priorities backwards."

The long drive combined with country air must have made me sleepy. I went to bed early, and drifted off almost immediately. But at some point later I awoke abruptly, aware that something had wakened me. For a minute I lay there, every sense alert, wondering what it was. And then I heard it again—the soft closing of a door. I sat up in bed. Was it my door that I had heard? No, I decided. Not this time. But even as I decided that, I knew that the noise I had heard of the first door closing, the one that had awakened me, had been my door.

That thought was so disturbing that I leaned over and switched on the light beside the bed and looked around the room. I saw it immediately, of course: a white rectangle lying in the middle of the dark green patterned carpet. Getting quickly out of bed I walked over and picked it up. The envelope had been lying face down. As soon as I turned it over I saw my name, Janet deMaury, typed on the front in capitals. The envelope had not, I noticed, opening it quickly, been sealed. The message inside, typed also in capitals on standard-sized paper that had been folded, read:

*Why don't you leave now? You'd be much safer.*

It seemed so simple, even gentle: a polite suggestion. Yet the shiver that flickered over me was not caused by the damp, chilly air that was blowing in through the open window. For a moment my reaction was all that the writer of that note could wish—a strong urge to dress, pack my suitcase and leave the house within the next hour. Suddenly, in front of my eyes I had a picture of my car downstairs in the old stables, waiting to be used the moment I turned on the ignition.

But that impulse, strong as it was, was swept away by an indignation that was all the greater (probably) for its having risen out of that cowardly first moment. Just who did Gideon think he was, dropping anonymous notes on my carpet in the middle of the night? Because I had not a doubt in the world that that note came from him. For a few seconds I toyed with the idea of marching down to his room, thundering on the door, and demanding an explanation. But a variety of second thoughts stopped me. For one thing, although I knew from Roger that Gideon's room was in the opposite wing, I didn't know which it was, and the thought of rousting out Roger, Benedict or even Mrs. Lowndes—although her room was most likely on the floor above—did not appeal to me. For another— my eyes slid to my traveling clock—it was two thirty in the morning. And although Gideon might consider this a suitable time for delivering unsigned notes, I did not feel that I could acquit myself well at such a bleak hour.

And bleak, I thought, was the right word. The sense of depression that I had experienced before, when standing in this room before dinner and when I was in the schoolroom, descended on me again. Fiercely rejecting all traitorous and atavistic memories of ghost stories, of tales of psychic phenomena and emanations, I reminded myself that any strange room, including that of the most plastic and mundane hotel, could, at two thirty A.M. bring on the blues; that rooms that were badly proportioned, or whose original shapes had been altered and thus distorted, could produce unease; that the heavy green curtains that Mrs. Lowndes must have pulled together when she turned down the bed were probably giving me claustrophobia.

Well, at least I could open those. I had always slept with curtains pulled back and blinds up, much preferring the sight of the night sky to feeling shut in. Not bothering to put a robe on over my nightgown, I went to the windows and groped for the draw string that would open the folds of green cloth. But these particular curtains were more old-fashioned and simply hung on big rings from a brass rod. Taking the edge of one, I gave a sharp tug, nearly jumping out of my skin at the noise it made. But either because of the weight of the lined curtain, or because the brass rings were a tight fit over the rod, the curtain did not move easily. Another futile pull seemed to indicate that I was too far away from it. Stepping forward, I placed myself almost between the curtain and the window, more or less facing the window, because the rod jutted back into the room several inches. Then, as I started once more to tug the curtain, I stood, frozen. The windows of my room were on the front of the house, and looked down the long avenue of trees to the gate. Because the curtain behind me shut off the light in the room, I could see the figure of a man walk quickly from what looked like a French window opening onto the front, run down the steps that surrounded the house and turn sharp right when he reached the gravel drive. The trouble was, I could not see him clearly, since, although it was no longer raining, the night was overcast, and he moved rapidly away from me around the other end of the house where the courtyard and the garages in the old stables were located.

I knew that if I went back to the bedside and turned off the lamp, I would see out much more clearly, but then, should he re-emerge quickly from around the side of the house, I would be likely to miss him. So, pulling the curtain back to join its mate, I stood in the dark between the curtain and the window and waited. In a few seconds, I heard the sound of a car starting up. Since it had nowhere else to go, I thought, it must surely come around to the front of the house and drive down the avenue towards the gate. But though I heard the car rev up, and knew that it was moving, it did not appear. On the contrary, after a pause, as though it were stopping before some other gate, the engine picked up and I could hear it driving far off to the right somewhere, the noise getting fainter by the second.

This time I did go and turn off the bedside lamp before returning to the curtains and drawing them back. Not that I thought anyone else was lurking outside or that he could see up into my window if he were, but the sight of a man—who could be either Gideon or Roger, or, for that matter, some other man whose presence around the house I had not been made aware of—driving away from the house between two thirty and three in the morning did nothing for my sense of security. Any more, I thought, than finding someone had come into my room and put an envelope on the floor where I could not miss it, a few feet from my bed, did anything for my sense of privacy—or safety.

But, of course, having turned off the light, I had to turn it on again in order to lock the door. I didn't think I would sleep anyway, but the thought of even trying to in an unlocked room, which had already been entered, was not much of an inducement. The key sticking out of the lock was a big, old-fashioned one. Furthermore, neither it nor the lock had been used in some time. For all my lack of weight and size I am quite strong, having played a fair amount of tennis, but I could not turn the key, not even after wrapping the handle in the skirt of my robe to keep from bruising or cutting my hands.

Tomorrow, I vowed, I would get that key oiled. And if anyone wanted to know the reason, I would be happy to tell them. In fact, I thought, carrying the light dressing-table chair and propping it with its back wedged under the doorknob, I would be happy to tell them—specifically Gideon—anyway.

If, I thought, getting back into bed after turning out

the light, Gideon went in for predawn forays into the countryside—(To see his redhaired ladyfriend? I couldn't help wondering)—that was his business. But it became my business if he took to dropping unsigned notes on my carpet before he left.

All of which sounded very brave and was, I knew in the depths of me, only bluster to fool myself into thinking I wasn't unnerved by the note and what it said: *Why don't you leave now? You'd be much safer.*

And I would, I knew without any doubt, be much safer if I left the following day. Why that was so I didn't know. But of two things I was quite sure: Gideon wanted me out, and would stoop to astonishing efforts—this note being one—to see that I left. The other was that someone—and I felt reasonably certain that that someone was, once again, Gideon—did not want me to look at the papers. Why, I couldn't imagine. I enjoyed writing, but I had looked upon the research among the papers as a boring job that should be gotten through as quickly as possible. Large parts of it would still, without doubt, be boring, added to which would be the tedium of having to put the papers back in some kind of order before they could even make sense. But one thing seemed clear: to someone, those papers were of vital interest. Because I did not, for one minute, buy Roger's theory that Benedict had emptied the papers on the floor to annoy his father. I didn't know why I was so certain of that, but I was. Whether the someone who emptied the papers on the floor and the someone to whom they were of crucial concern were both Gideon, I did not know. In fact, I decided, tossing around in the bed, I didn't know anything. I had beliefs, hunches, suspicions. But they didn't add up to the kind of evidence that justified the word "know." And it would be well if I remembered that in the confrontation that I would be having the following day.

I was dozing off when I heard another sound. Lying rigid, I waited to see if I had imagined it. No, there it was again, a faint whimper, and right outside my door. There followed then a soft scratching. Once more turning on the light, I tiptoed over to the door, silently removed

the chair and as quietly as possible turned the doorknob.
Then, quickly, I pulled the door open. There, sitting on
her haunches, was the small, tan mongrel.

"Boadicea!" I said softly. "Buff."

She gave a short, muffled bark, as though fully aware
of the hour.

"Come on," I whispered. "What are you doing here,
anyway?"

Moving with remarkable speed, considering that she
used three legs more than she did four, she was inside. I
shut the door and bent down. Rarely, I thought, as her
warm pink tongue found my cheek, had anyone been so
totally enthusiastic about seeing me, especially lately. And
equally rarely had I been so glad to see anyone else.

"I'm sure you're not allowed up here," I whispered.
"But I'm powerfully glad you're here." All of a sudden,
the room had lost some of its depressing quality.

"I don't know where you're going to sleep," I went on,
getting back in bed. "But I daresay you'll manage."

She did. Very well. Three legs or no she got up onto
the bed and snuggled herself down beside me, back to
back. I went to sleep almost immediately.

Undoubtedly as a result of my disturbed night, I did
not wake up the next morning until after nine. I lay
there, feeling slightly conscience-stricken. Had Gideon
mentioned any hour for breakfast? The thought of Mrs.
Lowndes toiling alone in a house of this size made me
feel worse. By a fairly obvious step of logic, that led me
to remember the man leaving the house at two thirty in
the morning who, I thought at the time, could be Gideon,
Roger, or some male retainer about the place. That, in
turn, brought me to the memory of the note. Flinging back
the covers, I turned towards the night table, where I had
placed the sheet of paper before going over to the
window the night before. I had refolded it, I recalled,
and placed it carefully under my traveling clock. I
couldn't have been mistaken about that, I thought, staring
at the golden brown polished fruit wood on which the
clock now sat.

Yet the night, or rather those bleak early hours of the morning, could play strange tricks, I reminded myself. Perhaps I didn't place the clock on it. Perhaps I just thought I did, or thought I ought to for safety, but actually, and carelessly, put the paper beside the clock, in which case it could have fallen down. But a thorough search both beneath and behind the night table and bed produced no note. By that time I was not only baffled, I was a little desperate. There's something peculiarly unnerving in having no evidence that I had done something that I so clearly remembered doing.

"If a thing isn't where it ought to be," a governess I'd had when small had said, "look for it where it shouldn't be."

Getting out of bed, I looked in my handbag, in the pocket of my robe, on the chest of drawers, in the drawers themselves, on the dressing table and in its drawers, and even, though by this time I knew my search had gone beyond the point of sensible action, in my suitcase, unpacked and stashed in the big wardrobe.

The note was nowhere to be found.

Then I remembered that, after letting Buff in, I had forgotten to replace the dressing table chair that still stood off in the corner between the door and the wardrobe. So the same person who had dropped the note could have come in and retrieved it.

"Why aren't you a better guard dog than that?" I scolded Buff.

Buff's reply was to make the whimpering noise I had heard the night before when she was outside the door. "It's all right," I said, smoothing her head, "it's not your fault. It's your revolting master's."

Her obvious reassurance gave me a pang. Someone had treated little Buff not well at all. My mind slid, once more, to Gideon.

"Beast!" I said aloud.

Well, I would have all the more to talk to him about.

When Buff and I went downstairs, we seemed to be occupying what felt like an empty house. Making my way to the dining room, I saw, at one end, one place setting, with a plate, butter, jam, cream and sugar around it, and propped up against the sugar bowl, what looked like a card. Picking up the card I read, *Please ring and I'll bring in your coffee, eggs and toast.*

With a return of my guilty feeling, I looked around and saw a bell beside the chimney piece. Ringing for servants was not something that came naturally to me, having been brought up in somewhat of a more informal way. Instead, I decided to go through the door that I assumed led to the kitchen.

Before the kitchen, I discovered, came what used to be called a butler's pantry. The kitchen was on the other side of that. Poking my head in I saw Mrs. Lowndes cutting up vegetables at a large table in the center of the room.

"Mrs. Lowndes?" I said.

"Oh, good morning, Miss deMaury. You should have rung the bell. I've kept your coffee hot and will do your eggs immediately."

"I feel very bad about putting you out this way," I said.

She gave me the cool stare at which, I had discovered off and on in my life, the British of all classes are particularly talented.

"It's not a question of putting me out, Miss deMaury. It's my job."

Fleetingly I reflected on the number of people I had known and worked with who resented some aspect of their jobs, however much they might be paid to do it. "Yes," I said. "I understand that. But I hadn't planned to be so late for breakfast. By the way, what time is breakfast, normally?"

"Well, Sir Gideon said that on your first morning you were to be allowed to sleep in, after your long drive and everything."

And after, I thought, my stirring night. "That's kind of both you and Sir Gideon," I commented hypocritically. "But I'm sure serving several breakfasts must be inconvenient. What time do Sir Gideon and Mr. Lightwood usually have breakfast?"

"Sir Gideon," the housekeeper said, going over and picking a rough pottery pot out of a pan of simmering water and pouring the steaming contents into a china coffee pot that had been warming on a wire rack above the huge range, "always has his breakfast at seven. Mr. Lightwood is rarely down before eight."

"Well, that's an hour's difference there and I'm sorry to have prolonged it by another hour and a half."

"It's no trouble at all. How would you like your eggs? Fried or scrambled?"

"I'd like them scrambled, please," I said, submitting, without too much effort, to be cooked for and waited on. "Would you happen to know where Sir Gideon is now?"

"Yes. He's gone out riding with his agent, who came over early this morning. They're going over to some of the pastures north of the house. Why don't you go and sit down in the dining room and I'll bring this in immediately. I'm sure you'd like your coffee right away."

As a matter of fact, I would, being one of those people who likes a cup of coffee as soon as possible after rising. But I stayed to ask one more question. "What time would you like me to come down in the future?"

"Well that's for you to say, miss. But any time between seven and eight thirty would be quite convenient."

I would far rather have been given a definite time, but a stubborn look had settled down on Mrs. Lowndes' face, and I knew she was not about to add to what she said. "All right," I replied. "I'll make it a point to be down at seven thirty." That would be halfway between the brothers, I thought, and would give me some privacy—another breakfast commodity I valued. And probably, I thought, they valued, also.

I had barely sat down when Mrs. Lowndes came in with the coffee pot, a small jug of hot milk and a glass of orange juice. "I'll bring in the toast and eggs in a jiffy," she said, whisking out.

The coffee was as good as the night before, and just as strong. I was glad to dilute it with the hot milk. I was still puzzling over what seemed like a grossly insufficient number of servants to administer to a house of such size when she came in with a plate of eggs in one hand and a toast rack in the other. I decided that however much it might scandalize her sense of form and propriety I'd ask her how much help she had.

"This seems an enormous place to keep up, Mrs. Lowndes. Surely you're not without some help."

"Oh no. I have girls from the village who come in on a daily basis. Not that they're much good. Girls nowadays are not trained the way they were in my young days. All they seem to care about are what they call their rights."

That didn't surprise me. The hierarchical world that had produced willing, uncomplaining and plentiful servants had been swept away, if not by World War II, certainly by the social revolution that followed it.

"It's worldwide, Mrs. Lowndes. An awful lot of kids come to apply for jobs wondering what you can do for them rather than the other way around."

"It's what I said to Lady Lightwood when she was trying to find someone to take care of Benedict when she was away so much. It's never been any good since Lady Lightwood died. Why, the way she—" But at that interesting point the elderly housekeeper snapped her mouth together. "But it's not my place to pass judgment."

"But what were you going to say about my cousin, Mrs. Lowndes? I'd be interested to hear."

"Your cousin, was she, Miss deMaury? She was a strange lady indeed. Why she—"

At that moment the door opened and Gideon walked in.

"Will that be all, miss?" Mrs. Lowndes asked, picking up her tray from the sideboard.

I could, at that moment, have killed Gideon, for all that I had a few topics of my own to talk over with the master of the house. But there was nothing I could do. I could hardly insist that Mrs. Lowndes continue what she was saying with Gideon in the room. "No, thanks. I won't be needing anything more. Everything is delicious."

"Good morning," Gideon said pleasantly, walking over and putting a copy of the London *Times* beside my place. "I thought you might want to look at this. Sorry I can't supply a New York paper. I hope you slept well."

It was so bold and barefaced that I found myself unable to believe that he had entered my room, dropped an anonymous note on the floor, and then come back again much later and retrieved the note from my night table. But unless I was willing to believe that I had dreamed the whole thing—

"No," I said. "I didn't." I took a deep breath. "Somebody came into my room at some point before two thirty this morning, put an anonymous note on the floor where I couldn't miss it, and then, much later, when I was back asleep again, removed it from where I had placed it on the night table."

Even before I'd finished I wondered if it sounded as unlikely and far-fetched—not to say incredible—to Gideon as it did to me. But I resolutely dismissed that thought. It had happened. I was almost certain Gideon was at the bottom of it, and I wanted to find out why.

Gideon, who had picked up the newspaper and was glancing at something on the back page, stared down at me. "You were dreaming."

"I was not dreaming. It happened."

"Where's the note?"

"I told you. It was removed." I stared back at him. "You don't believe me. You're standing there thinking I'm making this up."

"Rosemary always did say you had a lively imagination. She also said you were given to nightmares as a child."

"But I am not a child, Gideon, and I know the difference between dreaming and not dreaming. It happened!"

He put down the paper. "All right. What do you want me to do? Question everyone? Roger? Sheila? Mrs. Lowndes?"

I said bluntly, "I thought it might be you."

He laughed, and it struck me that that was the first time I had seen him laugh. "I see. Not very flattering. You know, Janet," he said, "if I wanted you out of here,

I really wouldn't have to resort to a silly and anonymous note."

"Oh," I replied, diverted. "What would you do if you wanted me out of here? I know you didn't want me to come. Your letter made that clear."

"Ah, yes. That letter. But I don't think that letter is an argument towards my having committed the anonymous letter. As I indicated, it wouldn't be necessary."

"What would you do if you wanted me to leave?" Curiosity won—for the moment—over my concern about the note.

"My dear Janet, if all else—all persuasion—failed, I would simply lift you up and place you on the other side of the gate, having, of course, driven your car, containing your luggage, out there first."

I looked into the cold light eyes. "Would you, now?" I asked.

His glance never wavered. "As I said, if all else failed."

"You believe in *force majeure*."

"In the last resort—yes."

"You know," I said, "your reaction to my news about the note left in my room and then taken from it is—to put it mildly—surprising. You don't seem horrified, or astonished, or even concerned."

"Please don't be offended. But, as I said, I think you dreamed it. You were tired after a long journey. This is a strange house—a house once lived in by a cousin with whom you had been closely brought up. People do have strange dreams in this house. I've been told that often."

All of a sudden I remembered the depression I had felt in my bedroom, not once but twice, and in the schoolroom. The link of the two subjects—strange dreams and unexplained depressions—did nothing for my peace of mind. I shook my head, as though I were getting rid of the suggestion. "Are you saying," I asked, with a deliberate light note, "that Tenton is haunted?"

"Who said anything about haunted?" a cheerful voice from the door inquired, and Roger, wearing an elegantly tailored pin-stripe suit that seemed in marked contrast to Gideon's rather worn breeches and tweed jacket, strolled in. "Are you telling her the family ghost stories, Gideon?" he inquired. "Ah, coffee. Now I wonder if there'd be a tiny bit left for me?"

I waved a hand towards the pot, from which I had hoped to extract an extra cup. "Be my guest."

"Janet's hardly had a chance to drink her own coffee, which is probably cold. I'll get some more." And, reaching across, Gideon rang a bell on the wall above the sideboard.

"Don't bother," I said quickly. "This is fine."

Gideon turned. "Are you sure?" he asked, bending that disconcertingly light stare at me.

My white lies are no better than any others I try to tell. I could feel the shaming blush rise up my cheeks.

"I thought that might be a polite fib. Mrs. Lowndes," Gideon went on as the housekeeper appeared around the door leading to the pantry, "—ah, you've anticipated us. You have brought some more coffee."

"I thought Miss deMaury might be needing some more, especially when I heard the both of you come in."

"Thank you, Mrs. Lowndes," I said gratefully, pouring myself out a steaming second cup. "You know," I continued, when she'd left, "this may be next to Wales, but Mrs. Lowndes, from her voice, might almost be Scottish."

"That's because she is Scottish," Gideon said.

"About the ghost," Roger said, pouring some of the fresh coffee into a cup he had taken from the sideboard, "have you been telling her about it, Gideon?"

"As far as I know there's no ghost, so don't put it into her head. She's imagined—well, dreamed—enough as it is."

"I did not dream it. And furthermore, Gideon," I reverted to the topic before last, "can you deny that you didn't want me to come here?"

"I didn't pretend to deny it." His voice was so grim when he said that that I caught my breath. "But as for this fantastic story about a note in the middle of the night—"

"What note?" Roger asked.

Gideon sighed and put down his empty cup. "Accord-

ing to Janet"—and there was something about his tone
that made me think of the statement, "the witness al-
leges"—"someone went into her room sometime prior to
two thirty this morning when she was asleep and dropped
an anonymous note on her carpet. Then, after she'd read
it and put it on her night table and went back to sleep,
whoever it was came in again and stole it."

"Put like that," I said drily, "no wonder you don't
believe it. It sounds like moon spinning."

"It does," Roger agreed. "But that doesn't mean it's
not true. I don't think Janet is the kind of person to
make up something like that, Gideon."

My heart warmed towards Roger. Just being in Gideon's presence, I was discovering, was like swimming
against a powerful tide or undertow. Without actually
putting it into words, he gave me the marked feeling that
he either disbelieved what I said on principle, or—
equally on principle—opposed it.

"I'm not implying anything at all about Janet," Gideon
remarked, untruthfully. "I'm simply saying that people
do have weird and vivid dreams when they're in this
house. Wasn't it Sheila, when she was spending the night
here when Benedict had his turn, who said that someone
opened and closed her door in the middle of the night?
Yet, according to her own admission, she'd felt nervous
enough to have locked her door before she went to sleep."

"Speaking of locks," I said, "I, too, heard my door
open and close. But since I *know* someone came in, I
don't think it was the family ghost or any other super-
natural agency. Anyway, when I tried to lock my door I
found the lock had rusted, or something. I couldn't turn
the key. Could someone find some oil for me, so I can oil
it? You may disbelieve my story all you want, but I
know it's true. And I don't want any more *billet-doux*
dropped on my carpet when I'm asleep."

Gideon bowed a little stiffly. "Madam, it shall be done.
I will, myself, go and get the oil, now." And he went
through the door towards the kitchen.

"He doesn't believe a word I say," I grumbled to
Roger.

Roger didn't say anything.

After a minute I said, hesitantly, "It occurs to me now . . . could it have been Benedict?"

"I thought you had Gideon picked for the villain of that particular piece."

I sighed. "I did. But somehow, though I think he's behind it, I am having difficulty in seeing him creep into my room at night. It seems much more likely that he'd have somebody else do it."

"Like Benedict."

"Yes. Like Benedict. His son. Does that seem strange or unlikely?"

"I'm just wondering what inducement he could have used. Except, of course, the usual one: fear."

Once again I found myself wondering what an eleven-year-old could do to defend himself against a man of Gideon's size, power and authority. But then I recalled the words, "No, I will not do as you say, and you can't make me." "From what I overheard yesterday afternoon," I said now, "it sounds as though Benedict could take care of himself—at least he isn't totally cowed."

"No. Gideon uses a combination of the stick and the carrot—with more emphasis on the stick. But every now and then he gets Benedict to do something by playing on his passionate desire to go away to boarding school."

"That's strange—that he should want to go away to school."

"Not for an English boy. It's the normal thing for a boy of his age and background to do. Besides, he's very lonely for children his age."

"Doesn't Gideon—or Miss Maitland—arrange for other children to come here?"

"It's a question of what other children. There aren't very many children here, and those there are, are village children. Yes—I know class distinction raises its head here. If he were well and could run around with the village boys, then if would be different. He'd have things like fishing and bird nesting and other—er—physical activities in common. But for them to be scrubbed up and brought to The Hall is something different. They're constrained and he knows it."

"Yes," I said. "I see. It's a pity. I see why he wants to go to school. The point is, will he ever be able to?"

Roger paused. "I don't like to say this, because I really don't want to criticize Gideon, or, of course, Sheila Maitland, who does pretty well what Gideon wants her to do, but I do think it's wrong for them to play up this burning desire of Benedict's. According to the doctors, there isn't the remotest chance that Benedict could go away at all, at least until university. So I think it's unfair of them to use it as bait."

"So do I," I said. "But if Gideon can twist Benedict in this way, how is it that Benedict would vandalize the Society's papers?"

"I must remind you that I didn't say he had, or imply that I thought it. I said that Gideon thought it was Benedict."

"Yes. Of course." I sat and thought about it. Somehow I, too, had accepted that Benedict had torn the boxes containing the papers apart.

"And now I must leave you. I'm driving in to Shrewsbury today. I don't suppose you'd care to come, would you? It's a lovely town if you haven't seen it, and has some of the oldest and most historic buildings of any town in England—if you like that sort of thing."

"I do—very much. And I'd love to. But not today. May I take what we call a raincheck? In other words, do it another time."

"Yes." He laughed. "I like that expression. You may indeed take a raincheck."

After Roger had left, it occurred to me that I should ask someone how to get to the attic containing the papers I had come all this way to see. My heart sank at the thought of sorting them out. But the fact remained that, with their present state of confusion, it was even more important than I had realized to get started on them immediately.

I hesitated for a minute, then pushed open the swinging doors into the kitchen area. Crossing the butler's pantry, I went into the kitchen and then stopped on the threshold. Sitting on a straight kitchen chair, chatting to Mrs. Lowndes, who was peeling potatoes, and looking much more human than I thought he was capable of being, was Gideon. On the floor between them, Buff was busily cleaning up a dish.

"I wondered what had happened to her," I said, waving at Buff. "She came into the dining room with me and then vanished."

"Och, the wee one came looking for her braikfast." Mrs. Lowndes dropped the last piece of potato into a pan with the others and got up.

Gideon rose. "May I help you?" He no longer looked human, I thought. He now looked like himself again.

"Yes. Please point me in the direction of the attic where those papers are. If they're in the mess you say, then the sooner I get started the better."

"I'll take you up there," Gideon said. "This way."

But when we were halfway up the first flight I heard the telephone ring, and Mrs. Lowndes appeared below. "It's the vicar, Sir Gideon. He'd like very much to speak to you."

Gideon hesitated.

"Just tell me where, Gideon," I said. "I can find it."

"All right. Keep on going up till you reach the second floor—third to you. Then go right and you'll find a narrow staircase going up to the attic from there. When you get to the top of those, walk through the room you'll find yourself in, through the next, and into the far one. The boxes are there. They're clearly marked. If there's anything you want, give a shout. One of us will come up and help you. All right, Mrs. Lowndes. Tell Mr. Theale I'll be right there."

I watched Gideon going rapidly down the stairs, then went on up to the second, or, by British parlance, first floor, and was about to mount the next flight when I heard, down at the other end of the hall, away from my room, the same voice I'd heard the night before.

"Please let me. I won't hurt myself. I promise."

And then there was the low sound of a woman's voice—Sheila Maitland's I supposed.

"But I won't, I tell you!"

I took my foot off the bottom step of the next flight. Everyone seemed most anxious that I should not meet Benedict. Well, I thought, to heck with them! It was high time I met Rosemary's son. Walking quietly to the door, I hesitated. Then I firmly turned the knob and went in.

# four

THE FIRST THING that struck me was that the room was by far the lightest I had been into since I had arrived at Tenton. Located at the back of the house, it was on the corner of one wing, and what sun there was poured through windows on two walls. My second swift impression was, again, of the vibrant quality of the tall, beautifully proportioned red-haired woman standing beside the fire. But the moment my eyes fell on the figure on the sofa beside the fire, I forgot everything else.

Curiously, the moment I saw Benedict I suddenly realized that what had been lacking, for me, in Tenton, had been any sense of Rosemary's presence. It was odd— more than odd—that a house in which she had lived for more than seven years, of which she had been mistress, should have been so completely wiped clean of anything that spoke of her to me. But as I looked at the thin, startlingly handsome boy, sitting up, with arms braced against the side and edge of the sofa, I knew that Rosemary's presence was alive and vital in this house and was, at this moment, looking at me out of Benedict's eyes.

"You're Cousin Janet, aren't you?" he demanded with an imperiousness that, for a moment, recalled his father.

"Yes. I am. How are you, Benedict?"

"I'm fine. Very well indeed, which is what I've been trying for the past hour to explain to Sheila. I *don't* have to be coddled. I *don't* have to be prevented from doing what I want."

"Benedict—" Sheila started.

"What is it you want to do?" I asked. His likeness to his mother was startling. Her fair, burnished hair fell loose and wavy about his face. Her features were there, the fine, patrician features that gave her the look of what the French call *race*. The hand clutching the side of the sofa was a boy's hand, but was long-fingered, like hers. But his eyes were more brilliant than hers. They were of a particular shade of blue, almost aqua, rather like, I found myself musing, the sea with sun on it. But whereas Rosemary's strength was inward, constrained, giving her reserve, her son's poured out and dominated everything within the room.

"I want to go to school, boarding school. The one my father and Uncle Roger and my grandfather went to."

"It would be difficult for you," I said carefully, "if you can't get around too well."

"I can get around perfectly well, lots of the time." And, moving stiffly and awkwardly, yet more swiftly than I would have imagined, he stood on his feet, still gripping the curved end of the sofa. "See? I can stand."

But it was spoiled then. The flush in his cheeks paled. He made a sound, and started to topple over.

"Careful!" I said, and plunged forward. Out of the corner of my eye I could see Miss Maitland move from her stance beside the fire.

But before either of us could reach him, Benedict caught himself, and then lowered his body to the sofa. "It's nothing," he said. "Just a dizzy spell. I tell you, I'm all right."

But his voice had lost its ringing conviction. Now, he

sounded like a boy who wanted more than anything in the world to be "all right." Yet knew that he wasn't.

"Here," Sheila said. "Let me put a cushion behind you."

"No," he almost shouted. "I don't want it."

"Don't speak to me in that voice, Benedict. I won't permit it." She sounded cool and in command. Nor could I fault her. If she was going to help him academically, or in any other way, she couldn't allow him to dominate their relationship by hysterical maneuvering.

He shut his mouth sternly, the lips tight together. And the silent tussle of wills went on. Then a look of defeat flickered over his face. "Sorry," he muttered.

"That's all right," Sheila said. She said it very nicely. Almost tenderly. But she had won, and everyone in the room knew it.

Be fair, I told myself silently. She had to win. My experience with children was not all that extensive. Yet I knew that Benedict was the kind of boy that, once dominant over any relationship between him and someone else, would be impossible to manage.

"You're not like my mother," he said suddenly, addressing me.

"No. I'm like my grandmother on the other side of the family."

"My mother was very beautiful. There's her portrait." And he nodded in the direction of the fireplace.

It was astonishing that I hadn't seen it. But I had been too much taken up with the people in the room, especially with Rosemary's living portrait sitting on the sofa. But there she was in an extraordinarily light and delicate painting. And I was struck again with whole worlds withheld behind that beautiful face.

"Yes," I said, walking towards the fire. "That's a very good likeness. More so than any photograph I've seen of her."

"It was done by Mansfield," Benedict said importantly, mentioning one of the outstanding portrait painters to light on the English scene in the postwar years.

"Yes. It looks like his work."

"I'm very like her," Benedict continued with so much the same sense of consequence that I wanted to laugh.

"Yes, Benedict, you are. In appearance, certainly. But I'm not sure you're all that like her in other ways. She was a gentle and serene person, and very reserved, and—"

I was unprepared for his reaction. Fists pounding the sofa, he shouted. "I am like her, I am, I am. You've no right to say that I'm *not!*"

While I stood, rooted, Sheila ran towards him. "Stop that immediately," she said, stopping in front of him. "How dare you raise your voice like that. Apologize at once!"

"She said—" Benedict said, in the same shout.

But at that moment the door to the room burst open and Gideon came in. "What is that disgusting noise about?" he demanded. And although I had been shocked and upset at the scene that was going on, I suddenly started to feel quite sorry for the boy. I would not, at any time, I thought, want to be responsible for the look on Gideon's face.

"Cousin Janet said I'm not like my mother," Benedict muttered, both sulky and plainly frightened.

"And for that you made an appalling scene?" Gideon moved towards the sofa. He looked so menacing that I said hastily, "It was tactless of me, Gideon. My fault. I should have seen how much . . . how much . . . being like his mother means to him."

He turned towards me. "Whether you're tactless or not has nothing to do with it. Such behavior cannot be permitted."

And what are you going to do about it? I wondered. Beat him? But Gideon had a subtler punishment. "Benedict, I wrote today to the headmaster of the school you want to go to, entering your name for next year. But the letter isn't posted yet, and in view of what I've just seen and heard, it will not be posted. For your own sake I wouldn't dream of allowing you to expose yourself in such a way to other boys your own age. You wouldn't last a month before you'd be pleading to come home."

"That's not fair!" Benedict yelled. He struggled up on his arms, somehow got to his feet, and took a step towards his father before falling.

Gideon took a step forward, but Sheila was faster. "Benedict," she cried, and I was astonished at the concern in her voice, a note I hadn't heard before.

"It's all right," Benedict said, sounding suddenly much quieter. "I can manage by myself. I can *manage*." Pushing her way, he reached over, grasped the sofa, pulled himself towards it, and by an amazing show of strength, pulled himself up. Sheila hovered around him, and the moment he was down on the sofa, pulled a wollen afghan over his legs.

"I don't want that," he said, and thrust it away.

"Thanks would be in order, Benedict," Gideon said sternly.

"All right. Thank you, Sheila. I'm sorry, Father. Now would everyone please leave me alone? I have . . . I have homework I have to do."

"I'll stay and help you," Sheila said, smiling.

"No, thanks. I'd rather do it myself. By myself."

"All right. We'll leave you. Carry on." Still smiling, Sheila joined Gideon. They made, I thought grudgingly, a handsome couple. "Come along, Janet," Gideon said. "Benedict says he wants to be left alone to work. I hope he means it."

Rather ostentatiously the boy put his hand out to a table, covered with books and notebooks, that stood, within his reach, just back of the sofa. All of a sudden I saw a quiver pass over his face. Once again he pressed his lips together hard. There was no question but what he would be a difficult, temperamental boy to handle, but my heart went out to him. I was just about to leave with the others when he said in an odd, reluctant voice, "Cousin Janet, could you stay a minute?"

Sheila, who was half out the door, stopped. So did Gideon.

"Of course," I said, rather flattered.

"What do you want to see Cousin Janet about?" Gideon asked.

Benedict didn't say anything.

"Perhaps it's a private matter," I said.

"I thought you wanted to be alone?" Sheila came back into the room. "If you're going to be temperamental, I'm afraid your father is right: you'd never be suitable for school life."

"It doesn't look like I'm going to get there, anyway."

"He can always post the letter, or write another—that is, if you show more of a steady tendency, Benedict. That's really all he wanted to make you understand."

I saw Gideon frown and start to open his mouth. Then obviously change his mind.

"I don't see that a few minutes' conversation with me could seriously damage his work," I said. I was beginning to be irritated. Such a fuss over nothing!

Gideon had already gone out the door again, and was halfway down the stairs, and Sheila followed him. I was about to close the door after them when Sheila said, "Miss deMaury. Just a minute—before you go in to talk to Benedict."

Unwillingly, I went back out into the hall. "Well," I said a bit ungraciously. "What is it?"

"Don't give too much weight to what Benedict might say," she said. "I know you think Gideon, his father, is rather harsh. I thought so myself. But Benedict is . . . undependable. . . . He swings from one side to another, from one mood to another in a very . . . well . . . unsteady way. I'm sure it's the result of his illness, and not any real . . . well . . . mental instability. . . ."

You mean, I thought, that you *do* think it's the result of mental imbalance. Clever. How to convey the idea that someone is crazy while at the same time appearing not to.

I said, calmly, "I'll bear in mind the various stresses and strains he's been under." Then I opened the door and went back in.

Benedict was sitting on the sofa, his legs up, a large pad on his lap and a pencil in his hand. "They warned you against me, didn't they?" he said matter-of-factly.

"Well . . ." I started. Those startling, penetrating eyes looked up suddenly and I found myself unable to lie, even to equivocate much. "I think Sheila—Miss Maitland—thinks you're a bit . . . unsteady."

He gave a short laugh. "Yes. That's her favorite word. Steady is good. Unsteady is bad. And she uses it at least once a day."

I walked slowly towards him. "You do swing up and down rather wildly, don't you?"

Suddenly he grinned, looking exceedingly normal. "Yes, I do, don't I?"

I stopped. "Do you mean you deliberately put some of it on?"

The corners of his mouth turned down. His amazing eyes seemed to sparkle. "Life gets very boring around here sometimes."

"You wretched child! Do you know you have your father worried, I'm sure, out of his mind. And probably Miss Maitland is, too."

The sparkle vanished. "Not her," he said rather rudely. "She likes to make out to my father that I'm far worse than I am. I *know*."

I was more than willing to believe ill of Sheila Maitland, to whom I had taken something of a dislike. But common fairness made me ask, "All right, Benedict. *How* do you know? Have you heard her talking to him?"

His face flushed, and for a moment he seemed to be back to being the hysterical boy I had seen when I first came in the room. "Yes, I have. When they thought I was asleep. She's always telling him that I'm far too unsteady . . . unstable . . . to go to school, or even to tell the truth."

"Well, you do play into her hands, don't you? I've seen you."

He stared at me for a while, then his eyes shifted and he looked down. "I told you. Life gets dull. Besides, sometimes I feel funny."

"Funny how?"

He shrugged. "Nervy. Like I'm going to jump out of my skin. Powerful—like I can do anything."

For all my desire to believe that Sheila Maitland distorted the truth because she had some ax of her own to grind, I couldn't help but see that Benedict gave her plenty of fuel. And what did I truly believe about him? I glanced down at the boy. Under his hand, some design on the pad on his lap was growing. I walked around to where I could look over his shoulder and received a severe shock. That he had talent was unmistakable. But the drawing that he was completing in a few swift strokes was a horror. A cat was hanging from a gibbet. A dog lay on a table, cut in half. A man sat at a desk; his head was on the floor. If Benedict had less skill, my feeling would have been one of disgust for the intent. As it was, I closed my eyes.

"D'you like it?" he asked.

"It's dreadful," I said, angry at my own shrinking. And then I jumped. Because Benedict put his head back and laughed, a laugh that went on and on, and as he did so he tore the paper off the pad and ripped it into pieces. "Got you that time, didn't I?" he said, sounding delighted with himself.

I turned on my heel and walked out of the room. I half expected to see Sheila waiting outside. But there was only Mrs. Lowndes coming upstairs with a small tray on which was a glass of milk and a bun.

"Is Miss Maitland in there with Benedict?" she asked.

I shook my head. "No. He's alone." Then, just as she was about to go in, "Mrs. Lowndes. What do you think of Benedict?"

She hesitated. Then she said, "I think he bears very careful watching, Miss deMaury. Not that he isn't watched —poor lad. Everyone in this house—and some who are not here all the time—watch him. And he knows it. Which is why sometimes he plays a part. But I mean—"

"Oh, there you are, Mrs. Lowndes. I was just coming down to get Benedict's milk. Thank you for bringing it up."

With a wide, gracious smile, Sheila Maitland swooped down the hall, took the tray from Mrs. Lowndes' hands and went into Benedict's room.

I was left with a great number of not very well formulated questions.

"I must be getting back to the kitchen," Mrs. Lowndes said. "We're short handed today."

Well, I thought, beginning to mount the stairs to the third floor, I might as well get on with what I had set out to do—go look at the papers. But I was very curious about a lot of things: Benedict's drawing, Sheila Maitland's role in all this, and what Mrs. Lowndes had been about to say.

Remembering Gideon's instructions, I mounted to the third floor, then stopped and looked around. There were the same long halls on either side of the landing as there were on the two floors below. But the ceiling here was lower and the halls narrower. Turning, I saw, to my right, the little staircase, visible through a small door to the right. It was a curious, winding stair, longer than I would have thought necessary between a third and fourth storey. The stairs were steep and narrow, and there was no handrail, though there were, attached to the walls, supports which looked as though they might once have held rails. "Somebody could break a leg on this," I muttered to myself as I wound up and up. Finally, at the top, where I least needed it, there was a short rail and then I was up in a long, low room. Sunlight poured in the dormer windows on one side, slanting across a floor covered with old carpets and lighting up the dust on furniture piled here and there: chairs; an old sofa, its cover frayed; a bed; two tables and many bookcases with books spilling out of them.

I have always loved secondhand stores and thrift shops more than I have liked the real antique stores. In the latter the furniture, usually of good design by the very fact of its being there, is polished for presentation. In rundown second- and third-hand establishments, on the other hand, nothing is dusted, and the good is shoved higgledy-piggledy in with the trashy, the whole with the broken, and book treasures are found piled with the garbage reading of previous generations. I have sometimes had a fantasy of being lost in a thrift shop and of being found, quite happy, several weeks later, having put back together all the broken furniture and read all the forgotten books.

And now, I thought, staring at the rich storehouse in front of me, my fantasy had come true. I could spend a month up here. But, I shook my head, that was not what Tony had sent me to Tenton for.

Walking through, I went into the next room, which was a smaller version of the first, and finally into the room beyond, the smallest of the three. Or perhaps it just seemed that way because of the cartons scattered all over the floor and spread from wall to wall.

"Ye gods!" I muttered. Scrawled in black crayon on the side of each carton were the capital letters STWU— Society Towards a World Union. But after walking around and staring at the boxes from all sides, I ascertained that, unless they were numbered on the bottom where I couldn't see them, the boxes were not in any order. Well, at least I could count them. I did so, not once, but twice, and felt no better for it. There were fifty-eight boxes in all.

And how long had Tony given me to run through them? Three weeks? At a quick calculation that meant almost three boxes a day. And those boxes were not small. The task was so staggering that I stood, just staring at them. Wouldn't it be better, I found myself thinking, if I had them shipped to the States? But I dismissed that, after a short meditation on the prospective cost of air-mailing several hundred pounds of paper. Furthermore, the cheaper surface mail could take weeks, and Tony's whole motive in sending me now was speed.

There really was, I decided, no choice. I'd simply have to go through the wretched cartons as rapidly and efficiently as I could. At least in that way I could weed out what I didn't want, and if the cost of air-mailing the rest were prohibitive, well, then that would be Tony's problem.

A motto on my desk back at the office read, *The best way to get something done is to begin.* Buckle down, old girl, buckle down, I sang to a well-known tune. And since there seemed no way of deciding where to start, I might as well begin with the box nearest to me.

Two hours later, my hands dry with dust, I had come

to a grim conclusion. Before I could make any decision
about the importance of any of the papers, I would have
to put them back into some kind of chronological order.
Whoever had messed them up had done a good job, and
they had been returned to the carton without regard to
year or even decade. In the first box I opened there were
letters and memoranda bearing dates of almost every
year since the Society was founded in 1929. My stomach
sinking, I wondered if this held true of all the boxes.
Getting up, I moved to the next and opened it. The first
two fistfuls of papers bore dates of twenty-four different
years. I dropped them back in the carton with a sound
somewhere between disgust and despair.

"Beaten before you start?" Gideon said from the door.

I looked back over my shoulder. "Do you have any
idea how muddled up these dates are?" I said.

"Of course. I put the stuff back in the boxes. Whoever
took them out and threw them around made very sure
that no lot from one year would be left in a single pile."

"But why?" I said, bursting out with my favorite query.
And then remembering what Roger had said about Gideon suspecting his son, I glanced up at him. Gideon's
mouth had closed in a way that reminded me strongly of
Benedict's.

"Roger," I said, taking a sudden decision, "thinks you
think that Benedict was responsible for all this muddle,
for vandalizing the boxes. Is that true?"

I don't know what I expected—a burst of rage from
Gideon, an angry denial or a curt suggestion that I mind
my own business. Instead, there was a flicker of pain
across his face, and then a stillness. "It's possible," he said.

"To annoy you? Or just to get your attention?"

"I don't think Benedict is lacking in attention from me."

"Perhaps he'd appreciate less harshness and more understanding of his feelings. Refusing to mail that letter
you had written was pretty rough."

"Sheila says—"

He stopped.

"What does Sheila say?" I asked.

Gideon stooped down beside one of the open boxes

and started idly taking out the top papers and looking at them. "She says, and I, of course, agree with her, that too much permissiveness will simply make Benedict worse, not better. That he needs firm boundaries as to what he can and cannot do."

"Firm boundaries are one thing. Dangling something he desperately wants in front of him, and then withdrawing it, is cruel."

"And how would you describe tearing open these boxes and throwing the contents around? Since you're the chief victim of that particular piece of drama, would you call it harmless childish high spirits?"

No, I thought. Considering the extent of the damage done, and also considering the intelligence of the boy who did it—who *supposedly* did it, I corrected myself—it could not be called harmless in any way. In fact, the more I contemplated the damage, knowing what putting it back in order would entail, the more appalled I was at both the vindictiveness and intelligence behind the act. If it could not be described as harmless, it could also not be designated as the work of someone stupid. It was no act of unthinking peasant anarchy, comparable to knocking over a statue or destroying a painting that represented some hated aesthetic arrogance. Whoever vandalized these boxes contributed a great deal of thought to the project. . . .

I glanced up to see Gideon watching me with such a forbidding look on his face that it jolted me.

"Roger doesn't think that Benedict did this," I blurted out, remembering belatedly that Roger, by that faint, but unmistakable shake of the head, had indicated he didn't want me to reveal to Gideon our conversation about Benedict and the boxes.

"So he says. But he doesn't offer any other plausible explanation. I don't believe that either Sheila or Mrs. Lowndes did it. That leaves Benedict, Roger—or me, of course."

"You sound like you've given the matter some thought," I said.

"Wouldn't you?"

"So, having eliminated everyone else, you decide your son did it. I realize he probably could do it—I'm told his hands and arms are strong and I've seen a little of that myself. But wouldn't it be hard for him?"

Gideon was walking around looking at the boxes. "As to his capability—there are times when he can get around, up and down stairs, very well."

"Wouldn't you know it?"

"Not necessarily. I'm away a fair amount, and I used to be away even more. I don't watch him every hour of the day. Keeping an eye on him is one of the things Sheila is here for. And besides—" He stopped.

"Besides what?"

He paused. Then, "Nothing. Now, can I help you with this in any way?"

It was a courteous question, but there was something in the way he asked it that made it obvious he was not asking out of an impulse of affection or even kindness. I received the strong impression that his motive would come nearer to an acknowledgment that the sooner I had accomplished what I came for, the sooner I would leave.

That being the case, I did not feel under any obligation to refuse.

"What would you suggest?" My voice was as cool as his own.

"Since you're the one who wants to go through them, I think the suggestion should come from you." He had neatly batted the ball back into my court.

I stared at what looked like, from where I was sitting, an acre of boxes. "Are they all like this?" I finally asked. "Letters and memos and papers representing practically every year since the Society was founded?"

"All of them."

I thought for a minute. "Then what would help me most would be two sturdy helpers and about fifty more boxes. By the way, were these the boxes they came in?"

"No, it was easier to get new ones than to try and tape the old ones back together; they'd been pretty much pulled apart. I simply ordered new box frames from a carton company, and put them together when they arrived. I can get more quite easily. Are you going to put the papers in chronological order?"

"Yes. I would suspect that an awful lot of stuff—flyers, printed posters and leaflets—could be thrown out on sight. But what's left has at least to be divided according to year before I can make sense out of any of it."

"All right. I'll ask the vicar if he can suggest a couple of helpers. He knows the young people hereabouts better than I do."

"They don't have to be young, even. Anyone who can read a date and put it into the right container would do."

"True. But I think that you'd do better with girls who'd worked in an office."

"Are there any such around here?"

"Oh, yes. Girls go from here to Shrewsbury, Chester and other towns—even London—and then come back from time to time for various reasons. I'll speak to Mr. Theale. In the meantime, I'll call up that carton company and tell them to send more boxes. They can put them on a truck and send them through here in a day or so."

I got slowly to my feet and looked at my hands. "I think I'll plan to charge Tony for a long manicure course. If my hands look like this at the end of two hours, I hate to think what they'll be like after I've sorted all those boxes."

"They'll show the results of honest labor."

"Well, I haven't sat around the rest of my life being waited on, you know. We didn't have wall-to-wall servants —why even this morning . . ." And at that moment I remembered the man's figure I had seen from my window the night before. Amazingly, I hadn't thought about him since.

"This morning what?" Gideon asked, shoving the open box out of the way of the door.

I was about to tell him, when I hesitated. Patronizing scorn would be a fair description of the way he received my news of the note left on my floor. If I added to it now a mysterious figure coming out of the house and then driving off without using the gate, what little credibility I had left would undoubtedly be lost. Not, I assured myself, that I gave a tinker's dam if Gideon thought of me as an overimaginative and slightly hysterical female. But I owed it to the job I was here to do to make as professional an impression as I could. So I held my tongue. Besides, if I had any queries about male servants in the household I could always ask Roger.

Gideon, Sheila and I had lunch at one o'clock, since Roger had not returned.

"He probably won't be back until dinner, if then," Gideon said, as we all sat down.

"Small blame to him for that," Sheila commented. "It can't be very interesting for him here."

Gideon helped himself to some shepherd's pie. "I can't think why he comes here at all. It isn't as though he'd been brought up here."

"Wasn't he?" I asked. "You were, weren't you?"

"Oh, yes. But Roger's mother had asthma so badly that my father took a villa on the Mediterranean, where she fared a lot better than she did among the damps of the English and Welsh climate. So Roger grew up there, mostly, except for the years he came back to England to school."

"I thought he said his mother was Welsh."

"She was. But even the Welsh get asthma."

I concentrated on the pie for a few minutes, finding it delicious, and listening to Gideon and Sheila talk idly about village affairs. One would think, I found myself reflecting, rather cattily, that she was in training as lady of the manor, future head and about-to-be patron of all the local women's societies. Down, Rover, I said to myself silently. No need to be spiteful. But the name Rover reminded me of something.

"I wonder where Buff is," I said aloud.

Sheila stopped in midsentence. "Sorry?"

"Buff," I repeated. "Boadicea."

"Boadicea?" There was a frown on the good-looking face. "I don't quite understand—"

"The little bitch that Parry and I got out of the trap," Gideon interpolated.

"It must be a joke then," Sheila said, "calling her Boadicea." Her nostrils arched. "An American joke. Anything less distinguished than that mongrel I can hardly imagine."

"That was the point," I said mildly. "Anyway, has anyone seen her? I haven't, since I went upstairs earlier."

"You *are* taking your responsibilities seriously," Gideon said.

"I put her out." Sheila spoke calmly. "You never know how well housetrained those mongrels are."

I surprised myself at the indignation that surged up. "Well, she spent a large part of the night in my bedroom without misbehaving. And it's raining."

"There are plenty of outbuildings she can take shelter in," Sheila said. There was a hard look around her mouth. "We're very fond of dogs in my family," she went on. "Real dogs, of course, not strays. But we never allowed them in the house."

"But I am adopting Buff and taking her back to the States with me. That was my understanding. Am I right, Gideon?"

Gideon put down his knife and fork. "Perfectly right. The dog is hers, Sheila. I should, of course, have told you. My fault." The iron look was back on his face.

Well, I thought, too bad if he was annoyed with me. "I'll try and keep her out of the way as much as possible. But I'd appreciate it, if she's in someone's way, if you'll let me know. There isn't a rule here about dogs having to be kept outside, is there?" That was a little mean of me, since I knew that the handsome Gelert slept on the hearth rug in the drawing room.

"No, there is not," Gideon said shortly.

I knew that I had put him in an awkward position and was not at all sorry for it.

"Then I'll get her after lunch and leave her in my room so she won't be in the way."

"Be careful she doesn't bite you," Sheila said.

"Buff? I can't imagine her biting anything."

"She's nipped me more than once. She's not trust-worthy."

Not only did I not believe her, I was convinced that she was trying to recover her lost face. And succeeding.

"If there's any question of that," Gideon said, "she'll have to go."

Sheila threw him a grateful smile.

Since the English enjoyed a well-deserved reputation as chief dog lovers of the world, I was puzzled by Sheila's antagonism to the almost ludicrously harmless Buff, and filed away the question for Roger when I next saw him. However, from what Gideon said, that would not be until much later in the day.

After lunch, when we got up from the table, Gideon turned to me. "Is there anything you'd like to do this afternoon, since I gather you have to wait for helpers and boxes before you can go any further with the papers?"

I thought for a minute. Since I had no desire to stay at Tenton Hall any longer than Gideon would have me stay, my choice would have been to spend every waking hour on sorting the papers. But he was right about one thing: it would be worse than useless to start taking the papers out and putting them into some kind of order if I had then to put them back into the same box.

"Well, it's true about having to wait to work with the papers. I think I'd like to find Buff, look over the house and then take a walk, in that order."

Gideon was leaving the dining room, but he turned at the door to wait for Sheila and me. "If you want to find Buff, as you call her, I suggest you go out through the kitchen, that leads to the stables and outbuildings."

The memory from the night before slid back into my mind. "Isn't there a door opening out of one of the front rooms?"

"Yes, there is. The bookroom. Why?"

"Because when I got up last night to draw the curtain," I said carefully, "I saw someone—a man—coming out of that door."

Sheila's brows went up. "At what hour was this?"

"A little after two thirty."

"I see," Gideon said. "You did have a busy night."

"Was that when you found that mysterious note?" Sheila asked.

So Gideon had already told her. Well, considering their relationship, I shouldn't be too surprised.

"Yes," I said, trying not to react to the tone in her voice. "It was."

"And what did the man do then?" Gideon asked in the tone of voice of someone indulging a child.

"He went around to the side into the courtyard," I said doggedly. "Then I heard the sound of a car starting. But he must have left by some other road since he didn't drive back by the front."

Almost before the words were out of my mouth Gideon said, "That must have been Parry. He lives in the gatehouse, and one of his jobs is to see that most doors and windows in the house are locked. I can't imagine why he'd be doing it so late. However, he may have been out for the evening, and come to do his lockup late."

"And the car?"

Gideon shrugged. "I don't know. I'll ask him. Anything else? Any more melodramas?"

I was tired of being patronized as though I were an imaginative and unreliable child. I knew the note had been left and then stolen. I *had* seen someone leave the house. I might be unfamiliar with the habits of English country houses, but I had a hard time believing that a gatekeeper would be locking up at two thirty in the morning and I didn't think for one minute he'd be driving by any route from the house to the gatehouse. Gideon obviously didn't believe me. Well, I didn't believe him. Parry's name came too fast and sounded too convenient. "I'd like to see the bookroom," I said. "*And* the door."

"Certainly. I'm going there now. I also use it as an office. Come along."

"I'll go get Buff and be right back."

Gideon continued to look amused. I could have slapped him. "All right," he said. "I'll wait for you there. It's the first room in this wing off the central hall."

But I didn't have to go out to the stables to find Buff.

As I went into the warm kitchen, I saw my protégée lying on a piece of old carpet right next to the huge range. "She looks comfortable," I said.

Buff, who had looked up at my entry, threw herself at me as though we had been parted for weeks and I had been in direst peril.

"Och, the puir wee thing," Mrs. Lowndes said, putting a clean dish on a shelf. "She was crying at the back door fit to break your heart. She's taken a strong fancy to you, I see."

"It's mutual," I replied, trying to calm Buff's transports. I hesitated over my next words, knowing that it was not the best form to appear to criticize the governess-tutor. "I take it Miss Maitland felt that Buff should go out."

"The wee doggie," Mrs. Lowndes said, "does not care for Miss Maitland overmuch. Miss Maitland thinks highly of the pedigreed animals."

The two statements strung together did not add much in the way of content to what I already knew. Yet I felt they came riding, in that dry, unemotional Scots voice, on considerable feeling.

"I tell you what, Mrs. Lowndes," I said. "I've decided to take Buff back home with me, and Sir Gideon has given his approval. So she's really mine now, and if there are any—er—orders regarding her, I wish you'd refer them to me. Especially if they mean putting her out in the cold."

"I'd be happy to, Miss deMaury." The housekeeper sounded as though she meant it.

As I stood stroking Buff between the ears and down her back—gestures that Buff was enjoying with closed eyes and a look of ecstasy—I pondered bringing up the subject of Rosemary, gambling that Mrs. Lowndes could be induced by guile or suggestion to finish her cryptic sentence, *"Your cousin, was she, Miss deMaury? She was a strange lady indeed. Why she—"* But there was no way I could introduce the topic—in the expectation of getting a quick response—without offending Mrs. Lowndes' sense of the proprieties. After all, Rosemary had been Lady Lightwood. At some point I would try to find a reason to be in the kitchen, or perhaps upstairs, when Mrs. Lowndes was, and when we could have a lengthy and, to all intents and purposes, rambling chat. Anything more abrupt than that would, I was quite sure, cause the elderly housekeeper to shut herself up behind the barriers of class and calling.

"Well, thank you for letting Buff in, Mrs. Lowndes. Come along, Buff, we're going to the bookroom."

Finding it without too much trouble, I pushed open the door. Buff scampered in ahead of me and pranced up to the fireplace where a wood fire crackled, combating the damp chill. Gelert, his magnificent length sprawled on the hearth rug, raised his head. I waited, prepared to leap to my pet's rescue. But after what looked like a stern glance, the handsome beast lowered his head. Like master, like dog, I thought to myself, and looked around.

"Well," Gideon said from behind a desk placed parallel to the windows, "do you see your mysterious door?"

"I'll come over and look," I said. "What a spectacular room this is."

It was. Long windows lined the front, and I could see immediately what Gideon had meant. From the door, any one of them could appear to be a French window. Two other sides of the room were lined with books from floor to ceiling. The fourth wall had shelves of books on either side of the chimney piece. The smell in the room was a combination of leather, old books, polish and potpourri, which latter came from a delicate bowl on a small table.

Strolling into the center of the room, my eyes were on the windows, trying to distinguish which one was, in reality, a door. But something to the left, above the fireplace, caught my gaze and I turned.

The woman's face that looked down from the portrait was arresting, the angles sharply delineated, the eyes brooding. "Who is that?" I asked.

"My mother," Gideon said, not looking up.

"She has an interesting face," I said. "Not beautiful, but—" I groped around for the right word, "compelling."

"She died in forty-nine when I was only fifteen, but I think that's the right word to describe her."

I was still looking at the painting. "Maybe it's the way she was painted—the style of the painter himself—but she doesn't look as though she came out of the English or Welsh countryside."

"She didn't. She was a concert pianist my father met when he went on a vacation to Austria. She was Austrian and Jewish."

I stared at him, thinking of the dates. "Well, at least she was over here during World War II, not in occupied Austria."

"Yes, but I sometimes wondered if she didn't almost wish she were back there. All of her family—two parents, three brothers and sisters and I don't know how many cousins—died in a concentration camp. To be safe when that was going on was not easy for her. As a matter of fact, I think the strain hastened her death."

# five

I STARED AT Gideon. "I didn't know any of that. I wonder, considering the closeness of the family connection, why I didn't."

"Well, she died in 1949. Rosemary and I weren't married until 1965."

"Yes, but—"

After a pause, Gideon said, "But what?"

"But you surely must have told her about your mother, and I'm just surprised she didn't tell me when I saw her both on the Continent and in the States. It's not exactly a common story."

"Especially for an English baronet," Gideon said drily.

"Having her be who she was and feel the way she did must have affected you."

He looked at me for a minute. I had the feeling he was watching me carefully. "In what way do you mean?"

"Well—you didn't grow up with your usual English upper-class schoolboy's view of current history and the modern world. I mean, I know your father's family must have been involved in World War II—"

"Yes. My father fought in Africa, Italy, France and Germany."

"But you were old enough to remember the war, weren't you? The business about the concentration camps?"

"Oh, yes. I remember well when they were opened up. My mother and I were in London when the first newsreels came in. I didn't see them, then. But I remember the afternoon she came home from seeing those films for the first time." He stopped. His voice had been unusually flat, yet a chill flickered along my skin. Meticulously he blotted the sheet on which he had been writing with an old-fashioned fountain pen.

"She . . . she must have been glad about Israel," I said hesitantly, "or did she live long enough to see it established? I forget the date—1948 wasn't it?"

Again came that watchful glance. I had the odd impression that I had said something rather important, although I hadn't the faintest idea what, since I had spoken out of nervousness, more to fill a silent space than anything else.

"What makes you say that?"

"Oh—I don't know. I suppose because I thought some of her relatives might have made it over there, except, of course, that you just finished telling me they were all wiped out."

"Not all. She had cousins once removed who went there before the state was established and fought for it. But you're right about one thing. I'm glad she lived long enough to see the beginnings of the modern state." He got up. "You surprise me."

"Why?"

"Because I always gathered from Rosemary that the fate of the dispossessed people, the founding of the state of Israel, was something you weren't terribly interested in. In fact, hostile to."

"Why on earth would she say that—?" I started.

"Well, it is true, isn't it, that the Society wanted you to come and help with fund raising and promotion because you bore your father's name, but that you had always rebelled against his idealism, which was why Rosemary came over to work with the Society in London instead."

"Yes, but—it isn't that I didn't care about people without homes, although the problem of the dispossessed people was different in the sixties from what it had been in the forties. It was just that . . ." I made a gesture. "It's hard to explain."

"You owe me no explanation," Gideon said coldly. "Nor have I asked for one."

"Nevertheless, I feel—defensive. And I'd like to explain what I did feel."

"Very well." It was hard to imagine him sounding less interested. I was determined to speak, out of some sense of self-justice, if for no other reason. Yet I paused, aware of the subtle, unspoken but quite palpable lack of interest—no, something much more active than that: antagonism—I was encountering in Gideon. He stirred restlessly. "As I said, there's no need—"

"Yes, there is." I took a deep breath. "My feeling about the Society was that it uttered, through my father and others, a lot of high-minded, abstract principles about great issues that sounded marvelous, but that they didn't translate very well into much good for the individual. Great for speeches, but not much good for people as people. I've realized, since I've got older, that there's a place for that. That people like that can have an effect on other people, or on that amorphous thing, world opinion, and that, in turn, does practical good. But just before my mother died something happened that made an impression on me. My father was delivering a speech, a terribly important speech, in New York, about world poverty. The press was all over him. He was interviewed on everything—the idol of every liberal and reformer. Almost that same week Mother discovered—I don't quite know how—that one of my father's assistants was about to blow his own brains out because of a mortgage and his wife's illness and the illness of two of his children. When she asked the man why on earth he hadn't said something to Father about it, he said it was because he felt so guilty allowing this problem to overwhelm him when he was supposed to be helping Robert deMaury establish peace and plenty for the entire world. I was quite small, but I knew about it because I walked into the living room just as Mother handed him a check and the wretched man burst into tears. After he'd left Mother said something like, 'It's probably very disloyal of me, but I sometimes think that if your father had started an ordinary business, making neckties, and given a hundred men jobs to work in his plant, he'd have done more good than founding societies for world peace and union. Always be practical in your help, Janet. Leave the great theories for others.'

"That's why I never could get very excited about Father's work. It was probably biased of me, but I kept remembering that. I was a lot older when I began to understand that some of the emotion behind Mother's argument might have come from the fact that my father spent his life—and Mother's life—trotting around the world doing good when he could have stayed home with his family. . . ."

"I see," Gideon said. He strolled over to the fireplace and stood staring down at Gelert. The big dog looked back up at him, his ears twitching. "That's not quite the way I heard it," Gideon added.

"What did you hear?" Beneath the level of our conversation it seemed to me something stirred, as though an element of which I had been totally unaware, showed itself briefly for a second.

After a minute he said, "It doesn't matter now." Turning, he waved in the direction of the windows. "Is that the door you were talking about?"

I walked over and looked. Sheila was right about one thing, the tall windows were almost identical. Only up close could one see that one was a door with a small latch. Opening the door, I stepped outside and looked up. The tall front looked bland, closed, the windows identical. It was impossible, from here, to tell which were mine and from where I would, the night before, have been looking.

"I can't tell," I said, stepping back inside. "Because I can't from here see which is my room."

Gideon came over to where I stood, stepped outside the door and looked up. "Those," he said, pointing. "The three just to this side of the central part."

"In that case, this is the door, because from there to here would be just about the right angle."

He came back in, closing the door behind him. "You're sure you saw this man."

"Yes, Gideon. I'm sure. But I suppose you put it in the category of the note on the floor which you have convinced yourself I dreamed."

Gideon's curiously light eyes were on me, as though he were thinking about something else altogether. "Could you have told who the man was even if you knew him? If it had been either Roger or me?"

I hesitated, because I had asked myself that. "I don't know. It was dark and, even though the rain had stopped, it was misty. In other words, I didn't recognize him. Whether I would have if it had been either you or Roger I don't know."

"All very mysterious," Gideon said, walking back to the fireplace. "If I remember correctly, your choice of activity this afternoon was to find Buff, look over the house and take a walk. Well, you've found Buff, do you want to look over the house now? Can you do it yourself or do you want Mrs. Lowndes to go with you?"

"I certainly do not want Mrs. Lowndes to stop whatever she's doing just to show me over the place. Maybe I'll reverse the order of things and take Buff for a walk."

He hesitated. "I thought I'd be riding this afternoon, but I've decided instead to go and call on Mr. Theale at the rectory. You can come along if you want to, and describe to the rector exactly the kind of helper you'd like to have."

"All right. I'll get my coat."

Fifteen minutes later we had left the side door, accompanied by Gelert and Buff, and were walking through the courtyard. "So there *is* a back road out," I said, thinking of the man I had seen and the sound of the car that had driven off.

"Yes," Gideon said briefly. "Behind the stables."

Back of the stables a partially graveled road wove in and out among trees, glistening here and there with puddles from the rain the night before. The road itself was neglected, with tufts of grass breaking through the pebbles and fairly deep declivities here and there.

"In New York," I said, jumping over one of them, "we'd call them potholes."

"That's what they are. But, like your New York City government, I can't afford to have them filled."

This was a surprise. "It's probably crude of me to mention it, but I thought a lot of money came with the title," I said. "Rosemary said once that she felt guilty about marrying so much money."

"Your cousin did not believe in inherited wealth, whether large or small. But that belief had little, if any, effect on her ability to live on a budget. She could, to put it at its most modest, be quite extravagant."

Some hot reply in defense of Rosemary sprang to my lips, but stopped there. It was all quite true. Her sudden onslaughts on some of New York and London's more expensive stores were as surprising as they were impulsive. Her spending streak matched nothing else in her nature.

"Maybe," I said mischievously, "it was her personal attempt to equal out the wealth she married."

"Modern taxation could be depended on to do that, plus double death duties within a rather short space of time."

"Why double? You mean someone besides your father?"

"Of course. My older brother inherited the title and estate. Then he was killed in Korea—in the Gloucester Regiment."

"I see." I remembered the famous British regiment that had been all but wiped out in 1951. "That was something else I didn't know."

"There seemed to be rather a lot that you and Rosemary didn't talk about. However," he added, before I could say anything, "I suppose she had her reasons."

I was back on the defensive, and reflected, once again,

that I had been in that state since I arrived. I could, of course, come out and ask why, but since the odds were heavy that I would receive one of Gideon's rebuffs, pride and anger held my tongue. I decided, for the moment, not to say anything at all. Let the burden of conversation be on him. Instead, as we broke through the trees into more open country, I looked around me.

The road had started to slope down. Then, on the other side of a gate, fell away much more steeply. Farther away, all around, rose hills, those in front of me, to the west, higher than those on either side. There was an overall, overwhelming impression of greenness. Trees, leafy and thick, lined the slopes above and below. At the bottom of the hill, out of sight, was the soft splash of a stream. Over to the right, under the hills, were pastures with red-and-white and black-and-white cattle grazing. Farther up were sheep. And far in the distance, visible between the folds of two hills, were receding lines of moors, changing from dark green to blue to purple as the lines disappeared into mist. I took a deep breath and a mixture of smells came at me—grass, wildflowers I couldn't identify, and cows.

"I haven't smelled anything like that since my vacations in Colorado and Wyoming. Only this is a little different, wetter maybe. In fact, wetter, definitely."

"I haven't been to your West," Gideon said. I had the impression that he was relieved to change the subject. "Is it like this?"

"No. This is more like New England, Vermont, mostly. Out west it's higher, colder, dryer, and the sky is bigger. But this is more mysterious."

He looked at me and, for the second time since I arrived, smiled. "Mysterious?"

"Yes. This feeling that everything is misted at the edges, as though at any point, if you walked far enough, you'd walk into another world, another dimension."

"Well, that's Wales you're looking at. And the Welsh are Celts, which goes with what you're talking about."

"Are you Welsh?"

"There was intermarriage further back, but the family is basically English."

Gideon's own ancestry, I thought—English, Welsh, Austrian and Jewish—was an even more interesting combination. I wondered, in passing, what effect it might have had in wrenching the tenor of his thinking from the orthodox paths of his distinguished but conventional landed gentry family.

"Well?" Gideon said sharply.

I jumped a little. "Well what?"

"You're looking at me speculatively." We walked down the last few feet of the path and he opened the gate, holding it for me.

"I was wondering how much your thinking was affected by your mother's background, by her and her family's experience. Or whether you cling to the true-blue Tory views of your squirarchy forebears."

"What makes you think they're true-blue Tory?" He walked through after me and closed the gate. "For all you know I might come from a long line of English socialist radicals."

"Do you?"

He grinned briefly. "As a matter of fact, no. But I dislike stereotypes."

"All right, Sir Gideon. Guilty."

He glanced at me as we started down the steep hill. "That was sometimes a bone of contention between Rosemary and me. She was rather fond of types: the reactionary lord, the noble peasant, the enlightened professor, the idealistic student, etcetera. One night, when we were in London, I managed to get together in the same evening a communist member of the peerage, an ultraconservative from the working class, a university don known for his narrow-mindedness and a student whose one expressed goal was to make a million pounds before his fortieth birthday, plus some other friends, including the vicar and his daughter, Gwyneth. It made an interesting dinner party."

"Did Rosemary enjoy it?"

"Not really. Nor did your father, who was also invited,

being in London at the time. The only person who seemed to enjoy himself was your boss, Tony Bridewell, who was also a guest."

"I didn't know you knew Tony. He didn't say anything to me about it."

"I wouldn't say I know him, I only saw him the few times when he was visiting Rosemary."

I tried to imagine what—beyond the family connection with Rosemary—the two men would have in common. "I can't envision the two of you together."

"Which of your types does Bridewell fit into?" he asked sardonically.

"Oh, if we're going to typecast—a member of the WASP elite, one-time liberal congressman, publisher of distinguished current affairs books, often by ex-New Frontiersmen. By the way, do you know the meaning of the acronym WASP?"

"Even here we know it means white Anglo-Saxon Protestant. But doesn't it carry a somewhat socially elite connotation? I don't think the term applies, for instance, to the poverty-stricken inhabitants of Appalachia, does it? Yet they would indeed be white Anglo-Saxon Protestants in the strict sense of the word."

"Yes. You seem to know a lot about current American mythology. I suppose that came from Rosemary."

"Here we are," Gideon said. "The rectory is just at the end of the street."

Tenton could easily figure in any English calendar as the idealized English village. Two rows of cottages, bisected by a stream and a road, ran for about a quarter of a mile. Three small stone bridges spanned the little brook, next to which ran a vividly green verge of grass, itself bordered on either side by huge trees, their abundant and leafy branches meeting overhead and providing shade to the houses on both sides. At the other end of the village, its squat tower half hidden by the trees, was a surprisingly large village church.

"I wouldn't think there'd be enough people in the village to fill that these days."

"No. Of course there are also parishioners from the

surrounding country houses. Even so, on a good morning
—Christmas or Easter—the vicar does well if he can
count thirty heads, including children."

"I wouldn't think that could support him."

"It doesn't. The 'living,' as we used to say, was in our
family."

"You mean the Lightwoods pay him."

"Past tense. We barely contribute now. Fortunately,
Mr. Theale has a small private income. And he lives in a
spartan fashion."

I could see that for myself when we were ushered into
the rectory, by far the largest house in the village itself.
Sitting back of the church in its own extensive garden,
the Georgian house looked as though it were built to
accommodate the immense families that were, at one
time, characteristic of country parsonages.

Gelert and Buff walked up the path to the rectory
door ahead of us.

"Gelert—sit!" Gideon commanded. "Buff—sit."

Gelert promptly sat down on the porch before the
front door. Buff came back and threw herself against
Gideon in sheer affection.

"Well, what can you expect?" I asked. "She hasn't
had time to be trained. You can't judge all animals by
that regimented guardsman of yours."

"Softly, softly. I was just seeing if in any previous home
your little friend had had any training."

"Buff, sit!" I said, surprised at how eager I was to have
her show up well.

Buff leant down on all fours, then leapt up to lick my
face. "Yes, all right," I said, a little embarrassed.

Gideon bent down and pushed Buff's hindquarters to
a sitting position. "Buff, sit." Buff lowered her ears and
waggled her tail.

"Sit!" Gideon repeated, and pushed her back again.
"That's a good dog."

The door opened suddenly. "Oh, good morning, Sir
Gideon."

I looked up. The young woman standing there was

shorter than I by inches, which was a rarity, since I am not tall. But a second glance showed why. The deformity of back and leg which reduced her stature was not immediately noticeable. But it was there, and when she moved, awkward and lopsided, the distortion showed. Her face revealed very white skin, dark brown waving hair and eyes so dark they were almost black.

"Good morning, Gwyneth. Is your father in and free to have visitors?"

"Of course. For you, any time."

It was a gracious response, yet it made me uncomfortable. The girl stepped back, holding the door.

We stepped into a wide central hall containing only a chair and a chest. The dark, polished floorboards were uncovered. A graceful staircase, its tread also uncovered, curved upwards from the hall.

"You know the way, Sir Gideon. Father's in his study."

"Gwyneth, I'd like to present my wife's cousin, Janet deMaury. Janet, Miss Theale."

"How do you do?" The dark eyes were fastened on my face with a curious intentness. "You're not at all like her—" Then the white cheeks were flooded with color. "Sorry."

"It's all right. No, I'm not."

She turned in some confusion to Gideon. "I was just on my way out to pick some mint in the garden. I'll see you after a while."

Gideon smiled. "How are the memoirs going?"

The distorted shoulder gave a slight shrug. "All right. Slowly."

Gideon turned towards me. "Mr. Theale is writing his memoirs—with emphasis on the years he spent as a chaplain in the army. Like my father, he was in the midst of the various points of invasion during World War II, and I think he was, for a while, a prisoner of war."

"That should be interesting," I said politely.

"It gives him something to do," Gwyneth said. And again I had the feeling of discomfort, as though something alien and angry had announced its presence. "I'll leave you, then," she said, and moved, with her uneven, staccato gait to the back of the hall.

"This way," Gideon said to me.

He led the way to a door opening off the front of the hall and opened it. "Mr. Theale?" Then he stepped aside and followed me into the room. I had a swift impression of a big room lined with books but sparsely furnished. Then my attention was taken up by the man who rose from behind the desk by the window.

He was as tall as Gideon, who is over six feet, and much handsomer. A magnificent proconsular face was framed in abundant gray and white waving hair. As he got up and came around the desk I saw that he was wearing a cassock.

"Gideon, how are you?"

"Very well, sir. May I present Janet deMaury, Rosemary's cousin?"

He came forward, his hand out. "Now, this is a pleasure. And how good of you to come and visit me."

It was impossible, I thought, shaking hands, that this warm, attractive man should be the father of that surly daughter. Then, remembering her deformity, I fought off a sense of guilt for my judgment of her, trying to make myself believe that whatever it was that made her so unappealing was unconnected with her physical problems. Nothing, my unobliging mind stated to me, was unconnected with physical problems.

By this time we had all moved forward towards the fireplace, in which, however, the few sticks of kindling and paper underneath were unlit.

"Now, coming from America I'm sure you must feel the cold," the rector said. "I'll just put a match to the fire."

"Oh, please don't," I said quickly, and marveled at my own vehemence. A damp chill penetrated the bare room and it was all I could do to keep from shivering. Yet more powerful than the damp was a sense not so much of poverty but austerity, of material goods held to a minimum, of comfort deliberately eschewed. To violate that would, in some way, be an admission of weakness.

"Are you sure?" The keen blue eyes bent on me. "I think you're feeling the chill. I'll just light it." And without further ado he put his hand up on the mantel, found a matchbox, struck a light and bent to the fire.

"There," he said, straightening. "That's better. Now, let me look at you."

I stood, waiting for the expected comment about my lack of resemblance to Rosemary. Instead, he smiled and said, "I expect you're tired of hearing how you're not like your cousin, aren't you?"

I laughed. "Frankly, yes."

"I don't know why people are so fond of remarking on resemblances, or lack of them. Something to do, I suppose, with the ancient sense of tribe and kinship. One gets used to it living in a small community." He glanced around. "Now, you must all sit down."

There were two stiff armchairs on either side of the fire, and the rector moved back behind his desk and brought out the straight chair he had been sitting on. "No, no. I insist. This really is my favorite chair," he said, firmly sitting on it and leaving one of the armchairs for Gideon, who had moved to sit on the uncomfortable one. I sat down opposite Gideon.

"Mr. Theale," Gideon said. "We came for your advice about something. Janet is going through all those papers that the Society shipped to me and they're in something of a mess. Since her time here is limited I thought she could do with some help. It occurred to me that you would probably be able to recommend someone from the village far better than I, since you work more closely with the young people."

"My dear Gideon, I certainly don't know more than you of young men hereabouts—less, probably." The old clergyman turned towards me. "Come harvest time, Gideon gets out with tractor and hay fork along with all the other farm workers." I glanced at Gideon in some surprise. Somehow this did not fit into my picture. "However," Mr. Theale went on, "it is true that I would probably know more about the girls, because those that are still here have done parish work at one time or another." He paused. "The trouble is, there aren't very many who are left. Glynis or Pamela might do very well, but they've just gone on holiday together to Cornwall. . . ." There was another silence, then I heard him give an odd sigh. "Of course there's Gwyneth. She did office work, in a rather high position, I believe, before she came home to look after me."

I saw, in my mind, the girl's dark eyes, intent with some hidden emotion. "I wouldn't want Miss Theale to bother herself with anything as . . . as boring as sorting through piles of papers. It's a filthy job and I really ought to have someone who wouldn't be put off by its tedium or . . . drudgery."

"Besides," Gideon said, "I'm sure Miss Theale has more than enough on her hands here." For once, I thought, Gideon and I were together, on the subject of Gwyneth Theale.

"Nonsense," the rector announced suddenly, rising to his feet. "It will make a break for the child. I'll call her."

"No, please—" I started.

But I was talking to his back, which was striding through the door.

"I really don't think she'd be right," I said to Gideon. "And I have a feeling she'd hate doing anything like that."

"Perhaps. But we can't refuse her if she wants to do it, and I can't stop the rector from asking her."

"She seems—hostile," I said.

"Well—" he started, and then, as footsteps approached the room, "we'll talk about it later."

The rector appeared in the doorway, dwarfing his daughter beside him. In her hand, I noticed, was a tightly clutched clump of mint.

"Here we are," the rector said. "I told Gwyneth that you had a proposal that might interest her."

I fought down a rising resentment that the matter had been taken so thoroughly out of Gideon's and my hands. Since her father had dragged the girl in, I could hardly refuse to offer her the scummy job I had in mind. "I can't see how it would interest her," I said firmly. "It's a dreary job, sorting through hundreds of papers to help classify them according to year. I'm sure Miss Theale would be bored doing anything so deadly."

Her eyes flickered, but she didn't say anything.

"Better than waiting hand and foot on me all the time. Wouldn't you like to get out during the day, my dear? Go up to the hill where you'd be with Miss deMaury?"

"Whatever you think, Father."

The submissive words were so at variance with whatever was going on behind her face that it seemed almost like a deliberate parody. But the rector swept over that, if indeed he saw it. "That's settled then. When would you like to have her? Tomorrow morning?"

"Father," Miss Theale said, an unreadable expression on her face, "you've hardly given Miss deMaury a chance to say anything. She might have some other kind of person altogether in mind."

"Of course, of course! How imperious of me. Now you shall tell me exactly what kind of person it is you want to have help you, and Gwyneth and I will do our best to find her."

By that time there was no choice. The offer to Gwyneth had to be made. "If Miss Theale wouldn't find the work too utterly tedious, I'd be delighted to have her help."

"Splendid," Mr. Theale said. "Now just tell us when."

"I can't do anything until the new cartons arrive. When will that be, Gideon?" I asked.

"I spoke to the place that sells them this morning. They can put them on a truck and send them tomorrow or the next day."

"Well, then, why don't I give you a ring when they arrive?" I said to Miss Theale.

Gideon and I took our leave shortly after that. The rector and his daughter saw us to the front door, where we were greeted ecstatically by Buff and with majestic dignity by Gelert.

"Bless my soul," Mr. Theale said. "I didn't know you had two companions with you. You could have brought them in if you wished." He bent down and patted Gelert's handsome head. Gelert put up with the attention with his usual regal air, but Buff lowered her head and backed towards my legs.

"She's shy," I said quickly.

"She is indeed," the rector said. "I wonder if she was mistreated."

"She's a stray whom Janet has adopted, so she may have been," Gideon said.

"She looks like she might have been one of Evan Williams' puppies," Miss Theale offered. "He certainly has a bitch exactly like her."

My stomach felt as though it had contracted. Foolishly, and without thinking, I said, "I'm sure you must be wrong."

Gwyneth Theale gave me again that odd, concentrated look. "Why do you say that?"

"Because she's determined to take the little mongrel back to the States with her when she goes," Gideon said drily. "If you really think she belongs to Williams, I'll go and negotiate some kind of sale with him."

"You'll have to have your wits about you," Mr. Theale put in.

"Why?" I was feeling more depressed with each word.

"Because," Gideon explained, "everybody knows he's a thief, a cheat, a liar, a poacher and a killer of almost anything that moves, but nobody can get enough hard evidence against him to haul him up before a judge." He looked at me for a minute. "But don't look so downcast. Buff was in poor condition when we got her—showing every sign of maltreatment—and I think the wretched trap in which she was caught probably originated with him."

"Would he put his own animal in a trap?" Mr. Theale asked.

"No. But he's capable of taking an unwanted puppy and abandoning it too far from home for it to be able either to get back or to feed itself."

"I'll buy it from him," I offered.

"Well, don't start mentioning a price," Gideon stated.

"He'll double it as an opener and claim the dog ran away. We'll start with the trap."

"And if that doesn't work," I went on, ignoring him, "I'll steal her."

There was a silence all around. I full expected the thunder of the Church to fall on my head. Instead, "If you need any help to accomplish that, Miss deMaury, just let me know," the rector said, "I'll be happy to assist."

I looked at him with far greater warmth than I had ended up feeling towards him. All of a sudden, his high-handedness became an endearing quality.

"I didn't hear that," Gideon said, with some amusement.

"Why not?" I asked.

"Because Williams is Gideon's tenant," Mr. Theale explained, "and man cannot steal from his own tenant, or countenance someone else doing it—officially, that is."

"Thank you, Mr. Theale. If I find I need help, I will certainly let you know."

"That's splendid." The big, shapely hand was held towards me. "Good-bye for now. Do come around any time, or get Gideon to bring you." A light look of worry tinged his face. "And you'll let Gwyneth here know when you need her, won't you?"

"I will." I found I was nowhere near as resentful of the rector's steamrolling as I had been.

Nevertheless, just before we reached the gate I heard the same dot-and-carry-one steps behind me. "Miss de-Maury!"

I turned. Miss Theale came up, her body jerking with her effort to walk quickly. "I just wanted to say, I know that Father pretty well forced your hand about asking me to work with you. It's not necessary at all. I'll completely understand if you think I can't do the work."

"There's no question of your not being able to do it." Quite suddenly and belatedly I understood the reasoning behind some of the rector's maneuvering. "It's just that it's stupid, boring work—the kind that I detest—and I felt that you'd probably hate it. It's not," I repeated a little overemphatically, "that you couldn't do it with your eyes closed—well, not that, but you know what I mean."

I would have felt much better if her face had relaxed, if she had given me any impression that she accepted what I said. But her face didn't change any of its watchfulness.

"All right," she said carefully. "Then I'll expect your ring."

"You know," I said to Gideon as we walked away, "I feel stupider than stupid. It never occurred to me that either the rector or his daughter would think I was dragging my feet about having her work because of her . . . er . . . infirmity. I wasn't even thinking about that, and now I feel like a heel. And I don't think she believed me at the end there."

" 'Dinna fash yourself,' as Mrs. Lowndes would say. Meaning, don't get upset. No one that I know, including Gwyneth's father, knows too much what she thinks. The only person who might have known was Rosemary, who used to have her up to The Hall quite often when she was younger."

"She's certainly not what I would describe as happy. She looks as though the remembrance of old sins—sins against her, old wrongs, I mean—were churning around in her. Is it because of her leg?"

"Probably. But I also think it's because she had to give up her job in town and come home to look after her father after he had a heart attack. She tried to get a leave of absence, I've been told, but couldn't do that, so the job had to go. On the other hand nobody suggested that her brother, who lives a sort of playboy life in London, should come home to help. I wouldn't be surprised if it weren't that that rankled."

"I couldn't blame her there. It seems in the worst tradition of male unfairness that nothing should be demanded of him."

"This is an old-fashioned part of the world. New ideas take their time penetrating."

"Even in this day of national television, when what's

thought in London or New York today appears on tubes in remotest living rooms the same evening?"

"Yes. I should have amplified what I mean. The young people hear and are influenced by the new ideas, but not their parents, who watch television but whose ideas haven't been shaped by it. That includes the rector, of course."

"Anyone who offers to help me steal Buff from your benevolent tenant has to be a good guy. I suppose, like anyone else, he has his blind spots."

"Yes. And to be fair to him, he knows he has. He feels guilty about Gwyneth's being there, though it would be very difficult for him to manage without her. Which is why he seemed overbearing in insisting that she come to The Hall to work with you on the papers."

"Well, the die is cast. The work is not only going to be boring, but all the bending up and down that will be involved in checking the papers, which will have to be on the floor because I can't think of anywhere else to put them, will not be easy for Gwyneth. How's her back?"

"Not too good. Perhaps I can put up some kind of trestle table, or move a table from another attic into the one with the boxes."

"That would be nice." I decided not to comment on the fact that he did not think of any such luxury for me.

"I was thinking about it, anyway," Gideon said, as though he had been reading my thoughts on a twenty-one-inch screen in his mind.

"Were you?"

"As you pointed out, it will be back-aching work. I have no wish to be faced—legally or in any other way—with evidence that I have contributed to serious back trouble to either of you."

"You put it so nicely."

Gideon didn't say anything, and we walked in silence the rest of the way home.

The next day I sat down and wrote to Tony, telling him exactly what had happened to the papers without mentioning any speculation as to who or what was responsible for their condition. *"And whether I can get through them in three weeks is more than I can say at the moment,"* I wrote. *"I'm hoping that a lot of the stuff can be discarded on sight. I thought at first that I might have it all shipped over. But then two difficulties with that spring to mind: one would be the cost of air-mailing such a load and anything else would be much too slow. The other was, where would I put them? Even if all the furniture were taken out of my apartment there wouldn't be room, and heaven knows there's no space in the office. There's no point in coming to grips with this problem until I see how fast the sorting of the papers goes. I've arranged to have a helper from the village, Gwyneth Theale, the local rector's daughter. And I'm thinking about asking Gideon for another. Anyway, I'll let you know in two or three days how the situation looks then."*

That evening at dinner I asked Gideon if he thought I ought to do anything about offering to buy Buff from Evan Williams.

"I told you," Gideon said. "Don't even mention money."

"You think then that I should just ignore the whole thing?"

"What's all this about?" Roger asked. He had stayed the night with friends and just arrived back that afternoon, looking, I thought, as though he might have been out on the tiles the evening before.

"Gwyneth Theale thinks Buff—Janet's adopted mongrel—might be one of the litter from Evan Williams' bitch."

"Yes, I rather thought that at the time," Roger said.

"Well, why didn't you say so?" Gideon asked. "At least we could have all been forewarned."

"Didn't think it was of any interest. It was pretty obvious that he'd just abandoned her, the way he does with animals he doesn't want—if he doesn't drown them. Why should he care what became of her—as long as she was just picked up around here? But I agree, if he gets wind of the fact that she's going to live a rich and luxurious life in America, his strong sense of property and bargaining will emerge with a bang."

"That doesn't make me feel better at all. Anyway, why should he hear?"

"Because everything, sooner or later, becomes known by everybody." He grinned. "People put their ears to the ground and by and by there are no secrets."

"That sounds almost sinister," I said.

"There's often a sinister undercurrent somewhere under the pastoral innocence of the country. Don't you think so, Gideon?"

"Meaning what?" Gideon asked.

"Oh—nothing in particular."

The following morning, with the boxes still not there, I was trying to decide whether to go for a walk or a drive, when I overheard Gideon mentioning to Mrs. Lowndes that Sheila Maitland, who had been there early, had left for the rest of the morning. "She's driving into Shrewsbury with her father, Mrs. Lowndes, so if you'll take up Benedict's morning milk and lunch, I'll be grateful. I'm not sure what time I can be up there, though I intend to spend some time with him."

Nice of you, I thought to myself, as Gideon walked out of the dining room, where we'd been having a somewhat silent breakfast. Well, I decided, I might go and visit Benedict myself. I toyed with the idea of following Gideon out into the hall and getting his permission. But since he had done nothing but discourage my visiting his son, I abandoned the idea. Why get defeated before I started? I argued to myself.

Armed with this admirable attitude, and taking along Buff, I knocked on Benedict's door.

"Come in," his voice called out.

"Hi," I said as I walked in. "I heard that Sheila Maitland wasn't coming today, so I thought I'd pay you a visit."

He was on his sofa, with the pad on his lap. His face, I

thought, looked paler than I remembered. "You don't like her, do you?" he said. His eyes had lost the blaze that had made them so striking before, but they were penetrating and remarkably shrewd for an eleven-year-old boy.

I was a little taken aback. "How do you know I don't?"

"I could tell the other day when you were here."

"I didn't know I showed my feelings that much." I stopped, realizing how much I'd given away. "What about you? Do you like her?"

He stared at me for a minute, then dropped his eyes to his pad. "I'd rather go to school."

My instinct was to say, perhaps you can, some day, but I recalled what Roger had stated: that he didn't think Benedict would be fit to go away until he had reached university level, if then. To encourage him in something that he could not do would not be kind. Bearing that in mind, I didn't know what to say next. But as I walked into the room, Buff following closely at my feet, I was overcome with a feeling similar to the one I had experienced in the schoolroom the night I had arrived—one of depression and dejection. What kind of life was this for a boy—immobilized, locked away from companions his own age by an indifferent father and a governess he had (I considered) outgrown both psychologically and socially? Granted the limitations of his illness, surely there must be some other solution, one that didn't isolate a boy that I felt quite sure was normally gregarious.

I stared for a moment out the window, where a pale sun reflected gold on the green slope opposite. Then, turning, I asked impulsively, "Would you like to go for a drive?"

"A drive?" He looked bewildered. "Where to?"

"Anywhere. Wherever you'd like to go."

"But I can't."

"Why not? Your father tells me that sometimes you can get around quite well with the aid of a crutch or a cane."

"But I haven't recently. That was months ago."

"Don't you want to try?"

"I've got to be careful. Sheila says so all the time. And her father, Dr. Maitland. If I do anything to my hip then they mightn't be able to put it right and I'd be a cripple for the rest of my life. And I can't bear the idea of that." Once more I heard the rising hysteria in his voice.

Every intuition in me pushed in the direction of urging him to try. Because I felt that, underneath his hysterical denial, lay a strong desire to do just that, an impulse towards freedom, towards the willingness to take a risk. It was, surely, I thought, a more natural impulse than the caution that had been hammered into him.

Yet something—was it common sense or cowardice?—made me hesitate. What did I know of diseased bones or of what might happen medically if Benedict fell in getting to the car, or was jolted by the car bouncing over a rut? And how would I feel if indeed he suffered some accident that prevented him from having the surgery that was supposed to correct his problem?

"You've got to see that," Benedict said in the same rather loud, frantic voice.

"Well, I—"

Was I glad or alarmed when the door opened and Gideon came in. "What on earth's going on?" he asked. "I could hear Benedict halfway down the stairs."

"Cousin Janet asked me if I wanted to go for a ride in her car. But I told her that Sheila and Dr. Maitland said it would be terribly dangerous. That I might hurt my leg for good. That's right, isn't it?"

On one level it sounded like an appeal for confirmation. Yet I wondered. Couldn't there be in his words an equally urgent desire to be released from the fear and unnatural caution that bound and governed his life?

"Cousin Janet said *what?*" Gideon's face seemed to go white. A muscle along his jaw twitched. Staring at him, I could almost feel his anger, held on a rigid leash. I could also see, because I was facing them both, that Benedict, who could, doubtless, read his father's face, was looking, not frightened, but a little titillated, as though deriving pleasure from witnessing the parental fury directed at someone other than himself.

"Do you mean to say," Gideon asked in a surprisingly level voice, "that without consulting me, you suggested to Benedict that he take a ride in your car, where he could not possibly keep his leg either up or straight?"

"I hadn't particularly thought about the position his leg might be in, I admit. But what on earth is so terrible about suggesting that he might alter his routine? Besides all of which he refused."

"I'm glad to hear that he has that much concern for his own welfare. Benedict, I'll come back to see you in a minute or two. In the meantime, could I speak to you outside, Janet?"

"I was right, Father, wasn't I?" Benedict's plea for commendation was so open, I wondered how on earth Gideon could miss it. Nevertheless, all he said was, "Obviously. Now get along with your assignment for this morning and I'll be back shortly."

I contemplated standing my ground in Benedict's room, refusing to go outside where Gideon could feel free to scold me with impunity. But, however much pleasure and amusement it might afford Benedict, I had to concede that to have a pitch battle—and it looked as though that was very much imminent—in front of him would do nothing to help what I felt deeply to be his confusion about his father, about his illness, or indeed, about anyone else.

"All right, Gideon," I said when we were outside and before he had time to open his mouth, "go ahead. Blow my head off! I can see you're longing to. And why get me outside? Why shouldn't Benedict hear? It might do him good to learn that someone can stand up to you."

"I resent your implication that Benedict can't speak his mind in front of me, just as I most emphatically deplore your dangling treats in front of him that he cannot possibly, in any safety, enjoy. My whole effort is to help him to be as content as possible with his lot, limited as it must be. If I didn't think it was so completely thoughtless, I would call it deliberately cruel. And, unfortunately, entirely characteristic of what I expect from you."

"What on earth are you talking about? What do you mean, it's characteristic of what you can expect from me? I've always been aware that you disliked me. Why, I've never quite known. I don't think I'm that dislikable. But it sounds as though you have some deep grudge of which I know absolutely nothing."

He was silent. I had the odd fancy that he had said more than he had meant to.

"Well?" I persisted. When he still didn't answer, I said, "I think you resent the fact—have always resented the fact—that it was Rosemary who got knocked down and killed and not me."

"That's ridiculous! Perhaps I said more than I should . . . or phrased it wrong. But I do consider it thoughtless in the extreme for you to invite Benedict on some outing that can do nothing except make him more discontented, at the least, and at worst injure what chances he has of recovering through surgery. . . ."

I gave up, and simply stood there until Gideon had run out of words. That I had certainly acted foolishly in suggesting to Benedict himself that he go for a drive without checking with either Sheila or Gideon, almost anyone would agree to, and was, indeed, typical of my tendency to act first and think afterwards. But in giving vent to his anger, Gideon was, I was, convinced, reacting to something more than that. Again I had the sense of something unknown, or at least unknown to me, moving beneath the surface of events as I knew them.

". . . there's nothing I can do now, but I would appreciate your not going into Benedict's room without my—or Miss Maitland's—permission. In fact, I must insist on it. If you do not give me your assurance that you will honor this request, then I will have to ask you to leave. As a matter of fact, Miss Maitland—but never mind that."

"Miss Maitland what?" I asked. I was now fairly angry myself, and the name of the red-haired governess acted like a spurt of gasoline on a promising fire.

"Miss Maitland said immediately after you arrived that I should declare Benedict's room—and his schoolroom—out of bounds."

"I wonder why."

"There's no mystery about that. Her close association with Benedict has made her extremely intuitive as to where his best interests lie and, conversely, where there'd be any threat to his health and safety. She obviously saw right away that your influence on him would not be salutary. I should have listened to her."

"What possible interest could I have in doing Benedict harm?"

"I don't pretend to understand your motives and am not, where Benedict is concerned, interested in figuring out what they might be. But on the most practical level I can only point out that on the two occasions when you have visited him you have upset him to the point where he's become hysterical."

"He seems to be hysterical, anyway. He doesn't need me to make him more so."

"I realize he's unstable. That's all the more reason why I want him subjected to as little . . . disruption . . . as possible."

"Well, I think he's protected and cosseted and hovered over until he seems to me to be in a strait jacket. You've now got him to the point where he's afraid to try anything."

"That's simply untrue. And I'd like to know what medical basis you have for that statement. Benedict is under the close care of a doctor—"

"Dr. Maitland. Miss Maitland's father—" I interrupted.

"Yes. Dr. Maitland, who *is* Sheila's father and whom you have never even met. You seem to be implying some accusation and I would like to know what you base it on."

I hesitated, because he had me there and I knew it. I had nothing to go on but intuitions of my own—plus, I had to admit, my own dislike of Sheila Maitland. "I'm not implying, or rather I'm not meaning to imply, anything against Dr. Maitland. What you call my—er—disruption of Benedict occurred because, on the first occasion,

I suggested that he, Benedict, did not appear to resemble his mother in temperament, and on the second, because I asked him if he would like to go out in my car. I wouldn't call either the deliberately provocative behavior that you seem to think it is. The fact that he reacted the way he did on both occasions springs from something within Benedict himself—not from some outrageous act on my part."

"I didn't suggest that you acted outrageously. That's the whole point. Benedict is volatile and—to be blunt about it—emotionally unbalanced. Do you think I enjoy telling you this about my son? It's my prayer that he will overcome this, and the medical care he gets through Dr. Maitland's frequent visits plus Sheila's supervision are all to that end. I'm not trying to keep you away from a normal boy with normal pursuits. I'm trying to protect one who isn't normal. Now do you understand?"

What I might have answered to that I don't know. Mrs. Lowndes appeared up the stairs at that moment, carrying her tray with the glass of milk and the bun on it.

"I'll take that in," Gideon said abruptly, and took it from her.

As Mrs. Lowndes went back down the stairs, there sounded, on the other side of the door, a short bark.

"That's Buff," I said. "I forgot about her. I took her in thinking that Benedict might find her amusing. Since you're here and can obviously prevent my doing Benedict any further damage, do you mind if I go in and collect her?"

I pushed open the door. Buff, front paws down, back-side braced up in the air, was watching a ball that Benedict, who was laughing and leaning down towards the floor, was about to throw. Except for the boy being on the sofa, it was the most natural, playful act involving Benedict that I had witnessed, and I felt a pang of regret for having to put an end to it. But I did not know when Sheila Maitland would return, and I did know that she didn't care for Buff. If she made some claim of Buff's misbehavior towards Benedict, I knew I could be quite sure that, as far as Gideon was concerned, that would be the end of Buff.

"Come here, Buff," I said.

"Can't she stay?" Benedict said. "We were having a game."

For a second I paused. But I had had more than enough evidence of Sheila Maitland's power and influence with Gideon. "I'm sorry, Benedict," I said as gently as I could, "but I'm going to take Buff for a walk now, and, anyway, I don't think Miss Maitland would want you to be left alone with Buff."

"Why not? There's nothing wrong with Buff. Please say she can stay here."

I glanced at Gideon, but then, as he hesitated, I made up my mind. I might have a variety of doubts about the governess, but one thing I was quite sure, especially when I remembered her claim that Buff was inclined to bite: she would not be pleased to find her with Benedict when she returned, and I had absolutely no doubt that she would make some complaint about her. What with Evan Williams' possible claims looming ahead, my ownership of the little mongrel was precarious enough.

Marching into the room I went across to where Buff was still flirting with the ball Benedict was holding. "Sorry, Buffie. But I'll get you another ball."

Leaning down I picked her up—she couldn't, I thought, weigh more than eight or nine pounds.

"That's not fair. Tell her she has to leave the dog, Father."

I could hear Benedict's voice rising up in its spiral of hysteria, and I was sorry for it. At that moment Gideon could be no more eager for me to get out than I was to leave. As I turned, something, glimpsed through the open door to Benedict's bathroom, caught my eye, something metallic that glinted. But I didn't have time to think about it or to register what it was.

Bearing Buff under one arm, I went out as quickly as I could, leaving behind me the contrapuntal sound of Benedict's shrill protests and his father's deep voice, telling his son, in no uncertain terms, to calm down.

It was not until I was walking over a neighboring hill, with Buff scampering over the grass and turf ahead of me, that the memory of that metallic glimpse came back. Watching Buff scrabbling frantically at a rabbit hole, I paused, nagged by the recollection of that one visual flash. What was it? I wondered. And why should it worry me? All of a sudden, just as I was about to give up, I saw it again and recognized what it was, lying on top of the shelf above the sink: a hypodermic syringe.

# six

THE BOXES ARRIVED the following afternoon and Gideon and Parry spent an hour or so putting them together and placing them where they could be used.

"There are not as many as I ordered," he said. "But you can put several years' worth of papers into each carton. They're pretty big. I also called Gwyneth Theale to tell her you would be wanting her tomorrow morning."

"Thank you," I said, not at all sure I was pleased by his high-handed management.

The next morning Gwyneth appeared at the top of the attic steps as I was busy arranging the old and new cartons in some kind of logical order for working. As good as his word, Gideon had put a rather battered but sturdy-looking table in the big attic room, where it could easily be used for sorting.

I explained how we would work; one box at a time, the papers would be taken out and placed on the table according to date.

"Keep the correspondence, memoranda and notes, and two copies each of all printed and mimeographed material. The rest can be thrown out in that big box there. We're not trying to keep a complete record—just collect the stuff that would be useful in a biography of my father."

Gwyneth nodded. "I see what you mean. Well, it may not be fascinating, but it should move quickly."

And it did. For some reason I had assumed that Gwyneth would be a slow worker, whether because of her infirmity or not, I wasn't sure. But she must, I decided, after about an hour, have been a blessing to whatever office employed her before she came back to the village. She was not only quick, she was extremely thorough, and produced efficient ideas of her own that hadn't occurred to me.

Sometime later I found myself thinking that the watchfulness Gwyneth had shown on the day I'd met her was nowhere near as apparent since she arrived to work, and seemed to disappear altogether as the morning wore on. Once or twice, it was true, I found her eyes on me, but they reflected a look that was almost puzzled, rather than speculating. However, I have always had a rather single-track mind, and the need to make some sense out of the deluge of papers—not only chronological sense, but sense in the meaning of relevance to my search— eventually blotted out everything else.

So absorbed were we that lunchtime had arrived before we paused. "Please," a breathless voice said from the doorway, "Mrs. Lowndes says lunch is ready and would you please come down."

I looked up to see a very young, and very pretty housemaid standing at the edge of the chaos. Tradition was served by the big, more or less white apron that seemed to envelope her. But underneath that she seemed to be wearing a blouse and skirt, rather than the cotton frock that had once served as the uniform for domestic staff.

"All right," I said. "Please tell Mrs. Lowndes we'll wash our hands and be right down." I looked at my grimy hands. "I feel as though a shower would hardly be enough." I straightened as the maid disappeared down the attic stairs again. "Come down to my room and use the bathroom there."

Neither Gideon nor Roger was present for lunch. When Gwyneth and I walked into the dining room, I was amused to see that Sheila Maitland had taken the chair at the end of the table.

"Do sit down," she said, with overwhelming graciousness. "Gwyneth, you're the guest today, why don't you sit beside me here," and she indicated the chair on her right.

Four places, not three had been laid: one at the head, two on the right of that and one opposite. I was contemplating this when Mrs. Lowndes, bearing a tray, came into the dining room. For a second she paused, her eyes on the end of the table. "I thought Sir Gideon was to be here for lunch," she said.

"Oh, didn't he tell you?" Sheila Maitland replied. "He's gone over to have lunch with Sir John Renfrew."

"I see," the housekeeper put her tray down on the side table.

I glanced quickly at Mrs. Lowndes. Her face was not one to give much away. Yet I thought she looked displeased. Or perhaps I just hoped that she did. Her mouth, as she placed a casserole dish on the mat in front of Sheila, was certainly closed in a thin line, but it could have been because the dish was hot.

"Have a care," she said, removing her hands rather rapidly. "It's overhot."

Whether Sheila meant for me to feel an outsider or not I couldn't have said. Very plainly leading the conversation, she seemed to keep it on local affairs, pausing every now and then to explain them to me in a kindly fashion. All of which made me feel more, not less, isolated.

This, however, suited me very well. I let my mind drift back over the morning's work. I had, some years before, learned the trick of running my eyes down a page and gaining a fairly accurate idea of its contents—at least in so far as they concerned some special interest. And my special interest on this occasion was anything that would aid in the writing of my father's biography. From that point of view the bulk of what we'd sifted through during the morning was useless. There were, by dozens, letters of commendation of my father's work—many of these from people of note in public life. A few could be used. But most were the kind of wordy, predictable statement that politicians of all stripes made when they wished to be on record as approving such indisputably worthy causes as motherhood, peace, aid to world hunger and the brotherhood of man. Almost any society dedicated to some social good could drum up drawers full of the same epistolary pat on the back. About my father, of course, they revealed nothing. Others, of course, did, and these I managed to check with a red pencil—another reason why Gwyneth was moving ahead so much more quickly than I.

It was curious, I thought, helping myself to some fruit salad, the kind of man that was coming through some of the more personal correspondence: a leader, yes. Considering the movement my father single-handedly started, and its considerable (if temporary) effect, at various points in history, on the sentiment and opinion of the day, he would have to be that. I had not been as prepared to find him a businessman and something of a shrewd politician. Especially, I thought, half listening to Sheila and Gwyneth discussing an outbreak of measles in the village, in consideration of my father's oft-stated views on the subject of businessmen and politicians.

". . . luckily," Sheila was saying, "Benedict has no reason to go into the village so there's no real danger of his catching the disease. Have you had them, Gwyneth?"

"Yes, when I was a child."

"And Miss deMaury?" Sheila turned towards me.

"Oh, please—Janet," I said. "Yes, I had them as a child, too."

"But since I live in the village, can I bring them to you?" Gwyneth asked anxiously.

"I doubt it," Sheila said. "Don't worry about it. We've all finished, haven't we? Then I expect I'd better let Mrs. Lowndes know she can clear up."

The days passed rapidly. Gideon disappeared on some business trip to do with the estate, Roger had gone to

London, and Benedict must have gone into a cooperative, quiescent phase because I heard nothing from or about him.

Any doubts I'd had about Gwyneth, either personal or professional, vanished, and I became increasingly grateful for her order and speed.

"You know," I said a week later, "when I think how discouraging I was about your working with me, it gives me cold chills. You've been marvelous."

The first real smile I saw on her face appeared. "Don't be too grateful. It's been wonderful for me, too. The only bad part is that it makes me realize how much I miss working at a job."

"I'm sorry about your having to look after your father," I said after a short pause. "I wish, for your sake, that some other arrangement could be worked out."

"So do I. So does Father. But there really isn't any other way. He doesn't need a professional nurse—just somebody to keep an eye on him and make sure he eats properly. He's perfectly capable of missing meals, then getting giddy and fainting, all of which puts a strain on his heart. He keeps saying he's all right and why don't I go back to London and try and get my old job back. And it's only because he's trying so hard not to be selfish. But I wish he wouldn't. It just makes it harder."

"I suppose a housekeeper wouldn't do," I said tentatively, wondering if I were being tactless. I didn't know what their financial situation might be.

"No. And it's not just the money problem. Between what I was making in London and a small private income that Father has, we could just about manage an elderly woman to live in and do the cooking, etcetera. It's that Father would ride right over her. He wouldn't mean to. He'd promise to obey at all times, and the first time she put dinner in front of him and someone telephoned for a sick call at home or he was in the process of brooding over his sermon, he'd simply act as though she and the dinner weren't there—you saw how he was."

I had indeed. "A benevolent despot," I said, picking up a handful of papers and wondering why even the words gave me a sinking feeling. Then, of course, I knew. "Our fathers had much in common. I'm not really reading these letters, but even glancing at them—the few that aren't just pablum—makes me realize that he managed the lives of everybody who came within reach—for their own good, of course."

"Speaking of that," Gwyneth said slowly.

But at that point Gideon suddenly appeared in the attic door.

"I thought you were away," I said.

"I just got back. Gwyneth, your father's on the phone for you."

"Oh, thank you, Sir Gideon. I expect he wants me to do something on the way home. I'll be back in a minute."

Putting down the papers she was holding, she disappeared through the door.

"Everything all right?" Gideon asked me abruptly. "I mean, is there any other thing—a table, a chair, more boxes—that I can get for you?"

Surprising myself, I gave him one of my best smiles. "I think with the boxes and the table we've got really everything we need. But thank you for asking."

I watched the black brows draw together. For a minute he looked at me in silence.

"Why are you so suspicious?" I said, looking, I knew, as though butter wouldn't melt in my mouth.

A glint appeared in the gray eyes. "My natural cynicism, I suppose. I don't associate you with such—er—sweet compliance."

"And I," I said, "don't associate you with such tender, loving concern."

"But then you don't know me very well, do you?"

The answer was unexpected, and my eyes flew to his. It was a strange moment, almost suspended, as though it bore no relationship to any other that had passed since I had been in the house. Then without thinking or looking I put the papers I was holding onto the table. Unfortunately, since I wasn't watching, I put them half over the edge and they scattered all over the floor.

"Damn!" I said, suddenly aware that for some unconnected reason my heart was beating rapidly. I started to bend down. I remember clearly—I will always, I think, remember—what happened then, though I had no idea why.

Hands grasped my arms, pulling me up. I lifted my face. And Gideon's mouth was on mine, gently at first, then hard with intensity.

I don't know how long we remained like that. Then, vivid as though she were present, Sheila's image sprang into my mind. I pulled away.

"Janet," he said.

There was an expression on his face that I hadn't seen before, but I didn't stop to identify it, because I was very angry. "You really are a bit of a turk, aren't you?" I said, pushing back. "Favors around for everyone. I always suspected that Rosemary had a lot to put up with. It seems I was right."

He stared down at me for a moment, his eyes expressionless, then, without a word, turned and started out the door. Behind him I saw Gwyneth approaching. Perforce, he stood aside to let her come in. As she passed him he said abruptly, "I take it everything is all right, Gwyneth?"

"Yes, fine. Just as I thought, Daddy wanted me to stop and see one of his parishioners on the way home."

"Let Mrs. Lowndes know if there's anything up here you need," he said, and left.

Buff, who had been with us all day, got up and started to follow him.

"Buff, come back here," I called.

Buff's ears went down, her tail waved, and she came prancing back.

"I think she has a crush on Gideon," I said.

"He's very crushable," Gwyneth astonished me by saying shyly.

"Et tu, Brute?" I asked.

She smiled. "I used to, a little. But I think that was partly because . . ."

I waited for her to go on. When she didn't I stared at

her and said, "For heaven's sake, don't stop there. Because what?"

"Well, I sometimes thought he seemed—it sounds incredible, somehow to say so—lonely." She said in a rush. "I hope you don't think . . . it sounds as though I were criticizing her—Lady Lightwood, your cousin Rosemary."

I was aware, suddenly, of a curious sensation; as though a door—a door I had been aware of but hadn't really paid any attention to—were about to open.

"What do you mean?" I asked slowly.

"I used to come up here a lot, before I went off to London," Gwyneth said. "Rosemary gave me odd jobs—sort of secretarial work. And since I could hardly wait to leave school and start working properly, I was terribly grateful, because I thought it would be good experience." The white skin stained red. "If you're lame," she said, and it was obvious that she was forcing herself to say this, "then you have to bend over backwards to make yourself not think that people are judging you because of that. But, no matter how much I tried, or how many rousing talks on the subject Father used to give me, I couldn't help but feel that if I had some experience before I even went to apply properly for a job in London, then I'd be at least equal to other people applying, instead of behind. I know I shouldn't think I'd be behind," she finished almost belligerently, "but I can't help it. And then the other thing that would happen—or at least I thought it might—was that people would hire me because they felt sorry for me. And that would be *worse*." She glanced at me. "I don't suppose you understand that—I mean, how could you?"

"Well, it's true I haven't had that particular problem. But I do understand a little. Not wanting to be given special consideration or even special notice was one reason why I left home to go to a college in the Midwest where most people had barely heard of my father, if at all, instead of to one of the eastern ones where he was considered practically a saint."

Gwyneth stared at me for a moment, opened her mouth and then closed it.

"What were you going to say?" I asked.

"Only—nothing really. But . . . well, I was just surprised. Rosemary, I think, did think of your father as kind of a saint."

"Yes. I know. In lots of ways she was much more his child than I was. What did you mean when you were talking about Rosemary before—that you didn't want to sound as though you were criticizing her, but that you had the impression that Gideon was lonely?"

Gwyneth, who had been, more slowly, sorting while we talked, distributed a few sheets onto their piles before she answered. Then, "It's hard to describe, really. As I was saying, partly to get some experience, partly to earn some extra pounds, I came up to The Hall to act as Rosemary's secretary, mostly when she was doing fund raising for the Society or involved in county work. I don't think she really needed me. I think she was just being kind. But I typed letters and made phone calls and arranged appointments. And a lot of the time when I was here I began to have the feeling . . . it's difficult to describe . . . but it was as though she and Sir Gideon, living in the same house, occupied different worlds. It wasn't that they didn't talk to each other, and it somehow wasn't the same atmosphere as when people who are in the middle of a fight have to stop and start being polite because a third person is present." She glanced at me uncertainly. "I'm sure you know what I mean." I nodded. She went on. "It was like they were that way all the time—civil, remote, and just sort of passing each other."

I was so intensely preoccupied with my inner vision of a door being opened that I didn't reply, just went on marking and sorting papers in silence. Why was I not more surprised? I wondered. Why did everything Gwyneth had to say fit in so completely with a picture of Gideon's and Rosemary's marriage that I must have formed long ago without realizing it? Except for the day of their wedding, I had never seen the two of them together. On what evidence did I form this picture? The evidence, I finally decided, was of the negative kind. I had seen Rosemary only twice in the seven years of her marriage, but we had exchanged numerous letters, and my impression came from the things she did not say. More than that, she talked and wrote as though the marriage did not exist—almost as though she lived in England because she happened to have a job that kept her there, rather than because she was married to a Briton. Neither Gideon nor Benedict were mentioned, unless I asked specifically after them.

Was I just noticing this for the first time? I wondered. Consciously, yes, I decided. But, unconsciously, I must have been aware of it for some time, only letting my recognition seep from the unconscious to the conscious when prodded by Gwyneth's words.

"You don't mind my saying this?" Gwyneth was asking anxiously.

"No. Of course not. I was just being surprised that I wasn't surprised."

"You mean you found the same?" She sounded relieved.

"No. I can't say that exactly. It wasn't the same because you saw them together, in their home, all the time. Except for the day they married, I never saw them together. But you know the way most married women talk about their husbands and families—I don't mean exactly talk *about* them, but their husbands and children are just part of the furniture of their conversation. I mean, they naturally crop up all the time. Well, with Rosemary, Gideon and Benedict never did. She never referred to them unless there was some terribly specific reason to—like my asking about them. And the moment you said that about Gideon I remembered that—at least it sort of came together in my mind."

We worked in silence for a while. Then, without thinking about my words before they were out, I said, "I suppose, therefore, and especially since Rosemary's been dead for five years, that it's natural Gideon should . . . well . . . find Sheila attractive." I paused, then burst out. "Good heavens—that sounds prissy. For all I know Gideon may have a score of girlfriends after and, from what we've been talking about, during his marriage. After all, isn't this supposed to be the day of the open marriage?"

"I can't see Sir Gideon having one of those—one affair after another," Gwyneth said.

I glanced at her. "Have I shocked you?"

"No. There's nothing new about married men having a bit of fun. It happens all the time—in a village as well as in London. But I don't think he's that kind of person. If he were, it might have been easier for him. My father once said . . ." Her voice trailed away.

Straightening, I put some papers on the table. "What did Mr. Theale say?"

"He once said that Sir Gideon was . . . was a throwback. That for all his English name he belonged to some Celtic past when people loved intensely—even killing for it."

All of a sudden it was as though the afternoon shadows not only lengthened, but filled the room. For no reason I saw again the headlights of the car careening towards Rosemary and then Rosemary's body lying where it had been thrown. Involuntarily, I shivered. "That's spooky."

The dark girl looked at me, her eyes unreadable. "Yes. That's what I think, too."

I wanted to say, what do you mean? Because I wasn't even sure what I meant. But the question itself made no sense.

It was the following day just as lunch was over and Gwyneth and I were leaving that Sheila asked casually, "How're the measles? Any new cases?"

Gwyneth looked back. "Tommie Morgan and Mary Leach—they got it from their older brothers and sisters who brought it home from school. They're thinking of closing the school for the next fortnight to see if they can keep anyone else from getting them."

"Probably best," Sheila said. "Don't work too hard." And she pushed through the swinging door into the pantry.

I glanced at Benedict's door as we passed on our way up. Whoever first called me rebellious was right. The fact that I had, in effect, been forbidden his room was enough for it to exert a powerful attraction for me.

"Do you know Benedict at all well?" I asked Gwyneth as we reached the top of the attic stairs.

She turned towards me. "Well, I did some years ago, when I used to come up here to The Hall. That was when he was younger, of course, before he had his accident."

"What was he like then?"

She stared at me. "Like? I don't—how do you mean?"

I thought about her question. "Have you seen much of him since then—since his accident, since Rosemary died?"

"No. I haven't seen him at all."

"Well, I've seen him twice. And he seems to me to be moody and volatile to the point almost of being hysterical." I described the occasions when he had flown off the handle: the first when I suggested he was not like his mother; the second when I offered to take him out in the car. "And then there was the little matter of the drawing," I finished, and told her about his macabre sketch and wild laughter when he showed it to me.

"He's always been terribly good at drawing and painting."

We moved towards the attic workroom as I asked, "But has he always been as—unstable?"

Gwyneth stooped down and collected an armful of papers and walked with her awkward gait to the sorting table.

"I remember that Nanny Hastings—she's retired now and lives in the village, but she looked after a lot of children around this part of the country—she took care of Benedict when he was younger and she used to say he was 'nervy.'"

"Meaning nervous—highstrung?"

"Yes. Once when Father and I called on her in her cottage she was fussing about him—" Gwyneth paused. I had the impression that again she'd come up against something she wasn't sure she wanted to say.

"What was she fussing about?"

"Well—" Gwyneth sorted rapidly through some papers. "You have to understand that Nanny Hastings's quite old—and very old-fashioned. I mean, she was looking after children as some kind of assistant nanny in World War One when women . . . when things were different."

I glanced at Gwyneth's face. "It sounds like she might have been critical of Rosemary."

"She kept wondering what kind of work would keep her away from her husband and child so much."

"But English women of the upper classes frequently left the care of children to nannies. Whole generations of Victorians were brought up by nannies. Their mothers may not have worked—but they certainly led lives that were too socially active for them to take over the care and feeding of their own offspring. So why would Nanny Hastings find Rosemary's behavior strange—especially if she were so old-fashioned herself?"

"I suppose because Rosemary was . . . different. She was involved in county affairs, of course. But she spent a lot of time in London working for the Society and lecturing on it around the country. And then she went abroad. And it was no secret that none of this was connected with her marriage. I mean, Sir Gideon was home a lot of the time when she was away. And when *he* was away at the War Office—those were the times she was at home."

I collected some papers from the bottom of a carton. "You won't believe this, but we've actually finished another of these boxes. What was Gideon doing at the War Office? I knew he was in the army. But I thought he got out of that a long time ago."

"I'm not sure," she said vaguely. "My father, who thinks the world of Gideon, said it was something very hush-hush, which I suppose means Intelligence."

"Hmm." I had carried my papers to the other side of the table and was running my eye down pages that seemed in some way different from the bulk of the material. As soon as I had satisfied myself that there was nothing there of any interest to me I started quickly putting them in the chronological divisions that we had established. "I somehow don't see Gideon as superspy," I said. "But I suppose Intelligence is nothing like spy stories, filled with blondes and gold and private eyes and drugs. . . ."

The word kicked off something in my mind that had been hovering there, waiting to come to the surface. "You know, when I was in Benedict's room, I saw a hypodermic syringe in his bathroom. Does Sheila give him shots or something? Is she a nurse?"

"She had training of some kind. In teaching as well as nursing. I don't know whether she finished. It was a little like me, you know. She was working or training in London, then had to come here to look after her father, Dr. Maitland."

"Maybe he taught her. When was this? When did she come here?" It was an idle question and I barely listened to the answer.

"I'm not sure. About two and a half years ago, I believe."

"I suppose she could be giving him injections of vitamins."

It was the following day at lunch when I suddenly asked Sheila, "Are you giving Benedict vitamin injections?"

"Injections?" Gideon interpolated before she could answer. He frowned. "What on earth are you talking about?"

"Insulin, isn't it?" Roger put in. He had just returned from London that morning. "Benedict's a diabetic, isn't he?"

"Yes, but—when was this development?" Gideon demanded. He looked annoyed, his brows forming a straight bar above his autocratic nose.

"I was meaning to tell you, Gideon," Sheila said, her face showing concern. "Daddy took tests on his last visit and said his—Benedict's—diabetic condition had suddenly grown more serious, needing actual injections of insulin."

"It would have been a good idea to tell me, I think," Gideon said. His voice was level, almost impersonal.

But I could sense, under that control, his anger. "When did this start?"

"Only a week or so ago. Daddy wanted to make sure before we worried you. I'm sorry, darling."

It sounded like a slip, a term of intimacy she was accustomed to using—but not when she and Gideon were with others. I glanced quickly at him. If he had looked irritated, I would not have been surprised. But he didn't react at all, which certainly, in my eyes, confirmed her right to the term and bolstered my opinion as to the freedom with which he bestowed his favors and how much those favors were worth. Finishing my lunch with a diminished appetite, I wondered why I felt depressed.

# seven

IT TOOK ANOTHER two days to clear the original cartons, filling the boxes that had been arranged according to date.

"And now," I muttered disgustedly, "the job is only beginning."

"You know," Gwyneth said slowly, "I can't be sure, because I've gone through the papers so quickly but . . ."

"But what?"

"Well, it seems to me that there are holes in the correspondence."

"Holes? What do you mean?"

"My father once said I had a mind like a piece of blue serge picking up lint. It's not brains—it's just a knack, like a photographic memory. But without particularly thinking about it, I've sort of kept a mental tally of the papers per year, and it seems to me that one or two of the years has noticeably fewer papers than the others. It probably means nothing—everybody was traveling or something."

I frowned. "Even if that were true—and you're probably right—I'm not sure what it would mean, if it meant anything. As you say. Everybody could have been traveling, or perhaps that year there were no rallies. Rallies were big events, or at least they were what produced this Niagara of paper."

"Well, it doesn't really matter." She gave her shy, rare smile. "I'm always coming up with facts that have no relation to anything and couldn't possibly be of interest."

I smiled back at her. "I have a very strong feeling that there are certain kinds of work in which that particular slant of mind is invaluable."

"By the way," Gwyneth said, "I found this while you were working with that other pile. It was clipped to a promotion sheet and fell off. It seems to be the carbon of a letter. I gather this is the kind of thing you're really interested in."

"That's right—personal letters, stuff like that. What did you find?"

"It's a letter from your father. The trouble is, it's page two and I haven't been able yet to find page one. On page two he seems to be discussing one of your American congressmen." Gwyneth picked up a sheet of paper and glanced at it. "He's expressing approval about something a Representative Bridewell did. It's a bit vague. He says somewhere something about an old saying. Yes, here it is. 'One good turn deserves another,' and so on."

I held out my hand. "I'll take it. You were absolutely right. It's the kind of thing I do want." I looked at the thin sheet. "I wonder where on earth the first page is. I think," I went on, "I'm going to find a smaller box, the kind that holds standard-sized paper, and use it for the really personal stuff. The trouble is . . ."

I stood with the sheet of paper in my hand, staring around me at the wall-to-wall boxes, only a few of which we'd gone through.

"The problem is," I repeated slowly, "what do I do now? To put these boxes into closer chronological order's going to take a lot more than the week left of my three-week leave of absence. On the other hand, it's a lot less expensive and generally less cumbersome to sort it here, than to ship it over to New York."

"Why don't you write and see if your boss would extend your leave?"

"Yes," I said doubtfully. "I suppose that's the thing to do. I should have thought of this sooner. It's going to take more than a week to get his answer even if he replies by return mail. Of course, knowing Tony Bridewell, he'd just pick up the phone and call."

I stared at Gwyneth. "Which, of course, is exactly what I should do. Do you think it would send the local operator into shock if I put a call in to New York?"

"Certainly not," Gwyneth said indignantly. "It may not be common practice, but I bet Sir Gideon's done it lots of times."

I grinned at her. "Did I offend your local pride?"

She smiled in reply. "A bit, perhaps."

"Sorry." I glanced at my watch. "Well, it would be about nine in the morning in New York. I'd better wait for another hour."

"You mean to say," Gwyneth said slyly, "that after all we've heard about how hard people abroad—especially Americans—work, you're not at your desks by nine in the morning?"

"It's safer," I said cautiously, not cracking a smile, "to call people in publishing at ten."

"By the way," Gwyneth asked, "that wouldn't be the same Bridewell as is in your father's letter, would it?"

"It would. The families have known each other forever. I wonder what the favor was my father did for him. I can't remember him ever mentioning anything like that." Standing there, I read the paragraph she referred to:

"The news from your New York and Washington press—at least as we get it over here—seems good. Tony Bridewell managed to do his stuff without incurring too much wrath which, considering everything, including the mood of the country, and the muscle of certain pressure groups, showed considerable deftness. Tell him the main thing to keep in mind—aside from one good turn deserving another—is that our Society has to be concerned with the overall good of the greatest number. A unified world is a peaceful world, and harsh as that may sound, that is more important than the fate of one isolated group here or there, however one may sympathize with their recent history. I feel sure he'll agree with us."

Being a carbon, of course, it was not signed. But in the space above his typed name, my father had squiggled his highly idiosyncratic RdeM, the sloping R leaning forward, dominating the other letters.

Strange, I thought, not all the memos and letters that I had hastily glanced through for the past two weeks had brought my father back to me. He had been dead seven years. Before his death I had escaped from his influence by deliberately choosing to attend a state university that, in his lofty eastern view, he considered inconsequential, and in the years since he had died I had, without making too much of a conscious effort of it, thought about him less and less.

But in this letter, with its characteristic assumption about the inevitable rightness of his world view, I saw again the quality in him that always—even when I was a child—raised my hackles, and when I was older became the final barrier. For a second there flashed across my memory that appalling scene I had walked into as a child: my father's middled-aged assistant, a quiet, dogged man who had always been kind to me, as godlike in his invulnerability as I assumed all adults to be, standing, his face convulsed, tears streaming down his cheeks, staring at the check in his hand that my mother had given him. Years later, after my mother had died, I told my father about my small role in this episode and how devastated I had been to see a grown man cry.

"Yes, yes," my father said. "Your mother reproached me quite strongly about it. She seemed to think that I should have noticed or done something. Well, I did know about it. Someone told me, but, besides the New York speech, we were planning our first big rally in one of the Iron Curtain countries. You were only a child, so you can't imagine the kind of opposition we encountered in the cold war atmosphere of the time. I kept running down to Washington to bolster what little support we had. And he chose that moment to get into a fuss about his mort-gage and medical bills. I suppose I was abrupt with him . . . But when so much larger issues were at stake . . ."

But, like my mother, I had a mind for the concrete rather than the abstract, and it was that difference that divided my father and me to the point that when we met we confined our talk to family matters, because my mind had a fatal tendency to wander when he embarked on a discussion of whatever the Society was doing at the moment. In later years I realized this was not so much boredom, as I thought at the time, as a form of defense. Because, underneath much of what my father said to me, was his anger that I, his only child, did not share his enthusiasm; that, unlike my cousin, Rosemary, I did not spend my college vacations doing volunteer work in one of his offices, stuffing envelopes, licking stamps, carrying the occasional picket. This was an anger expressed, as I recalled, only once, when during a lunch the two of us were having, after my attention had once again strayed, I was brought back by his voice, icy with outrage. ". . . But I see I am boring you by all this dreary talk of how human beings can learn to live without murdering one another. Let's discuss something that really interests you—now what would that be? The football games so prominent at that university you've chosen to attend? The dances—proms, I believe you call them?"

As it happened, neither football games nor college dances had been of much interest to me. My current enthusiasm had been for a column I had talked the local paper into letting me try (for nothing) on animals. And I spent most of my spare hours at school picking the brains of various town vets. But I stared across the lunch table at my father, startled into silence by a bitterness that I had never seen before.

"Well, you've never cared much about what I did," I blurted out. "You've always been too busy saving the world."

"And you couldn't have less interest for that kind of thing, could you?" he said, rising, a tall, handsome, elegant figure in the magnificent club dining room where he had taken me for lunch. "I think we might draw this unfortunate lunch to a close. Let me know if you need any money," he finished, laying down his napkin.

And that was the last time we had tried—just the two of us alone—to have a conversation.

Now, standing in the attic with this letter, the old feelings—the bitterness, the anger, the defensiveness of both sides—came flooding back.

"I shouldn't be writing this book," I said. "I'm the wrong person. Much the wrong person."

Gwyneth was staring at me. "Why, what do you mean? Why should you be the wrong person?"

I looked at her. "It's too long to explain now, Gwyneth. But, unlike Rosemary, I was never heart and soul for my father's causes. That's putting it mildly. In fact, I was hostile to them. I don't mean they weren't good causes— I'm sure they were. But they always seemed to me to be bought at the expense of something else. It's hard to be clear . . ."

She sighed. "I think I might know. I have the same a bit, with my father. He's deeply religious, and somehow— I can't seem to help it—I've shut all that out."

I turned. "I'd better go down and brace Gideon for my expensive telephone call."

But Gideon seemed undismayed by my request to telephone New York on his phone.

"Of course," he said almost absent-mindedly, when I ran him to earth in his bookroom. "You can use the telephone in here. I have to go out anyway."

I tried not to think about what happened in the attic between the two of us and—following immediately on that in my mind—Sheila's astutely placed "darling." Needless to say, I didn't succeed, which made my voice stiff as I said, "Thanks for letting me call New York."

He gave me a hard stare. Then, "Hope you get through to them," he said.

The door closed as I dialed for the local operator.

Reaching the New York office proved astonishingly easy, and Cynthia Harris's voice was as clear as though I were calling from twenty blocks rather than three thousand miles away.

"Hello, Janet, how are you? Long time no see. When are you coming home?" Tony's secretary sounded so bouncy and full of herself that I felt a vague apprehension. There was palpably, even at this distance, a "school's out" quality about her that was usually a sure indication her boss was not there.

"Fine. And I don't know when I'm coming home, Cynthia. That's what I'd like to talk to Tony about. Is he there?"

"No. He isn't coming in. He said day before yesterday that he'd be away for a few days and would be in touch."

"And no hint as to where?"

"None," she said.

"Damn!" Not only was I annoyed at having spent all that money for nothing, I was irritated at having to wait around until Tony took it into his head to return from one of his uncharted specials—a term Jason had thought up for the occasions when Tony would disappear for a day or two without telling his secretary where he could be reached or what he was doing.

"He might call in," Cynthia said. "Shall I tell him to phone you?"

"Yes. Please do. Tell him . . ." I paused, trying to find a way to telescope what I wanted to say. "Tell him that it would be easier for me to stay longer here and finish the close sorting of the papers than to have them shipped over there. Ask him to call me so that I can talk to him about it. The number here is—" And I read off the number on the instrument I was using.

"Okay. Any other message?"

Mischief took hold of me. "Yes," I said deadpan. "Tell him my helper, Gwyneth, and I are getting a strange view of his goings on when he was a congressman."

"Okay—" I could almost see her writing it down word for word. A sense of humor was not among her many assets. "See you."

"Did you reach him?" Gwyneth asked when I got upstairs.

"No. He was away. I'll just have to wait and go on doing what I'm doing."

The following afternoon around four I straightened up from bending over one of the boxes and added a few sheets to a growing pile sitting on top of one of the up-turned empty cartons. The trouble was, it was situated between two drafty windows, and since many of the sheets were onionskin, they kept blowing across the room or behind others of the boxes where it was difficult to retrieve them.

"I'm sorry," Gwyneth said. "I've looked everywhere for a small box, the kind you described. There must be every size and shape of large box or carton going up here, but not one to store standard sheets in. I know I have one at home somewhere—Daddy's always ordering more paper. I can bring it in tomorrow."

I stretched, easing the back muscles that were protesting from more stooping and bending than I'd done in years. "I think, instead, I'll walk down to the village. There's a stationery store there, isn't there?"

"There's a general all-sorts shop—sweets, cards, newspapers, writing and typing paper. I'm sure you'll find a box there."

"You walk home, don't you? Buff and I'll go with you."

"As a matter of fact I usually cycle, but I'll walk and wheel the bike."

"No, don't. It would be an awful bore for you, particularly after standing about all day."

"I don't mind. It'll be fun to walk to the village with you and Buff."

This time we left by the front gate, creaking it open and then making sure it shut behind us.

It was about a two-mile walk along the main road coming through the village and passing west by The Hall. Our progress was, inevitably, given Gwyneth's painful gait, slow. Too slow for Buff, who showed a curiosity and boldness I'd not seen in her before, streaking out ahead of us for a while, and then running, flat out, straight back to make sure we were there. The road, which wound as it followed the river, was not much frequented, but from time to time a car or truck would pass. "I wonder," I said, "if I should put Buff on the leash. I don't think she has sense enough not to run in front of a car."

"Probably," Gwyneth agreed doubtfully. "But she's having so much fun it'd be a pity."

So I let her run free, salving my conscience by keeping a close eye on her and calling her every time she showed any inclination to desert the low bank next to which we were walking and run across the asphalt. Idly, it occurred to me at that moment that we were on the wrong side of the road. English traffic drives on the left, so it is safest to walk on the right where the cars come from the front and both car and pedestrian can readily see one another.

"Shouldn't we be walking over there?" I asked Gwyneth, waving to the right side of the road.

"Strictly speaking, yes. But there's no bank there for Buff to play on."

I glanced over and saw Gwyneth was right. The high stone wall forming the boundary of The Hall's grounds rose straight up from the roadway.

"True. So we'll stay here and trust to the excellent manners of English drivers."

Gwyneth, who was wheeling her bike, smiled. "Most drivers around here are pretty sedate—that is, if they're local. We get a few travelers speeding through in their sports cars or on their motorbikes."

We strolled on, with Gwyneth and her bicycle on the outside and me between her and the grassy bank where Buff was running backwards and forwards investigating promising smells. Every now and then she'd spring down and run along the road for a few yards before I whistled or called her back onto the bank again.

"Back!" I yelled once.

Buff turned, her ears up, then raced up on the bank, her ears flat and her tail straight out.

"She seems to know what you mean," Gwyneth said.

"I'm sure she does. I think the whole thing is her little

joke. Every now and then she prances down to the road to make sure I'm noticing what she's doing."

After that the conversation drifted on to Gwyneth's years in London and her work there. "What kind of work was it?" I asked.

"Oh, it was a branch of the civil service."

"That covers a lot of territory. At least it does with us. You could be anything from a policeman to a pundit at city hall to an aide in a hospital."

"As a matter of fact," Gwyneth said rather shyly, "it was a branch of Intelligence, which makes it sound as though I dealt daily with vital secrets, which I didn't. Not everything in Intelligence holds the fate of the country in its hands or is terribly hush-hush."

"You mean they still have to have typists and dogs-bodies and personnel and general management?"

"And people to get the boss's tea and buns," Gwyneth finished cheerfully.

"Didn't you say Gideon was in Intelligence?"

"Yes. But that was military. I wish you'd tell me more about your father's work. I know you said you didn't share his zeal—and I do sympathize with the reason. Still, it must have been interesting, to have a sort of worm's-eye view of the Society."

I was fairly sure that Gwyneth had turned the conversation more because she didn't want to discuss her previous work than because she had any avid interest in my parent and his causes. But, if I were right, I still had to accept her lead with, perhaps, the mental reservation that her job was less banal and routine than she would have me believe.

"Well, my father—" I started, when it happened.

A car came around a bend in the road about thirty yards off. Idly, I watched it approach us, most of my attention on Buff, who was scampering at my feet. Then, quite suddenly, its lights blazed on. There was a roar as it accelerated, veering towards us. My action was reflex. Flinging myself sideways and forward, I managed to grasp Buff by the scruff of her neck with one hand and with the other to yank both Gwyneth and her bicycle with me, so that all of us, including the bike, finished up in a heap on the bank above the road.

"What on earth—are you all right?" I said, rolling away from Gwyneth.

She sat up holding her leg, a white look on her face. "Yes. I'll be fine in a minute."

"I'm sorry—but that maniac! He must have been going at eighty miles an hour. Are you sure you're all right? We're more than halfway to the village. I could easily run ahead and get Dr. Maitland, or somebody with a car."

"No. My . . . foot was just twisted for a minute. But it's fine now." Putting her hands on the ground she started to struggle to her feet.

"Here," I said. "Let me help you."

"I'd rather—if you don't mind—do it myself."

Something in her voice made me realize she meant it. I stepped back and turned my attention to the bank, looking for Buff. She was standing shaking herself after my rough handling. "I'm sorry, Buff. But I had to get you out of the way."

Her ears went down and she wiggled her backside. I was already seething with anger at the driver, and the sight of Buff, who had so nearly been killed, gave a fresh spurt to my rage. "I wish I had that man . . . whoever it was, in front of . . . in front of *my* car. I'd run him down so fast—" I glanced back towards Gwyneth. She had got herself up and was brushing her coat.

"Okay?" I said. I didn't want to fuss over her, but her face had been almost gray. Even now it was paler than her usual creamy whiteness.

"Yes. Entirely okay. I think it was just the surprise. I wonder if my bike's all right."

The way the bicycle was lying it looked, at first, as though it might be a casualty, but when raised seemed no more than a little scratched here and there.

"I'm afraid I flung it down rather abruptly," I said. "Or rather dragged it."

Gwyneth and I lowered it to the road. "Well, it's thanks to you that it's not a heap of scrap metal and I'm here at all," she said, and this time color dyed her cheeks. "How on earth can I possibly thank you?"

"Don't try. It was *sauve qui peut!* I don't think I even realized what I was doing. Are you sure you want to continue the walk?"

"Oh, yes. My father would be ashamed of me if, no more than a bit shaken, I didn't get back up on the horse and ride again, metaphorically speaking."

"I think your father's charming and interesting, but he sounds a bit hard to live up to."

"Yes, but he doesn't ask of me or anyone else what he doesn't do himself."

"I've heard that said before about various people, but I've never found it a comfort." I walked around her, putting her between me and the bank. "I think I'll walk on the outside this time. I can watch Buff just as well, and if we should encounter another maniac, I'll just push you on the bank, instead of dragging you." I paused while we got ourselves sorted out. "By the way, did you get any kind of look at who it was, or what kind of car? I'd dearly love to report him to the authorities."

There was a pause. "No. I'm afraid not. I wasn't noticing. Did you?"

"No—something funny occurred right before it happened, only I can't remember what it was. But I have no picture of anything else—not the driver, not the car, nothing."

"You did say," Gwyneth said hesitantly, " 'he' when you spoke of the driver. Was that just 'he' as in 'one'— impersonal, I mean. Or did you really mean 'he'?"

"Did I? I can't remember." I tried to recall any impression of any kind that made me assume the driver was a man. But the screen of my memory was blank. I could see nothing except the front of the car, the lights like two eyes. "I can't remember seeing it was a man—or that it wasn't a man. I don't think I saw. I must have used 'he' in the general sense."

We walked in silence the rest of the way. Even Buff's spirits seemed somewhat dimmed. She kept up on the bank religiously, turning every now and then to assure herself that we were following. As it turned out the incident must have occurred more than halfway to the village, because we came in sight of the first houses quite soon afterwards.

"Where's the all-sorts store you were talking about?" I asked.

"About halfway down the street. I'll take you there. It's on my way."

The "all-sorts" shop turned out to be a tiny establishment tucked in the middle of a row of little houses. We left Gwyneth's bicycle outside while we went in and Gwyneth introduced me.

"This is Mrs. Evans," she said to me, with her shy smile towards the elderly woman behind the counter. "She was giving me a penny's worth of sweets when I was six years old."

When Gwyneth explained to her what I wanted Mrs. Evans said, "Let me just see if I have an empty one."

It turned out that she still had one that had been emptied only the day before. "I was going to throw it out, but am glad you can find a use for it."

We were leaving when something made me turn back. "Mrs. Evans, you can see the street from where you are behind the counter, can't you?"

"Oh, yes. Of course," she replied, looking faintly puzzled. "Why?"

"Did you notice a car speeding through the village—oh, about twenty minutes ago?"

"With so many cars passing I'm sure Mrs. Evans wouldn't notice one," Gwyneth said. "Besides, it may not have been speeding then."

"There hasn't been much traffic this afternoon," Mrs. Evans said, "and nothing to notice particularly. I did notice a dark red car, probably because it was red and a bit larger than most cars you see around here, but it wasn't speeding or anything. Just driving through."

I had the odd, sudden impression that a light had flashed on and off and I glanced outside, wondering if one of the cars parked next to the narrow sidewalk had turned on its lights. But that was impossible, I decided. There was no one in any of them.

"What's the matter?" Gwyneth asked.

"Nothing. I thought one of the cars out there had flashed on its lights for a second."

"There's no one there at all," Mrs. Evans said.

"I'd better be getting home. Thanks, Mrs. Evans." Gwyneth started limping towards the door.

"Buff and I will see you the rest of the way," I said.

"There's absolutely no need," Gwyneth said. "Truly."

"We want the walk. Besides, it's only a few steps along, isn't it?"

Five minutes later I was delivering Gwyneth to her door. "Please come in," she said. "Daddy would love to see you."

"I think we'd better be getting back," I said. "How's the leg?"

"It's absolutely fine. No damage——" The carved front door swung open.

"Hello, hello. I thought I saw you. Do come in, Miss deMaury." The big figure of the rector stood there, the long black cassock making him appear even taller than he was.

"I don't think——" I started.

"Nonsense. You have time for a cup of tea, I'm sure. My child, what happened to you?" This last was addressed to Gwyneth.

"Nothing, Daddy. Nothing at all. I just——"

"No. Don't lie to me. Something happened. If you don't wish to tell me what it is, then I must accept that. I have no right to pry. But please don't tell me an untruth. Come in, Miss deMaury."

I had no desire whatever to go in. There was a tension between Mr. Theale and his daughter that I did not wish to be a part of. But just as I was about to refuse again, I encountered a look from Gwyneth that seemed to hold an appeal.

"Thank you," I said reluctantly. "For just a minute, then."

Gwyneth placed her bicycle against the wall of the porch. "I'll put on some tea."

She disappeared towards the back of the house as the rector led me to his study.

"And how is Gideon these days?" he said, drawing an armchair towards the fire and waving me to it.

"Oh, fine," I said, sitting down.

"And Benedict? And Miss Maitland?"

Was there a different note in his voice? I glanced up to see the rector's eyes on me. They were, I found myself thinking, a curious smoky color, a combine of blue, green and gray, as brilliant and striking as all the rest about him. "To be truthful," I found myself answering, "I don't know how to reply to that. The two occasions I've been with Benedict have not ended particularly well."

He was staring at me over his clasped hands. "Could you tell me more exactly what you mean?"

"Well, each time he appeared to get hysterical over what seemed to me nothing." I described the two encounters in as much detail as I could remember. "Of course," I finished up, "I realize he's a diabetic. I don't know how much effect that might have on his emotional make-up."

"Oh," the rector said. "I hadn't heard that—that he had diabetes."

"I don't know why I'm surprised that you haven't." I smiled. "Perhaps because you and Gideon seem such good friends. I would have thought he'd tell you."

A wry look came over the rector's handsome face. "As you saw at the front door, closeness doesn't always imply a . . . a . . . readiness to confide."

He paused. Part of me felt it was up to Gwyneth to tell her father what occurred on the road. Yet I found myself saying, "What happened just now was that a speed maniac, going eighty miles an hour, nearly ran us down on the road when we were walking here. In getting out of the way we all landed in a heap on the bank, and I think Gwyneth may have twisted her leg a bit."

Mr. Theale stared at me. I felt as though those amazing eyes were probing around in my head, almost, I thought, like headlights—and once again there was that flash in my mind of something I'd seen. But whatever it was, was gone before I could remember.

"I see," he said, but that still, penetrating look had not left his face. "I don't think, however," he said slowly, "that whatever was troubling her—and something was, indeed, troubling her—was because she twisted her leg. Gwyneth has had a lot of physical discomfort—even pain—in her life. But it has never been that which disturbs her."

There came again to my memory that strained, gray look on her face. I had put it down to her bruised leg and, perhaps, to shock. Shock, I thought now, might very well be right. But shock at what? At the actual near accident?

"Tell me more about Benedict's illness," he said. "How severe is it. How long has it been going on?"

"It seems to have got worse suddenly. At least that's what Miss Maitland said. Apparently, until recently, it had been controlled by diet alone. But then, when I mentioned seeing the hypodermic syringe in his bathroom and asked her the other day at lunch if she were giving Benedict vitamin shots, she said his diabetes had become worse and she was giving him insulin."

"Unusual," the rector said "—ah, here we are." I turned to see Gwyneth come in with a tray bearing three cups and a pot of tea.

"It's really late for this," she said, "but Daddy was right. It will give us all a lift."

"I could offer you sherry," Mr. Theale said suddenly, as though remembering his responsibility as a host. "How forgetful of me. We do have some, don't we, my dear?"

"Yes, of course. Janet, would you rather have some sherry?"

"No, I'd much prefer tea, thanks."

The rector drew up a table and another chair, and Gwyneth, sitting down, poured.

"Why?" I asked, after I'd had a sip of the hot tea,

"did you say 'unusual' when I was telling you about Benedict's diabetes?"

"My younger brother had it as a child, and I had occasion to learn a fair amount about it. . . ."

Even before he had spoken the words, I knew what he was about to say. Details from a book on children's diseases I had worked on suddenly returned.

"You mean that it's very rare for a child's diabetes to be controllable by diet."

He glanced at me. "That's right. I see you know about it too. When a child has the disease, it's nearly always much more severe. It's adults who acquire it later in life who can use diet alone to control it." He glanced at his daughter. "We're talking about Benedict's diabetes. Did you know he suffered from that?"

Gwyneth shook her head. "No. I didn't. Which is strange."

"Why?" I asked. "I mean, why should you know? Lots of people keep that kind of thing secret."

"Yes, I know. Only one of the odd jobs I do around here is general bookkeeping for Mr. White, the chemist, and help him to order the supplies. I know of three people in the village who have to have daily shots of insulin, for which he orders the ampules—through Dr. Maitland's prescriptions, of course. But I didn't know about Benedict."

"Well, according to Miss Maitland," I said, "Benedict's case has only recently become much worse. Which is what Mr. Theale and I were discussing. I once did editorial work on a book about children's diseases, and I just remembered now—as your father also recalled—that it's extremely rare for children's diabetes to be controllable by diet, as Miss Maitland claimed Benedict's was until a short while ago."

"If it was that recently, then I wouldn't have known about it. I haven't done any work for Mr. White for more than two months."

"We must remember," the rector said, "that none of us is an expert. My dear, Miss deMaury told me of your near accident. Is your leg all right?" Those keen eyes, I noted, were on his daughter's face.

Gwyneth's attention seemed to be on the hot water jug as she poured some of its contents into the teapot. "What I'm sure Janet didn't tell you was that she saved my life. I wasn't watching the road, but Janet was, on account of Buff, who kept running from the bank down, and she hauled me onto the bank only just in time."

"No, Miss deMaury certainly didn't tell me that." He turned towards me. "I am indeed indebted to you."

A little uncomfortable, I tried to pass it off. "Well, actually we're all indebted to Buff here. It was because I was watching her that I saw it in time." I touched my brogue to Buff's back, where she lay curled in front of the fire. Buff's small pointed muzzle twisted back towards me. Her ears, which had gone up inquiringly, lowered. Her tail thumped the floor.

"Who ever thought you'd be such an agent for good?" I said.

More thumping.

Bending over, I scratched her behind her ear. Buff closed her eyes in ecstasy. "I must say, she's an appreciative little creature."

"Speaking of being saved," Gwyneth said, "heaven knows what would have happened to her by now if she hadn't been rescued."

"She'd be kept in the shed by Sheila Maitland," I said somewhat grimly, and added, "I wonder why she dislikes Buff? I can't imagine anything less offensive."

"Because you have befriended her, probably," the rector said.

I looked at him. There was a rather grim note in his voice, which surprised me. Then I shook my head. "No. Roger, Gideon's brother, told me the first night I was here, when I had said I wanted to take Buff back to the States with me, that Sheila would be delighted. She must have disliked her then—before I arrived. But I can't think why. Because she doesn't object to Gelert, Gideon's German shepherd, who can, indeed, be fierce, as I know. He frightened me half to death when I arrived."

"Gelert is Gideon's," Gwyneth said.

I took that in. "I see." Then, "Is it . . . do I take it that she doesn't like animals in general, with the exception of Gelert, because he's Gideon's?"

"I don't really know," Gwyneth replied. "I don't know Sheila that well—just what I've told you about her training in some way in London, and I got that from Mr. White. She didn't grow up here, you know. She and her father only came here a few years ago. I think he'd been in practice in London. Then old Dr. Piers died and Dr. Maitland bought the practice and he and Sheila moved here."

"There's something about that young woman that disturbs me," the rector said.

"That doesn't sound very Christian," Gwyneth said teasingly.

He transferred his compelling gaze to his daughter. "On the contrary. If one feels one is in the presence of great wrong—evil perhaps—then it is one's duty to say so."

"Evil's a pretty strong word, Mr. Theale," I said. "I don't like Sheila because I think she's bossy and domineering and doesn't like Buff, and . . ." My voice trailed off.

"And?"

I looked at the austere old man. That single word had been spoken almost like a command. I paused while I arranged and rearranged sentences in my head. Finally I said, "You implied, when I first commented on Sheila Maitland's dislike of Buff, that it was from jealousy of me. I wondered what made you say that, because she hasn't the faintest reason to be jealous—" At that moment the traitorous memory of that long kiss up in the attic flashed vividly into my mind, and I could feel the color come up into my cheeks. "I mean," I went on confusedly, "Gideon seems—" But that, too, I was unable to finish.

"What do you mean?" he asked more gently.

"I'm not sure. I assumed . . . Roger led me to believe, that there was an . . . understanding between

Gideon and Sheila. I have no reason to think he wasn't telling the truth. Certainly, she seems very sure of her status in the household. And there's absolutely no question but that Gideon trusts her completely as far as Benedict is concerned."

"I ascribed jealousy to Sheila Maitland," Mr. Theale said sternly, "because I think—I'm sure—that she cannot tolerate a rival."

"But I'm not a rival! That's what I've been trying to say. Not personally, not as far as her position at The Hall is concerned, and most of all not with Benedict."

"I didn't say you *were* a rival, my dear. I said that she could not tolerate a rival. And I think that she would see any young unattached—or even attached—woman in that light, particularly, if you don't mind my saying so, if she had charm and good looks."

"Thank you," I murmured, somewhat overcome. I felt that the rector would bring his full theological integrity to bear even on such an untheological matter as paying me a compliment.

"Not at all," he said. And this time there was a twinkle in his handsome eyes. "Neither age nor holy orders can prevent me from recognizing a pretty girl when I see one." The twinkle then faded. "But I have—what do the young people call it today?—very strong vibrations about Miss Maitland, and they are not good. Also—but I won't speak of anything until I'm sure of what I'm talking about."

"Well, you've certainly made me feel less—" I was about to say "bitchy" but hastily censored the word. In an effort at modernity the rector might rise to "vibrations." I did not think he'd like "bitchy." "Less malicious in my dislike of her."

"I doubt," the rector said seriously, "whether you could be malicious."

"Yes. So do I," his daughter agreed, smiling. Then she said, "There's one thing . . . it probably has nothing to do with anything . . . but when I was in London I once or twice saw Roger Lightwood and Sheila Maitland together. Once in a restaurant. Once at a party given by people we both knew."

"What does Roger do?" I asked curiously. "Half the time he's not at The Hall for lunch or dinner, but then half the time he is. Doesn't he have a job? Or is my puritan ancestry showing too much?"

The rector laughed. "No more so than a lot of people's. Roger has had one or two quite good jobs. One had something to do with export-import. The other, I think, was with a brokerage firm. I believe he also worked in some capacity or other for one of the film studios. But he never stays very long away from The Hall, which is strange."

"Why strange?"

"Because he wasn't really brought up here. His mother far preferred the Mediterranean coast, and after his father's death in 1959, when Roger was six, she stayed there almost permanently. Of course, later on he came back to school. But all holidays were abroad, and except for the odd visit with Gideon, he was almost never at Tenton. That changed when his mother died when he was in his last year at school. Since then he has been here quite often." Mr. Theale sighed. "She—the second Lady Lightwood, I mean—was an unhappy lady, very different from Gideon's mother."

"Gideon told me about his mother. She sounded remarkable."

"She was. I'm told by people who knew that she was a great pianist. She stopped playing professionally pretty much when Gideon was born. I think she felt that he needed her by him. Then there was the war. . . . I don't think she was happy, not because there was anything wrong with the marriage, but because of what was happening to her people and her family back in Austria. Then after the war she died. Sir Gareth, Gideon's father, was fearfully cut up. In a curious way, I think that's why he got into trouble—but I am gossiping."

If it had been anyone else I would have cried shame on stopping there. But something about the rector's long upper lip told me that it would be worse than useless. I glanced at the clock and rose rapidly out of my chair. "Good heavens. It's almost dinner time. And Buff and I have to get back."

The rector rose immediately. "I'll be happy to drive you."

"No, no. Buff and I can do a brisk trot back, it shouldn't take more than thirty-five or forty minutes."

"I insist," Mr. Theale said. "No. Please don't argue."

And once again I saw an example of his kindly meant, but unquestionably streamrollering ways.

While I was still protesting, he strode out of the study—with me following—swung a cloak over his cassock, and flung open the front door. "This way," he said.

"It's no use," Gwyneth said from behind me. She limped up to where I could see she was smiling. "You might as well give in."

We drove back through the village street in the long English dusk, Buff sitting on my lap. "I suppose," the rector said suddenly, and totally unexpectedly, "that you feel it was unfair of me to stop short as I did when talking about Gideon's father and the trouble he got into. I think, perhaps in fairness to Roger, so that you will understand him a bit better, I will finish what I didn't say. The young people today, of course, think the concern of my generation with such matters as legitimacy, and what we used to call morality, straining at a gnat in a world of war and death and starvation and atom bombs. . . ."

His voice ran down. "Sometimes I wonder if they aren't right. Anyway, Sir Gareth, who had married young and had had, I think, an extraordinarily happy marriage. was extremely lonely. He was a good-looking man, had been a member of the House of Commons quite a large part of his life, was prominent in London social and—I suppose through Gideon's mother—artistic circles. Anyway, he met Roger's mother. I'm told there was something in the gossip columns about his being seen with her. She was an actress, or trying to be. Very ambitious. Then, rather suddenly, they were married. They left almost immediately for the Continent, and a short time later, Roger was born. Whether that hasty, rather undignified way of doing things has ever bothered him or not, I don't know. But in a part of the country like this—

where rather old-fashioned standards are adhered to—it might have."

"But you said he was almost never here as a boy."

"That's true. But that wasn't his choice, I feel, but his mother's. As I told you, after she died he came here quite a lot. And I think it's been made quite plain to him, both by the county and by the village people, that they really don't consider him part of the family."

"I see. Yes, that might be hard to take. To feel like an outsider in your own home."

The rector dropped Buff and me off at the gate of The Hall, refusing to come in. We slipped through a door at the side of the tall gate and all but ran up the drive. Off to the left, behind the house, parked in the courtyard, was a car I hadn't seen before. Vaguely I noticed that in the dusk it seemed—though I couldn't be sure—a dark red.

Streaking upstairs, I washed my hands, combed my hair and slipped out of my sweater and skirt and into a dress. Then, with Buff at my heels, I went downstairs and into the sitting room.

As I walked through the door a familiar figure rose from one of the armchairs before the fire. "To think I'd come all this way to see how you're coming along, and you're not even here to greet me."

"Tony!" I cried, and was enveloped in a hug.

# eight

I WAS A LITTLE surprised at the warmth of his greeting, Tony never having been one to toss around indiscriminate hugs. But I experienced that same little *frisson* of pleasure, combined with some other, less definable, emotion, that I had had in his office when he came around the desk and took my hands in his that famous last day before I left New York.

"What brings you here?" I asked, moving away a little and playing for time. Not only had Gideon and Roger both risen when I came in, Sheila Maitland, looking striking in green, was sitting on the sofa, her tawny eyes on Tony and me with a watchful expression.

"I was in London anyway on business, and after your letter describing the muddle I thought I'd take a quick trip up here to see how you were faring." He glanced at Buff. "You seem to have acquired a friend."

"Yes," I said, rather carefully not looking at Sheila. "I'm going to take her back to the States with me."

Tony bent down. "What's her name?"

"Buff. After Boadicea."

"Well, Boadicea—you don't look like an early British warlike queen to me." He held out his hand. Buff sniffed at it delicately. Then, to my vast amusement, trotted over and raised up on her hind legs with her front paws on Gideon's leg. Everybody laughed.

"Yes, all right," Gideon said, rubbing her head, "but I don't have anything for you. You'll have to make love to Mrs. Lowndes after dinner."

"You're going to have to keep an eye on her, Janet," Sheila said, and I noted, in passing, that this was the first time she had called me Janet. "I heard over the wireless that there had been some kind of rabies scare around."

"Rabies?" Gideon said. "When on earth did you hear that? There hasn't been any rabies in England since the last century. That's why the laws about incoming animals are so stringent—to keep it out."

"I heard the announcement," Roger said. "But you've got it wrong, Sheila; it was somewhat near the channel coast of France that there was a report." He was lounging back in his chair, looking very much the indolent, handsome young man. I glanced at him gratefully, remembering a little what the rector had told me about him. But his eyes were on Sheila.

There was a short pause. Then, "Yes, I think you're right," Sheila said. Odd, I thought. It was almost as though he had sent her an instruction.

"How are you coming on the sorting of the deMaury papers, Janet?" Tony asked.

"It's going quite well," I replied, accepting a glass of sherry from Gideon. "We've sifted out the huge quantities of promotional material and got the rest down to being grouped by decades. Now, with new boxes kindly ordered by Gideon, we're starting to sort them more closely. By the way, I called you yesterday to tell you this, and also to tell you that it's going to take longer than the three weeks you originally said I should be here. But Cynthia said you were away on one of your uncharted specials, and—"

"My *what*?" The silence stretched for the length of one breath. Staring at Tony, I sensed, once again, that unknown quality in him. Whatever it was, it made me feel as though I were again sitting in front of his desk back in his big New York office.

"It's just an . . . an expression," I stammered. "Meaning those trips you take every now and then when no one, not even Cynthia, knows where you are."

"I see," he said easily, and smiled, and the tension disappeared. "Well, sorry I wasn't available. This trip to London came up suddenly one night after a phone call at home. I didn't think I'd be gone long enough to bother Cynthia with the whys and wheres. Was there anything else?"

"Nothing really," I said, still rather rattled, and angry with myself for being that way.

"Where are you doing all of this interesting work?"

"Up in one of the attics, spread over the floor and every other available surface. It's quite a sight. Will you be around? I mean, are you staying in the village so you can see what we're doing tomorrow morning?"

"Sir Gideon has very kindly offered me a bed here tonight, which I have gratefully accepted. The inn I passed on the main road through the village looked a little primitive."

"The village inn is extremely primitive," Gideon said, pouring Tony some more sherry. "Sheila?" He held up the decanter.

"Just a little." She held out her glass.

Gideon walked over to where she sat on the sofa. I found myself watching the two of them. Sheila's amber eyes were on Gideon's face as he poured more sherry into her glass, but as far as I could see he kept his gaze on the dark gold liquid.

"Well, then you can come up and see our labors tomorrow morning," I said to Tony.

Mrs. Lowndes appeared in the doorway. "Dinner is served, Sir Gideon."

It was Buff who woke me, pawing at the door and whimpering. The noise dragged me up from what felt like a fathoms-deep sleep. I lay there, for a minute, wondering what had waked me, when I became aware of the soft scratching against the wood of the door and an occasional whimper. I sat up and turned on the bedside light. "What's the matter, Buff?"

She abandoned whatever she was doing and came and jumped on the bed, then paused, her head cocked to one side, listening. I heard it then: the soft sound made by feet in some kind of slippers. Jumping off the bed, she went back to the door.

"Well," I whispered to her, "what's so funny about that? Somebody's going to the bathroom." I glanced at the little traveling clock beside my bed: it was three thirty. "Come on back here, Buff. Settle down." I patted the bed, and that obedient little dog came and jumped back on it. Putting my hand on her back, I pressed it down so that she lay as she had been when I had originally gone to sleep, curled in a bunch against my middle. "That's a good girl," I said sleepily, turning off the light and snuggling into my pillow.

I must have dozed off, because I was waked again. Buff was back at the door. "Damn it!" I said aloud, sat up and turned on the light again. Then, as the obvious and unwelcome probability that it was Buff herself who wanted to visit the bathroom dawned on me, I moaned, pushed aside the covers and reached for my robe.

"What have you been eating or drinking," I said crossly to my companion as I wrapped the robe around me and hunted for my bedroom slippers. Fortunately, unlike the mules I had at home, these were a traveling pair made of thin, very soft leatherlike material that fitted around the foot and, when packed, folded into a case not much larger than a matchbox.

"All right," I said. "Come on."

Just before I opened the door I thought to put in my pocket a thin flashlight that goes with my overnight case. If there was anything I didn't want to do, it was to wake the household by falling downstairs.

But once outside in the shadowy hall, Buff made straight for the stairs going up to the next storey.

"Come back here," I called after her in a loud whisper.

Now that I knew she was not being pressed by nature, I was ready to administer a severe scolding for rousting me out of an excellent night's sleep. "Come back here," I called more loudly, and then glanced back to see if any curious heads appeared around doorways.

But others, too, must have been enjoying the sleep of the just. The hall behind me lay silent and undisturbed, lit only by the windows that appeared at either end where the dark was a lighter gray, and a faint illumination came from stars and a high, pale moon, just barely visible at the edge of one of the windows. If a door had been open, I wouldn't have been able to see it, but I could certainly hear if someone had opened a door while I was standing there.

When I turned back, Buff had disappeared; whether down or up I didn't know. I switched on my thin but strong flashlight and turned it on the hall immediately in front of me and on the broad flight of stairs going up. But there was no sign of her.

"Buff!" I whispered. And then more loudly, "Buff!"

Where had she gone, up or down? It was a toss-up, but remembering that she had been going in the direction of the flight going up, I decided that she was more likely there than on the ground floor. Well, I thought, feeling the tug of my warm bed, why didn't I just go back to my room and let her return when she felt like it? Perhaps she'd heard a mouse. By the looks of her there was unquestionably some terrier in her make-up. She was most likely just having an atavistic attack and was now in pursuit of the unlucky mouse, and I was extremely foolish standing there in a cold, dark, drafty hall worrying about it. But then I remembered it wasn't a mouse that had sent her ears up in that alert way. It was footsteps, footsteps that I had assumed were taking someone to one of the hall bathrooms. But in all the nights I had been at The Hall, and Buff had spent in my room, she had never behaved in this fashion. True, the previous nights there had not been two visitors. Besides Tony Bridewell there was Sheila Maitland, who, having been asked to stay for dinner, was occupying the bedroom that, I understood,

was often put aside for her use. Which meant that there
were two extra people who would be using the bathrooms
in this wing. But if that was the case, why did Buff go
upstairs, as I was by now quite sure she had?

There was no answer to that. Oh, drat the dog, I said
to myself, and turned back to my bedroom. What harm
could she come to? But as I put my hand on the doorknob, I remembered that Sheila, who was spending the
night here, did not like Buff.

Damn, blast and hell, I muttered softly, and turned
once again. Then, getting a firm grip on the flashlight, I
marched to the foot of the ascending staircase and started
up to the floor where the servants—what servants there
were—slept.

But when I got to the top and shone my light up and
down the long hallway there was no sign of Buff. Just to
make sure I called softly, "Buff! Buff!" And stood, for a
minute, straining my ears.

Of course, I thought, if any door were open along the
hall, there was nothing to prevent Buff from going in,
especially as most of the rooms were empty. But from
where I was standing I couldn't possibly see whether any
door were open or not. My light was strong within a few
feet, but it was thin, and if I tried to cast it further than
the immediate vicinity, it paled to nothing. Well, there
was nothing for it but to go up and down the hall looking,
which I proceeded to do, getting crosser by the minute.
"You are a miserable hound," I muttered to myself, passing one door after another and seeing them all firmly
shut. "Just wait till I get hold of you!"

It was a long walk, through both wings of the sprawling house, and before I was halfway finished I would
have been extremely glad of Buff's company. I knew I
was not a nervous type, had never thought I believed in
ghosts and was not psychic (to my knowledge). Yet as I
crossed the center part of the house and proceeded to the
opposite wing there was a curious prickling at the back of
my neck.

At one point I stopped and said in a loud whisper,
"Who's there?" and then I stood in that dark, silent hall,

listening to the silence, trying to hear—something, if nothing but breathing. Because I could not rid myself of the growing feeling that I was not alone, that out there, just below the level of my hearing, was somebody, or something, waiting. It was not a pleasant sensation.

As I stood there, I realized that my hand holding the little flashlight was shaking, the light itself jiggling along the floorboard. "Buff!" I whispered again, and then forced my lips into sounding a rather quavery whistle.

But for all that I did not feel alone, I knew that it wasn't Buff near me. And then, suddenly, a spurt of panic for her rushed through my system and shook me out of my paralysis. Quite why I was so convinced she was in danger, I don't know. But to find her became suddenly of the utmost importance.

I was moving back towards the center when my light shone on the narrow entrance to the stairway going up to the attic. Of course! Why hadn't that occurred to me? Since I had spent every day for two weeks up there, and Buff with me, it seemed incredible to me that I wouldn't think of her going up there.

But I was, although resolved to go up, oddly reluctant to start. Finally, almost in the spirit of a rite, I whispered, "Buff!" loudly, and the name seemed to echo back to me from the hallways. Then I gathered the skirts of my robe up and, holding the flashlight in one hand, proceeded to mount the steep winding steps to the attic.

They seemed to go on forever, and I wished again that whatever handrail had been there originally had been left. As my head came level with the attic room floor two things happened: I heard a sound that I immediately recognized as a muffled whimper from Buff, and I became gripped with the absolute conviction that I was not alone.

I was extremely frightened. But that sound from Buff had done something to my nervous system. It was not a case of making a decision. I could no more have gone back down and left that silly, defenseless mutt up there than I could have taken off on the nearest broomstick.

"Buff!" I whispered, stepping onto the attic floor. "Where are you?"

There came that sad little sound again, off to one side. I turned, shining my light around in that direction. The sound came again. Following it, I walked slowly across the carpet covering the attic floor, trying to remember the jumble of furniture, chairs, shelves and piles of books that I had seen up there, and nearly jumped out of my skin when my shin encountered some object that went across the room with a clatter. What on earth could it have been? I wondered, standing there, frozen. After a moment my memory produced the picture of a high footstool that had always stood to the right of the stairway. "Buff," I breathed as I let out my breath.

Again there came the sound, this time behind me, nearer to the stairs I had just come up and to my right. "I'm coming," I said, as much to reassure myself as her.

I saw her then, lying near the open stairwell, her muzzle tied with a piece of rope, struggling in some kind of knitted afghan or rug that had been wrapped round and round her.

"Poor baby, never mind." I bent down, put down the flashlight on the floor and untied the rope around her muzzle. Then I groped for the edge of the afghan to free her. It was as I was unwrapping the last of the folds, with Buff wriggling loose, that I heard a sound behind me. Grabbing up my flashlight I stepped back and turned. The slender beam of light revealed a pair of heavy shoes. After that, darkness descended, and that was all I remembered.

I woke up lying still in my robe on my own bed, and lay there feeling muddled and a little sick. "What . . . who?" I started to sit up.

"Lie still," a voice said. For some reason I found it comforting, and relaxed. After a few seconds my stomach felt better and I remembered what had happened up to the moment I started unwrapping the robe from Buff.

"Buff," I said. And this time managed to sit up.

The next thing I was aware of was two front paws on

my lap and a tongue licking my face. I gave her a hug and looked around. My room seemed full of people. The voice that had spoken to me, I realized then, was Gideon's. Dressed in turtleneck sweater and trousers, he was standing at the end of my bed. Next to him, in pajamas and robe, his hair tousled, was Tony Bridewell, and grouped around the other side were Roger and Mrs. Lowndes, in robes, and Sheila in a long, sweeping housecoat of much the same green as the dress she had worn at dinner. I glanced at their feet. All except Gideon, who had on shoes, wore slippers.

"What happened?" I asked. "Why are you all here? Somebody hit me on the head."

"What hit you on the head was the attic stairs as you fell down them," Gideon said.

"With a mighty clatter," Roger added, grinning. "What on earth were you doing up in the attic in the middle of the night? Making everything neat for the boss?"

"Buff ran upstairs," I said, putting my hand on the culprit's back. "She pawed at the bedroom door and woke me up. But when I opened the door, she ran upstairs and I went up to get her. Then I found her, all trussed up, and was undoing her when I heard something behind me. I turned around—" At the last minute I stopped myself mentioning the shoes that my light had picked out.

"You turned?" Gideon said. "And then what?"

I looked him in the eyes, painfully aware of the fact that of all the people present he was the only one wearing not bedroom slippers but shoes. "Somebody hit me on the head."

"Who?" This was from Tony.

"I don't know," I heard myself say. "I couldn't see. I had a flashlight with me, but it's tiny and pretty ineffective except for shining directly on something."

"But who could it have been?" Mrs. Lowndes said in a shocked, worried voice. "The house is locked up every night. Of course, there are windows—one or two—that do not lock properly. This is terrible! Was anything taken, Miss deMaury?"

I decided—for the moment—to go along with the suggestion that it might be an intruder. "I don't know, Mrs. Lowndes. I haven't really had a chance to look in my room, and certainly not anywhere else." Again I looked eye to eye at Gideon. "You seem to be up and dressed. Have you had a chance to see if anything in the house is stolen?"

There was an icy edge to Gideon's voice as he replied. "When you fell down the stairs, making, as Roger justly said, a lot of noise, I threw on the nearest and easiest garments, since Mrs. Lowndes has my robe for mending. After that I ran out and found you at the bottom of the attic stairs with your wretched companion barking her head off beside you and waking whatever of the household had not heard you fall."

"I did *not* fall," I said indignantly, and then winced as pain shot through my head. "There's a bump on my head." I put my hand up. "I can feel it."

"There's an awful lot of stuff up there in the attic," Mrs. Lowndes' Scottish accent somehow seemed to lend great sense to what she was saying. "You might have heard a noise all right, and turned, and hit your head. There are chairs and tables and bookshelves up there. All manner of stuff. And then after you'd hit your head you fell down the stairwell. There's no guard rail on that side."

It was on the front of my tongue to say, "But I saw feet in heavy shoes." But I didn't. Quite why I didn't, I wasn't sure. One element at least in my hesitation was a sense of my own danger. I have never been a quick thinker, but it was obvious even to me that if my assailant were one of the people now standing around my bed, then for me to provide more evidence of someone up there in the attic would be to invite another attack. Another possible cause in my hesitation I glanced at briefly and dismissed. That it might have anything to do with my feeling towards Gideon made me extremely uncomfortable—Gideon, who was now building such a firm case for my having struck my head on a piece of furniture, fallen down the stairwell and knocked myself out.

"And all for your little dog," Sheila said in a soft, silken tone. "I know you think I'm prejudiced, but even you will admit that she's been the cause of a lot of trouble."

A hot rejoinder to the effect that the trouble lay with whoever was in the attic and knocked me on the head, almost fell out of my mouth, but as my senses cleared I saw my own danger in holding to my story and not appearing to accept Gideon's version.

"What do you want me to do?" I said coldly to Sheila now. "Put her outside in the shed? Have her destroyed? Give her back to the man who abandoned her near one of his own traps? Would that make you happy? She's such a large threat to you."

"Sheila hardly merits that, Janet," Gideon said rather forbiddingly. "And there is no doubt about it that it was your pet that caused the whole episode."

"And where does Gelert sleep?" I shot back.

Gideon paused a fraction of a second. "In the house. But then Gelert doesn't get me up in the middle of the night and send me wandering through the attics."

*Oh, doesn't he? I thought. Then who did?*

"This seems a lot of fuss over a harmless little beast," Tony said soothingly. "I suggest that what Janet needs now is some rest."

"Indeed she does," Mrs. Lowndes agreed, wrapping her robe around her even more closely, "and I shall bring her a warm drink."

"No, Mrs. Lowndes," I said a little guiltily. "Please don't trouble. I shall be fine."

"Go back to bed, Mrs. Lowndes. I'll bring Miss de-Maury her warm drink." This was from Gideon, who stalked out of the room before I could say anything.

Tony lingered by my bed after Sheila and Roger had left. "Are you sure you're all right?"

"Yes, Tony. Thanks. I really am."

He stared at me for a minute. "You got rather sat on

for your suggestion that anyone could have whacked you on the head. But—I wonder." He smiled a little at me. "You've always struck me as extremely down to earth. So I ask myself, if that was indeed your impression, who could it have been—and why?"

I shook my head, and then winced again as the pain shot through.

*"Something,"* Tony said, rather emphasizing the word, "gave you that blow on the head, which, I take it, is forcing itself on your attention every time you move."

There was a short silence. I felt strongly that Tony was telling me he believed me. Not surprisingly, this touched me, and I found it even more reassuring after Gideon's determination to force his version on me. "Tony—" I started, reaching out my hand.

"Yes?" He took my hand in his. Lightly he touched my head.

"There was—" I began. But at that moment Buff sprang off the bed with a bark and trotted over to the door. With the briefest of knocks Gideon appeared holding a napkin wrapped around what looked like a glass of milk. Tony released my hand. "Good night, Janet, my dear," he said and moved towards the door. As he left I had the rather desolate feeling that my last friend had disappeared.

"Here," Gideon said briefly, putting the glass, with the napkin on top of it, on my bed table. "Drink this. You should be able to go back to sleep. And as for you—" He looked down at Buff, who had reared up on her hind legs, her front paws on his leg. "Let's have no more wandering and barking. And, Janet"—he glanced up at me—"if this benighted animal should try to get out again, put your head under the covers and ignore her."

I looked at him steadily. "You don't believe a word I said, do you?"

"Having had a few blows on the head in my time, I know how the mind can play tricks—produce pictures of events that never happened. I am not accusing you of lying. I think you think the events as you recounted them were true. That doesn't mean you couldn't have hit your head on one of the many pieces of furniture up there and fallen down the stairs. The alternative is to believe that one of us—Bridewell, Roger, Sheila, or myself, or even Mrs. Lowndes—why leave her out?—launched an unprovoked assault on you. And I find that a lot harder to believe than that the knock you gave yourself, plus the knocks you got falling down the stairs, played tricks with your memory. Good night. Sleep well."

After he'd gone, I sat up in bed for a while, thinking and staring at the milk. I had read and heard enough to know that Gideon was right when he said a blow on the head could play tricks with the memory of what had gone immediately before. There was a lot of furniture piled higgledy-piggledy in that first attic. I had been bending down over Buff and could have risen suddenly, hitting my head. But if the whole thing had been some kind of unlucky accident started by Buff's midnight ramble, who tied her muzzle? Or was that, too, part of an illusory memory produced by my whacking my head on a protruding shelf or table?

How long I sat there after Gideon left, my mind going back and forth between possibilities like a pendulum, I don't know. But after a while, a familiar and repetitious noise intruded on my cogitations. It was Buff pawing the door, which, I realized, she had been doing ever since Gideon had walked out, just as she was pawing it earlier that night when she first woke me. Buff was indifferent to Tony and Roger and actively disliked Sheila—with good reason. The only person around The Hall, other than myself, that she would try to follow was Gideon, on whom she had developed a foolish crush. Logic pointed unanswerably: it was Gideon Buff heard going up to the attic; it was Gideon who was wearing shoes; it was Gideon who rode like a steamroller over my story to replace it with a more acceptable one. Ergo. . . .

I had flunked an elective course in logic at college, largely because I got bored and refused to attend class. Nevertheless, the most basic logic now pointed inexorably to an unpleasant conclusion, a conclusion a large part of me was unwilling to accept.

Nevertheless . . . getting up, I picked up the glass of milk, then, keeping Buff firmly away from the door, carried it down the hall to the bathroom and disposed of it down the toilet. The unmistakable odor of warm milk came up to me as I poured. But, against every desire not to, I wondered if milk was all that was in the glass.

To my intense irritation, Gideon knocked on my bedroom door before breakfast and told me that Dr. Maitland, who had made an early call to check on Benedict, would look in on me when he was finished.

"That was unnecessary," I said, tying my robe.

"How did you sleep?" he asked, strolling into the room as I left the door open.

"All right, considering." I was still angry at Gideon for refusing to believe my version of what happened to me, although he had succeeded in planting doubts in my mind as to whether or not he might be right. Feeling unable to cope with a recapitulation of the argument, I said, rather grudgingly, "I'm sorry to hear that Benedict has diabetes. When did you discover it?"

"Not too long ago—perhaps a year. Dr. Maitland discovered it."

"And he hadn't known before about it?"

"No. There was no reason to consider it. But Benedict had developed some symptoms which Sheila had told her father about, and, as I said, he ran a test."

Odd, I found myself thinking, that the doctor wouldn't have discovered it before, if he was watching over Benedict that carefully. . . . I was recalled to reality by Gideon's voice.

"Yes, in here, Doctor. This is Janet deMaury, my wife's cousin. Would you just look her over? As I told you on the phone, she fell downstairs and gave herself a nasty knock on the head. Janet—Dr. Maitland."

Thinking that, again, he had produced his own version of affairs, I turned, curious to see Sheila's father.

Although there was not much resemblance between the doctor and his daughter, I found myself thinking that he, too, must once have been a good-looking man.

Now he seemed oddly seedy. Tall and, for the most, spare, he had a small paunch that gave him a curiously flabby appearance for a countryman—more like a city dweller who, through poor eating habits and lack of exercise, had allowed himself to run to fat. His skin, too, showed pale by contrast to Gideon's windburn and tan.

"How do you do?" he said with an attractive but oddly vague smile,

"I meant to ask you," Gideon said. "Is there some special reason for your visit to Benedict this morning? Or is it just a routine call?"

"Sheila thought I might give him a once over—especially with measles running rampant. She said he seemed a little off his feed yesterday."

"You know—" Gideon started, then paused. "I'm torn between wanting him to have every possible medical attention—certainly all that is necessary—but not wanting him cosseted to the point where he grows up feeling that every time he has a twinge of any kind doctors must be sent for."

"Well, you can't judge him by your own sturdy health, Gideon. He'll probably need extra care all his life, not only for his leg, but his other problems."

"Such as his diabetes," I found myself saying.

The doctor glanced at me, his eyes almost black in his sallow face—no not sallow, I found myself thinking. More grayish. "Yes," he said. "It can be quite serious in young people."

"I think," Gideon commented with a sharp edge to his voice, "that you should have let me know that his condition had deteriorated to the point where he needed injections, rather than just careful diet."

There was a longish pause. I don't know how I expected the doctor to react: be indignant, or a little uncomfortable, or display dispassionate medical calm. But as the pause lengthened, it seemed almost, I thought, as though he were fishing around for something in the back of his mind.

"We wanted to be sure," he finally said, which more or less matched what Sheila had given as a reason.

"Well," Gideon said with some impatience, "how did you find him this morning?"

The doctor seemed to look more cheerful, as though this were a question he liked answering. "Quite stable. Everything is going as well as can be expected."

There was a pause. Then Gideon said, "When you say as well as can be expected—"

"I mean, of course, given the condition of his leg and his diabetes."

"I see. Well, I'll leave you to look over Miss de-Maury." And he went out the door.

The doctor smiled, a smile that seemed to have no effect on the black eyes above. "Sheila has spoken of you," he said pleasantly.

I'll bet, I thought. But I, too, smiled and wondered if my smile looked as phony as it felt. "I'm perfectly all right," I said. "Gideon shouldn't have bothered you."

"No harm in making sure. Let's just have a look at you."

Sitting me down on the bed, he felt my head, asking me from time to time if the pressure of his fingers hurt, lifted one eyelid and asked me how I felt.

"Fine," I said.

"No dizziness or weakness or any blurring in your vision?"

"None at all."

As it happened, my answers were perfectly true. Yet the terseness with which I replied had less to do with my impatience at what I considered unnecessary fussing than it did with a disturbing sense of discomfort in the physician's presence. Covertly I glanced at him, a little surprised at the strength of my desire to have him out of the room and away from me. Further, I had the strong impression that his mind was somewhere else. Yet there was nothing fumbling or uncertain about the way he examined my head.

"Yes," he said. "I think you'll do. You have a slight swelling back there, but nothing serious. It should be entirely gone in a day or so."

Rather slyly I asked him, "What do you think could have given me a bump like that?"

He snapped his black bag together. "Oh—anything might have done it. Falling against some furniture, or tumbling downstairs, as I understand from Sir Gideon you were unlucky enough to do."

"Or a blow on the head," I said.

"That, too. Although I gather there's no question of that." He smiled. "Mustn't have you taking away a bad impression from our corner of the country."

I rose up off the bed. "But I gather from the rector that you and Miss Maitland aren't native to this part. That you had a practice in London."

"Oh? I wonder why Mr. Theale said London. How strange! Well, the rector's getting on. It's a pity to see a mind like that give in to age. But I suppose it happens to all of us. Actually, it was in the north that I had my practice. As I said, no need for you to worry about your head. Good-bye."

Ten minutes after he left I was dressed and upstairs in the attic only to find Gwyneth already at work.

"Guess who's here," I said. "Or perhaps you already know."

She turned then, and I saw the whiteness of her face and the shadows under her eyes.

"Hey," I said, before she had time to speak, "are you okay? That fall you had yesterday must have shaken you up worse than you let on."

"No, I'm fine."

"You don't look fine."

"Well, I didn't sleep too well. That happens sometimes. Nothing to be upset about." But she was upset and I could see it, despite her valiant efforts to keep me from noticing.

"What's bothering you?" I asked bluntly.

There was a hesitation. Then she gave a wry smile. "I think I did, after all, twist my leg. It's quite sore. Do you think you could do without me for a day or so?"

"Of course. Are you going to stick it up and rest it?"

"No. Daddy has to go to London for something and I thought I'd go with him and see the doctor there that I've always been to."

"By all means. And don't worry about the work here. As a matter of fact, as I started to tell you, Tony Bridewell, my boss, dropped out of the blue and was here last night when I got home. He'll probably want to see what we've accomplished and we wouldn't be able to get much actual sorting done until he goes."

"Oh, well, that's all right then. Do you mind if I go along now? Daddy was making noises about starting out today if it could be arranged."

"No, of course not. Would you like me to drive you down? I can put your bike in the back of the car."

"No, that's all right."

"I'm sorry you won't get to meet Tony—particularly since you've been so involved in the work."

"Yes. It's a great pity. But another time." She was collecting her coat and beret quite hurriedly.

"By the way," I said, "Dr. Maitland came to see me this morning to look at my head—I had an adventure last night that I'll tell you about in full, glorious detail when you get back—and I mentioned to him idly that your father said he, the doctor, had been in practice in London. Apparently it was the north somewhere. Not that it matters."

Gwyneth was putting a scarf around her neck. "Did he say where in the north?" she asked, without looking up.

"No. I don't think so. I don't remember that he did."

She looked up. "What happened to your head?"

"It's a longish story involving Buff and ghoulies and ghosties and long-legged beasties going bump in the middle of the night. I know you're in a hurry, and I don't want to bend your ear."

"Oh, I can wait to hear that," Gwyneth said, putting on her coat. Her eyes were on my face with an odd intensity. They were dark brown eyes, I found myself thinking, as opposed to the doctor's, which were black.

And black eyes were an unusual color for someone in this part of the world to have. . . .

"What happened to your head?" she asked again.

As briefly as possible I told her everything until the moment I blacked out, leaving out only that my light had shone on shoes. "I thought—at first—somebody had whacked me on the head," I said. "But, of course, I don't really remember. And everybody else seems convinced that I banged my head on a piece of furniture and then finished off the job by falling downstairs."

"I wish you'd go home," she said.

"Why?" I asked, astonished. "Because I hit my head?"

"No—I can't talk about it. But everybody'd be much happier if you would."

"That doesn't sound very nice. Why would everybody be much happier?"

"I'm sorry. I didn't mean to be—not nice. I've loved working with you. But there are things you don't understand."

"What things? You sound as though you think somebody *did* knock me on the head deliberately." Perversely, having almost persuaded myself that I had knocked my own head on some furniture and was suffering delusions of memory as a result, I was disturbed that she should be arguing my original viewpoint.

"First there was the car last night," she said. "Now this. How many accidents of that kind do you want to have before you take the hint and go?"

She sounded so unlike the calm, good-humored young woman I had been working with for the past few days that it was hard to believe we were having this conversation.

"You really believe somebody's out to get me? You seem to forget that the car would have hit you before it hit me. You were on the outside."

"No. I haven't forgotten that." She looked up at me. "Janet, please be careful." Reaching out, she touched me on the arm. "Good-bye."

I went on sorting papers, wondering what had happened to Gwyneth in the course of the night. That the near accident could have shaken her badly, I was prepared to accept. Yet, when I left the rectory, she neither looked nor sounded as she had this morning.

I'd been working about another half hour when there were footsteps coming up the attic stairs and through the adjoining rooms. I glanced up to see Tony surveying the scene from the doorway.

"Good God!" he said. "I begin to see what you mean. I had no idea there'd be this much stuff. I heard it was far less—just a few boxes."

Something about what he said bothered me, and I hesitated while I tried to catch onto it. But whatever it was vanished, and I decided I was imagining things. "Well. I wrote you it was a mess. Didn't you believe me?"

He grinned. "I thought you were indulging in understandable exaggeration. I'd hate to think what shipping all this stuff air-mail would cost. My New England parsimoniousness cringes at the mere idea. You'd far better stay here and finish it."

"That's what I thought," I said, gratified that he'd discovered I was telling nothing but the truth.

"By the way," he said, "I called Cynthia just before I started from London, and she mentioned some message about some kind of goings on when I was a congressman. What was that all about?"

"Oh, it was just a bad joke. It was a page of a letter from my father commenting on your doing your stuff or some such in the teeth of pressure groups. I hadn't a clue as to what he was talking about. Do you?"

I looked up at him and found him watching me. "I'm afraid not," he said. "Are you sure you have it right? Sounds pretty garbled."

"Well, since you doubt me, just for that, let me show you." I went over to the place where I had carefully placed the thin sheet of paper along with one or two others I thought might be of particular interest. All the rest were there. But though I shifted through the shallow pile half a dozen times, and looked all over the floor, there wasn't a sign of that particular letter from my father. "That's odd," I said.

"What is?" His voice sounded sharp.

"The letter—it was only page two and a carbon—was here. I could swear it. In fact, I even bought a special box which I have downstairs. I was going to use it for letters and papers of particular interest, and it was that letter that inspired me to get it." I went through the papers once more. "But I can't find it."

"Maybe your helper—what did you say her name was? Gwyneth—put it in one of the larger cartons."

"Well, I suppose that's possible, on the theory that if something isn't where it should be look for it where it shouldn't be. But she was the one who held it out to show me as being different from the rest."

"Wouldn't hurt to look," Tony said.

I was familiar with this bulldog streak in Tony, but reflected rather sardonically that it was usually asserted over something more worthy of his doggedness. However, reminding myself that he was the boss, paying handsomely for my being here and for my work, I turned to the big carton in which all correspondence from the sixties had been placed.

"It'll take a while to go through this," I said, a little crossly.

"I'll help you." He had strolled over and was staring down at the sixties box as well as the others in the immediate vicinity. "That box doesn't seem to be as full as the others, anyway," he said.

"No. There seemed to be more correspondence in some years than in others. As a matter of fact, Gwyneth remarked on that. In fact, she even seemed to think, in her hasty run-through, that there might be correspondence missing out of some of the years. There were holes in the correspondence, as she put it."

"Interesting. Here, you take half and I'll take half." And he swooped down into the box, emerging with his arms stacked with papers of all kinds. "Where can I dump these?"

"On this table. I'll clear off a space."

Tony, I decided a while later, could rival Gwyneth in the speed and thoroughness with which he went through those letters, memos and carbons. "What a pity you were born rich, with a publishing house in the family," I said, watching him. "Somebody has lost a great executive secretary."

He laughed. "That's probably why good executive secretaries hate to work for me. I think I know their job better than they do. I can't see anything here like the letter you described."

"Well, it's really not that important, Tony. Not by itself. But I must say, as Father's future biographer, I would like to interview you on what the blazes he was talking about. What did he mean when he wrote about your doing your stuff in the teeth of pressure groups?"

There was a silence.

"What pressure groups are you talking about?" Tony asked then. His voice was pleasant. Yet I had the feeling he had suddenly become taut. "The civil rights groups? The Arabs? The Birchers? Dreyfus and his crowd—all of those headline hunters, paranoid to boot?"

"Whoa, Tony!" I said. "What set you off—? Oh, hello, Gideon."

Tony wheeled around. "Crepe soles for silence, Lightwood?" he said. There was a caustic edge to his question. Evidently Tony realized it because he gave a sort of laugh and said, "Sorry. You startled me."

"So I gather," Gideon's tone matched Tony's. The lines in his face looked deep this morning, I thought, and his mouth grim. "I came up to ask if there was anything I could do, or anything you wanted. I apologize for startling you. You may notice that old carpets cover a lot of the attic floor."

"Yes, of course. Sorry, old chap."

There was something going on here that I didn't understand, as though I had stumbled on some ancient antagonism between the two men.

"I also came to say," Gideon continued, "that if some carpenters start working just below the attic, near the stairs, pay no attention to them. They're doing some long-overdue repairs that I commissioned weeks ago. In this day and time they appear when they feel like it."

"I hope," I said pointedly, "since I was supposed to have fallen downstairs last night, that you are going to have the banister replaced. The brackets are still there. It's bad enough going up the stairs. Coming down is wicked."

"Yes, and, of course, the stairs are unusually high to allow for that—but none of that concerns you. I'm thinking of driving into Shrewsbury on business. Is there anything I can do for you while I'm there? Get for you, Janet?"

"Architecture is one of my minor hobbies, Lightwood," Tony said, glancing through the papers in front of him. "I noticed that the steps leading up here seemed unusually high, as though the distance from the floor here and the floor downstairs was greater than in the previous flights. Which is odd, as ceilings usually get lower the higher in a house you go."

"Oh, it's something to do with the flooring," Gideon said. "Not being particularly interested in architecture, I've never understood it. But one of the panels below the stairs started buckling in a peculiar way, so I got some construction experts in and they said they'd send along carpenters to fix it. Now they've telephoned to say they'll be out today. Mrs. Lowndes will show them where to work. I take it, by the way, Janet, that your troublesome dog is up here somewhere."

"No, of course not. I left her to go down to the kitchen after breakfast, the way I always do."

"Strange. Mrs. Lowndes said her food had been put out but she hadn't touched it. I assumed she was in your bedroom, but when I knocked, looking for you, and then opened the door, she wasn't there. Are you sure she's not up here?"

"I didn't realize you were that fond of her," Tony said lightly.

"I'm fond of peace in the household," Gideon said coldly. "Janet seems to feel there are dark plots against the wretched mongrel, and I'd like to forestall, before they occur, any—er—untoward accusations."

I didn't have to be Sherlock Holmes to figure that one out: Buff was missing, and Gideon was defending Sheila before I'd even had time to suggest she'd done anything. I put down the papers I was holding. "No need for anyone to jump before they're hit," I said. "I'll go and look for her."

"Yes, do. She's probably hiding somewhere, and it would be better—as well as more considerate—to be sure she hasn't gone on some ramble of her own before you set everyone by the ears."

The tone I read in Gideon's voice was one of arrogance and contempt for what he considered foolishness, and it had the effect on my temper of a lighted match to cleaning fluid, as Gideon should have known if he had taken one moment's thought, I reflected savagely as I plunged down the stairs.

"Hoi," Tony called. "What about these papers?"

"They'll have to wait," I called from halfway down the attic stairs.

Privately I cursed the day I had allowed that inept and brainless cur to get such a hold on my affections and sense of protectiveness. "You're being ridiculous," I said aloud to myself as I thrust open my bedroom door. "Buff!" I called.

But the only occupant of my room was the pretty housemaid that I had seen once before when she came up to the attic to announce luncheon.

"Buff—my dog—isn't in here, is she?" I asked.

The maid, who was making the bed, straightened. "Oh, no, miss. I haven't seen her this morning."

"I'm told she didn't eat her breakfast."

"No, miss. Mrs. Lowndes was speaking of it, and we were bothered because of what Parry said."

"What did Parry say?" I stood in the door, an unpleasant premonition settling down on me.

"Well, nothing really, miss. Only that he'd seen Evan Williams up in the woods behind the house."

My premonition, I thought unhappily, had proved well

founded. Every time that man's name was mentioned it betokened no good for small animals. "Why?" I asked nevertheless. "What would he do to Buff? He must know she belongs to the house here."

"Oh, yes, miss. But he often steals animals and then sells them back to the owner. Especially if he thinks you're rich."

That artless statement certainly fit in with what I had heard before. But it just fed my exasperation. "Well, why doesn't someone call him on it?"

"Call him, miss?" The pretty, childish face looked blank. I was, I realized, venting my irritation on the wrong person.

"Never mind. I'll go and find Sir Gideon."

I ran Gideon to earth in his bookroom. "The housemaid says that that charming tenant of yours, Evan something or other, has been seen in the vicinity and that he might have stolen Buff with the idea of selling her back to me."

"Yes. He's a strong upholder of the principle of free enterprise."

"Well, why do you let him get away with it?"

"We don't. He gets hauled up before the bench from time to time, when we have evidence on him of one kind or another. He grumbles and pays the fine and promises to be good—until next time."

"Do you think he has Buff?"

"Janet, how would I know? All I know is what Mrs. Lowndes told me. She could have hidden anywhere in the house."

"I don't believe she has. She's never done it before. Why should she? I'm worried that that horrible tenant of yours may do something to her. Where does he live?"

"You're making a big fuss—"

"All right. I'll ask someone else," I said, and started out the door.

"If you must go haring off after Evan Williams," Gideon said, "I'd better take you myself. He could swear blue he didn't have her with him, and then where would you be?"

"But he'd listen to you?"

"Oh, yes," Gideon said, closing a drawer in his desk and locking it with a key he put back in his pocket. "He'll listen to me." He glanced at me. "Are you ready to go out, or do you want to get your coat?"

"I won't be five minutes," I said. Running upstairs, I snatched my raincoat and bag, went up to tell Tony where we were going, and rejoined Gideon in not much more than that.

Leaving the house by the side door, we ran into Roger, who seemed to be coming from the direction of the stables.

"Where are you two off to?" Roger asked.

Gideon replied, "We're off to find Janet's dog, who seems to have disappeared."

"Good heavens! She shows a marked talent for getting herself in trouble. Well—good hunting!"

"Why should Evan Williams listen to you if he won't listen to anybody else?" I asked, picking up the conversation where we'd left off.

"Because he's my tenant, living in what is technically my cottage, on my land. If worse comes to worse, I can evict him, and he knows it."

"I can't understand why you haven't done it before, what with his stolen animals and his traps and his generally unlovely ways."

"That's because you don't come from around here— or from around anywhere where people have lived for hundreds of years. Evan Williams' father's people have lived in that cottage for almost as long as Lightwoods have lived at The Hall."

"He seems to have some queer power over people."

"That's because his mother was a gypsy, and although they won't exactly admit it, some of the local people think he can put the curse on them and their houses. So when he steals an animal and asks for money in return, they consider a few pence, or even a pound or two, a cheaper price than to have him work one of his spells."

By this time we were in Gideon's car, driving out the back way to the main road. "It's hard to associate that,"

I said, "with such contemporary signs as the television aerials and the jeans I see in every village I drove through."

"People who live where their ancestors have always lived manage to amalgamate modern customs with ancient superstitions quite well. Living in New York nearly all your life as you have," he said, "you'd probably have a hard time understanding that."

"You're right," I replied rather brusquely. "I would."

We drove in silence for a while. At some point Gideon turned off the main road onto a narrower one that wound around curves and up and down hills but which climbed steadily into wilder and barer country. The houses and farms got fewer and fewer and I realized after a while that I had seen no cultivated fields, just slopes with sheep dotted here and there.

"Is this still part of your property?" I asked firmly.

"Yes. I'm taking you the long way around because it's a nicer drive. We're heading towards the northwestern part of it. The boundary lies about two miles on the other side of Williams' cottage."

"Do you think," I said, voicing something that had been bothering me increasingly since we had started, "that he'd do something to Buff before we arrived?"

"I seriously doubt it. Why should he? He'd not only not get any money from us, he'd earn my displeasure, and he knows it."

"Nevertheless and despite what you say, I'm still not clear as to why he'd do all this—given the fact that Buff lives at The Hall and now belongs to one of your guests. I should think the risk would be too great."

"I told you," Gideon said in a reasonable voice that made me want to kick him, "he's a believer in free enterprise. And as any businessman will assure you, free enterprise entails risk."

"I find the combination of free enterprise entrepreneur and gypsy worker of ancient spells very hard to put in the same package. I suppose you're going to say that that's because I don't come from around here."

"I can also say it's because you lack imagination. After

all, you have the same not too far away from your part of the world. I seem to remember driving through parts of New York City and seeing windows in Puerto Rican sections advertising Espiritism—right there in your center of urban sophistication. And you find it all the time in the Caribbean: tourists happily spending money to watch voodoo rituals, at least some of which the native population takes seriously."

"I suppose so," I said grudgingly.

"Here's the road to Williams' cottage," Gideon said, turning the car into what looked like a dirt track. The track started on what looked like a bare, bleak part of the moor, but dipped then, following the line of the hill into a shallow valley with bushes and trees dotting the fields. The track, which was narrow, got narrower.

Gideon drew to a stop near a bend shielded by trees where the track became abruptly much narrower. "We'll have to do the rest of the way on foot," he said. "I can just turn here, but not if we go further."

"It looks like extra earth has been dumped on the side of the road so that a car can't get up it."

"That's undoubtedly Williams' doing. I'm sure he'd rather have his callers approach on foot where he can keep an eye on them. Can you get out all right?" Gideon got out his side and started to come around.

I eased my door open. "I can manage," I called to him, and spoke too soon. As I wiggled out the narrow opening of the door, which was wedged against the dirt bank, I felt my foot slip against the soft earth and lost my balance.

"Ouch!" I said, as my hand hit some sharp, slaty stones buried in the dirt. It was an undignified sound but it saved our lives. As Gideon started forward past the front of the car to help me, a shot rang out. There was a whizzing past my ear as the bullet missed him by inches.

"Run!" Gideon yelled as more shots sounded.

I felt my hand yanked forward, and I was dragged up over the dirt bank, down into a ditch on the other side that ran between the bank and the field, and then pulled forward into the shelter of trees.

# nine

||||||||||||||||||||||||||||||||||||||||||||||||||||||||||||||||||||||||||||||||||||||||||||||||||||||||||||||||||||||||||||||

"My God!" I said. All of a sudden my knees were shaking. "Somebody tried to kill us!"

"Yes," Gideon said grimly.

"But who?" I asked.

"I'd rather like to know that myself." He glanced at where I was still rather crouched in the narrow ditch. "Are you all right? Did you twist your foot?"

"No. It just slipped."

"If it hadn't, we'd both be dead. I'd like to know where that bullet came from."

I got shakily to my feet and looked in the direction he was facing. I found we were at the edge of a little wood thick enough so that I could see neither straight ahead nor to my right. "Someone can see us," I said. "But we can't see whoever it is."

"No," Gideon said slowly. "I don't think anyone can see us now, but they—whoever it was—could see us when we started to get out of the car. The immediate question is, does whoever fired that shot know that we got away?"

"That *is* rather an important question," I said sarcastically, trying hard to keep my teeth from chattering. "If they thought we hadn't, they might be heartened enough to have another try."

Gideon turned and looked at me. "I want you to stay here. Get down in the ditch. You'll be shielded by the shrubs and trees. I'm going up ahead."

"Are you crazy? Whoever shot at us is up ahead."

"I'll be shielded by the trees until I cut across to where the road doubles back. Besides, I have a feeling that whoever fired that shot is not straight ahead."

"Maybe not. But that doesn't mean he won't have another try as you stroll down the lane."

"If he's going to try again, he can do so just as easily if I go back the way we came. Behind the car the track is equally exposed. And I don't think that the person concerned has hung around to see how his efforts came out."

"What makes you think that?"

He hesitated. "Intuition. What you call a hunch."

"Your intuition wasn't too alert in coming down the lane."

"No. You're right. I didn't count on— Anyway, I think he's gone. Stay here." Gideon put one foot out of the ditch.

I got up with him. "Not on your life."

Gideon turned back. "I'm not taking you with me," he said firmly.

"Maybe not. But you can't prevent me from following you. I don't relish going up ahead—or back towards the main road, for that matter. But least of all do I relish being left here to be picked off in case your hunch is wrong. Besides, how do I know it's not me they're after, instead of you?"

"You'll be much safer here—and I'll be much better off not having to worry about you."

"Well, I'm sorry. But I'm not going to be stuck here. If you think the man has gone, then we'll both be safe."

I could tell, by the set of his jaw and the way his lips were clamped together, that he was not at all pleased by my refusing to stay put. "Very well," he said finally. "But listen to me, Janet. You will do exactly as I tell you. If I say fall flat on your face, you'll do it, without question, and immediately. If you don't give me your word about that I will see to it that you will stay where I choose to leave you, and there will be nothing you can do about it. If you think I would hesitate to knock you out and tie up your hands and feet if I thought it necessary, then you don't know me very well."

"With what?" I asked rather brazenly, more to give myself courage than anything else.

"I have a tie, a belt and a handkerchief. You have a scarf. Don't worry. I'd find a way. Now stay immediately behind me."

Without waiting to see whether I agreed or not he started forward, walking along the ridge above the ditch, but well behind the trees.

It was impossible to tell from where we were how wide the belt of trees was. Common sense, and a vague memory of how the road bent, indicated that the wood would not be deep. Yet though the trees were neither particularly high nor thick, there was an eerie quality about the silence. The slight breeze I had been aware of before had fallen and there was, as we walked, a stillness, which grew more marked as we entered the wood, walking on grass and leaves and earth. Once, without thinking, I stepped alongside Gideon.

"Get back," he snapped in a whisper.

Noting the almost soundless way Gideon walked, I thought about Tony's sneering comment, "Crepe soles for silence, Lightwood?" because Gideon had a countryman's ability to walk without noise, whereas every step I took seemed to rustle and scatter leaves and twigs. The slight sun of the morning had faded by the time we had left The Hall. Now I had the impression, from what little sky I could see among the tops of the trees, that it was suddenly overcast.

As abruptly as we entered the wood, we came to its edge. One minute we were surrounded by trees, the next, we were looking across a clearing to a low, thatched cottage. I peered around Gideon's arm. The cottage bore all the signs of being inhabited. There was the sound of animals in the back—a dog whining, the honk of a pig—and a wisp of smoke trickled from the chimney. Yet I had never seen such a desolate-looking place. A little way behind the house the ground rose steeply in a wooded slope. As we stood there, watching, there was, from behind the house and its back enclosure, the noise of a car starting up and driving off away from us up through the trees at the back where a thin line, marking a break in the trees, indicated there might be a road.

"I think," Gideon said, "that could be our friend leaving us."

"That's nice," I said. "Can we depend on it?"

"Well, now's the time to find out." And he started over the ditch and down to the road which ran right below.

I jumped down after him. "What do we do now?"

Gideon glanced down at me. "What we came to do. To buy your pet back from Evan Williams, if he's there."

I had by no means forgotten Buff, but the events of the past half hour—such as being shot at—had distracted my attention. Now my concern for her pushed back. "Do you think she's there?" I asked it anxiously, because for some reason I couldn't define, I felt strongly that she wasn't.

"We'll soon find out."

We crossed the track and up the worn-looking turf to the cottage door. The moment Gideon knocked, the dog at the back started to bark frantically. After waiting for a few seconds Gideon knocked again, this time more loudly. Then he laid his ear to the scarred wood of the door.

"Can you hear anything?" I asked.

"No. I think I'll see if I can get in." The door was fastened by an old-fashioned latch. Suppressing it, Gideon pushed open the door and walked in. I followed. Gideon's tall, broad-shouldered form prevented me from seeing anything right away, but nothing could stop the stench of the room from hitting my nostrils.

"Piew!" I said. It was a smell combined of animals,

food and unwashed humans. Gideon moved then, and I could see that the entire cottage was one low-ceilinged room, dimly lit by tiny, dirty windows. An unusually large fireplace, with various black pots around it and a roasting skewer above it, indicated where the household cooking was done. In a corner was a sagging bed on top of which was a pillow without a pillowcase and a torn and dirty blanket. Skins hung from the beams, and off to one side on a chest lay small dead animals—a rabbit, a couple of squirrels and what looked like a badger.

Anger and nausea seemed to rise in me at the same time. "What a horrible place," I said.

"Yes. It's not very toothsome. I wonder where Williams is. By the looks of things he might have left hurriedly."

"Why do you say that?"

He pointed to the fireplace. One of the pots was on the hearth. Beside it, a cracked plate was half covered with food, a bent spoon laying across it. "Something tells me he was about to eat. Also, his beer on the table there is half drunk." I looked over at the table. Sure enough, a tumbler half full of dark liquid sat at what could have been called, at a liberal pinch, a place setting.

"The sanitation," I said, breathing through my mouth, "is not all it might be."

Gideon glanced at me. "I don't think," he said wryly, "that Williams was a believer in the maxim 'Cleanliness is next to Godliness.'"

"Well, if he's your tenant, why didn't you do something about it?"

"Because he wouldn't have stood for it. I have a hard enough time scraping together the funds to repair the houses and cottages of those who want it done. He may be my tenant, but he has the right to live the way he wants."

"Including killing all those animals?"

"If he got them by poaching—and it could be proved—then we could fine him. But there are areas where he can legitimately take a gun."

"I don't think there's anything legitimate about killing animals."

"I'm sympathetic to that viewpoint, but the sportsmen of old England would rise up in horror at you. And from what I hear, those in your own country would, too."

"Yes," I said unhappily. "I'm well aware of it. I wonder where Buff is. She doesn't look to be here."

Gideon went around the room peering in the dim corners under the table, the bed and back of a couple of chests. "No, she doesn't." There was an odd, grim note in his voice.

"You sound," I said, "as though you were quite sure she was."

"Well, I explained that this morning. Stealing animals and selling them back at a profit is one of Williams' favorite tricks. I'm going to look out back."

He opened a door to the left of the hearth and I followed him out. The same sense of desolation that had struck me when I first saw the cottage washed over me again. A rickety-looking fence surrounded an area partly covered with grass and part bare dirt. In one corner, fenced off by posts and chicken wire, was what looked to be a pen occupied by a heavy, dirty-looking sow. On the opposite side chickens pecked at the unrewarding ground. Frantically barking in the middle, where she was chained to a post, was a bitch with the heavy teats that suggested multiple litters of puppies. I went over and looked at her. She stopped barking, whined a little and ducked her head when I put out my hand. She was bigger than Buff, with longer ears and heavier build that suggested hound as well as terrier in her ancestry. Nevertheless there was the same pointed muzzle and tan with black shading, and something about the expression in her eyes that made me say, "I bet this is Buff's mother."

Gideon glanced over. "Probably."

"She looks like she's had many families."

"She undoubtedly has."

"I wonder what happened to all the other puppies."

"Drowned, most likely, those he couldn't sell."

Absently I stroked the bitch's head as I looked around every yard of the enclosure, unhappily confirming something I already knew. "Buff's not here."

"No." Gideon was standing in the middle, his hands in his pockets. "She isn't. Nor, obviously, is Williams."

"Do you think . . . do you suppose . . . that he's taken Buff somewhere to try and sell her?"

"I don't know what to think."

"But why should he? He must have known I'd buy her back, for anything he could get from anyone else."

Gideon didn't say anything.

"Wouldn't he?" I persisted.

"Wouldn't he what?" Gideon took his hands out of his pockets and strolled towards the back of the fence.

"Wouldn't your charming friend Williams know he could get as much money from me for Buff as he could from somebody else," I said. Between exasperation and fear my voice was louder than I intended. "Or would he," I went on, giving words to the anxiety that was growing in me, "think that I would simply accuse him of stealing Buff and not only not pay him, but hand him over to the police, or get you to?"

"I don't really know," Gideon replied after a minute as though his mind were on something else. "I hadn't thought."

"Well, then, I wish you'd think," I said. "This is what we came for, to get Buff. You were the one who discovered she was missing, and you were the one who thought Williams might have her. Now you act as though you didn't remember any of it."

He turned towards me. "Has your monomania on the subject of Buff made you forget that we—either you or I or both of us—were shot at by someone who was firing from somewhere over among those trees behind the cottage? And that all of that could have something to do with the fact that neither Williams nor your dog is here, though I strongly suspect, as I said when we were in the cottage, that they were here until a short while ago?"

"You say 'they.' What makes you think that Buff was here, too?"

He pointed down to the ground not far from the fence. I saw then the tin dish and the smaller, cracked saucer. "It's not what could be called incontrovertible proof. But

I suspect the tin dish belongs to his own dog and he added the saucer for yours. It's at least a suggestion that she was here."

I stared at the two dishes. After a while I said, "Are you saying that Williams was the one who shot at us—and if so, why should he? Or do you think he ran away—with Buff—when he heard someone else shooting?"

"I'm not saying either one or the other. I'm only stating the obvious facts that we were shot at and that both Williams and your dog are absent. We may as well go."

He turned to go back through the cottage.

"Should I just leave this dog here?"

"Of course. We have no right to interfere with his property."

"Don't you think we could at least let her off the chain?"

"And what if she ran away?"

"I wish she would," I said angrily. "She doesn't look happy."

"But nor does she appear ill-used. I don't see a mark on her, do you?"

I had to admit that I didn't. Nevertheless I grumbled, "If I took his dog I could maybe use her to get mine back."

"If you think sentimental attachment to anything, animal or human, would move Williams more than the thought of ready cash, then you have less common sense than I thought. Come on, let's go."

I followed him back through the house. "What about leaving a note?" I asked.

Gideon looked at me in some irritation. "I doubt if reading notes is one of Williams' accomplishments. But do so, by all means, if you want."

I tore a sheet off the small notebook I carry in my bag, located a pencil and stood poised for a second, trying to compose a simple, straightforward and unmistakable message. Finally, I settled for PLEASE RETURN MY DOG. I WILL PAY, all in block letters.

"Do you think he'll get the drift?" I asked Gideon, holding it out.

"He'll understand the word 'pay' with no trouble at all. You do realize, don't you, that, regardless of how the dog is returned to you, you're obligated now to hand over some cash?"

"Yes. That's all right."

I put the note on the filthy table and weighted it down at one corner by the half-empty glass of beer. "He can't miss it there," I said.

We walked out the front door of the cottage. "Why don't we call in at the police station on the way back and report that Buff's missing, and perhaps offer a reward?"

"If we can use the car."

"Why shouldn't we?"

"I have a feeling that some of those bullets hit a tire. If so, we have a long walk ahead of us before we can get near enough a telephone to have someone pick us up, let alone call on the police."

We went on in silence until we came to the car. Even a few yards off I saw both of the front wheels resting on their rims, the tires flattened out beneath.

"Well," Gideon said, looking at it. "It seems I was right. It's going to have to be shanks' mare. Let's cut across the field here to the road."

It was a strange walk under the overcast sky that looked as though it might empty itself of rain at any moment. The track climbed steadily, wide enough here for a car. As we pulled out of the small valley where the cottage was hidden, the trees thinned out. Far in the distance, green moors, dotted here and there with patches of brown and a purplish blue, climbed to the low horizon. Back behind us the air had been heavy and still, but as we pulled up onto the hill I felt the occasional stirring of a breeze against my face.

"How far are we, actually, from a telephone, do you think?" I asked after a while.

"Not too far as the crow flies. But it's going to rain at any moment, and I think we'd better stick to the road. Perhaps six or seven miles." A true New Yorker, I calculated this in blocks. "Ye gods, that's more than one hundred and twenty blocks. If you started off in Greenwich Village you'd end up in the middle of Harlem."

For the first time that morning he smiled. "But you won't find it as hard going as concrete pavements."

"Well," I said philosophically, "I suppose I should be glad I put loafers on this morning."

Gideon glanced at my feet. "They don't look too sturdy to me. Brogues would have been better."

"But I didn't know I was going to have the pleasure of a cross-country ramble, to say nothing of being shot at." I shifted my shoulder bag higher onto my shoulder. "Gideon—what happened? And why did it happen?"

"I don't have any answers, just a few ideas. But that's all they are. Janet, if I asked you, would you go home immediately, back to New York, tomorrow?"

I looked at him. "Why?"

"I'm not prepared to give you my reason."

A shiver of fear went through me. "You think it's me they're after?"

"You talk about 'they.' Who do you think 'they' are?" He turned and looked at me as we walked.

It was not until he asked that, that I realized I had, in my mind, been avoiding a great number of signs pointing in a direction where I didn't wish to look, including my apparent obliviousness to the shots that had so nearly finished us off. Another way of putting it was that I had come up against a brick wall. And the brick wall was Gideon. It was Gideon's shoes I saw up in the attic right before I received that blow on the head, and it was Gideon who had almost convinced me that I had done it to myself by knocking my head on a piece of furniture. Whatever my feelings for him might be—and I had consistently shied away from any examination of them— I could no longer avoid the strong evidence that whatever danger lay at The Hall for me, came from him.

But nor could I sidestep the fact that the bullets that had missed us by inches had come at us—or me—while Gideon was with me. But a small treacherous voice within me said, they *had* missed us. Perhaps, instead of its being an accident that the bullets had missed us, that had been the whole intent from the beginning, a charade that Gideon had set up with——? With whom? The missing Williams, possibly.

The skies suddenly delivered themselves of the promised rain, the soft, not very soaking rain that seems to fall only in the British Isles. There was nothing to do, no umbrella to put up. As a slight and useless gesture I raised the collar of my raincoat. After a while, I knew, my hair would coil into ringlets all over my head, a tendency I'd spent all of my adolescence and most of my twenties trying to repress. Well, I thought, it would just have to curl. I glanced up. The horizon seemed to have come much nearer, and the green fields had a drenched look. Only the sheep on the slopes appeared indifferent, cropping away, their wool more than a match for the falling wet. At least, I thought, as we squelched off the track and turned onto the paved road, I'd be a little drier underfoot than on my head.

Almost against my will my mind went back to its unhappy maze. Wasn't it Gideon who uncharacteristically drew my attention to the fact that Buff was missing, who suggested that we find her at Evan Williams' cottage, and who had insisted on driving over? But why? One answer seemed obvious enough: to get rid of me. Hadn't he just suggested that I leave for New York immediately? But again, why?

Even as that word echoed in my head the image of Sheila slid across the screen in my mind. Sheila, who, in the words of the rector, saw any halfway personable woman as so much of a rival that she extended her dislike and jealousy to a particularly inoffensive dog. I thought about the striking-looking governess and the moments when her power seemed almost palpable, when her need for domination pulled compellingly on everyone else in the room. If Sheila Maitland wanted to get rid of me, she would certainly make it her business to see that Gideon did also. But surely there were easier ways than this elaborate setup. As we trudged on the path that rose to meet the moor, I toyed with this idea, viewing it from various angles, but nagged also by something I couldn't quite get hold of, something I almost remembered. Then oddly, and without any reason that I could think of, there appeared in my mind the attic room stacked with the big tan boxes and piles of papers . . . papers, some of which appeared to be missing. . . .

"You haven't answered my question," Gideon's voice beside me said. "Who do you think 'they' are?"

I couldn't bring myself to say, you, you and Sheila Maitland, whether out of cowardice or for lack of logical reason (apart from being in his house, what did the deMaury papers have to do with Gideon, let alone his son's governess?) or for some other unacknowledged reason, I couldn't be sure. Instead, I took refuge in the debater's trick.

"Who do *you* think 'they' are?" I asked. "After all, it's your land, your house, your tenant."

"But you seem to be the one to whom things are happening. You are the one—according to your story—who got whacked on the head last night. You're the one who nearly got run down by the car. . . . Hello, I wonder who that is. What's the matter?"

I had stopped still, halted by two things that seemed strangely linked: the car lights coming towards us, flashing on and off, and Gideon's words: *You're the one who nearly got run down by the car.* But I didn't have time to sort anything out because the approaching car had drawn up.

"Hello," Roger said, his face sticking out of the passenger window. "What are you two up to? Where's your car?"

"It suffered an accident," Gideon said. "Someone was shooting up in the trees around the back road behind Williams' cottage and hit a couple of tires."

"Good God! You could have been killed!"

"Yes. That rather occurred to us. What brings you here?"

"There was a trunk call from London. Someone wants you to call back before two o'clock. Bridewell said you had set off for Williams' cottage so I came to hurry you up. Did you find Buff?"

I was aware that Roger was looking at me, but my mind was still in a turmoil.

"No," Gideon said. "Nor did we find Williams."

"Odd," Roger commented. "Or do I mean two plus two equals four?"

"Meaning Williams did the shooting?" Gideon asked. "But why should he want to dispatch us?"

Gideon opened the passenger door of Roger's car. "Get in, Janet," he said.

As I crawled into the rather cramped bucket seat, I reflected sadly how strange it was that only because it was Roger's car, and because Roger was driving it, did I feel safe.

"By the way," Roger said, after he'd turned the car and we were on the way back, "I should have mentioned this first thing, perhaps, but Benedict took a turn after you left."

"Yes, I rather think you should," Gideon said from the back. I could hear the sudden anxiety in his voice. "What do you mean by turn?"

"I'm not entirely sure. I do know that Sheila was rather hastily sending for her father. He's there now."

There was a silence. "You mean," Gideon said in a sharp voice, "you didn't see whatever it was that alarmed Sheila enough to send for her father?"

"I'm afraid not, Gideon. I did try to ask, but she was rushing for the phone, and all I heard was her end of the conversation in which she said what I told you—that he'd taken a turn for the worse."

"But you said Dr. Maitland was there now, which means Sheila was off the phone and you had time to talk to her."

"I should have said I assumed Dr. Maitland was there now, because Sheila said he was on his way, and he'd certainly have arrived by this time. But all I actually heard was what she said to her father—that Benedict had taken a turn for the worse."

"I see."

After a few minutes Gideon said, "You don't know who the trunk call was from?"

"I don't think—oh, yes, it was someone named George Tillbury, who said he was calling from your club."

"Oh. Probably something to do with the annual dinner."

I saw Roger glance at Gideon in the rear-view mirror. "That's pretty expensive—to call about an annual dinner."

"Well, it's the big shindig of the year."

We returned through the back road, leading up the hill behind the house and down into the courtyard. Gideon was out of the car almost before it stopped, leaping up the shallow steps to the side door.

"I wonder what happened to Benedict," I said to Roger.

"I didn't like to say so to Gideon," Roger replied, starting to back the car into one of the open garages, "but I heard Benedict shouting this morning, and he must have been yelling at the top of his voice because I heard him from the floor below."

"Why didn't you want to say that to Gideon? Surely as Benedict's father he has a right to know. In fact, he should know."

"Because Gideon gets very upset when Benedict puts on a show like that. It's not the kind of pukka sahib behavior that he expects of his son."

I thought about Roger's statement for a while. "That's pretty old-fashioned, don't you think? I thought that kind of thinking went out before World War Two—and certainly when the Empire finally came to an end."

"Well, you've been around Gideon now for some time. Don't you think he's pretty archaic in his notions?"

I didn't answer that for a minute. Then, "Some of them," I admitted.

"And he's even more archaic in some of the punishment he metes out, too." Roger put on the hand brake and opened his door.

I got out, too, closing the door beside the passenger seat, and walked to the front of the car where Roger was standing. "Just what do you mean by that?"

"He was brought up not to spare the rod. It wasn't spared on him when he was a boy, either at home or at school, and he feels that he should—er—chastise his son the same way."

"Even though Benedict is . . . is . . . crippled?"

"He wasn't always crippled. Now look here, don't run away with the idea that Gideon is a monster. Caning is not considered the black sin over here that I gather it is in your country. It's certainly done in the best schools. I had my share, too."

"I still think it's pretty inhuman for a boy who can't walk."

"The fact that he can't walk doesn't mean he isn't spoiled. In fact, quite honestly, I think Benedict's used that—his being lame, I mean. And I think one of Sheila's tasks has been to try and steer the middle path: not to spoil him too much on one hand, but not to punish him too severely on the other."

I strolled over to Tony's car parked on the other side of the garage. Roger joined me.

"Bridewell does himself pretty well in cars, doesn't he? That's not your usual run-of-the-mill bus you get from a car rental agency."

"Maybe he owns one and keeps it here. He's over here often enough," I replied.

"Perhaps. I'm going back in. I want to see what the verdict is on Benedict. Are you coming?"

"Yes," I said, abandoning the car with an unsatisfied feeling as though there were an unanswered question. But there was something on my mind far more important. "You know, I've seen the way Gideon talks to Benedict. I just don't buy this statement of yours that sometimes he's too soft, spoils him."

"You haven't seen them together the way I have. I think it's to make up for the fact that Gideon feels guilty about losing his temper and wielding the rod a bit too vigorously. It's very hard for him you know, Benedict being the heir and all that."

Unfortunately, I thought, as we walked towards the house, that part of it sounded all too true. As we started mounting the steps I said suddenly, "I thought you didn't like Sheila Maitland."

"I don't particularly, why?" Roger, who was a few steps above me, stopped and looked down.

"Because I was surprised that you spoke kind words about her when you said she was trying to steer the middle path with Benedict."

"Well, the fact that I may dislike her, particularly in the role of my future sister-in-law, doesn't mean I can't be fair to her."

It was odd, I thought, staring up into Roger's face, how different he looked. He didn't seem at all the amiable, volatile young man, but a grim, rather frightening stranger.

"You needn't look so . . . so punitive. I just asked a question."

Quickly then his face changed. He turned away. "Sorry. I suppose I'm like Gideon in that"—he glanced down at me—"in that I believe in giving the devil his or her due."

I followed him into the house, through the various rooms and into the central hall. There we found Sheila Maitland, her father and Gideon.

"I must insist, Lightwood," the doctor was saying. "This is a very good nursing home. Benedict will have the closest care. He needs to be under the most careful, controlled condition—"

"He's not leaving here," Gideon said flatly. He turned his head a little as Roger and I approached.

Sheila put her hand on his arm. "I completely understand how you feel. But I do think that what Daddy says is the best for Benedict. You weren't here when he passed out—"

"He's come around now," Gideon said. "I don't want him away from home."

"These diabetic comas—" Dr. Maitland started.

Gideon turned towards him. "But you've just given him an injection which brought him out of it."

"Yes, but I feel most strongly that he should be where his injections, his insulin intake, to say nothing of his diet, can be most carefully supervised."

"You have Sheila here to watch over him at all times.

His diet comes under Sheila's eye. No tray goes to his room that she doesn't see."

"But, Gideon," Sheila said gently, "I'm not here during the evening. You know how boys are. He probably persuades one of the servants to bring him something he shouldn't have from time to time, and as we all know, he isn't always confined to a couch. He can walk himself."

"If anyone has brought him something he shouldn't have—or anything at all without checking with me first, when you're not in the house—then whoever it is has violated my strictest rule." Gideon looked towards the doctor. "When Sheila's away no one is allowed to take him anything without asking me first. I repeat. Benedict is not leaving the house."

"Then I must protest your interference," Dr. Maitland said. He lifted his bag off the hall table. "As Benedict's personal physician I feel responsible for his care. I will not be answerable if he has some kind of turn for the worse when neither Sheila nor I is here."

"Sheila's welcome to stay here at night. She often does. However, I don't think there's any need. Tell me what I'm to do, and I'll have a bed made up for myself in the room next to Benedict's."

"That won't be necessary," Sheila said. "Gideon, I think you're making a serious mistake not letting Daddy and me drive Benedict to the nursing home. He needn't stay there long—just a week or two. But it could make all the difference to him."

"Just as a matter of curiosity—not because I've changed my mind—what nursing home is this you're talking of? St. James's Hospital?"

"No, it's a private one where I'm one of the consulting physicians," the doctor said. "I have nothing against St. James's. It's an excellent hospital, but Benedict is a private patient, and I think he'd do better in a private home."

"It can be the best home in the country," Gideon said, "but Benedict is not leaving here."

"Then I cannot be held responsible," Dr. Maitland said. It occurred to me that he was angrier than I had realized. The hand down by his side seemed to be shaking. How very pig-headed of Gideon, I thought, but how well his blind stubbornness on this point fitted in with what Roger had said about his see-saw swing from over-severity to overpermissiveness brought on by guilt. I had seen something of that tenacious clinging to a point for the sake of clinging in my father. And it was, to my mind, one of his least lovable qualities.

"Why don't you let Benedict go, Gideon?" I said, knowing I had no right to interfere, and would most likely be reminded of that fact.

I was. Gideon swung around. "This really doesn't concern you in any way, Janet."

Gideon frequently had a forbidding expression on his face, but I had never seen him so formidably intimidating as he was now.

"All right," I said, undaunted. "But I think you're being pig-headed to Benedict's disadvantage."

There was a pause. I could almost feel his tightly controlled rage. "A while ago, Janet, at Williams' cottage, I suggested you leave tomorrow for New York. At that moment I was concerned for your safety. Now I am repeating that request, with the added information that if you interfere with Benedict in any way whatsoever, I will see to it that you leave immediately—and as we've discussed before, I can do so very easily."

I have a fairly volatile temper of my own, and was about to respond in kind when I glanced up the stairs. Coming down in a leisurely fashion from the landing was Tony.

"May I be of any help of any kind?" he asked. And such was the power of his personality that for a moment the tension in the hall seemed to relax.

"None," Gideon said briefly. I saw then that he had not been touched by Tony's calming influence.

There was a short silence. Then Tony, who was standing on about the fourth step from the bottom, turned to me. "Did you find your dog?" he asked.

"No," I said. Buff had by no means slid to the back of my mind, but to worry over her aloud when Gideon was so upset—and understandably so—seemed, if nothing else, tactless.

"I'm sorry," Tony said. My heart warmed towards him. I smiled at him and he smiled back.

"Yes," Gideon said briefly, "we'll have to look for her somewhere else."

"And besides not finding Buff," I started, about to tell Tony about the shooting, when the telephone rang.

Sheila was nearest. But while she was reaching for it Gideon took one long step and picked up the receiver. "Yes, hello. Yes, speaking. Hello, George. I was going to ring you back. . . . Yes. . . . Unfortunately, no. . . ."

Since Gideon's end of the conversation seemed as pointless as most half-heard telephone conversations, I turned back towards Tony, who had come down the rest of the stairs. "Did you find the carbon we were looking for when I left?"

"No, as a matter of fact, I didn't."

"That's too bad. I wonder what on earth could have happened to it."

Gideon hung up the receiver and turned away from the telephone. "By the way, Bridewell, did those carpenters turn up?"

"No. They didn't. It seems to be an international certainty, these days. If people are supposed to turn up, they don't. Or they do at some crazy hour when they're not expected to." He hesitated, then went on. "I realize you all have serious and worrying things on your mind, but I was wondering if I could invite you to dinner this evening at an inn I know of not far from here. It's plain, but excellent food, and they have a good wine cellar. You probably know the place better than I do, Lightwood."

"Are you talking about The Golden Pheasant?" Gideon asked.

"Yes, that's the one. One of my authors entertained me there on my last trip. It would be a great pleasure for me if I could take you all there."

"Sounds like a sound idea," Roger said. He eyed Gideon and seemed to backtrack a little. "But it's up to you and Sheila, Gideon."

"Well, I must be getting on," Dr. Maitland said. His one hand, I noticed, still seemed to be shaking. Vaguely I wondered if he were at the onset of one of the degenerative diseases that strike the aged. Then I felt embarrassed when I saw him glance in my direction and notice me watching him. If there were any doubt in my mind as to whether or not he saw me looking at his hand, it was removed when he brought that hand up to the other and grasped it around the handle of his bag.

"Nonsense, Dr. Maitland," Tony said. "The invitation includes you, of course."

"I really don't think . . ." Dr. Maitland said hesitantly.

"Oh, come, Daddy." Sheila linked her arm in his. "You haven't had a night off since I don't know when. Gideon, please persuade him." There was an uncomfortable pause. I saw the red-haired young woman flush a little. "I realize we're not in agreement on what's best for Benedict at this moment, but there's no necessity in letting that . . . argument . . . spoil other things, is there?" And with her other hand she reached out and touched Gideon on the arm.

I had to hand it to her, I thought. It was a graceful, reconciling gesture. And it worked. Gideon seemed almost visibly to relax. "No, of course not. All right." He glanced at Tony with a somewhat rueful smile. "If my acceptance leaves something to be desired, my apologies. As you can gather, I have other things on my mind. But—thank you. I accept. Always supposing that Benedict remains all right. I'd like the doctor to have another look at him. You say your injection has brought him round and leveled his insulin to the right amount. Do you think he'll have another attack?"

There was another short pause. "I can't go back on what I said before," he started. But his daughter stopped him.

"Daddy, we'll talk about it another time." She pressed her hand against his arm. "For now I think you can assure Gideon that Benedict won't take another turn today." She turned back to Gideon, "Actually, considering what he's been through today, he's most likely asleep. I really believe it would be better if he were allowed to continue. But I'll take Daddy up just in case he's awake, and he can give you a final assurance."

"I'll go with you," Gideon said.

"Yes, do, and then you can see for yourself."

The three of them went upstairs. Tony, Roger and I were left in the hall.

"I must say," Tony said in a slightly lower tone to me, "I really don't see what Lightwood can object to in having his son taken to what I gather is a highly regarded private nursing home." He glanced at Roger. "What do you think?"

"I'm rather inclined to agree with you. But then, as Janet and I were discussing before, Gideon is rather unbalanced in his treatment of Benedict: the Victorian father one minute, and overcosseting him the next. It's difficult all around." He paused. "As Janet knows, I'm not Sheila Maitland's greatest admirer, but I do think she has a difficult time as far as that aspect of her job is concerned."

"Well," Tony said. "I'm glad he's agreed to go out later. Janet, is there anything I can do to help you find that hound of yours?"

"Nothing I can think of. I'll go out and see Mrs. Lowndes. Perhaps she might have some helpful suggestion. All of which reminds me, whatever happened to lunch?" I glanced at my watch. "It's two o'clock."

"Well, with you and Gideon gone for heaven knew how long," Roger said, "Sheila asked Mrs. Lowndes to serve some sandwiches and coffee in the library, which she did. I'm sorry, I never thought about your lunch. I suppose Gideon hasn't had any either, but we thought you might go on into Shrewsbury after you'd found Buff. I'm sure Mrs. Lowndes would be happy to make you a sandwich. Shall I ask her?"

"No, that's all right. I'm not that hungry, and I want to talk to her anyway to see if she can throw any light on what might have happened to Buff."

But Mrs. Lowndes had nothing to add to what Gideon had told me before we set out: that Buff hadn't eaten her breakfast. "I'm that sorry, Miss deMaury. She's a sweet wee thing. Didn't you find her over at Evan Williams'?"

"No. We didn't find Williams there, either. In fact, before we even got to his house, somebody shot at us. We didn't get hit, but the car did."

The housekeeper, who was sifting some flour into a bowl, stared at me, her hands motionless, holding the old-fashioned sifter. Hers was a blunt-featured, square face that showed little emotion. Yet, in the not very bright light of the kitchen it seemed to me that her face was the color of her gray hair, and that there was a look of fear in the pale blue eyes. After a few minutes, her hands started their rhythmic motion again. "That's wicked, awful thing," she said, her Scots accent sounding unusually pronounced. "Did Sir Gideon think it was Evan Williams?"

I remembered then, his questioning of me. "*Who do you think 'they' are?*" But when I asked him, in effect, the same question, he refused to answer.

"I don't know who he thought shot at us, Mrs. Lowndes." There was another silence while I watched the soft white powder drop into the bowl. My own culinary endeavors had always been minimal: hamburger and salad; occasionally a chicken part, wrapped in cellophane in the supermarket, bought and brought home and broiled or baked; more often bought ready-roasted; the ever-useful sandwich. Yet it occurred to me that the concentration and manual effort required for the old-fashioned, from scratch, step-by-step effort to bake a cake, might be an effectively soothing therapy. But did anybody but the Mrs. Lowndeses of this world do it from scratch?

"I wish I could do that," I said suddenly.

"It's not difficult," she said, and her face relaxed. "Have you a good range at home? One that has a slow oven?"

I glanced at the huge iron affair that seemed to stretch one full side of the room. It not only gave off warmth, I decided, but helped make the kitchen by far the cosiest room of the house. In winter, I thought, were I to be there, I'd move my bed next to the iron monster. It gave off some sort of obscure comfort.

"I think, Mrs. Lowndes, if you saw the oven in my apartment, you wouldn't stop, you'd turn right around and go back to Kennedy Airport and get the next plane home."

"It's probably no worse than those gadgety little things they have in flats in London. My niece has one. I wouldn't boil an egg on it."

I watched her as she broke some eggs into another bowl. "Were you here when Benedict took his turn for the worse?" I asked. "Sir Gideon is very upset about it." I knew my saying this came under the frowned-upon category of gossiping with the servants, but I found myself vaguely reluctant to leave the warm and comforting presence of Mrs. Lowndes and her big range.

"I heard Dr. Maitland arrive. I couldn't quite understand what the trouble was."

I explained what I knew about diabetes as well as I could. "Apparently Benedict went into what's called a diabetic coma. Evidently the illness has got a lot worse in the past week or so, because Miss Maitland and her father were explaining to Sir Gideon that watching Benedict's diet is no longer enough. He now has to have injections of insulin. Although," I said, as much to myself as to the housekeeper, "from everything I've ever known about the disease, it's practically unheard of for children, if they have diabetes, not to have a severe enough case to have to have injections right from the beginning."

"But he's been having injections for some time now," Mrs. Lowndes said, picking up the eggbeater.

"What do you mean?"

"I mean many's the time I've seen Miss Maitland washing one of those syringe things in Benedict's bathroom. Once or twice she spoke sharply to me when I'd gone into his room without knocking and seen her, but it's hard for me to remember to knock when it's a child I've taken care of since he was a baby. I thought then anyone would suppose she was doing something she didn't want me to see. But then she said she was giving him vitamins by injection because it was stronger that way."

I stared up at the housekeeper's face. "Are you sure?" I asked after a minute. "I mean, are you sure that you saw those syringes before a week or ten days ago?"

"Positive. I've seen them for the past six months at least." She stared back at me for a few seconds. "Yes, six months. I remember because Sir Gideon was away. Mr. Roger was here. I didn't mention the matter to him. But with Sir Gideon not being here I felt that I should ask him, Benedict being his nephew. And it was after that that Miss Maitland explained to me about it's being vitamins. And now you say he's getting this insulin stuff by the needle."

I'd been sitting on a kitchen chair drawn up to the big table in the middle of the room. But I got up now and started walking around. I was doing that when the door opened and Roger came in. "Well, did you have your sandwich?" he asked.

"No. I forgot. Is Gideon demanding food?"

"Not that I know of."

"You mean you and Sir Gideon didn't have lunch before all that happened to you? I'll fix you some bread and butter and cold meat immediately." And Mrs. Lowndes wiped her hands on her apron and went towards the pantry.

"Any helpful hints about Buff?" Roger asked.

"None," I said briefly. "Tell me, if Evan Williams had her, and wanted to sell her to somebody—me or anyone else—how would he go about it?"

Mrs. Lowndes, who had come back with a loaf of bread, answered. "He'd take her around from door to door, when he's selling anything else, like rabbits or firewood or some such. He knows the folk who are soft on animals, and he'd be sure to take them there. But mostly he tries people who are passing through. The people in caravans or those who are camping, or the people who look like tourists. Or he'd just . . ." Her voice trailed off. I looked up to find her watching me as she sliced bread.

"Or what?"

"Well," she said, putting a cloth back on the end of the big brown loaf. "Ye'll not like it, but he puts them down in the field."

"You mean he abandons them."

"Yes. He's not a kind man."

I sat there thinking. Every common sense approach to the problem suggested that Evan Williams would wait to sell Buff back to me. After all, who would pay so handsomely for a little mongrel cur but the Yankee, who, by this time, must be known far and wide as having taken a fancy to her? But then, why did he shoot at Gideon and me, if it was he who did the shooting? And if it wasn't? If it had nothing to do with him at all, wouldn't the sensible thing for me to do be just to wait until he turned up at the back door, Buff under his arm?

That was undoubtedly the sensible thing to do, which therefore did not explain why I felt a rising urgency to go and look for my lost companion. Absently I put a slice of the cold meat Mrs. Lowndes had placed in front of me onto a piece of the excellent bread, and watched while Mrs. Lowndes arranged more meat, bread and tomatoes onto a tray.

"I'll just take this into Sir Gideon," she said, and glanced at Roger, who had helped himself to some bread and butter. "Would he be in the bookroom, Mr. Roger?"

"He might be by now. He was upstairs in Benedict's room with Dr. and Miss Maitland, but he's probably come down by now."

"Where's Tony?" I asked as Mrs. Lowndes went through the door into the pantry. "I really ought to be upstairs working."

"I'm not sure where he is. When you came in here I think he went back upstairs." Roger hesitated a minute. "I came in here, Janet, to see if you could use what influence you have over Gideon to persuade him to let Benedict go to this private nursing home. It's not just that his illness could be treated under controlled conditions. I honestly think he would benefit from being away from this house—from the somewhat overemotional atmosphere that exists between him and Gideon."

I said doubtfully, "That's the first time I've ever heard anyone describe Gideon as overemotional."

"He isn't, around anyone except Benedict. But that's where the damage is done. And you *have* seen that."

"Yes," I said slowly. I thought about Gideon's threats to Benedict not to send him away to school, his refusal to send the letter he had written to the headmaster, and Benedict's hysterical reaction.

"Well, anyway," Roger said, "I just thought that if you had a chance you might put in a word for the nursing home. In this, I must say I think Sheila—and her father, of course—are right. But do what you think is best."

"I'm afraid anything I could say would do more harm than good. He's already told me not to interfere. I'd better go now, though, and look for Tony. Being fired for neglecting my job at this point would solve nothing."

Roger smiled. "Somehow I don't see that happening. I doubt if Tony would fire you for anything."

I looked at him sharply. He grinned. "I mean—you'd have to be blind."

"Rubbish," I said, with a vehemence that surprised me.

"Not so. You underrate your charms, dear Janet."

I took the last bite of my sandwich and chewed it. Then I took my plate over to the sink and rinsed it off. "Roger," I said, going out of the kitchen, "you have all the makings of an old gossip or matchmaker. But you're wrong."

He was shaking his head as I pushed through the door. I was a little surprised to see the swinging baize door leading into the dining room still moving, as though someone had just come in—or gone out. As I stood there I heard Roger's steps in the kitchen. Had the kitchen door been closed when we were talking after Mrs. Lowndes left? If so, what could they have heard? Only Roger asking me to use my influence with Gideon to get him to allow Benedict to go to the nursing home. And his foolish insinuation concerning Tony's feelings towards me. Foolish?

As I pushed the swinging door into the dining room and walked through into the big hall I wondered if it were foolish. Tony had always been a man attracted by and attractive to women. Even when he was issuing brusque, not-to-be-argued-about orders at his publishing house, there was a subtle but powerful difference between his address to men and women employees. It was, I was convinced, quite unconscious. Or was it? I started climbing the stairs. And what did it matter anyway. Such speculations were along the which-came-first, the-chicken-or-the-egg debates. Was it his initial manner towards women or women's immediate and inevitable reaction to him that made the difference? Either way, whether Tony was inviting one to dinner or asking one to put a memo through the copier, his awareness of one as a woman came through loud and clear. So what did all that add up to in terms of Roger's innuendo?

By this time I had arrived up on the third floor and paused at the foot of the attic steps. And I stood there, rather astonished that my own reaction to all this was not one of pleasure, as it was when Jason Bradshaw, the gossipy publicity and advertising director, had said approximately the same, but of something else altogether. I was pondering this as I paused at the foot of the steep winding stairs down which I was supposed, according to Gideon, to have fallen. I could see where the panels that Gideon spoke of were buckling. Along one vertical line it looked almost as though the wood had parted company with the frame next to it. And there were little chips of white paint, plainly from the white painted panel, lying at my feet. Putting my fingers up I felt along the edge. Then I peered more closely. They seemed to have come from there. My hand was against the side of the panel, covering the crack where it had expanded or contracted so that it had split off from the frame. After a few seconds it occurred to me that I was feeling a slight movement of cool air against the palm of my hand.

Curious, I thought. For all that it was summer, the big house was dank and chill except in the rooms where fires had been lit. So for the air against my hand to feel chilly by comparison with the air of the little foyer there below the attic stairs meant it had to be cold indeed. I took my hand away and stared at the crack, and as I was doing so heard steps behind me.

"As you can see, it needs mending," Gideon's voice said.

I turned around. "There's cold air coming against my hand when I put it up there against the crack."

Even as I spoke I heard footsteps coming from above down the stairs.

Gideon glanced up at the stairs, then said to me, "Well, that's not surprising. This is an old house that leaks at every joint. If you got behind the walls and under the floors, you'd probably feel cold drafts coming from every direction. Hello, Bridewell. Did you find that missing paper, whatever it was?"

"No, I'm afraid not. As I was telling Janet." He came down the rest of the way. "I was going to ask you, Janet, if you'd had news of your dog from Mrs. Lowndes?"

"No. She just repeated what she said to Gideon earlier, that Buff hadn't eaten her breakfast."

"That's really too bad. I'm sorry." He glanced at Gideon. "Isn't there anywhere you could take her around the vicinity here where she might possibly come across her? I gather from what Roger said that your tenant had the habit of selling animals to people who are passing through or are in the nearest town, or even just putting the wretched creatures down somewhere."

"Yes," Gideon said. "I was thinking that myself. But I'm afraid I have to wait for another call from London this afternoon, and I was wondering if I could impose on you to take Janet out this afternoon and look around with her."

There was an odd, frozen second or two. I had never in all the years I had known Tony seen him disconcerted. Yet I had the feeling that for that moment he was thrown off step. And as I stared into the open, rather magnetic eyes, I found myself thinking of what my father had said. "Tony burns."

Then, "Of course I'll take Janet out. But can I? I mean, would I know the proper places to look?"

"Oh, I can direct you about that. Come downstairs and I'll tell you where you should go."

Gideon stood behind us, a little, I thought, like a shepherd driving his flock before him. Again I had the impression that Tony was reluctant, and that some sort of silent tussle of wills was going on between the two men. If anyone had asked me before which of the two men would win in such an unspoken contest, I would have, without hesitation, elected Tony, such was the power of his personality. But, I realized now, I would have been wrong. Perhaps, I thought, as the three of us went downstairs, it was because Gideon was on his own home ground that his will emerged as the ascendant. Briefly, I glanced up at his face. No. His strength was more hidden, his face less open, his power less visible. But on his own or anyone else's turf he would be able to meet Tony on level ground and win.

"Now," Gideon said, stepping down into the hall, "I think we have a map here." And he walked over to an oak chest that stood to one side of the dark paneled hall. Pulling out a drawer, he took out a folded map which he unfolded. "This is a fairly large-scale ordnance map of the immediate country, showing the back as well as the main roads. Come over here," he said, "while I show you where you should drive."

He laid the map flat on top of the chest, and Tony and I went and stood on either side. "Here and here and here," Gideon said, taking a pencil from his pocket and marking thin black lines that showed around and back of the house. It was, as he said, a large-scale map of the area, criss-crossed by lines indicating roads, some of which were blacker than others. "The dark ones," Gideon said, "are the main roads. You don't have to pay too much attention to them. Stick to the ones around the fields here. You can get out and look around the fields. If you don't have any luck there, then come back and we'll think of something else."

"I must say," Tony said, and there was a bite in his voice, "I don't think much of your tenant's ways. Isn't the local Justice of the Peace or whatever he is able to put a crimp in his style?"

"First you have to get the goods on him. When he sells animals to people who are passing through, that's what they're doing, passing through. No one knows their names, where they're from or where they're going. So they can hardly be called as witnesses. We have rules of evidence, you know." He hesitated a second. "As a one-time congressman with a strong liberal reputation, you should approve of that." Was there a tinge of malice in his tone?

Tony went over to the hat rack that stood in a small room off the hall. "I do," he said curtly, putting his coat on as he came back. "Janet, are you putting anything on?"

"Yes. I'll get my raincoat." I went upstairs and snatched my raincoat out of the wardrobe and rejoined the men.

"Well, see you," Tony said, his hand against my back. "Why don't we go out the side door?"

As we reached the bottom of the steps leading to the courtyard he said, "Wait here. I'll bring the car out of the garage."

I glanced up at the sky. "It's a dark day. It looks like it might storm at any moment."

"If it will help in the search I'll turn on the headlights." He paused, putting on driving gloves, and I stood watching him, wondering why it felt as though the word "headlights" had pressed some kind of button in my head.

"Does it occur to you," Tony asked, "that Lightwood was trying to get rid of us?"

"Good heavens!" I said, struck with the idea.

"Yes. Quite. I must admit, I wondered why. I wonder what's behind it?"

He gave me a sardonic grin. "I'll go and get the car."

I was still trying to sort out the meaning when he brought the car from the dark depth of the stable-garage. True to his promise, he put on the lights that blazed suddenly at me.

I knew then what a rabbit felt like, frozen by the lights, unable to move before the oncoming death.

# ten

<hr>

"WELL," TONY SAID agreeably, as he drew up beside me, "what are you waiting for?"

As I opened the passenger door and climbed into his handsome red car I realized why the sudden blaze of lights had sent the alarm through my system: lights had flashed on seconds before the speeding car had nearly killed Gwyneth, Buff and me, as though the blaze had been a deliberate effort to blind and immobilize us and thus decrease the chances of getting away. It was, I reflected grimly, a swift, efficient way of setting up a victim. In the panic of the moment, my mind had blotted out that memory, but it had nearly come to the surface several times since then, most particularly that morning when Roger's flashing lights, in conjunction with Gideon's words, *You're the one who nearly got run down by the car,* had almost connected in my memory the lights with being nearly run over. Realizing all that, I thought, as Tony put the car in gear, nailing the memory, so to speak, should make me feel better, or, to be more accurate, at least relieve my sense of being nagged by something. But I still felt nagged, as though the recollection, like a sore tooth, had not been fully drawn. There was something left, something that still nagged, something that was important. . . .

"Here's the map Lightwood marked," Tony said, putting it on my lap. "Can you tell me which way I should turn when we get to the gate?"

I picked it up and started to unfold the stiff paper. "Of course," I said.

I saw him glance sideways at me. "What's the matter?"

It was on the tip of my tongue to tell him about my flash of memory, but something—perhaps not wanting to be thought fanciful by my attractive, compelling boss, or maybe because of that odd, unsatisfied feeling, as though there were more memory to dig up—prevented me.

Instead, I said, "I'm worried about Buff." And then added, to explain my hesitation (why should I hesitate to express my concern for Buff? The whole world was privy to it!), "I keep having the feeling that if we don't find her this afternoon, then I'll never find her."

"You're really attached to that little mongrel, aren't you?"

"Does that surprise you?"

He didn't reply for a second. Then, "I don't have your sentimental feelings about animals. All right, we're at the gate. Where do we turn now?"

I directed him as we negotiated the gate, which was open, but whose opening was narrow. Going right, we proceeded up the hill towards the road that ran back of the house. It was then that for the first time that afternoon I thought I heard from somewhere behind us the sound of a car.

"Somebody following us?" Tony asked.

I saw him looking into the rear-view mirror.

But although we were silent for a few minutes, and Tony took his foot off the accelerator so that we coasted silently, there was no further indication that a car was anywhere near us. After a bit Tony put his foot back on the pedal. "Now where?" he asked, and there was an irritable note in his voice.

In the next hour we must have driven over every winding lane within miles of The Hall, stopping frequently to get out and look over fields, in ditches, along hedgerows. Twice more I thought I heard the sound of a car. Once Tony actually turned the car around and went back, driving rapidly, to see if there were a car behind us. But when we came to where the road we were on crossed a much wider one, he turned the car again. I stole a look at his face.

"It could have been anyone on this highway," I said, indicating the much wider motorway that crossed the narrow lane we had been following.

"Yes," he said.

Irritated was not the word I would have used to describe the way he looked at that moment. Angry would have come much nearer. But there was another element there, and I was surprised to find myself thinking of my father, which astonished me. What on earth did those two men, one dedicated to an idea, the other dedicated to . . . to what? . . . have in common? *Tony burns,* my father had said. And he should have known. Because he burned, too.

"This is an idiotic errand," Tony said savagely, pushing the car in gear with a scraping noise. "Even if that wretched dog were in one of these fields or ditches, how the hell would we know if it weren't making some kind of noise? I'd give very much to know what Lightwood wanted to get us out of the house for so much that he'd send us on such a fool's journey."

I opened my mouth again, and once more heard the sound of a motor behind us. But this time the sound came nearer. Tony stopped the car and turned in the seat. Turning myself, I saw a car come slowly around the bend immediately behind us, and come to a stop right behind the car. To my utter astonishment, I recognized, behind the wheel, the thick white hair of the rector.

He got out and came towards us.

"I came after you," he said, approaching the driver's window, "to tell you that I have Miss deMaury's little dog. I'm so sorry I wasn't able to get in touch with you sooner, but you had left before I was able to reach The Hall."

My first feeling was one of almost sick relief. Then I bent forward, staring at him past Tony's head. "How on earth do you happen to have Buff?" I asked.

The vicar lowered his handsome white head to peer through the window at me. "I had come back to the house after some morning calls and was, I'm afraid, succumbing to the temptation of a short nap—a piece of self-indulgence I have lately fallen into. Anyway, I awoke, thinking I had heard the sound of a dog outside, whimpering, and got up to look. I opened the door and found the little mongrel tied up to one of the posts in the rectory porch. I thought I recognized her, and when I took her to The Hall, Gideon confirmed the fact. He told me you were out looking around here so I came to find you."

"I'm so glad. I know it's absurd, but—well, anyway, I'm relieved more than I can say." Something stirred around at the back of my mind. "I thought you and Gwyneth had gone to London."

"At the last moment I decided not to go. But Gwyneth's there, and I have been rather hoping to hear from her. I expect she'll ring later on."

It was hard for me to see him closely, but as he straightened, the light fell on his face, and it struck me he looked strained.

"Is everything all right?" I asked.

He hesitated, then said in a strange voice, "All shall be well and all shall be well and all manner of thing shall be well."

After a minute's somewhat surprised silence I said, "That sounds like a quotation."

He glanced down at me. "Yes. The Lady Julian of Norwich, a fifteenth-century mystic. Forgive me. I must get back. I'm a little concerned about Gwyneth."

"Why? Did something happen to her, I mean?" It was awkward, straining my head to see past the silent Tony.

"She was supposed to ring me as soon as she got to London. . . . But then, where she's concerned, I'm afraid I'm something of a fidgit. I'll be getting back."

And he swung on his heel and returned to his car, his gray tweed coat flapping around him.

Tony waited until the rector had gone past with a wave of his hand before he started turning our car in the narrow lane. "Well, Janet, I'm glad your pet is restored to you. But I must say this has been a wasted hour."

We drove in silence for a few minutes, then Tony said, rather abruptly, "Did Gwyneth Theale tell you anything at all about the deMaury papers that are missing?"

I stared at the road in front of me. Who would think, I wondered, that it was summer? Everything was gray—the sky, the rain that was falling again, the road, which was dark, sleek gray under the leaden clouds, even the fields and hedges. It had been gray like this—though not actually raining—the evening before, when there was the flash of headlights from the car seconds before it came hurtling out of the dusk.

"I asked you a question," Tony said. And the tone of his voice was the tone he sometimes used in the office, and never had to use twice to the same person on the same occasion.

"Sorry, Tony. I was wool-gathering."

"You seem to be doing a lot of that here. I sent you to do a job, not to become absorbed with rescuing stray animals or disappearing into some kind of mental fog of your own where you can't seem to keep track of important letters. If I had known you were going to be like this—" He jammed on the brake as we approached another road cutting across ours.

Out of wounded feelings and sheer reflexive habit all the old pangs had started to assault me. It was most unfair. Besides, Tony had never spoken to me like that. Others—after a lot of provocation—yes. But not me. . . . Then some kind of new sanity asserted itself. There was something about this that didn't make sense.

"Why are you angry, Tony? You've been here less than twenty-four hours. It's not like you to be so impatient. Nor is it my fault the papers were in a mess. I'm sorry I lost the one I mentioned on the phone to Cynthia, but I don't know why you're in a state about it. You are, or can be, such a patient man in the office. Not always, of course, but I've seen you put up with some awfully dim people for quite a while if you thought they needed more of a chance than usual. And I don't think I'm being either dim or slow."

It was true. Within certain limits Tony could be very patient; extraordinarily so, I thought, as several examples of his patience trooped across my mind.

I could almost feel Tony exerting an effort to relax. "I suppose I'm upset because that business deal in London that I came over to negotiate didn't work out quite the way I planned." He reached out and patted my knee. "Sorry it washed over on you."

And that, too, was strange, I mused. In all the years I'd known and worked for him I'd never heard him apologize. We relapsed into silence. Perhaps it was because I was still feeling a touch of wounded self-esteem, but I found my mind running back over the people for whom Tony had shown such lenient forbearance as had nearly driven the rest of the office mad:

There was that young editor, bending the ear of anyone who would listen to him about his personal philosophy of editing, but who, it turned out, couldn't write a decent reader's report. Tony put up with him long after any other editor in the house had stopped giving him manuscripts or carefully sent out those he had read to be read again. . . .

There was the girl who said she could type fifty words a minute, which turned out to mean fifty words an hour. Why did we keep her on for so long? Because Tony said she thought she was being discriminated against for being a woman and should be given an editorship immediately. Even the managing editor, who was a woman, didn't buy that. Nor did I. . . . Then—if I was to be honest—there was myself. . . . When I heard there was a job open, I came to Bridewell and Denby, Publishers, with a B.A. degree and no salable skill of any variety. I was given a typing test along with all the other applicants who had turned up that week. My showing was appalling. I could type—barely—having learned to do so because one of my professors would not read handwritten term papers. But my speed was bad and my accuracy worse. By sheer accident, and because I had gone to school with the girl who had administered the typing test, I learned that a young boy who had taken that same test had scored the most brilliant words-per-minute of anyone who had ever been tested. But I got the job. And I got it, I later learned, because Tony had insisted that I be given it. . . . That was one of the reasons that Jason had always teased me about his having a *tendresse* for me. I had felt a little guilty until I had learned that the boy who had lost out to me had found a much better job in another publishing house. And I assumed that Tony had given the job to me (Oh, vanity!) because he had known me before and thought I would be a bright, competent, apprentice who would, in short order, be a bright competent editor. . . .

There were others, but we three were enough to go on with for the moment. What did we have in common for the usually impatient, imperious Tony to show us such forbearance? Not sex. Not even race. The girl with the good degree who couldn't type was black . . . the daughter of a prominent black congressman. . . . Another penny slid into the slot. The young philosopher was the nephew of a leading electronic journalist. And I? I was my father's daughter. Nearly eight years before, when I applied at Bridewell and Denby, my father was still alive, and though his influence was nowhere near what it had been in the fifties and early sixties, his name, his idea and the Society he founded still had a lot of clout.

I glanced at Tony's profile, dark against the gray-green hedge we were passing. . . . What was it one newspaperman had called him when he was still in Congress? Kennedy-esque. Another described him as a legacy of Camelot. Many of the young politicians who had been around the Kennedy brothers were his friends. Then he was defeated in an election and took over the family publishing house. It was odd, I pondered, that anyone that attractive, with those credentials and friends, a liberal man from a liberal state, should have been voted out of his seat. I was still in college when that happened, but I remembered now the puzzled reports. One of the newsmagazines, trying to discover what might have happened, dug out the surprising fact that a large element of the Jewish vote in Bridewell's area had voted against him. When asked about it in a poll, several local residents had stated that when a couple of bills on aid to Israel had come up in the House, Bridewell had not been there. One man in particular, someone named Dreyfus, the representative of a Zionist organization, had been quoted as saying, "Whenever our friends had to stand up and be counted, Bridewell was always off on some junket."

"You turn left here," I said, as the back gate came into view.

"I know," Tony said, and obediently turned the car into the road leading to the back door behind the garage.

I was out the door almost before he had the car stopped, and up the steps to the back door.

"Where is she?" I said to Mrs. Lowndes, bursting through the back door into the kitchen. "Where's Buff?"

Mrs. Lowndes turned from the range. "That silly little dog went straight up to your room and won't come away. I put food out for her there, but she won't eat it until she sees you."

It was true, I discovered after I had torn upstairs, her dish in hand, and thrust open my door. She must have heard me coming and started her rhapsodic barking as I came up the last of the stairs. When I opened the door, I received her in my arms, like a small cannon ball, out of her head with delight. We had an emotional reunion.

"You silly thing," I scolded, putting down her dish. "You haven't eaten a bite." But even as I spoke she was wolfing down the various tidbits that Mrs. Lowndes had donated to tempt her. In the middle she suddenly thought I might have disappeared again and we went through the whole greeting business once more.

There was a brusque knock on the door, and without so much as waiting for me to say come in, Gideon pushed the door open.

"Well," he said, not too kindly. "I'm glad you've been

reunited with your tiresome pet. Now for God's sake keep your eye on her so we won't have to go through this again."

I looked at him. "Mr. Theale said he found Buff tied up outside his door when he got home. Why do you suppose your friend, Evan Williams, if he was the one who shot at us, should bother to do that?"

"Did I say he was the one who shot at us?"

"No. But you didn't say he wasn't, either. And the bullets did come from behind his house. And he wasn't there," I finished.

Gideon stooped down and rubbed Buff between her ears. "What a girl you are," he addressed her. "I think you should be confined to this room, except for sedate walks at the end of a leash."

"I'm inclined to agree with you."

I glanced down at Gideon's feet. He was wearing, I could have sworn, the same shoes my flashlight had lit up the night before. And I was back to the brick wall—Gideon, and my previous doubts about the whole morning's mission, back to . . . Like a well-programmed animal treading a familiar maze, my mind went to the papers in the attic . . . to the deMaury papers, that Tony had become so surprisingly impatient about.

"Gideon," I said. "What's going on?"

He straightened. "What do you think's going on?"

"It's something to do with the papers, the papers up in the attic, isn't it?"

He didn't say anything for a minute, just stood looking at me. Then, "Almost, you know, you persuade me."

"I persuade you of what?"

He had left the door half open. But he shut it now, came back towards me, and grasped my arms with his hands.

"Do you trust me?" he asked.

I looked into the long, narrow gray eyes that I had so often found cold. Their expression now was not cold, but it was unreadable.

Pushing down an irrational desire to answer his question with a resounding "yes," I reminded myself that it was his shoes I had seen up in the attic, that it was he who declared Buff missing and then took us on that jaunt to Evan Williams', where we got shot at, it was he who sent Tony and me on that wild goose chase for no discernible reason.

I said as steadily as I could, "I would like—I would like very much—to trust you. But for a variety of reasons I find it a little difficult."

He stared at me. "I could say very much the same." Then he dropped his hands. "But you're right, of course."

Two hours later, the three men—Gideon, Tony and Roger—and I set out for the Golden Pheasant. At the last minute Sheila, who had gone to put on her coat, came down the stairs and said that Benedict, although by no means ill, was not as well as she would like him to be if she were going to be away from him.

"But Mrs. Lowndes will be here," Gideon said. "If he's not ill, and you say he's not, then I don't think he should be spoiled by having you forgo this dinner. What about Dr. Maitland?"

"Well, Daddy was hoping very much to go, but one of his patients has acted up. He rang just a while ago to say he must, regretfully, refuse."

"That's too bad, not to have either of you," Tony said.

"Yes. I'm awfully sorry. But I would really, honestly, feel better staying. I'm sure you understand."

"Of course I do." Tony smiled. "Although very sorry."

"Perhaps we ought to call it off," Gideon said. He glanced towards Tony. "My thanks for the invitation remain, but we can do it another time."

"But who knows when I will be back here again? Come now, Lightwood, let's not abandon the whole thing. I've been looking forward to another dinner at that place all day. And I'm sure Janet has."

"Why don't the three of you go? I agree that it would be a shame to miss it."

"Well, if you're going to be that stubborn, Gideon," Sheila said, "then I'll go with you. I think for you to give it up is absurd. But it does seem unfair to Mrs. Lowndes."

"Why should it be unfair to Mrs. Lowndes?"

"Well . . ." Sheila said, and glanced towards Roger.

"As a matter of fact, Gideon," Roger said, "I was out in the kitchen when Mrs. Lowndes happened to mention that she hadn't seen her nephew and his family in a long time. You know how fond of them she is. So, thinking we were all going to be out, I suggested she go and see them this evening. I should have asked you first, of course, or at any rate told you about it, but it slipped my mind and I didn't think at the time that you'd have any objection."

"And with Benedict's condition being a little tricky right now," Sheila chimed in, "I really feel that Mrs. Lowndes or me should be here. However, if you're really determined not to go unless I do, I'll speak to Mrs. Lowndes."

There was something in the governess's voice that made me look up to where she was standing on the staircase a few steps above the rest of us. As I stared at her glowing eyes and cheeks and tried to define the quality she seemed at that moment to exude, the word "authority" occurred to me. That was what it was. Always before, she had made some gesture towards deferring to Gideon. But she spoke now as though any need for that had passed. My heart felt as though a hand had squeezed it. I had never before been sure of the relationship between them despite what Roger had said, despite what Sheila had, by tone and occasional word, implied. Something important between them must have been settled. Idly, and aware of my growing unhappiness, I wondered if an announcement would shortly take place.

Then Gideon said, "I see."

There was a pause that seemed much longer than it was. Perhaps, I thought, Shelia assumed that Gideon would now say something about their engagement. Instead, he said, "In that case then Sheila, of course, you must stay. I'm afraid you won't have much dinner. Can we bring anything back for you?"

"No. There's the remains of a pie I can hot up, and

Benedict's dinner is ready for heating. Don't worry about anything. And have a good time."

When the four of us got to the garage an amiable argument arose between Gideon and Tony as to whether we should all go in one car or split up and go in two.

"My dear fellow," Tony said. "I can easily carry all of you. There's plenty of room."

"I'm sure you can," Gideon said. "And I'll admit that the car I have left is no more a thing of beauty than the other was. But there's some business I might have to do after dinner, and I certainly don't want to tie up the rest of you. Janet and Roger, I'll be happy to take either of you, though I'll admit you'll have a cushier ride with Bridewell."

Roger grinned. "Don't I know it. That's for me."

Gideon looked at me. "Janet?"

I thought again of his question, Do you trust me? And my reply which, in effect, said no.

"Go with Bridewell," Gideon said. "You'll be more comfortable." Pushing open the door to the second stable or garage, he revealed one of the smaller British cars.

Tony looked at it. So did I. It was impossible not to compare this little box on wheels to Tony's magnificent Mercedes. "Lightwood's right," Tony said. "Come along, Janet, and we'll put you in the front seat."

"I'll go with Gideon," I replied and marched over to Gideon's Mini.

"You'll probably be sorry," was his gracious response, as I folded myself into his front seat. He leaned out his side. "Why don't you go first, Bridewell?"

Tony leaned across Roger who was in his passenger seat. "Sail before steam," he said graciously.

"Not this time," Gideon waved his hand. "After you."

I watched the dark red rear of Tony's car disappear down the drive. Dark red, I thought. Why did those words bother me, give me an unpleasant feeling?

"Where's your boon companion?" Gideon asked, switching on his ignition.

"Buff? Upstairs, in my room."

"Umm. Let's hope she stays there."

"Why? What are you talking about?" A flicker of alarm went through me.

"I don't have to tell you that Sheila doesn't care for her. If Buff starts annoying her or getting under her feet, she might very well put her out. Which would hardly be a major disaster, but if you found her gone when you got home you'd set the house by the ears all over again." He eased the car out into the court beside the house.

"Well, she's in my room with the door firmly closed. If you think that Sheila might go in there . . . is that what you're saying?"

"I'm not saying anything except what I said. If you want to take her to the rectory for the evening we can pick her up on the way home."

I was surprised, alarmed and baffled, but I didn't pause to ask questions. Getting out of the car I ran upstairs to my room, grabbed a surprised and delighted Buff, put on her leash and went back down to the car, carrying her under my arm.

It occurred to me as we shot down the drive, at rather more speed than was warranted, that Gideon looked unusually grim.

"What do you think might have happened to Buff?" I asked, as we sailed through the opened gate and turned right towards the village.

"I told you, for God's sake."

"Well, you needn't try to kill us in the car. What's the matter with you?"

He pressed his lips together and did not reply. But, as we pulled up to the rectory gate, he said, "That dog of yours is a lot luckier than you realize. A lot luckier than—"

I was halfway out of the car, Buff under my arm. "Than whom?"

He waved his hand. "Go on in and take her to Theale. We've delayed enough as it is."

I fully expected having to launch into an elaborate explanation to the rector, as to why Buff was being deposited on his doorstep again. But it wasn't necessary. "Yes. That's quite all right," he interrupted me right after asking him if I could leave her. "We're good friends now, aren't we Boadicea?"

I had forgotten about her original name, and the ludicrousness of it struck me all over again. "I take it you don't believe in nicknames?" I said.

The tall rector bent down and patted Buff's head, then lifted her up in his arms. "She was named for a great queen," he said. "I think she should know that. I'll just see you to the gate."

"Did you get your call from Gwyneth?" I asked, as we walked down the path.

"No. I'm afraid not."

I glanced at him. Like Gideon, his face showed great strain. "Are you really worried about her, Mr. Theale?"

He didn't reply for a minute, then, as we reached the car, he said, "It's a little . . . a little disconcerting that she hasn't been in touch. But . . ." He looked down at Buff, took her pointed muzzle in his hand and shook it with gentle affection. "To quote the Lady Julian again, 'All shall be well . . .'"

I saw Gideon, who had been looking at Buff, glance quickly up at the rector's face. His gaze stayed there for a moment, then he said to me. "Come along, Janet. We're going to be late."

We had driven for a long while in that endless dusk of an English summer when I broke the silence. "Nothing makes sense."

Gideon pointed the car up a hill. "My mother used to say that—in moments of great bitterness."

I thought about his mother and all of her relations who had died in concentration camps. No, I thought, not all. Some of them had lived to go to Israel. And she herself had lived to see Israel become a nation. "What was your mother's name?" I asked.

He didn't answer for a moment. Then, "Dreyfus," he said. "Lisa Dreyfus."

Dreyfus . . . a famous Jewish name. . . . There was the Dreyfus affair in France. But the name had an echo in my mind that was considerably more recent than the last time I had thought about the notorious French court-martial. Much more recent. Like someone with a piece of food caught between two molars I worried at it. So many things had nagged at my mind lately that it would be a relief to be able to run one down. . . .

"Oh!" I said suddenly.

"Now what?" Gideon slowed the car as we came down a hill. We had, I noted idly, been following a winding up and down road.

"I was trying to think of where I'd heard the name Dreyfus recently and I suddenly realized that Tony had mentioned it this morning."

"Oh? In what way?"

"Nothing world shaking, I suppose. Just that ages ago, when Tony was defeated in Congress, the head of some Zionist organization, a man named something Dreyfus, said that whenever aid to Israel came up in Congress, Tony wasn't around to vote. Which, I must say, seemed awfully strange, in view of Tony's impeccably liberal—"

"Nathan Dreyfus," Gideon said.

". . . record—What did you say?"

"I said his name was Nathan Dreyfus."

After a long minute I said, "You sound as though you knew him, or knew about him."

"I did. And do. My mother also had American cousins, and he was one of them."

"But—were you aware of what he said about Tony?"

"Of course."

It was, I thought, like picking up a skein of wool, tangled beyond hope. For a minute I felt dizzy, as though, as the scientists, or perhaps it was the metaphysicians, said, time was not linear but circular.

"Gideon," I said. "Stop the car. I've got to find out something. Is anything that's going on now to do with that?"

"I can't stop the car. For one thing we'll be late, and it's important that we not be, and for another we're almost there. But, to answer your question . . . Damnation, there's the village. I wish I could stop. I see now how wrong I was about . . . But I don't have time to explain."

He turned towards me, slowing the car so that for a few seconds it crept along. "Janet, I can't explain now . . . I should have before. But trust me. Please trust me."

For a brief moment our eyes met. For the first time since I'd known him his were neither hostile nor inscrutable. There was something in them that made my heart give an odd jump. With his free hand he picked up mine, turned it over and kissed it. Then he released it, put the car in gear, and drove the remaining yards up to the inn.

I had, of course, heard of the Golden Pheasant, noted as much for its age and its location as its cuisine. Situated at the edge of a village, itself now a suburb of a much larger town, the inn sat at the top of the highest hill in a cluster of hills, with the village dribbling down the side of the hill towards the town that lay by the river in the valley below.

As we drove up to the sprawling, half-timbered building, Roger stepped out of the front door.

"What kept you?" He bent down to the window beside the passenger seat. "We practically sent out the local constabulary."

"Janet forgot something," Gideon said, blackening my character without a blink.

"Oh. Well, there's the car park behind, if you like. But it's pretty crowded and whoever is directing the cars has made a fine mess of it. Getting out's going to be a problem. There's also a garage down the street. Costs a bit more but makes life a lot simpler."

"Yes, I know," Gideon said. "I think I'll take the garage. Janet, do you want to get out now or will you drive down with me?"

Roger opened the door beside me. "Come on, Janet. We have a dry martini all poured out and waiting."

"Yes, go on in," Gideon said. "I'll join you in a minute."

I followed Roger as he went up a few steps to the entrance, and turned right into a bar which managed to look at the same time ancient, simple and expensive. The floor and the bar were made of dark oak. In the rest of the room were small tables, also of oak. Several people were standing at the bar when we walked in, but Tony was seated at one of the tables, gazing absently at what looked like a dry martini.

He rose as I came up. Sure enough, as Roger had said, a slender glass stood at my place filled with a clear liquid.

"That looks like a dry martini," I said to Tony as I sat down.

"It is. This is one of the few places outside London that understands the American approach to a dry martini."

"Why don't you call it straight gin and have done with it?" Roger asked, sitting down. "All of this mystique about the extra dry martini is a lot of palaver."

Tony sat down again. "As a matter of fact, there used to be a cocktail lounge in New York that arrived at the same conclusion. It made all martinis so dry they almost blew away. If somebody asked for one extra dry, they just poured straight gin or vodka on the rocks. Even then, the barman once told me, there were those who ordered a second with the instructions to make it drier."

"Exactly," Roger said with satisfaction. "That's precisely what I mean."

"Gideon parking the car?" Tony asked.

"Yes. He elected the garage down the street."

"Sensible man. Ah—here he is. We didn't order for you, Lightwood," he said as Gideon came up. "Because I didn't know whether you wanted to stick with your usual sherry or order one of these?" And he waved at the colorless liquid in front of him.

"Thanks. I think I'll just have a whiskey," Gideon said. "No—I can get it at the bar. Don't ring the bell." Tony, who had been about to press the bell beside him in the wall, dropped his hand. "As you wish, but the barman has strict instructions that it's to go on my tab, so don't think you'll pull a fast one."

Gideon hesitated for the fraction of a second. Then said, "Thanks," and went towards the bar.

Long afterwards, someone asked me whether the

Golden Pheasant had lived up to its reputation for gourmet cuisine on the one occasion I had been there. And I spent the following fifteen minutes trying, off and on and between other topics of conversation, to remember what I ate. To this day I can't remember. Nor can I recall what anyone else had. From the moment Gideon sat down, it was as though a powerful agent had been added to a chemical mix changing the atmosphere from one that had been relatively relaxed to one of increasing tension. Yet, in the bar and later in the dining room where a deferential waiter had led us, conversation—at least on the surface—flowed on: about the inn, its history, its reputation, its food, which slid by obvious steps to Anglo-American cooking, with amusing and sometimes calamitous stories of culinary disasters in travels on both sides of the Atlantic, which led to amusing and affectionate anecdotes pointing up the differences in folkways between the two countries. Tony was particularly entertaining at those.

So it seemed a perfectly natural extension of everything that had gone before when Gideon said sometime in mid-meal, "I hear you're up for that ambassadorship that's about to fall vacant, Bridewell."

Tony made a face. "That's still in the rumor stage. You know what newspapers are: they'll take somebody's educated guess, make a headline out of it, and run with it."

"I should have said it was more than that. Your name had been mentioned as the strongest contender by even our most conservative papers over here."

Tony shrugged. "That must have been a lean day for news."

"That's not true, Tony," I put in. "I heard about it at the office before I left. Don't be so modest." To me, Tony's disclaimers were beginning to sound a little phony, perhaps because I had always found exaggerated modesty as much of an attention-getter as outright conceit. . . . Attention-getter, headline hunter . . . My mind moved along with the words that echoed and re-echoed from something this morning. What was it Tony had said? *"All of those headline hunters. . . . Dreyfus and his crowd. . . ."* Dreyfus. Gideon's mother, Lisa Dreyfus. Her cousin, Nathan Dreyfus . . .

It was then I committed my insanity. I have said I remember nothing about the actual meal. That's not entirely true. I was nibbling a piece of almost paper thin toast, and then rolling my fingers over the crumbs that had fallen onto the white cloth, when, without a single preceding thought that I can recall, I opened my mouth and said, "Nathan Dreyfus."

"What?" Tony said.

I raised my eyes to his and it was, for a second, like looking at another man. Under the table a foot touched mine.

"Who did you say?" Tony repeated.

"I was just thinking about a cousin of Gideon's in New York," I said, hoping that I didn't sound as frightened as I had suddenly become. It felt, I thought, as though the safety catch had been taken off a loaded revolver. Yet I would be hard put to describe why I thought so. No one had made a move—except for that soft pressure under the table. And other than Tony's bland question, no one said anything.

"I hadn't realized you knew him," Tony remarked and then blinked rapidly twice. Curious, I thought. Tony only blinked like that when he thought he'd put a foot in it.

"I don't," I said.

"Ah, Lightwood must have been mentioning him." He smiled, then suddenly looked at his watch. "Sorry, Roger, I forgot to remind you about that trunk call."

"Oops!" Roger got up, putting his napkin on the table. "A fine reminder you've turned out to be. Sorry, everybody. Be back shortly."

"What Roger needs is a secretary," Tony said. "He can't even seem to remember his own business deals."

"I didn't realize you knew Nathan, Bridewell," Gideon said.

"Everybody knows who he is. Zionist. Leader of one of the Jewish defense agencies. I didn't know he was your cousin." Those azure eyes seemed to bore across the table. "Seems like an unlikely cousin for you to have."

"Oh? Not really. My mother's maiden name was Dreyfus. She was Austrian. And she was Jewish."

"I see. That rather explains your interest in the deMaury papers, doesn't it?"

I was thinking that was a very odd connection to make when Gideon replied, "Partly. Of course, the fact that Rosemary was my wife as well as Robert deMaury's protégée could also explain it. I'm surprised that you didn't know about my mother—that Rosemary didn't tell you. She told you so much, didn't she?"

"What do you mean by that?"

It was like a duel, I thought. Naked, the buttons off the foils, the safety catch off the pistols, as though the two men were alone, not in a pleasant, civilized dining room, with a score or so of other people seated at the other tables scattered around the room.

"I mean that time she saw you in Rome. At the contessa's apartment—the one with the balcony above the piazza—a few hours before she died. She thought a crowded party would be a good place to have your chat. But she was overheard, nevertheless."

As the silence stretched, the tension became unbearable. I was trying to think of something—anything—to say, when I became aware of one of the red-jacketed bar waiters standing at Gideon's elbow.

"There's a telephone call for you, Sir Gideon."

# eleven

GIDEON WAS GONE only a moment, but it seemed much longer as Tony and I sat, waiting in silence. Finally I said, "I didn't know you were in Rome, Tony."

"No," he replied, his voice—under the circumstances—unbelievably casual. "You didn't come to the party."

"No. I had a party of my own to go to and she hadn't said anything about your being in Rome."

"I expect she didn't. Rosemary was a very discreet girl." Tony's gaze, which had seemed focused on his plate, suddenly lifted. "Wasn't she?"

Rosemary's incredible reserve, I found myself thinking. Even as an adolescent she had not been confiding. Oh, we had giggled and laughed over things at school, over the boys on whom we—no, not we, I—had crushes. I was always in and out of love. First it was the Gray boy, then Johnny McCarthy, then Timothy Craig whom I found, pimples and all, devastatingly attractive. . . . What's the matter with me? I thought now. Why am I thinking about that now?

"Yes," I said. "Rosemary never really said anything much about . . . anything. Except—"

"Except what?"

"Except about my father, and the Society. And then she didn't actually say much. Once she talked about it, really talked. She was angry that I didn't feel the same. . . ."

"If one could be said to have an Oedipus complex for someone not really one's father, Rosemary had it for yours. Perhaps it would be more correct to say she was in love with him."

"With my father?" A mental image of that austere, driven man loomed in my mind. "My father never loved anything except his own idea. Not even my mother, I don't think. That—his idea—was his one and only love."

"Yes. You're quite right." He laughed suddenly. "Is it the—Ah, Gideon. Nothing too serious, I hope."

"I'm afraid it might be. That was Mrs. Lowndes. There seems to be some kind of trouble at home—Benedict has had another turn—and I'd better get back. Sorry, Bridewell, to be leaving like this. Tell Roger—Oh, here he is."

Roger came up. "Where's everyone going?"

Tony had risen. "Your brother got a phone call from Mrs. Lowndes. Benedict's not well and he has to get back."

"I thought Mrs. Lowndes had the evening off."

"Apparently she didn't take it," Gideon said. "Janet—"

As he turned towards me, I said, picking up my handbag, "I'm coming with you."

Gideon looked at me. No one said anything. Then Tony said, "If you feel you must, I can certainly understand."

"I'd like to go with you," Roger looked troubled. "But I was coming back to say that I was going to ask Bridewell to put me on the nearest train to London. I should have made that telephone call sooner, and now there's some kind of muddle over a business thing I'm involved in. I'm terribly sorry."

"Of course," Tony murmured. "I'm sorry about Benedict, Lightwood, and also that no one is getting dessert. This was not the best possible evening for a dinner, I'm afraid."

"I'll see you later, then," Gideon said. "Are you coming, Janet?"

As we left the hotel Gideon said, "This way," and turned right. We walked along the village street in silence, our feet echoing over the old stones. It was as dark as it ever gets in midsummer in Britain. But the rain clouds had blown partly away, and a few stars had appeared, looking high and chilly. After a few minutes we came to a low, fairly modern building set back from the street, with petrol pumps in front. A few cars were parked out on the apron on either side of the pumps and I could see more through the open double doors of the garage.

"Here we are," Gideon said.

I saw first Tony's big car, its paint shining dark red under the naked bulb above, parked against the back wall, looking like a thoroughbred, as did an impressive array of Rolls-Royces, Bentleys, Jaguars and other automotive aristocrats parked around. Off to one side as though unworthy of such company, was Gideon's Mini.

Dark red. I *did notice a dark red car. . . .* Although no voice sounded, the words were as clear as though someone beside me had spoken them. But who? It was a woman in the shop in Tenton Village. What was her name? Mrs. Evans. And she was answering a question we had asked her: had she noticed a car speeding through the village some twenty minutes before? "*I did notice a dark red car. . . .*"

"My God!" I said, and stopped. "It was Tony."

Gideon was walking towards his Mini. "What are you talking about?"

"It was Tony," I repeated.

He looked up and stopped where he was. "In Rome? Yes. I've always been pretty sure of that. Stay there, Janet. You won't be able to get in your side. I'm going to drive the Mini out a little."

Obeying by some reflex action, I watched as Gideon folded his long body into the car, turned on the engine and began backing out. I was a little surprised when, instead of stopping beside me, the car seemed to go on and on. I had one glimpse of Gideon's astonished face before the back fender gently ran into another car.

I heard Gideon make a sound. He got out. Going past me, he went back to where the Mini had been and stood staring down at the garage floor. Like most garage floors it was dirty with oil. But there seemed to be two fresh pools of some thick liquid.

"Well, well," Gideon commented.

"Well what?" I asked. "Gideon, would you mind explaining that comment of yours? The one before last. About Rome."

"How unsubtle," Gideon said, as though I hadn't spoken. "Reith!" I jumped as he called out the name.

There was the sound of footsteps from deep in the building to the left and back. In a few seconds a muscular young man appeared, wiping his mouth. By the paper napkin tucked in his collar I would have guessed him to have been at dinner.

"Reith," Gideon asked. "Do you have a car I could hire for this evening?"

"Hire, Sir Gideon? Is something wrong with your Mini?"

"Come and look and tell me."

The young man came and stood beside Gideon. "Looks like brake fluid," he said.

"Yes. That's what I thought. Particularly since I couldn't stop the car. The brakes wouldn't work."

"Let me look underneath."

Giving his mouth a final swipe, Reith went down onto the floor on his back, then wiggled himself under the car.

"Yes," he said, getting up after a while. "It's your brakes. Somebody's fiddled with them. I don't like that. It's never happened in my garage before. I don't like it at all."

"Neither do I. But I don't think it's your fault. How long have you been at dinner?"

"Twenty minutes. Half an hour. I've never worried

about leaving the cars. We've never had any trouble before." He sounded upset.

"Since you were at dinner, I don't suppose you saw anyone coming over here?"

"Nobody but Mr. Roger, who came to get something he wanted out of the Mercedes. But to answer your question, I don't have one single car I can let you have. There are only two that I sometimes hire, and they're both out."

"Too bad," Gideon said. He was looking at the Mercedes. "Well, I think I'll ask Bridewell if I can borrow his, or if he'll drive us back. Did he leave the keys with you, Reith?"

"No, Sir Gideon. He was very particular about parking the car himself—some gentlemen who own those big cars are."

"All right. Sorry to bother you, Reith. Go back and finish your dinner."

"I can stay if I'm needed, Sir Gideon."

"No, no. You're not."

"I can't think who'd do that to you, Sir Gideon."

"Nor I. Someone with a perverted sense of humor probably. I'll leave it here for you to fix. Janet, come back and lend your persuasion with me."

Grasping me by the hand, Gideon led me out of the garage and down to where the street curved towards the inn. Then he stopped and dodged into a little lane that led back to the fields between two of the cottages. "We'll wait here," he said.

"It was Roger, wasn't it, who did that to your car?"

"Yes. But keep your voice down. Sound travels at night."

I found, to my surprise, that I was shaking and my teeth were chattering. Either Gideon heard them, or he sensed how I felt, because he put his arm around me and said, "It's all right. It's going to be all right."

I was reminded of the rector's "All shall be well, all shall be well . . ."

A whole kaleidoscope of images came together in my head: the dark red car that nearly ran Gwyneth and me down . . . Tony in Rome . . . the headlights right before the car hit Rosemary . . .

"It *was* Tony," I said. "It was Tony who nearly killed Gwyneth and me. It was Tony who killed Rosemary."

"Quiet! Yes, it was Tony. Now we're going back to the garage. We've been gone long enough to look as though we had permission from Bridewell."

But I was still thinking about Tony. "But *why?*"

"Shh! Later."

When we got back to the garage there was nobody around.

"Let's hope and pray he left the car door open," Gideon said, going towards the Mercedes. Grasping the handle he pulled open the door by the driver's seat. "Good," he said.

"Why is it so important to have the door open?"

"Because the hood wouldn't open if the door were locked. And to start the car without a key I have to open the hood."

I watched as he proceeded to do this. "Now," he said, lowering the hood, "get in."

"That's a useful piece of knowledge to have," I said, as Gideon got in his side and started to ease the car out of the garage.

"In the course of an extremely chequered career I have picked up some interesting and often quite illegal bits of information."

Reaching the street, Gideon turned left. In a minute or two we passed the inn, a mellow light shining from its windows and doors.

"It's hard to believe," I said, still numb from shock, "that in that cosy bit of old England sits a man I've known all my life and worked for for the past several years, and . . . and even thought myself in love with . . . who is a murderer."

"Two men," Gideon said. "The only reason Roger isn't a murderer is that he isn't as efficient. He did his best—or worst, if you prefer."

"You mean fiddling the brakes in your Mini?"

"Yes. And, I'm pretty sure, taking pot shots at us this morning from behind Williams' place."

"But *why?*"

"Your favorite question. Well, Roger's motive is the oldest and simplest of all. He wants what I have: the land and the title. God knows why. It's a night-and-day struggle to keep it still together and going. Except, perhaps, that he was, because of his mother and the hole-in-the-corner way she and my father were married, always made to feel an outsider. It became a symbol for him."

"What about Benedict? Wouldn't he inherit from you?"

"He would. That's been on my mind. Probably Roger thought he wouldn't live long enough. Possibly . . . probably Roger would *help* him not to live long enough."

I thought about what the rector had said. "And you've known this? And let him stay around?"

"No. Stupidly, I didn't see just how serious he was about this till this morning. Oh, I knew he resented me. And I felt sorry for him. My father wasn't very nice to him, probably as some kind of extension of the way he finally felt about Roger's mother—that he had been more or less cornered into marrying her. He—Roger—has never really held down a job for very long. He's always dabbled around in the kind of businesses where he thought he could make a packet fast: some kind of dubious import-export firm, an international film corporation, South American mining bonds that turned out to be bogus—he just missed being in real trouble over that. . . ."

"But what made you think he was serious this morning?"

"Because after we had been shot at I started trying to put together who was behind that gun. As far as I knew there were only two who knew we were going to Evan Williams' cottage. I dismissed Williams. He's careless and dirty and a poacher. But he'd have no reason to want to kill me and far too healthy a respect for his own safety to try anything so stupid. Then I thought about Roger and I remembered that he saw me when I was talking to Evan Williams before breakfast."

"You talked to Evan Williams?"

"Yes. I gave him your dog so that I had a good excuse to get both of us out of the house. Why, I'll explain later. Getting myself out was easy. Finding something that would get you away from that attic was not so easy. The one thing I was fairly sure would distract your attention was your dog. So, having arrived at this brilliant plan, I was then stuck with the necessity of finding a reasonably credible excuse. At that moment, I happened to be looking out of my bedroom window and saw Williams traipsing home through the woods at the back, with his gun and a brace of rabbits slung over his shoulder. So I got out the car, drove up the back road and intercepted him. Told him I'd hand him the dog and for him to put on an act of trying to sell it back to you. By that time it was late enough for you to have come downstairs and brought Buff down for her breakfast. I simply waited until Mrs. Lowndes had gone into the dining room and then kidnaped the wretched little beast as she was about to dip into her dish. I handed her over to Williams, who was waiting back of the stables, with dire threats as to what would happen if he didn't take good care of her. It was when I was returning that I happened to glance up to Roger's window. He stepped back as soon as he saw me looking, but I was pretty sure he was there. Then, of course, we met him on our way out and told him we were looking for your dog. So he must have added an obvious two and two and come up with four."

Gideon put the car in gear as we started up the first long hill beyond the village. There were no lights now except for our own headlights, and the midsummer midnight blue seemed darker. I shivered.

I saw Gideon glance up to the rear-view mirror for the third or fourth time.

"Why do you keep looking up there?" I asked. "Are you expecting somebody to come after us?"

"Yes. I don't think he would have waited very long to follow us to the garage. When he discovers that I left the Mini and took this, he'll know that we—or at any rate I—know what he's up to and he won't have any choice but to follow. It'll just be a question of whether he can steal one of the other high-priced cars before Reith gets through with his dinner."

"Gideon—my head is reeling. What about Tony? You say he killed Rosemary. He also almost killed Gwyneth and me a few days ago. We were walking to the village and this car came out of nowhere, blazed its lights and then bore down on us. We barely scrambled up the bank in time. I didn't realize . . . I just saw now when I noticed the car's dark red color in the garage . . . that it was Tony. I know now, too, that it was his car that came at Rosemary. But in either case I still don't know why. And yet—in some way or other—I think I do. It's something to do with the papers, isn't it? The deMaury papers."

"Yes. It has everything to do with those papers. . . ." And then I wondered if Gideon's sanity had suddenly snapped, because he started to laugh. "If you only knew how . . . how ironic it was. But I can't explain now. Look in the mirror."

I looked. For a moment all I could see was the blackness of the hill under a dark gray that was the sky. "I don't see—" I started. And then I did. Two lights suddenly rounded one of the crests behind us. "Is that them?" I asked ungrammatically.

"Yes. I wonder what car they've been able to beg, borrow or most likely steal. Now sit tight."

I hope I will never have a ride like that again as long as I live. I've never liked even the kind of speed that is generally considered acceptable on an open straight road. This road was neither open nor straight. It wound up and down with blind corners and narrow turns that bent back on themselves. As Gideon's foot pressed lower and lower on the pedal the highly sprung car swayed alarmingly. After a while I put my hands out to the door on one side and down on the seat on the other, to keep my body from being flung about.

"Don't press on that door," Gideon snapped. "If you got flung out, you wouldn't have a prayer."

"I'll lock it," I said, groping for the catch.

"No. I don't want you imprisoned in here, either."

Taking my hand off the door I grasped the leather seat instead. Every now and then a car coming in the opposite direction on the narrow road would sound the horn protestingly, and the noise passed in a blare. One man yelled at us. I could hear and appreciate his anger but could not possibly distinguish what he was saying.

After a while it was easier to close my eyes, but then I found myself opening them to look in the rear-view mirror. The lights seemed in about the same position.

"They're not gaining on us, anyway," I said.

"No," Gideon said. He did not sound reassured.

Almost immediately I felt the car's speed diminish.

"You're slowing down," I said after a minute, when the speed did not pick up again.

"I'm trying an experiment." He sounded so grim I glanced at his profile, the vertical forehead and thrusting aquiline nose, in the dim light from the dashboard.

"Watch them in the mirror for me," he said. And I felt the push as the car speeded up again. "Are they the same distance behind?" he asked after another minute.

"Yes. They must have speeded up when we did." I paused. "I wonder what that means."

"It could mean a lot of things, among them that he's waiting for something to happen to this car, or one of them is. Janet, I'm going to speed up suddenly in about one minute. There's a turn coming up which is hidden from behind by a bridge, a stone wall and some trees. I'm going to slow down there. Get out immediately and hide in the trees."

"But—"

"For Christ's sake don't argue. I'm trying to save your life—and mine. Now."

The car gave a spurt forward, and a second or two later I saw the turn he was talking about. The lights picked up the gray wall and the tops of the trees, but I couldn't see the other side. Turning the corner on what felt like two wheels, he slowed abruptly, flinging out a hand to keep me from hurtling forward.

"Go quickly," he said.

The car was still moving as I opened the door, pulled my legs forward and jumped, landing on soft earth and leaves. Then, with a roar, the car speeded up and hurtled down the road. In a minute or two I heard the sound of another car coming up from behind and scurried forward to the protection of small trees and bushes. They were perfectly adequate to hide me from the car that then passed, mostly because no one in it was bothering to look for me. But I could see, from where I was crouched, both cars on the road ahead that skirted the side of a hill. Below, the hill fell away to a valley. It was a strange, almost aerial view. From where I was standing the road went down. From time to time Gideon's Mercedes was hidden from me as it disappeared behind the rise of a hill and then reappeared. I had just stood up when the big German car disappeared again. Anxiously I waited for it to reappear, aware of the car behind that seemed to be maintaining its even pace.

Then, as I watched, the lead car, the Mercedes, veered off the road to the side, appeared to hang over the edge of the slope and then tip forward. It all seemed very gentle and slow motion until, as it rolled down the hill, there was a huge red flash and then an explosion that seemed to rip the hill apart.

I stood there among the trees, trembling all over, watching the ball of fire roll down the rest of the hill and stop at the bottom. Then, in the glare, I saw the second car draw up to the same edge and I watched as two men got out and looked down.

I had no idea how far from me that burning car was—a mile, two. Distances at night could be deceptive. I did know that no one could have survived either the explosion or the fire, and I found myself praying that Gideon had died instantly. Then, as the first smell of burning oil sprayed across my nostrils, I leaned forward and was violently sick. It felt as though I was losing everything I'd eaten all day, and when that was gone, I continued to heave and retch. So it was a few minutes before I struggled up from my knees and looked across the wide expanse of hill and valley again. The flames had died considerably, although the car was still burning. But the other car had gone.

There was nothing to do but walk. So with unsteady knees I set out on the road. There were things I knew I had to think about. Questions—questions about Tony, about Rosemary, about Gideon himself—that lay somewhere back of the pain that seemed to fill my mind. But the pain was all-encompassing—pain that Gideon was dead, pain all the worse because I had not known how I felt about him until I had seen him go over the side of the hill in flames.

Most urgent of all, now, was the thought of Benedict. With Gideon dead, he stood in immediate danger. I wasn't sure what I could do, but I knew that between Roger and Sheila Maitland Benedict would need help and would need it now. Somehow I had to get back and to get back quickly.

It was not easy going. There was a thin moon high up and a few remote stars, but the only light anywhere near was the reflected glow from the burning car that was, itself, only occasionally visible. As the road wound, the curve of the hill cut off sight. Twice I stumbled and once I went down on one knee.

And then, with seeming abruptness, it was not as dark. Light washed out onto the road from behind me. I turned. I had been too numbed and absorbed to hear it, but a car had come up.

"I say," a pleasant English voice said. "Are you all right? Is that your car down there?"

The car had stopped. A man was getting out of the passenger seat and a woman was looking out the window on her side.

"Are you all right?" the man repeated.

I'm not usually a quick thinker, but just as I was about to say "That's Sir Gideon Lightwood's car," I knew that that simple statement would almost certainly involve me in heaven knew how many hours of explanations and questions. I would have to face them sooner or later, but the immediate need was to get back. There was nothing I could do now for Gideon, but I might be able to help his son.

"If that was your car . . ." the man was saying.

I licked my lips that felt dry. "No, it's not that. You see . . ." What could I say to make them pick me up and take me immediately to the nearest place where I could get a car or a lift of some sort? And then a story that would make my hesitation look like maidenly embarrassment struck me.

"You see," I said, drawing a breath, "we . . . some friends and I—there were two cars—were coming back from a dinner party, when we saw the wreck down there. So everyone got out to have a look, and I decided . . . well it had been a rather long drive and we'd had a lot to drink and I stepped away a few minutes, if you see what I mean. . . ." I let my voice run down.

"I quite understand," the nice man said.

"Anyway, when they got back in the cars—there were quite a lot of us—I suppose each lot thought I was in the other car. Before I could get back, they drove off."

Would they buy it?

Perhaps if I had not been a foreigner they would not have. But innate courtesy to strangers (helped, probably, by an equally innate belief that foreigners were given to doing strange things) asserted itself.

"Oh," said the woman from the car window. "Bad luck. Well, you'd better let us give you a lift. Where shall we take you?"

"Is there somewhere further on I could get a taxi or a car?"

"Where are you going?" the man said.

I hesitated for a moment, disliking to mention Tenton. But I didn't have time to be delicate about that, I decided.

"Tenton Hall. Outside Tenton."

"You're in luck," the man said. "It's on our way. Hop in."

The ride seemed longer than I had remembered, or perhaps it was my growing sense of urgency. The couple, identifying me as an American, asked the usual questions, and I answered as well and as calmly as I could, while underneath my whole being was saying *hurry, hurry, hurry*.

Finally, through the dark windows, I saw that we were entering what I recognized as the village of Tenton. Yes, there was the church, with the rectory behind, and halfway along, Mrs. Evans' shop. Then we were through, and driving rapidly along the the tree-lined road towards The Hall. After a few minutes the headlights picked up the gray wall on one side and, as the car started to slow, I saw the tops of the gateposts.

"Here it is," I said.

I barely waited for the car to stop, but opened the back door and got out. "Thanks so much," I said.

"You'll be all right?"

"Oh, yes, fine." And before they could ask any more questions, I had waved my hand and was running towards the gate. It was then I noticed that the gate itself was open, which struck me as unusual. In the whole time I had been there the gates had been opened only to allow a vehicle to enter, and then immediately closed.

For a minute I stood still, listening. There was a light from the cottage beside the gate, from which I deduced that the gatekeeper and his family were there. Yet I felt strangely reluctant to knock on the door and suggest that the gate be closed, even though I felt increasingly strongly —even if for no reason I could nail down—that it should be closed.

So I walked between the gateposts and stopped at the outside edge of one of the gates. Tentatively I put my shoulder against the big iron frame. Somewhat to my surprise, it moved rather easily. Putting my hand against it, I found myself walking the gate shut, pushing it with my hand. I didn't try to be particularly quiet about it, yet I stood still again when I had closed one half to see if anyone had heard me. But there was nothing except the wind stirring in the trees. Then I walked across and did the same with the other gate, which closed with a click. After which I turned and went up the drive as quickly as I could, given the fact that I couldn't see the ground under my feet. It occurred to me that by closing the gate I might have done the worst possible thing. Supposing Benedict and I should want to get away in a car? This had not occurred to me before, so I stopped for a second or two to see if I felt an equally strong urge to go back and open the gate. But I didn't. After a minute I went on.

Glancing up I noticed that some of the windows in The Hall were lighted: one or two on the ground floor, including Gideon's library, one or two on the second and third floors, and the dormer windows of the attic. I paused for a second to see if I could see any figures moving around in the rooms. But either there weren't any or they were too far into the room for me, standing below the steps, to see them.

Skirting the steps, which were slightly lit by the re- flected glow from the windows, I walked around into the courtyard at the back, circled a large car parked in the shadows, and went up to the kitchen door. As quietly as I could I thrust it open.

I don't know exactly what I expected to find, so its emptiness was almost a letdown. Mrs. Lowndes had called Gideon—or at any rate, that's what he had said. But she wasn't in here. Consciously pushing back the pain that Gideon's name had brought, I trod as noiselessly as I could across the big kitchen, through the pantry and to the green baize door that led to the rest of the house. But be- fore I opened that I put my ear to it. Hearing nothing, I pushed it open, and was therefore considerably surprised to see, standing in the hall, Tony, Roger and Sheila Maitland.

If I was surprised to see them, they were even more surprised to see me. There was a sound from Roger. Sheila's face flushed red; Tony's seemed to grow even more still than it was. But it was he who, after a second, spoke.

"Good God, Janet! What happened to you?"

Even knowing what I now knew about him, it was hard not to believe in the innocence he was portraying so convincingly. Instinct rather than thought made me aware of how much my safety lay in persuading him that I did indeed accept the role he was playing. Just in time I snatched back the words, *But you saw, you were there, after the car went over the cliff.* Instead, I said, "Gideon is dead. His car went off the road down the side of the hill."

"You mean it was you and Lightwood who went over? We saw the burning wreck, of course, when we passed. We didn't dream it was you. How terrible! But thank heaven you escaped!" Three long strides brought him over to me and I felt his arm go around me in a hug.

I glanced up at him. "Gideon took your car," I said, wondering what he would reply since he obviously already knew that fact. "So it was your car that went over."

"Yes. I was glad he did when I realized something had happened to his. Luckily one of the for-hire cars came in at that moment and we were able to get it. But this is frightful news about Lightwood. . . ."

As his voice went on and on I found it almost impossible not to believe the role of concerned friend, kindly boss, possibly even would-be lover that he was playing so movingly. No wonder he had, for a while, anyway, been such a successful politician. Politician . . .

The exchange that back at the inn had made no sense to me came back at that moment word for word:

Gideon had said, ". . . . *My mother's maiden name was Dreyfus. She was Austrian. And she was Jewish.*"

And Tony had replied, *"I see. That rather explains your interest in the deMaury papers, doesn't it?"*

The links forged themselves in my mind: Nathan Dreyfus, Zionist, Tony Bridewell, liberal politician, the deMaury papers . . . But there was, of course, a link missing—the link between Tony Bridewell, liberal politician, one-time politician, *about to be ambassador* and the papers.

All of this went through my head in a second or two. Tony's arm was still around me. Roger's and Sheila's eyes were on me. They, at least, were not skilled actors. There was no mistaking the hostility in their faces. All of which reminded me that there was something more urgent than the missing link I had just discovered. There was Benedict.

"How's Benedict?" I asked, moving as casually as I could away from Tony's arm.

"He took a bad turn and fainted," Sheila said. "We're taking him to the hospital."

"We felt sure that that was what Gideon would want," Roger said. "And we couldn't understand, of course, why both of you weren't here. Now that he's dead," Roger went on, beginning to rival Tony's acting skill in the sorrow reflected in his voice, "there's really no choice."

Oh, isn't there, I thought. But how on earth could I hope to stop them? I could, of course, tell them that I was onto their game, but what would that do besides making sure that I was dispatched with the greatest possible speed?

"How did you manage to save yourself?" Sheila asked, and I almost laughed. Her tone did not convey any sense of pleasure or congratulation that I had achieved this.

I was hesitating how to answer when all four of us were startled by hearing a loud knocking on the front door.

For a second no one moved. Then it occurred to me that since all my enemies were right in front of me, I might find an ally. I went towards the door. The fallacy of this reasoning became immediately apparent as I swung the huge door open and saw Dr. Maitland standing there. For a second I stared into the grayish face and black eyes. Then he pushed the door further open and walked past me.

"I thought she was dead," he said in a conversational tone.

"Be quiet," Tony rapped out. "Sheila, your father's not well. I think you should take him into the bookroom."

The silence crackled for a few seconds. Then, "Oh, very well," Sheila said. "But we don't have much time. When is the ambulance coming, Father?"

"I thought we would take him in the car," Dr. Maitland

said. "No need to have any more people involved in this, don't you think? By the way, I thought I told you to leave the gates open. They were shut. Now if we're to get Benedict safely tucked away— What are you doing?"

This last was addressed to his daughter, who by now had him by the arm and was tugging him. I moved so that I could see the doctor's face more clearly in the hall light. There was something about those black, black eyes that was pressing itself on my notice. Something that, on some level, I had known all along. . . . And then I saw. The pupils of his eyes were so large they had almost blotted out the dark brown of the iris. From everything I had heard and read, dilated pupils could mean, among other things, drug addiction, which went also with his face, his unreal manner and . . . Of course, I thought, it could explain so much about the strange couple. I looked then at Sheila and knew that not only was I right, but that she knew I knew.

"There's no need to take my father to the bookroom," she said. And her voice betrayed not only her anger but a curious kind of gloating pleasure. "Janet knows. What a pity you got away," she said to me. "However you managed it. We'll have to do the job all over again."

There was a taut silence. Then Tony said in a voice that was like a knife, "You're a stupid woman, Sheila. Stupid as well as greedy and vindictive."

"What the hell do you mean?" Sheila said.

"Now, look here," Roger started.

But Tony brushed them aside. "I mean that Janet is not and never has been very quick on the ball. Bright, yes. But gullible and trusting." He smiled at me. "Such a useful quality. And if you"—he turned back to Sheila— "hadn't threatened her, we might have just managed to get home clear without having to do anything about her which only increases our own risk. I have never been able to endure stupid people."

Tony's anger at Sheila was real and dangerous. He did not like people getting in his way or endangering his aims, and having now, through her bungling, to get rid of me, did just that. I started to slide my feet back as soundlessly as I could towards the kitchen door. *Tony burns,* my father had said. Well, it took one to know one. And although they nominally burned for different causes—Father for his Utopian society, Tony for his own ambition—the result was oddly the same. Well, let him burn now, burn with rage towards Sheila. Anything to distract him for a moment while I got away.

I was almost across the hall to the baize door when Tony saw me. "Oh, no, Janet," he said. "I'm afraid now we can't let you go."

I was through the kitchen door as he spoke. And I almost made it. If the kitchen had been smaller, so that I could have got through the back door and into the dark outside, I might have. It was Roger who caught me, twisting my arms to my back. There was no one to hear, of course, no one who could help me. Nevertheless, by instinct, I let out a loud scream and continued to scream until his hand went over my mouth.

"Why bother stopping her?" Sheila's voice asked back of me. "There's nobody to hear."

"No need to take any chances," Roger gasped. I was giving him a hard time. Years of athletics had made me strong and Roger was slight. I felt a sudden give in his arm as he spoke, yanked my head free, gave another scream and managed to scramble loose. But by this time Sheila had come around and was between me and the kitchen door. I turned to make a last desperate run through the house, and as I did so, saw her arm go up with something in her hand. Then everything went black.

I came to lying on the floor. My first sensation was one of pain. That was rapidly followed by a feeling of nausea. For a few minutes I fought that and it passed. Then, as I remembered what happened, I lay still, having no idea whether I was alone or not. After a while, although I heard no sound, I became quite sure that I was not alone. Cautiously, I turned as well as I could, considering that my wrists and ankles were bound, and I got myself into a position where I was able to some degree to look around. I was right. I was not alone. A man, also bound, was on the floor, his back to me. Friend or foe? Well, on the theory that the enemy of my enemy—and obviously he was no more liked around here than I at the moment—was my friend, I was about to speak when it occurred to me that I had better look further. There might, for all I knew, be a third person, unbound, and more than ready to knock me out again. So, wriggling and shifting as well as I could, I looked around.

I was in a large lighted bedroom lying at the end of what was obviously a twin bed, the other bed being some feet beyond my own feet. It was certainly not my bedroom. Nor, I thought, beginning a process of elimination, was it Benedict's. It did not look like a boy's room. The master bedroom—Gideon's? The name brought back another kind of pain. I'll have time for that later, I told myself, and made myself look around the room again.

Then I saw an open suitcase on one of the beds and I knew that I had seen it before, in New York. It was one of those flattish cases that looked part traveling bag and part brief case, and Tony used to bring it into the office on days when he would leave direct for Kennedy Airport on a trip. Which meant that this was Tony's bedroom. I took a last, searching look around, although I was sure by now that my bound companion was the room's only other occupant. Then I rolled back, preparatory to speaking, when the door opened. Hastily I shut my eyes, wondering if I was approximately in the same place I had been put in when I had been brought here, or if Tony—or whoever had just entered—would notice if I were not.

I had just decided there were two people when I heard Tony's voice.

"Thanks to Sheila's idiocy we're now going to have to get rid of Janet as well as our other friend over there. I suppose setting fire to the place is the only way. Well, it will be your loss, not mine. My God, you're welcome to one another! How can you stand that harpy?" There was a pause. "Or was it that you needed her?" I could almost see Tony's inquiring glance. "Yes, I suppose that was it. You needed her to aid in getting rid of Benedict. Just as a matter of curiosity, how were you planning to do that?"

I heard Roger's voice. "Are you sure they—Janet and that man—aren't conscious and can hear?"

"What difference does it make? They're not going to take the information anywhere. But you can check and see if you want."

"I thought I was fairly cold-blooded, but—" Roger said. "All right. I'll look."

I heard his feet walk past me and stop. After a minute the steps came towards me. I held my breath, thankful that the way I had turned my head quickly when they came in had made my hair fall over my eyes. Then I felt a hand on my wrist and realized Roger was feeling my pulse.

"They still seem to be out cold. I wonder who and what that man is—some sort of henchman of Gideon's I suppose. If you hadn't hit him so hard and so fast, Bridewell, we might have learned something."

"And he might have turned around and got a good look at me. No thanks. You haven't, by the way, answered my question. What were you planning for Gideon's son?"

There was a pause. Then I heard Roger's voice. "You know, I really don't think that's any business of yours. We've been able to aid each other's plans, it's true, but to use an Intelligence cliché, I believe in the need-to-know theory of giving out information."

"Suit yourself. But when the scandal breaks, and the press, knowing I've been here, starts nosing around and asking me questions—to say nothing of the police—then I hope that what I say fits into your interests."

Pause.

How clever of Tony, I thought! And how like him! I could almost hear his voice quoting a favorite maxim of his: always appeal to a person's self-interest; that's the best way to get him to do what you want. For a minute I almost laughed, and then stopped myself just in time.

"I suppose"—Roger's voice sounded more the sulky adolescent than the smooth young man I had first met—"I suppose you're right.

"Well, it all began about six months or so ago. Benedict's leg had improved enormously. He was getting about quite well and nagging his father to go to boarding school. Gideon even put his name in for his own old school for this September. We—Sheila and I—knew that when Benedict went away to school the game—our game—would be over."

"By this time, I take it, you two had formed a . . . a mutual aid society." Tony's voice held amusement as well as—I could hear—contempt. But then I knew him. And in the past hour or so I had come to see how much contempt he had—had always had—for everyone.

"Yes. I had been observing Sheila's efforts to charm Gideon into marriage on my occasional visits to Tenton. It occurred to me to put a spoke in her wheel—I'm quite good at that, as I'm sure you can imagine. After all, it didn't serve my interests to have Gideon marry again and produce more sons. But, luckily for me, I didn't—mostly because I wasn't quite sure how best to go about it. But then she played her hand too hard—subtlety was never her strong point. Gideon's interest obviously waned, and I saw how her mania to become Lady Lightwood could be used to our mutual benefit. So, I encouraged her to think that if she threw in her lot with me and helped me to remove the obstacles to my inheriting the title, that she would indeed achieve her heart's desire. Not being so obvious about transferring her affections, of course, as to arouse Gideon's suspicions. Anyway, it was shortly after that that Gideon entered Benedict's name in his old school, and I knew Sheila and I had to make our move.

"You're right, of course, when you call her a harpy." Roger's voice contained all that charming candor that had first attracted me. "But, as you noted, our interests did indeed coincide. Sheila has an old-fashioned obsession to be lady of the manor, something quite pre–World War II. I think it had to do with her mother, who—in an equally *passé* phrase—married beneath herself and never failed to get a dig into her husband—Dr. Maitland—about it. Who knows? Maybe that's what drove him to drugs. Anyway, the late Mrs. Maitland instilled into Sheila that being a lady, especially with a capital L, was the only thing in life that mattered. So for the first year, while Sheila was here looking after Benedict and presumably preparing him for school, she worked her considerable charms on Gideon, who was not totally invulnerable. After all, what with, I gather, was a bad marriage and Rosemary's sudden death, and his preoccupation with Benedict's illness, he had led a pretty spartan life.

"But just about the time he was almost ready to come out of his shell, she started making mistakes, overdoing it a bit here and there, and he began to sheer off."

"Why didn't Lightwood get rid of her?"

"Because he needed someone to help with Benedict, preferably, for the boy's sake, someone young. And it's not easy to find somebody for a remote place like this, especially if you can't pay them too well. Also, his disenchantment didn't happen all at once."

"Yes, all right. And then what?"

"At that interesting point yours truly drifted in."

There was a slight sound of creaking bedsprings. Behind the curtain of my hair I half opened one eye. Roger had settled himself on the twin bed opposite Tony, who, his back towards me, was leaning against the footboard of the bed near me, his hand on the open top of the suitcase.

Roger leaned back on his hands and went on. "I had just run out of a job and came back for a bit of free board and lodging and to see how my nephew was doing. After all, if anything happened to him I stood next in line to inherit."

"To inherit what, for God's sake?" Tony asked impatiently. "A crumbling house that would cost more than the estate provides to put back in repair and a title in a growingly socialist state?"

"Well, being an American, you probably don't understand. We may be a socialist state. But titles—particularly one as old as this—still mean something. And as far as money is concerned, Gideon owns large tracts of land that are unentailed and I just happened to learn from a man I know who has a friend in financial circles that Gideon's been offered a big sum—in the millions—for a hunk of it; the part near the town—for housing estates. Only the idiot turned it down. I can tell you right now I wouldn't. In fact, come about six months, I won't."

"Why did Lightwood turn it down?"

"He's some kind of wildlife fanatic. Said that's one of the few stretches of country left in these parts where the local flora and fauna can survive. And the naturalists' societies kicked up a rumpus."

"I see. So when you came here you and Sheila realized that your interests—if not your hearts—beat as one."

"Quite. I think she knew then that she might not get Gideon. So we—er—merged. Sheila's part was to reverse Benedict's recovery as rapidly as possible, without alerting Gideon so that he smelt a rat. The whole idea being to make him appear unstable enough so that in six months or so his being institutionalized would seem the only logical thing. Once he was institutionalized in, of course, a private institution of Dr. Maitland's choosing, then the good doctor would take care of the rest, and I would be free to turn my attention to Gideon. For these purposes, Benedict's original accident—the one with the pony— was perfect. On the pretext of building him up with vitamins, Sheila started feeding him alternately stimulants —mostly amphetamines—and sedatives, so that he began to swing between moods when he appeared high one time and languid a few hours or a day later. Not too much at first, of course, but getting slowly more pronounced over a longish period."

"And I suppose she got all those pills and drugs easily enough from her father. I'm surprised Lightwood didn't catch on."

"Why should he? He didn't know anything about medicine. All he knew was that when he came home from various business trips Benedict would either be frenetic or languid. And when he was frenetic, and Gideon tried to control or discipline him, then the boy'd get hysterical. Besides, during a lot of this time Gideon was still under Sheila's spell, although it was getting weaker.

And, don't forget, she trained both as a nurse and as a teacher, which Gideon, desperate to find the right person for Benedict, found pretty impressive."

"So impressive that when she seemed amenable to working for slave wages he should have smelled a rat—a large one," Tony commented wryly.

"Not if part of the stated attraction for Sheila was, as she told Gideon, that she could be near enough to live at home and take care of her father. Gideon's very much for the old stout virtues. It was given out, when the Maitlands arrived here, that the good doctor had given up a busy city practice for reasons of health. In a way it was the truth—or at least part of the truth. He retired for health, all right. He's a drug addict. After one or two incidents it began to be known that he was taking his own drugs and he sold the practice before legal action was taken."

"Did Sheila know this?"

"Of course."

"Does she drug herself?"

"Not much, not addictively. I think she rather fancies what you Americans call speed—amphetamines. It keeps her stimulated and she likes that. But it's when she's up that she makes her mistakes, so she tried to keep it under control."

"And she told you all this?"

"Oh, no," Roger said languidly. "I made it my business to find out one or two things when I discovered her here. A few discreet inquiries among certain circles in London yielded *very* revealing details. After all, unlike Gideon, I do not particularly admire the solid virtues, caring for an aged parent, etcetera, nor did I find the wench attractive. So no wool was pulled over my eyes."

"I see. You blackmailed Sheila into your merger."

"Oh, it appealed to her own interests, too, though a little pressure made her even more amenable. But"—here Roger's voice lost some of its amiability—"she could never leave well enough alone. It was when I wasn't here that Sheila hit on the scheme to have Benedict be a diabetic. She gets these brainstorms and doesn't check herself. Her father in one of his less drugged moments told her it wouldn't wash, that it could be too easily checked, and that it was too dangerous. But you've seen what she's like when she gets a notion in her head—it's probably due to her pet drug. Anyway, he told her—I know because he told me—that the kind of diabetes children develop is almost invariably the serious kind, not the relatively mild variety adults can get in midlife that is controllable by diet."

"Why did she bother with it? Wasn't she building up a strong enough case with the other drugs?"

"I told you," Roger said impatiently. "She likes to fiddle. Elaborate. Also," he added grudgingly, "Gideon, in one of their growing quarrels over Benedict, said that she was cosseting him, that physically he was getting better—which was true—and that perhaps his instability was due to too much spoiling and too little exercise. That's when she had her brainwave about saying he—Benedict—had diabetes. It established a physical disease in Gideon's mind. And you've got to remember that Gideon comes from a long line of stoics and soldiers who still believe that anything in the head is not really a disease and is therefore not quite credible. Something that is physical that can be tested under a microscope is different. But then Sheila made a mistake. She had said the diabetes could be kept in control by watching Benedict's diet. Of course, when Janet saw the syringe—which Sheila was now using in her carefully escalated program of amphetamines and sedatives, since injections are more powerful than pills—then she realized she had to cover herself by saying that Benedict's diabetes had got worse and now had to be treated by shots of insulin. What a pity you had to send Janet over here! Everything was going so well! But her presence precipitated things. Sheila can't bear another woman to have what she doesn't—particularly if she'd tried for it herself. And Gideon's obvious attraction to Janet made her behave stupidly: needling Janet about her wretched dog, playing lady of the manor, calling Gideon darling in front of Janet—knowing Gideon, it was the worst thing she could have done."

"And then I turned up," Tony said, snapping his case shut. "Too bad."

"Well, it rushed things," Roger said. "But as everything turned out, it may work just as well."

His voice was so exaggeratedly casual that I opened an eye. He was, I noticed, not looking at Tony, but appeared to be examining the fingernails of one hand.

"Just as a matter of curiosity," Tony said, almost as casually, "why did you shoot at Lightwood and Janet when they went over to see that tenant, Evan whatever his name is? Weren't you running a risk?"

"On the contrary. It seemed a heaven-sent opportunity. I saw Gideon talking to Evan from my window. Then I saw him come back into the house and emerge again with Janet's dog. When I bumped into Gideon and Janet on their way, they said, to look for the dog, I realized he had set up the whole thing—probably to impress Janet with his tender care for her interests. So I knew where they were going. And it was too good a chance to dispatch Gideon and get someone else blamed for it.

"Of course, it reversed things a bit in our plan: Benedict was to go first. But he was well on his way to an institution. Now I had a way to remove Gideon without anyone's suspecting. Poor Williams' reputation with the gun—not to mention strong drink—was so well established. He's a crafty old fox but I didn't think he could stand up in the kind of murder trial that would result. Anyway, it was a chance and I took it.

"So I got there ahead of them and told Williams that Gideon had changed his mind about coming and wanted him to take the cur immediately to the rector, which lay in nearly the opposite direction from where Gideon and Janet would be coming."

"And he believed you?"

"Why not? He used to be shrewd enough, but large and frequent potions of daily and nightly beer have not helped his reasoning. Besides, I gave him some money."

"But he would have heard the shots. Couldn't he have implicated you?"

"How? It would be his word against mine. As I said, given his reputation, who would believe him? Besides"— Roger went on with one of his charming smiles—"who could tell what might happen to the old rascal?"

"And you called me cold-blooded!" Tony said somewhat grimly.

I opened an eye in time to see Roger grin. "I may be cold-blooded, but I'm not as stupid as popular mythology would make out, for all that Gideon was always supposed to be the bright one. And he must have been far from bright, or far gone in love, to leave you alone to nose out that room beneath the attic, behind the paneling, where he'd hidden those papers, especially as it didn't take you long to find the entrance, did it?"

There was another pause. I would have given much to see Tony's face. But given the look of little boy triumph on Roger's, I could easily imagine that Tony, who was skilled at manipulating people into making damaging admissions, was leading him on. Watch it, I tried to send a message to Gideon's half brother. Not because he wasn't as much a murderer, or would-be murderer, as Tony. But because if I were lucky, and my enemies were about to fall on one another, I would rather be left having to cope with Roger.

"No," Tony said. "It was quite easy when one realized the entry was from above through an opening in the attic floor usually covered by the rug. I discovered that the night I was up there when Janet got knocked on the head."

He said it coolly. Again, I had to prevent myself from making a sound.

"So it was you who knocked her on the head, the way she insisted?" Roger said.

"No. It wasn't. I gathered it must have been Lightwood, which meant that she was getting near something he didn't want found out. I was in the far attic with the papers and with the door closed. But when I heard the hubbub outside—she kicked something—I stayed where I was. Eventually I heard someone moving about and then going downstairs. I waited until the coast was clear and came out. I had a flashlight with me, and could see that where Janet had fallen, she had pushed the rug aside, and I saw the trapdoor then."

"And you found the missing papers," Roger said. "A small but interesting lot, meant, of course, for Robert deMaury's memoirs, which he never got to write. I had a look at them myself. After Janet's cable there was a flurry of activity in the attic—the discovery of the vandalization and the arrival of the cartons. So, because I like to keep on top of things, and because that lower room was always used to hide odd bits and pieces the Lightwoods didn't want people nosing into, I went down there to see what I could see." Roger grinned. "It was a worthwhile trip. The papers weren't totally conclusive, but were more than enough to convince any American Senate committee that had to confirm your appointment as ambassador as to your unfitness. As you can see I've kept up with American politics! Copies of those papers, alluding to that timely contribution to your campaign expenses from the Arab oil conglomerate would be of absorbing interest to any one of the Zionist or other Jewish agencies in the States. You might even go to jail—I don't know enough about your American laws to be sure of that. But I do know enough to know that that would be the end of your political career. What I am slightly baffled about, though, is what Robert deMaury, secular saint and peace laureate, was getting out of blackmailing you about the contribution? What did he hope to get from you?"

"Not from me," Tony said almost casually. "You've got the cart before the horse. From his Arab friends. They were willing to underwrite that last tribute to his ravenous vanity, that World Union Congress in Moscow, just before he died that turned out to be such a fiasco. Along with the money, they gave him this tidbit about me—the contribution made long before when I was running for Congress, so, as a quid pro quo for the Moscow financing, he could use it to control me for their interest and, incidentally, his own."

"Why didn't they blackmail you direct?"

"Because that egotistical old fakir was one of the few people who could bluff them at their own game, and they, along with a lot of other people at that time, overestimated his influence in world affairs. Playing around in Western politics was something fairly new for them then, and they made mistakes. Robert deMaury was one of them. They didn't realize how old hat he and his precious Society were. But, I suppose, from their point of view it wasn't such a mistake. When deMaury talked about world union he always meant Russia. And with Russia, of course, stood the Arabs. And there Israel was, a thorn in the flesh to his friends, the Arabs, and therefore—if you'll excuse the mixed metaphor—a fly in the ointment to his great vision of a world united."

"But then Robert deMaury died. How convenient for you! So you were free at last from one of your blackmailers, with no one the wiser. . . ."

Lying there, my eyes now dangerously wide open out of sheer shock, I could almost see Roger's facile brain ticking over while he paused, figuring the logic of the next step.

". . . no one the wiser," he continued, "except perhaps, Rosemary. The spiritual daughter, the worshiper at the shrine, who died in front of a hit-and-run car in Italy. Well, well . . ."

Tony's move was so smooth I almost missed it. One moment he was standing relaxed. The next he was holding a gun.

"And it's no use waving that gun at me, Bridewell," Roger continued in that same voice. "I know you've got the papers in that suitcase, but I have copies. Killing me will do no good. Sheila has the copies and she's just as interested in money as I am. In fact—"

"If you're interested in blackmailing me," Tony said a little grimly, "why did you place that explosive in my car that blew up as it took your brother over the side?"

"I didn't," Roger said. "Gideon did. To get two birds with one stone—both you and me." He was eying the gun a little less confidently.

"Won't wash, Roger. Why should he want us out of the way? And if he had, why use the car himself?"

Roger shrugged. His *sang-froid* before Tony's gun was beginning to fray. "He wanted to get rid of you, Bridewell, because he'd read those papers. Have you forgotten he's half Jewish? Practically all his mother's family died in the camps. As for me . . . well, there's never been any love lost between us. And he may have begun to suspect some kind of alliance concerning Benedict between Sheila and me. And as for getting in the car himself—perhaps he miscalculated the timing, or planned to put it across the road so that if we were pursuing him we would be blown up. Who knows?"

It was obvious to me that Roger was now badly frightened. Despite a strained attempt at his usual grin, his face showed it. And I knew that if I saw it, the far cannier Tony would see and know just how to use it.

"Good effort," Tony said approvingly. "But I have another version. Would you like to hear it? You wanted me out of the way for the simplest of reasons. There were to be no witnesses left to the plans you and Sheila managed so beautifully. Certainly not a witness who might know how to use his knowledge for his own benefit. And having read those papers, you were not under any —er—illusions about my high-minded motives. That's about it, isn't it?"

Almost I felt sorry for Roger. The expression on his face revealed not only that Tony had scored a bull's-eye, but that Roger himself knew now that he'd been outmatched.

"I wonder," Tony said musingly, "whether you were going to find some entirely acceptable reason for me not to drive you to that train you said you were going to catch, or whether the bomb or whatever it was was set to go off after the train had left, when I was alone in the car? I don't suppose now I'll ever know. I'm afraid, Roger old chap, yours is going to be one of the bodies hopelessly charred by the tragic fire that will break out and take so many lives. Such a pity to lose an old house like this, but the timbers must be dry as dust—"

"All right, Bridewell, drop the gun. The police are here—"

The voice came from the door. I literally could not believe my ears. Two shots rang out, one right after the other.

"Gideon!" I cried. To have him alive and then to have him killed was unthinkable. Since Tony was still standing I assumed he was unhurt. Then I saw him drop the gun.

"Damn you to hell, Lightwood," he said. And I saw the blood oozing from the arm that had held the gun.

# twelve

"GIDEON, DARLING," I said as he untied me. "I thought you were dead in that car."

"No, I got out before I steered it over. And only just in time. That little explosive device Tony was talking about that Roger had put in the boot went off a few seconds after the car plunged down the side." Gideon straightened up. "Even so, Roger, you almost got away with that, at least. Two seconds later and the explosion would have been assumed to be the gasoline tank."

"Did you know it was going to blow up?" I asked.

"I guessed, when their car kept an even distance behind. If Roger hadn't been pretty sure I'd blow up, anyway, he'd have moved heaven and earth to catch up with me. Luckily I tumbled to that in time to get you out and then myself when I was around a curve and no one could see. Then I steered the car straight for the edge. Yes, thanks, Jacob. Keep the gun on them. The police will be up here shortly."

Sitting up and rubbing my wrists, I was astonished to see my erstwhile bound companion sit up of his own accord and then get to his feet. In his hand was a service-able-looking revolver.

I looked up at his face. "You're the man I saw outside the old Society headquarters in London."

He smiled and said with his slight accent, "That's right."

"But—but if you could get up that easily, if you weren't really tied, why didn't you get up sooner?"

"Because," Gideon put in, "he had two jobs here, one of which was to collect any evidence he could. Were you able to get anything on tape, Jacob?"

The man put his free hand inside his jacket and brought out a flat, oblong object. "I turned it on while they talked," he said. "Which was one reason, Miss deMaury, I didn't get up as you just asked. As soon as I realized they were going to spill some information I lay there—just as I suspect you did—giving all the appearance of being out cold."

"How did you know I wasn't really out?"

The narrow, seamed face smiled. "I've had a lot of experience. More, luckily, than Mr. Roger Lightwood here. I was about to get up and untie you—having managed to get my own hands untied—when they came back in and started talking. I decided that it was more important, as Gideon said, to collect the evidence against Mr. Bridewell, here."

I glanced over at Tony, who was now sitting on the other twin bed, one hand gripping his arm. Blood was seeping through his fingers. The blue eyes were looking at Gideon, this time with open hatred. "Tapes are not always permissible in court," he said. "Your so-called evidence could amount to nothing."

"Perhaps not," Gideon agreed. "But I can imagine that any one of several agencies I could send a copy to of that tape in New York would know how to publicize the contents."

He strode forward towards the bag lying on the near twin bed. I saw Tony make a move. Jacob's pistol came up. "Sit where you are, Mr. Bridewell." Out of the corner of my eye I noticed that with his other hand he touched some kind of a switch on the recording device and placed it on the bureau behind him.

"So that's why you wanted those papers," I said to Tony. "All that bit about a biography of my father was so much cover."

Tony's eyes never wavered. But he didn't open his mouth.

"What I can't understand," I said, "is how you ever took that money in the first place."

"Do you want to comment on that, Bridewell, or shall I?" Gideon said. When Tony still didn't speak, he went on, "All right, then." He looked over at me. "Some time before the 1967 six-day war between Israel and Egypt, when Bridewell was running for the House of Representatives, he found himself in need of money—even the richest run short sometimes in campaign spending, and that was well before the laws limiting the amount that could be spent. Anyway, he tried to raise it in various places without much success, and was then offered a sizable contribution by a Mideast oil combine—an Arab outfit, not to put too fine a point on it. And he took it. In return for that largesse he was not expected to do anything radical, like filibustering against aid to Israel— anything so obvious would be self-defeating. But not to lend such aid any support, and, wherever he could, without endangering his own interests, to discourage it. And this negative influence from someone generally considered to have the liberal cause at heart might well sway those who couldn't make up their minds. So when the various pro-Israel groups in and out of Congress looked around for help from those they expected to give it, he managed never to be there. That's what my cousin Nathan Dreyfus pointed out, remember? And Bridewell had such splendid liberal credentials in all other respects that it took his fellow liberals quite a while to notice this. When some of them did, he lost enough support to be defeated at the next election. So Bridewell returned to his publishing house.

"But other than this strange anomaly—that Bridewell was out to lunch whenever any kind of support for Israel came up—no one had anything to go on. There were those both in Israel and in New York who would have loved to pursue this further. But there were no visible grounds. So there the matter rested, except for a few pig-headed types like Jacob here and Nathan and myself and one or two others both in New York and Israel.

"But no matter how much we dug we found nothing. And then one day Rosemary"—he paused here and then went on—"Rosemary accidentally let something fall. We were having one of our, by then, frequent arguments over the Society your father founded. It was an argument that went on, unfortunately, for years, and . . . and, I suppose, helped to destroy the marriage. To Rosemary, the Society was your father, and she looked on him as a devout Catholic would look on a saint. He could do no wrong. I think she honestly considered him the greatest influence for good in the twentieth century. . . .

"Anyway, the argument could be boiled down to whether peace was worth it at any price. To Rosemary, as to your father, the prerequisite of world union was world peace, so the answer was yes. To me, feeling as I did about the holocaust and Israel, the answer was no: some prices—such as the destruction of Israel—were too high.

"In the heat of argument after a dinner party in which politics had been the main topic of conversation, and Rosemary had had more than her usual one drink, she said something—I can't remember the exact words—but it included something about Robert deMaury's hold on Bridewell being an example of the end justifying the means.

"I asked her what she meant, but she refused to say anything more. So I started looking around at the other end—Robert deMaury's end. I was in British Intelligence then and there was considerable liaison with Israeli Intelligence. So some friends in both groups and I started asking ourselves the old question: Cui bono? What would be in a deMaury-Bridewell linkup for deMaury or his pals?

"Slowly we put the pieces together. I always wondered

where your father got the money for that final disastrous splash—the congress in Moscow. Tony was about right when he called it the last tribute to deMaury's ravenous vanity. . . ."

Gideon glanced at me. "If this wounds you—"

I shook my head. "It doesn't—that much, anyway. It's no great shock. Mother never used those terms, neither did I—but we might have. But I still don't see why he needed money. Think of some of his supporters! The Red Peer, the Red Dean, the pundits, the double domes, as mother sometimes called them—all of them willing to drop everything and run when he summoned. To them he was supposed to rank with Gandhi as *the* twentieth-century saint."

"To be fair to him, Robert deMaury probably did start out as an idealist. But he always was one of the greatest egotists that ever played politics with kings, presidents and prime ministers. And he ended up confusing the sanctity of his ideas with universal law."

"But why couldn't he get the money, what with anti-Vietnam war peace groups coming out of the woodwork at that time?"

"Because he wanted something more than a collection of hippies, college radicals and other dissenters. Remember, in the midsixties, the Establishment was still sitting on the sidelines and the peace movement hadn't really grown teeth. What he wanted were heads of state, or at least their ministers, leading intellectuals, ranking clergy and so on. I honestly think he believed that if the Peace Congress as he saw it went through, he'd be the only man in history to be awarded the Peace Prize twice. But all that cost money—especially if the expenses of some of the main attractions and celebrities were to be paid. And when the Society sent out its usual solicitations, they got back a fraction of their normal haul. DeMaury was stunned to discover that the Society and its members were considered old hat, passé. The new peace people were on the streets in jeans, not in embassies, chancelleries and universities in pinstripes. The other drawback was the original idea for the Society—world union. In the thirties and forties it sounded like a noble concept. But by the sixties, so far from wanting union, most of the developing nations were spinning off on their own, and in the United States, when the young weren't marching for peace they were busy asserting their ethnic and racial identities and unmelting the melting pot.

"When deMaury started trying, without much success, to raise money elsewhere, some bright Arabs saw in this excursion into vanity the opportunity they had been looking for. Along with the money they handed over the information about Bridewell.

"This had two advantages for them. One: they could operate from behind deMaury, a deeply respected figure; and two: they knew that by this time deMaury was so blinded by bewitchment with his own idea, plus a useful residue of anti-Semitism, that his interest and theirs would be pretty much as one. And Bridewell played up, didn't you?"

Gideon, still holding his gun, faced Tony, who was now sitting on the bed holding his arm, his face white.

"Do you want me to bleed to death before your copper friends get here?" he asked.

"By no means. I want you to be alive and well when all this comes out, so you can be around to enjoy it. Cover me, Jacob."

Going over to him, Gideon used two handkerchiefs and my scarf to fashion a serviceable bandage and sling. "You're going to live, Bridewell. It's not serious."

As he backed away I asked, "What do you mean by Tony playing up? Not supporting Israeli interests?"

"That and feeding on deMaury's incessant demands for public attention. How many times was your father summoned to Washington to testify before some committee? A committee, I need hardly add, that Bridewell was on. According to Nathan and various New York friends he became a regular feature—whether he had anything genuinely useful to say or not.

"And then in 1970 he died. By this time Bridewell was defeated and out of Congress, but with deMaury dead, he must have known that one hook was taken out of him. But then he discovered that Robert deMaury had told Rosemary. And Rosemary"—again Gideon hesitated—"Rosemary, who also knew the uses of power, let Tony know she knew. Remember that dinner party I gave for all the nonstereotypes—the communist peer, the capitalist student? Well, Rosemary did not think it was so funny, although Bridewell, who was, as you may remember, also there, did. When I was seeing the other guests to the door, I heard him run the needle into her a little. So Rosemary needled him back. All she said was a half sentence about campaign contributions, but there was a chilly silence when I walked back into the room."

Gideon turned to Tony. "So you bided your time, Bridewell, didn't you? And your opportunity came a year later in Italy when Janet and Rosemary were going to meet in the piazza after that late party which you had left earlier. Who would associate you with a hit-and-run killing? And it worked so well, in fact, that I suspect you succumbed, like the gambler you are, to the temptation to try it again on Janet here a few days ago."

Tony's eyes, which had been fixed stonily on Gideon, flickered.

"That was it, wasn't it?" I said to him. "Because of that idiotic message I left with Cynthia as a joke, you knew I had come across some reference to your Arab oil ties."

His eyes glanced in my direction and then down and I knew I was right.

"But, even with Father and Rosemary dead," I said then to Gideon, "his Arab friends knew about his contribution—since they'd given him the money. So he wasn't really off the hook."

"What hook? The Arabs certainly weren't going to blow the whistle on him as long as he showed a reasonable concern for their interests—nothing dramatic, just a steady anti-Israeli influence in high places. Anyway, the matter by then was academic because Bridewell was out of Congress. Not for one moment had he given up his drive for power. He was just lying dormant for the time being—letting the dust settle. And then the gods must have seemed to him to smile on him again. The American ambassador in London fell ill and was forced to resign for reasons of health. Bridewell's name started being mentioned as a possible, and then likely, and then certain candidate. And it would assuredly be a stepping stone to higher things."

"But wouldn't your cousin Nathan Dreyfus and other Jewish agencies point out his anti-Israel bias?"

"Of course. But what proof did they have? Absenteeism when votes came up? There were plenty in Congress who had done exactly the same. He could always claim that the Zionist forces were hysterical and paranoid—that he was merely a U.S. congressman putting, as he should, his own country's interests first. And, as I repeat, there was no proof—at least none that he knew about at the time. Bridewell was clever enough to make sure that any contribution he had received had been laundered enough for it to look legitimate. . . ."

"The deMaury papers," I said, looking at the suitcase. "They were the proof."

"Precisely." Gideon went forward, opened Tony's suitcase, threw out the clothes and pulled out a handful of papers. He turned and looked at Tony. "You found these in the room under the attic, where I intended you to find them—hence all my elaborate hints about the room and the paneling. It was the confirmation I needed, which is why I removed Janet and me for the trumped-up reason of looking for her dog."

Watching, I saw Tony's eyes flicker again. At that moment, two men in plain clothes appeared in the doorway.

"We have Miss Maitland and her father," one of them, a stolid-looking man in his fifties, said. And added almost laconically, "They admitted everything almost immediately."

"My son?" Gideon said.

"He's come around from the sedative she gave him. The police doctor is with him. Says he'll be fine."

Some of the strain went out of Gideon's face.

"I'm glad," I said. And meant it. Gideon looked at

me. So often I had found his face unreadable. Now what was there was unmistakable. I felt my heart skip a beat.

"We're ready to take Mr. Bridewell," the police said.

"I've committed no crime in this country," Tony said. He had shifted so that he was facing all of us.

"Well, I don't know, Mr. Bridewell," the other plain-clothesman said. "Knocking an old woman on the head, tying her up and locking her in her room is a crime."

"Mrs. Lowndes," I said. "I'd forgotten about her."

"Well, we hadn't."

I looked at Gideon. "How did the police know to come?"

"Because when I had crawled out of the car before steering it over, and saw you given a lift, I flagged down the first car I could, hitched a ride to the nearest police station, called my friend John Renfrew, who is chief constable around here, and he got in touch with the local C.I.D."

"The man you had lunch with that day, Sir John Renfrew."

"Yes. I told him what I was up to—as much as I could—and alerted him."

My mind was looping back. "And it all started because Tony met Myron Weatherby, secretary of the Society. Was that just a lucky coincidence for you, Gideon?"

"Of course not. I don't believe in coincidences. We, Jacob and a few like-minded friends and I, set it up that these papers should be found and shipped to me. It wasn't difficult. The Society in London had dwindled to a few well-meaning but somewhat dim-witted codgers of both sexes. Since they were about to lose their space, they accepted with avidity the suggestion that I, the late Rosemary's husband, should store the deMaury papers, and were perfectly happy to ship them to me. They were also fed the idea of a commemorating biography, which they obediently and happily passed on to Myron Weatherby, along with the suggestion that Bridewell and Denby would be the obvious house. Weatherby, amiable and not very bright, could be depended on to pass it along to Bridewell. Which he did.

"Bridewell saw, as he was meant to see, an opportunity to get hold of any deMaury papers that might implicate him in that original contribution. I don't think he thought there *would* be any records. But he sent you over here, Janet, to make sure."

"But why me? Why didn't he come himself?"

"Well, that, of course, was what I wanted him to do, which will explain the curtness of my letter to you, and the less than cordial reception you had when you arrived. It was not at all what I planned in this elaborate setup to get Bridewell over here. In addition to which, I had always assumed—please forgive me—that you were more or less in cahoots with him. And when you turned up in his place, I was sure of it." He glanced at me. "I'm sorry, Janet."

"It's all right. I understand. I mean, how could you think anything else? But I still don't understand why he sent me."

"It was a risk, of course. But I suppose he weighed the danger of having you see something you shouldn't—after all he didn't think there were any incriminating documents—with the greater danger, at this point in his career, of showing too much interest. Also weighing heavily on the side of his sending you was the fact that he believed, as did most of the people around you, that you were so in love with him that you could be depended on to see no evil, or, if you did, to remain loyal. If push came to shove I think Bridewell would have been quite willing to marry you to prevent that."

I could feel my face getting red. "What a boost for my ego." I frowned. "Then who dropped that note on my floor?"

"Oh, that was Roger. He and Sheila found your presence, at such a delicate point in their own plans, rather inconvenient."

"And I suppose," I said, "that that man I saw going out of your door in the middle of the night was Jacob here?"

Gideon nodded. "He came straight up here after seeing

you in London and managed to keep out of sight during the day practically all the time. I'd heard that Bridewell was over here, and I wasn't taking any chances with either of you—particularly since I'd heard Bridewell's suspicions had been aroused."

"How did you know that?" I asked.

Gideon smiled. "You have a very gossipy co-worker named Jason Bradshaw. One of Jacob's and my friends in New York has been cultivating him assiduously. And there is nothing around your office—including Bridewell's calls to his secretary—that he doesn't winkle out of somebody."

"Gwyneth!" I said, suddenly remembering her. "The rector hasn't heard from her."

"He has by now. She's fine."

"Was she in all this too?"

"Oh, yes. I recommended her for her first job—in the same government department I was in. She went to London to get the records on Maitland. The call from George Tyrrel—same initials, made at her request by a male friend—told me about the good doctor. By the way, she thought she recognized Bridewell behind the wheel of the car that day he nearly ran you down. Evidently her angle of vision was different, and she wasn't quite as blinded by the lights." Gideon looked down at Tony. "You made quite an impression on her at that famous dinner we had, Bridewell." He glanced back at me. "And that was the reason why she was so upset, Janet, and why she wanted you to leave for New York."

"Why didn't she tell me that she thought it was Tony?"

"Because she wasn't positive. And because she thought that telling you might put you in even greater danger." Gideon paused, and then said, "Well, Bridewell, you're right about one thing. You're an alien, so I'm not sure what we can do about you over here. But I'm fairly certain a copy of that tape to an American newspaper would go far to keep you out of political life."

Tony's eyes were like blue flags. His terrible drive seemed at that moment to be at work inside him in some massive convulsion. Gideon might know everything about Tony's politics. But I had known him almost all my life, and I was aware of an eerie, but urgent, sense of danger.

"Gideon," I said.

But he had turned to the two men at the door. "You can take him now. And . . . and my brother. I suppose the others are downstairs."

"Yes. They're with Sergeant Anthony."

I had totally forgotten about Roger, even though he was sitting on the same bed as Tony, only a few feet from him. And then everything happened at once.

As Gideon's attention had strayed, Roger had leaned forward to snatch at the gun in his hand. At that moment Tony sprang for it. There was a struggle among the three men. Then Tony stood with the gun. Before anyone could stop him he turned the muzzle to his head and pulled the trigger.

Much later, Gideon and I were in the library. The police had taken Roger and Sheila away and a mortuary van had removed Tony's body. The rector had delivered Buff, who had proceeded to act as though our separation had been one of years, and then, exhausted by emotion, had gone sound asleep in front of the fire that Gideon had lit.

"I wonder," I said staring at her, "if things would have been exactly the same if Buff, who seemed like such an accident, had not happened along in my life."

"Probably not. I think she was something of a catalytic agent. If it hadn't been for her, I don't think Sheila, for one, would have lost her head so much. I'm beginning not to believe in accidents, either."

"That sounds rather portentous," I said. "Rather like John Knox or John Calvin. Something Presbyterian and full of predestination."

But Gideon didn't smile. "I owe you such a huge apology, Janet. And I don't know where to begin. I thought you, like Rosemary, knew all about your father's and Tony's goings on, and went along with them. I also— God forgive me—thought you might have known about

Tony's killing Rosemary, and because you were so in love with him, justified it to yourself in some way. And if all that wasn't enough, it was I who knocked you on the head in the attic, my darling. I'm sorry."

"I realize that. I'll even forgive it. But why? And why did you go on insisting that I had fallen downstairs? That bothered me almost as much as being hit on the head."

"I knocked you on the head because I had followed Bridewell upstairs into the attic where the papers were. I had stayed up deliberately to see if he would do something like that. The fact that he'd get up in the middle of the night to go up there was all the confirmation I needed. And then your wretched dog turned up. I could hear her coming upstairs. Then I saw her with my torch. I knew any second that she'd bark and give away my presence, so I tied her muzzle up with a piece of string that was lying around, and then wrapped her in the afghan. Just when I thought I had her settled, you appeared. I had been originally convinced, as I said, that you knew what Bridewell wanted and were in it with him. But you had been at Tenton for a while, and I was finding it harder and harder to believe that. Besides, if you were in league with him, you'd hardly be coming upstairs calling your pet. You'd be calling Bridewell. That was the first time I seriously considered the fact that you mightn't know what he had been up to. In any case, I didn't want to risk either distracting Bridewell from what he was doing, or having him come out and turn on the light, in which case he would see me, and the game would be up.

"So I hit you. I tried to hit you as lightly as I could to do the job. But I insisted, later, that you had fallen downstairs partly for your own safety. Bridewell would know he hadn't hit you. If he thought someone else—I, for instance—had, he would not only be alerted to danger for himself, he would certainly know that someone suspected him, and if that were so, you might be involved. So, because I was beginning to believe in your innocence, and knew I had also to keep him from suspecting that I was on to him, I thought it wiser all around to state, firmly, that you had hit your head yourself on a piece of furniture and then fallen downstairs."

"Thinking all that about me, no wonder your letter was so full of warmth and charm. When did you change your mind?"

He shrugged. "After you arrived."

"You mean my integrity of character and purity of motive impressed themselves on you."

He smiled slightly. "Not exactly."

"Then what?"

He made a gesture with his hands. "Everything. Also, there was something about your single-minded devotion to this really tiresome dog—"

"—she's not tiresome."

"—that made it hard for me to put it together with the other qualities I had always thought you had had— ruthlessness, in the manner of your father and cousin, for one thing. Besides, you kept taking time out for her when, if you had really been here to destroy any evidence against Bridewell, you would have kept your nose to that particular grindstone. Besides . . ." He paused.

"Besides what?"

"I fell in love with you," he said. I stepped over Buff towards him and his arms went around me.

Still later I turned my head against his shoulder. "Rosemary," I said. "I'm sorry about her. Sorry about your marriage. Sorry she died the way she did."

"Yes. I hadn't loved her for a long time. She looked so different from what she really was. And I fell in love with the way she looked. But in getting Tony Bridewell, one element was to pay back what he had done to Rosemary."

"Benedict?" I said. "Will he be all right?"

"According to the police doctor, who took some samples while he was here, Benedict does not have diabetes—not that I thought he did—and says that after he's recovered from the effects of some of the drugs he's been fed, he should be all right."

"He wasn't the one who vandalized the papers, was he?"

"No. I did that. Right after I got your cable. I wanted to have an excuse to keep you long enough over here so that Bridewell would get nervous and come himself." Gideon took a deep breath and dropped his arms. "The person who really paid most for this . . . this caper, I suppose I could call it, was Benedict. Between setting the trap and waiting and watching and keeping in touch with Jacob and other Israeli friends, I didn't pay attention to him. I barely noticed him. If I had, I would have known immediately that somebody must be giving him something—most obviously Sheila. I hope he will forgive me."

"Perhaps you didn't suspect her because you were in love with her," I said slyly, hoping he would deny it.

He did. "No. Never that. She was attractive and I was lonely and felt . . . well, attracted . . . at the beginning. But that didn't last long."

"None of this would have happened if my father hadn't decided to keep notes—memoranda—of all of his papers for his memoirs. I suppose it is the obvious thing for a man like him to do. But he never said a word about it."

"That's because he didn't."

"Didn't what?"

"Keep notes for his memoirs." There was a silence while Gideon looked at me, his gray eyes long and narrow in the firelight. Down in the fireplace something crackled and a short jet-like flame flared up.

"But you just said——"

"Yes, I know. That was the trap. You see, Janet, there were no deMaury papers."

There were no deMaury papers. In the silence that followed I repeated these words to myself, trying—and failing—to take in their meaning. Finally I said, "I don't understand."

"Oh, there were long boring letters and endless flyers and posters. But there were no memoirs, no notes, no nothing about any campaign contribution for Bridewell."

"But Tony *saw* them. *I* saw them."

"They were forgeries, Janet. I forged them. All of them."

I stood there a long time, just staring at him.

"I had to get him over here in some way and trick him into admitting everything he'd done. So Jacob, who spends most of his time tracking down war criminals, Nazis hiding out, but who decided that helping me in this was well worth his effort—Jacob and I set the whole thing up. God knows, we didn't intend for Bridewell to die— just to stop him politically, keep him from climbing towards a place where he could seriously influence United States policy."

"Is all this going to come out, Gideon? I mean, when the papers report his suicide."

"I hope not—not if I can help it." He paused. "Do you still love me?"

"Yes," I said. "I couldn't imagine now not loving you. But I can't help thinking, isn't that what you accused Rosemary—and my father—of? Justifying the means by the ends?"

"Yes. I've thought of that. Often." He went over to the desk. "Here they are, the forgeries. They've served their purpose. I thought I'd put them in the fire. But I'll give them to you. Anyone who really took the trouble— any court of law, for instance—could discover in a second that they were forgeries. Here."

"You mean I can have them to hold over your head? No thanks. Let's burn them."

We watched as the thin papers curled, then browned, then burned. I tried to make out some of the typed words, but I couldn't. "Somewhere," I said, "I think it's in Eliot's *Murder in the Cathedral*, there's something about the final treason, doing the right deed for the wrong reason."

"What I did was the other way around. I did the wrong thing for the right reason." As he spoke he glanced up at the portrait of Lisa Dreyfus Lightwood, his mother.

"Did you do it for her?" I asked.

"It would sound horribly sentimental to say yes. Yet I

think I did—partly. When she died, I tried to think of something I could do . . . I was fifteen, an idealistic age. It seemed like a wild romantic fantasy, but I wished I could do something for Israel—it meant so much to her. As a sort of memorial."

"I expect one could call what you did that," I said.

And then we both watched as the rest of the deMaury papers burned.

# Sylvia Thorpe

*Sparkling novels of love and conquest set against the colorful background of historic England. Here are stories you will savor word by word, page by spellbinding page into the wee hours of the night.*

| | | |
|---|---|---|
| ☐ BEGGAR ON HORSEBACK | 23091-0 | 1.50 |
| ☐ CAPTAIN GALLANT | Q2709 | 1.50 |
| ☐ FAIR SHINE THE DAY | 23229-8 | 1.75 |
| ☐ THE GOLDEN PANTHER | 23006-6 | 1.50 |
| ☐ THE RELUCTANT ADVENTURESS | 23426-6 | 1.50 |
| ☐ ROGUES' COVENANT | 23041-4 | 1.50 |
| ☐ ROMANTIC LADY | Q2910 | 1.50 |
| ☐ THE SCANDALOUS LADY ROBIN | 23622-6 | 1.75 |
| ☐ THE SCAPEGRACE | 23478-9 | 1.50 |
| ☐ THE SCARLET DOMINO | 23220-4 | 1.50 |
| ☐ THE SILVER NIGHTINGALE | 23379-9 | 1.50 |
| ☐ THE SWORD AND THE SHADOW | 22945-9 | 1.50 |
| ☐ SWORD OF VENGEANCE | 23136 4 | 1.50 |
| ☐ TARRINGTON CHASE | 23520-3 | 1.75 |

**Buy them at your local bookstores or use this handy coupon for ordering:**